DOES ANYONE CARE?

Steven Trinkwon

Michael Terence
Publishing

First published in paperback by
Michael Terence Publishing in 2018
www.mtp.agency

ISBN 9781977011466

DOES ANYONE CARE?

Steven Trinkwon

To Jill Spires with fond memories.

PREFACE

My name is Alex Forrester, and I am forty-six years of age. I live in Norwich and work for Norfolk Constabulary within the MASH* unit.

This novel style 'written account' came into being for two reasons. First, because of my desire and need to record the truth! To have something extra and not just rely on official documents which might require filling in one day?

Second, I have fulfilled an ambition held since I was in my late twenties. Namely, to write a meaningful and enthralling, I assumed it would be, Crime Fiction story, with the use of artistic license afforded to the undertaking of producing a creative piece of authorship.

Never did I ever consider my first attempt will turn out to be the story of investigations into three crimes I was involved in; one way or another?

Multi-Agency Safeguarding Hub.

PROLOGUE

Today is Sunday, November 2, 2008. I'm listening to my favourite song ever as I begin writing this story. It's called, "Jungleland" by Bruce Springsteen and the E Street Band.

My tell-tale starts with what happened at two very different events which I attended. One took place six years ago at Norwich Crown Court, Court 3. The other was at an Annual Grand Summer Fête in the village of Heydon, in 2004.

September 2, 2002

My presence in court is mainly on a professional basis. By way of plying a trade as a Forensic Profiler. Three days ago I gave evidence in this trial as a witness for the prosecution.

It is 10 am and head of Norfolk County Council's Children Services legal department, Maxine Stewart, watches Judge Crystal Frampton take her seat. The "Glam Judge" is a pet name Maxine uses for the only female Judge in Norfolk!

Crystal's presence feeds Maxine some reassurance despite there still being quite a few butterflies in Maxine's tummy. Albeit they are now flapping more lightly. The aflutter began fifteen minutes ago when Maxine realised a fiercely held ambition which is to represent the prosecution from the front in a court of law!

Maxine has often expressed to some acquaintances, colleagues and friends, "I want to demonstrate I am a skilled all-rounder. I hate having a reputation for what I did when defending men and women accused or charged with harming children."

Crystal begins today's proceedings, 'Good morning everyone. Yesterday, via a video link, we heard from seven-year-old Jordan Wye. A brother and half-brother to our respective alleged victims. It is in the best interest of all three children, why I have decided not to adjourn proceedings this morning! You see, Barrister for the prosecution, Mr Horatio Armstrong-Pollock, was abruptly taken ill twenty-five minutes ago.

Under the Judicial Proceedings for Minors Act 1994, it is **obligatory** for me to ensure that no suffering is caused to a child by way of an avoidable delay in any Minor proceedings. The same act also states, "In the exceptional circumstance whereby a Barrister is unable to perform his or her assigned duties in court, the first solicitor can step in. Thus avoiding delay and means their client can continue to be represented by a person they know and who has a holistic knowledge with regard to the details of the case."

It is my view it is incontrovertibly the case it is in the interest of Jordan Wye and his siblings for this trial to continue uninterrupted. Yesterday ended with the defendant being questioned by his Barrister. Therefore, I invite the Prosecution's lead solicitor, Mrs Maxine Stewart to begin her cross-examination.'

Maxine gives Crystal a friendly smile before saying, 'Yes your honour, I call, Oliver Stubs please.'

A chaperoned Stubs begins to walk toward the dock. Almost at once, each juror can see Stubs broad grin. His pleasure enhances by noting ten out of the twelve avoid eye contact. Instead, they pretend there is a need to adjust the position of their respective computer screen.

As Stubs begins to take the oath, he spots Jordan Wye's parents. Stubs stare at Damien Wye comforting Deborah Stubs suggests he is not scared of anything or anyone! Appearances though, do sometimes deceive!

The return look in Damien Wye's eyes is intimidatory and knowing Mr Wye, I'm pretty sure he's thinking, 'If I'm ever alone with **you,** I will tare you to shreds!'

High on Adrenalin, Maxine begins, 'Can you please confirm for the court that you are Oliver Stubs and you currently reside at Twenty-Eight Little Mead Crescent, Marlingford, Norfolk and your date of birth is the ninth of April nineteen seventy-one.'

'No.'

Damien and Deborah look at one another in shock. Crystal places her pen on top of her notepad, and she looks up and across too late, to see the witness smiling.

Maxine remains assured. 'Mr Stubs, I must warn! You are under oath and if you continue to insult this court you are in contempt. A grave offence! So, I repeat, can you please confirm for the court that you are Oliver Stubs and currently reside at Twenty-Eight Little Mead Crescent, Marlingford Norfolk, and your date of birth is the ninth of April nineteen seventy-one.'

'No, I am not Oliver Stubs. No, I do not live at twenty-Eight Little Mead Crescent. Yes, my date of birth is the ninth of April nineteen seventy-one. But.'

Stubs savours the atmosphere and glares at Maxine. It is identical in a manner to that of his brother. The sort that fires a shot from each eye right through you. It hurts. So much so, Maxine is consumed by the horror of realising the true identity of this witness. With her whole body turning to jelly, Maxine nearly collapses as she hears, '**My** name is **Isaac** Stubs. I am Ollie's identical twin. I live in ninety-six Somerset Drive, Nor...'

Oh my god! Ollie is free! But how? cries Maxine silently. Shock waves are also pinging chaotically inside her brain. Remarkably, Maxine regains enough control to fire at Isaac an assortment of expressions with more contempt than any court can offer.

'How do we know you're not lying?' says Maxine.

Isaac remains buoyant with his reply, 'You know I'm Isaac, don't you! It's in your eyes! We swapped places, pretty ...'

'Shut up Stubs,' orders Crystal and he does. All the same, Isaac enjoys the annoyance in her voice.

'Clearly, we must adjourn Mrs Stewart. Please meet me...'

'What a fucking farce,' is shrieked in absolute rage by Damien Wye who is sitting at the back of the court. He is unable to stop now. 'You've fucking lost him, haven't you! You useless cretins...' and as Damien continues to speak, he directs his damming words at DI Alan Oaks.

Oaks own expression hides thoughts of having every sympathy for his accuser and wants to clap Mr Wye for being so human. Make no mistake though; DI Oaks is seething too!

'...and why the fuck was he on bail for Christ sake? And who the fuck is in charge of this circus and...'

'That is more than enough thank you, and I am in here Mr Wye,' reminds Crystal.

Damien then adheres to her command for him to sit down. She then continues with absolute clarity and authority, 'I do sympathise with how you feel and I apologise unreservedly. With all the politeness I can muster I ask you to please leave quietly. I sincerely do not want **you** to be found in contempt of court, too.

Please believe me Mr and Mrs Wye; I too find this morning's event an unacceptable shambles. I will guarantee there is a thorough enquiry into how this situation occurred. More important than that, ensure **everything** that needs to be done to find Oliver Stubs, **will** be done! On the assumption this offensive activity is not a double bluff, please take this Stubs down, n**ow!** I will sentence him at two pm this afternoon.'

The usher is anticipating Crystal will give her signal to leave and dutifully watches for eyebrows to come together. 'All rise,' she says.

As you might imagine, not a day in court everyone involved wants to remember. But, no-one can forget! Not detected for a few years henceforth, immediately after the usher spoke, a member of the public gallery in Court three rushed out to meet a friend. In less than half an hour James Hawker reached their rendezvous. It was a bench near a lake in Colney, which is a tiny village south of Norwich City.

September 2, 2002

Sat on this bench, at opposite ends, is Clive Verity and Harold White. Clive is on leave from the Army and most people who meet Clive agree he is quite charismatic by nature, although in a most non-attention seeking way. Harold is a man of pensioner age waiting for his friend, James Hawker. Clive and Harold met by chance only half an hour or so ago. A conversation began because Clive helped Harold get to his feet following a fall. A fall caused by entanglement between Harold's Zimmer Frame and some Kissing Gates.

As Harold catches sight of his friend, he interrupts Clive, 'Excuse my rudeness, Clive. But, can you see that man over there?'

'Yes.'

'He's my nephew, Tristan. He's got marital problems and asked us to meet discreetly to chat about things. Sorry, its just he's a worrier and you being here might put him off.'

'I get it. No problem,' says Clive who then stands up and offers his hand before adding, 'Nice meeting you Eddie. Perhaps we will again. Do you fish here at all?'

'No. I don't have the patience but I sometimes join a friend over there. You have to pay to be allowed time over there though.'

'OK. Do you know how I apply for membership? I love fishing!'

'The person you need to see lives behind us,' replies Harold. Both men turn their heads and Harold points, 'Over there in Swan Close. I think its number seven,' he says.

'Thank you, Eddie, and look after yourself eh? I assume it's a hip problem you have? Are you waiting for a replacement?'

'Yes it is and I am actually.'

'Are you high up on a waiting list?'

'No. I'm paying private as it happens. I'm due to have it done a week tomorrow.'

'Hope it goes well,' Clive says as they shake hands for the second time.

Harold says, "Look after those girls in your life. I imagine they'll both really miss you when you return to Germany. Or are you being posted on a front line? You SAS fellows seem to be always needed somewhere in the world.'

In good humour, Clive replies, 'I didn't confirm or deny I'm SAS remember, Eddie? You take care, bye.'

Harold watches James and Clive share a courteous nod as they go by each other and then contemplates with excitement: I wonder how pretty she is?

Clive disappears out of sight as James puts on a spurt and crashes onto the bench.

'Who is that Harold?' James asks.

'Tell you later. So, what happened?'

'Oh Harold, you'd AV loved it. It worked a treat. Isaac was brilliant and that fat pig Oaks is spitting blood like Niagara Falls.'

'That's nice. So, no hiccups at all?' asks Harold.

'None. Ollie sent a text saying all OK. And, we won't be hearing from him for quite a while,' replies James gazing right into his best friend's eyes.

Harold opens his arms and they hug. 'Let us celebrate, eh boy,' Harold whispers into an ear.

Clive left Colney that day, oblivious to the fact that his new acquaintance lied seven times during their conversation.

July 3, 2004

Heydon is a gem amongst many village jewels in a neck of the woods affectionately known as, "The Heart of Norfolk." No doubt, its beauty and amity go a long way when ticking boxes to host this region's annual Grand Summer Fête.

Within the boundary of an encircling forest, Heydon is hidden to the rest of the world. The vast majority of travellers pass on by and do so without the slightest hint of learning they have done, just that!

Heydon village belongs to Lord Reginald and Lady Eva Chalice-Hermitage and before them first born ancestors from successive generations. The estate, in which all these titled owners have lived, is the village's grandest property and it's called, unsurprisingly Chalice Hall." The hereditary chain goes back to when the Hall first stood in the sixteenth century.

When on holiday in Malaysia Reginald, more than Eva, haggled a bargain price for a street craftsman to make a wooden placard. On its front aspect is scripted the patron saint of England. The sign hangs above the front door of their living quarters which is cordoned off from the rest of the Hall. The choice of St. George's stems from the synchronisation of Reginald and Eva being born in the same year on April 23. This date is also their wedding anniversary and they tied the knot twenty-nine years ago.

When visiting Heydon, most people feel an aura they are stepping back in time. The village has a well kept central green and beyond it are the substantial grounds of the impressive Chalice Hall. In the early nineteen seventies, the Hall was derelict and the then Lady Chalice-Hermitage paid for its restoration to its former original Elizabethan glory.

There has not been any new building in Heydon for over one hundred years. With less than twenty homes there is the Hall, a pub, an ancient church, a blacksmith, a unisex hair salon and a thatched house whose downstairs has evolved into a general store which also accommodates a quaint tea room. In 1971 Heydon was appointed a conservation area and it has won the "Best Kept Village in Britain" award twenty-two times. I would suggest a significant reason for such recognition is its prettiness and halcyon ambience. Of which, is tangible once you are within its invisible parameter!

Reginald is a frustrated actor due to his responsibilities as a Judge and member of the House of Lords. However, he has on a handful of occasions negotiated with five directors' of cinema films to use the wonderful facilities Heydon has to offer. In one of these films, Reginald was thrilled to play a cameo role in the film's opening court scene. Financially, the royalties have been kind too. It is the fourth best British made film in history. That is if you make a judgement by measuring success on monetary remuneration alone!

For today's Grand Summer Fête Reginald, and all other residents of Heydon, voted yes to what is an annual request from Loxley Parish Council's Social and Recreational Activities Committee. This protocol has been a tradition since the first Fête took place in 1585.

The committee member with the leading province for coordinating arrangements necessary for the smooth running of today's Fête is Councillor Mrs Rosalind (Rosa), Thorpe. It is 5 am.

'Are you sure you don't mind coming to the Fête?' Rosa asks me.

'Of course not. Thanks for inviting me along Rosa. I'm just sorry I can't stay all day. I'm hosting a World Cup party. Not every day England get to a semi-final.'

'Sounds like good fun so perfectly understandable,' replies Rosa before adding, 'To be honest, I've been dreading the drive to Heydon this year. What, with losing my Willie to the angels not very long ago. Its twenty-two years we attended the grand Fête together.'

'I'm sure he's with you in spirit,' I say hoping it is supportive and I then draw on a straw in a cup of coffee.

Rosa says, 'Thank you, how sweet...'

I interject, 'Thanks again for joining me at the concert last night. Not to mention your hospitality after that.'

'You're very welcome Alex. Although, it's me who needs to thank you because seeing Jools Holland live now means I had the pleasure of ticking off another of my boxes. Forgive me for rushing you Alex; we do need to leave soon.'

'Ready whenever you are Rosa,' I reply.

***

Rosa is a lone driver on what is the only road from which you can turn into either of the two entrances to Heydon village. It is a glorious morning, weather-wise. The sun's light pierces through gaps in branches of tall overhanging trees. They form an arch and are rooted in an entire row on both sides of the road. Many of the leaves have speckle patches tinged with red and blue, and all this brightness causes Rosa to squint both eyes. She then curses, 'Drat! I have forgotten my sunglasses.'

As a double check, Rosa fondles contents of a leather handbag nestled on her lap. She says, 'If I had left my handbag behind Alex, I would have had to go back!'

'Sure. Bound to need something in it sometime during a day, eh?'

Rosa laughs briefly and replies, 'Oh yes, see what you mean. No, that isn't why Alex. The handbag is with me everywhere I go because Willie bought it during our second honeymoon in the Gambia. While there we also enjoyed a ceremony to renew vows on the day of our twentieth anniversary.'

'Lovely to have special memories,' I say.

Rosa steers right onto the village's shingled communal driveway and then wipes tears from both eyes. 'Such a lovely green,' she whispers bravely.

Soon, we park outside a church. In the distance near the Hall, we can see half naked men emptying equipment from lorries to build a fairground, gymkhana course and a pen for the sheep-dog trial.

Rosa gently holds her handbag and says, 'Willie, I do so hope you like the new memorial cup bearing your name. It is this year's prize for the winner of your favourite event. So fitting because, we both did so love our rides out, didn't we darling!'

Rosa then steps out of the car, and as she helps me open my door, I say, 'Thank you, Rosa. I think walking around the whole site is a bit too ambitious. Perhaps, after you've checked things are hopefully progressing as they should, you will join me in the tea shop and let me treat you to breakfast?'

'Yes, of course. Splendid idea. So, see you soon,' replies Rosa.

'Good luck,' I say as Rosa heads toward the nearest stall which is still in the process of being erected. She is soon close enough to say cheerily, 'Good morning Phyllis.'

'Hello, Mrs Thorpe. It's such a beautiful day, isn't it!'

'Fabulous. Can I give you a hand with anything Phyllis?'

'Thank you for offering Mrs Thorpe, but I think we're winning. Kenneth has just gone back to the car to fetch our chairs. Hope to get a chance to top up my tan.'

'I see. You obviously have Kenneth well trained. Good for you,' Rosa suggests.

Phyllis chuckles and says, 'Good luck for today Mrs Thorpe.'

'And you Phyllis,' replies Rosalind who then makes her way toward Chalice Hall to check all is well there.

***

Rosalind enters the tea room, 'Are preparations going well Rosa?' I ask.

'Marvellous. Have you had breakfast, Alex?'

'No. Waited for you and so now I'm looking forward to some.'

'You daft sausage, you shouldn't have done. I do beg your pardon, hello Janet. How are you?'

'Good, thank you. Can I get you anything, ma'am?' asks Janet.

'A cream tea for me please Janet. What do you want Alex?'

'A Grenole with a cup of decaffeinated coffee and a straw please,' I reply.

Janet says, 'Both coming right up.'

Rosalind joins me at a table beside a tiny front window. She cowers to watch the organised chaos transforming the landscape and character of the village. Soon, Mrs Strumpshaw brings breakfast.

'Thank you, Janet, it looks delicious,' says Rosa.

'Thank you, ma'am. And here is yours, sir.'

Thank you,' I say.

Janet then says to Rosa, 'They say the proof is in the eating.

So, hope you still feel the same then eh?'

'I'm sure it will be delightful,' replies Rosa who then bites into a mountain of cream, savouring the taste!

***

Rosa is re-filling her cup with tea as we both hear a soft creaking sound. It induces us to see who is entering the front door?

Rosa raises both eyebrows and her forehead as she says, 'I've just started on a fresh pot. I'd be delighted to share some with you, Reginald. Please, join us?'

Rosa gestures at the empty chair.

'Thank you, Rosa. I must say, given the time of day, you look wonderful. I mean you always look wonderful, it's just, no, stop digging a hole Reg. Rosa, I do apologise,' says Reginald.

Rosa replies, 'It's perfectly all right Reginald. I think I know what you mean. The fact that **you** think I do is a cherished compliment, so thank you for giving me a much-needed boost. Now then, I'd like to introduce you to a friend of mine. Alex works at the same police station in Wymondham where my young son-in-law to be was recently posted. Alex, this is Reg, Lord of the Hall and who kindly allows us to use his land for our annual jamboree. Lord Chalice-Hermitage, please meet Alex Forrester.'

Reginald replies and as he says, 'Delighted to meet you,' the Lord offers a hand to shake. He then adds, 'I think I've heard your name before. Do you work in Sir Roger's division?'

Reginald is looking a bit perplexed why his arm is still outstretched and untouched. I reply, 'Please excuse me. I am unable to use my hands for most things. Yes, I do. A pleasure to meet you.'

I'm pretty confident Rosa is also feeling embarrassed in some way at this precise moment.

Reginald then says, 'Oh, yes. I remember saying to Rog, Sir Roger. It sound like your new profiler will gain you a lot of PC brownie points with the county's Police and Crime Panel. Good to meet you. And, bully for you despite...'

I interrupt deliberately, 'It's the first time I've spoken with a hereditary Lord. Hope you don't mind me asking as I'm genuinely interested to hear: Which side were your ancestors on during the English civil war?'

I can see Reginald is looking even more nonplussed and we are interrupted by Janet placing another cup and saucer on the table. 'Do you want something to eat Reg, my Lord?' asks Janet.

'No, just popped in for a taste of your wonderful Rosie Lee, please Janet. Thank you all the same,' Reginald replies.

Rosa says, 'Thank you, Reginald, for agreeing to judge the William Thorpe Memorial Cup. I know you said you wouldn't ever be a judge at this fête again after that fiasco fifteen years ago. It means a lot.'

'A hon...'

***

It is ten minutes after midday, so reluctantly Rosa prizes herself away from the firemen who look very smart in their uniform. 'Fascinating and thank you for letting me see the inside of an engine, most interesting,' concludes Rosa.

'You're welcome ma'am,' says Chief Officer David Neil who then shakes hands with Rosa.

I then say, 'I'm going to head home now Rosa. Taxi booked for twelve, twelve thirty. I'm happy to find my way back as I know you're off to the WI stall next. Shame, as I've enjoyed it here.'

Rosa replies, 'No, of course. I understand.'

'Thank you, Rosa. Enjoy those cakes you're about to judge.'

Rosa smiles and says, 'That's a certainty Alex. Well, I enjoyed your company and hope the party turns into a historical celebration.'

'Now, that's not a certainty Rosa,' I jest before adding,

'Goodbye Rosa and good luck with the rest of your day.'

'Au revoir Alex, and keep an eye on that son-in-law to be of mine, Finley is his name. He's a lovely boy but, like Kristina was raised sheltered from the rough and tumble of life and a big city.'

'Noted. See you soon,' I say and then take my leave.

***

Rosa arrives at the tent erected by the Women's Institute. She is ushered to the back of the Marquee by Cindy who is Chairwoman of the local WI. They exchange small talk briefly and then both go forward until they reach a long table. Upon which, there are all the adorned cakes are placed in two rows across it. Each entry created and baked by a member of the Institute. First prize is a pair of vouchers for a weekend at a Norfolk spa retreat called, "Top2Toe."

Cindy steps back and Rosa contemplates the dreadfully pleasurable responsibility of choosing the winning cake and baker. Although conscious of a crowd watching her every move, Rosa enjoys sampling the first morsel. After what seems an age to the excitable spectators, Rosa decides as many women buying shoes do! Namely, settling for the very first one they tried.

Rosa whispers her choice to Cindy who likewise discreetly gives brief information about the winner. Cindy then places an upright finger to her closed mouth. The murmuring of the crowd recedes into a hush.

Rosa takes this cue to begin revealing the lucky winner, 'I would like to offer, on behalf of everyone here, a whopping thank you to all involved with the Women's Institute.'

Applause.

'Not just for their fund-raising effort today but more importantly for their ongoing dedication to helping people in our communities who are in need!'

Applause.

'I would also like to thank you for giving me the honour of judging your wonderful cakes. All sixteen are scrumptious! So, well done all of you,' says Rosa as she claps the crowd.

The crowd clap back and cheer loudly. Familiar cries amongst a few are, 'Bravo, here here, girl power and well said!'

Rosa holds up her hands and cheers fade to be replaced by a nail-biting silence.

'The winner is... the Lemon Drizzle Sponge cake baked by WPC Sally Underwood.'

Sally cannot contain her excitement. Sally's joy is not for herself, it is for her mother who taught her the recipe. Sadly, in January this year, Sally's mother passed away due to Breast Cancer. So, given the Race for Life Charity is this year's Fête beneficiary it is literally, for Sally, the icing on the cake.

Sally makes her way to the front of the WI tent and by now the clapping and cheering is a level worthy of football supporters in the South Stand of the Madejski Stadium in Reading.

Rosa moves forward and as she shakes Sally's hand she notices a tattoo of a star in each of a two-link chain circling Sally's right wrist. Of course, Rosa is unaware each star represents a loss of a loved one.

'Well done Sally,' Rosa says heartedly.

'Thank you. I'm glad you like it,' Sally replies.

'Cindy has just told me the sad news about your mother. I'm sure she is watching with pride. The cake is truly delicious!'

'Thank you again,' is all Sally can say and she accepts the prize sealed in a gold envelope. Sally then rejoins the crowd of gracious and envious competitors. Everyone wants to offer their congratulations though.

Rosa shakes hands again with Cindy and strides briskly away. I need to sit down. So, a visit to see Pauline next, she muses.

Pauline's stall is only three along from the WI and on arriving Rosa can see Pauline selling a jar of one of her excellent range of home-made Jams. Rosa waits until the customer has been served and says, 'Hello Pauline. Seems to be going well!'

'Hello, how lovely to see you, Rosa. How are you? So many responsibilities. I expect your head is spinning, isn't it? Hope you are getting time to enjoy today!'

'I am actually. It's nice to take a break, mind you. I'm sure I can get away with a half hour or so.'

'Wonderful, take a seat and I'll get us a sherry. Would you like something to nibble too?' asks Pauline laughing.

'Very funny. I'd love a Rosie Lee please Pauline.'

'Coming up.'

Rosa sits down and in the distance beyond the grand marquee, her eyes follow a red hot air balloon drifting serenely in a blue sky. One day I must take a ride. I bet the views are marvellous, muses Rosa.

'There you are pet,' says Pauline.

'Thank you, Pauline,' says Rosa before enjoying the wetness on her lips and giving out a fairly loud sigh.

'My, are you sure you're OK Rosa?' asks Pauline.

Rosa replies, 'Fine, just good to relax and feel a bit stuffed, to be honest.'

'I bet! Don't suppose you even want one of your favourite biscuits,' says Pauline with a tempting smile.

Rosa leans forward and replies, 'You know I can't resist one of your macaroons. So, yes please Pauline.'

Pauline disappears behind her stall. Grabs the macaroons and on returning is bemused to find Rosa is walking away.

Rosa is heading toward a stall run by a Helen Thompson. The prompt for Rosa to leave so urgently was seeing Lilly, who is Helen's daughter, break a tail end of a conversation between her mother and a man clothed in a Roman tunic. This man's name is Luke Stewart but Rosa doesn't recognise him as someone she knows. It was Lilly's gesticulations toward her mother and the frenetic-ism of them which instinctively concerned Rosa.

Immediately after Lilly interrupted Luke left to resume entrance gate duties, he's sharing with three other Roman guardsmen. Luke's wife Maxine and step-daughter Milena are away on a 'Hen's and 'Chicks,' long weekend in Amsterdam. Therefore, Luke took this opportunity to visit the woman who runs the 'Hand Made Wedding and Christening Dresses' stall. Luke asked Helen if she would make something a little different to those on display, just for him? Helen agreed and sealed a deal.

Within earshot now, Rosa asks, 'Is there a problem Helen?'

'Oh hello, Rosa I was about to look for you. I certainly hope not,' Helen replies.

'What is it, Helen?' asks Rosa.

Helen replies, 'Lilly and her friend Joanne went to queue for a pony ride and because the queue was long, Joanne went to buy them ice cream.'

Rosa looks to her right and the queue to ride a pony hasn't shortened. She nearly speaks but she knows there is more.

'And because Joanne went about twenty to twenty-five minutes ago, Lilly gave up on waiting and went to look for her. She checked the queue for ice cream in the Grand Marquee and had just come to tell me. Oh, Rosa, I'm scared.'

'Understandable Helen. Where are Joanne's parents?'

'In the Peak District for a weekend with army friends from Germany. Although, Joanne's father has now left the army. He, it's not important why, is it? Sorry, I'm babbling. It's just, I'm worried Rosa,' exclaims Helen who then takes a deep breath.

'Of course, you are. Now...'

Helen interrupts, 'Right, to explain better. Joanne is staying with us because she and my Lilly wanted to come to the Grand Fête for the first time, together.'

'Where are your two youngest?' Asks Rosa.

'Each is with their father for the weekend.'

'Are they here or visiting later?' asks Rosa.

'No, neither are coming here Rosa,' Helen replies.

'I see. Well, I think we need to start looking for Joanne. Surname please Helen? asks Rosa.

'Verity,' replies Helen.

'How old is Joanne, Helen? And a brief description of what she looks like and is wearing will help too please?'

Helen replies, 'Yes. Sure. ERM..., Joanne is fourteen, same as my Lilly. Joanne has long jet black hair, a slim build but a bit taller than Lilly. Pretty sure Jo's wearing an all in one pink and white dress, is that right Lilly?

'Yes mum,' replies Lilly.

'Thank you. Come on; we'll start with the Marquee again. There are lots going on in there so someone is bound to have seen Joanne,' says Rosa positively.

Helen begins replying, 'Yes, of course. You're right,' Rosa uses a walkie-talkie to call the coordinator of the Red Cross and St. John Ambulance stewards gathered in a large tent on the other side of the green.

Helen's anxiety rises steeply because Rosa's conversation with the coordinator sounds like Joanne has disappeared?!

***

Helen's level of anxiety at the Fête bares no comparison to how it is now. She is at home and it is nearly twelve hours since Joanne Verity was formally declared as a "Missing" person.

Sangria Creek has at least one candle lit in every downstairs room. And, on a sofa adjacent to a dimly lit fireplace, Helen is cradling Lilly who is simply unable to stop crying.

Joanne, it seems, has vanished without a trace. Police and other statutory public agencies are intensely involved with a painstaking search to find her. In addition, the police are attempting to manage the hundreds of people from Norfolk and neighbouring counties who made their way to Heydon, keen and determined to volunteer their help with the search.

Joanne's parents are in turmoil, at Norfolk Constabulary HQ in Wymondham.

CHAPTER ONE

It is three years and twelve days on from the date Joanne Verity Went missing, and she still is. While the investigation remains open, to all tense and purpose, the activity on it has come to a halt!

The only significant sighting of Joanne is in a statement to the police by Lady Anne Ellen from Stratford-Upon-Avon. Lady Anne attended the Fête to be a volunteer steward following an invitation to do so from her friend, Rosa Thorpe.

In her statement, Lady Anne confirms seeing a girl matching Joanne's description walking into the Ladies Toilet when, following completion of an inspection, Lady Anne was walking out.

The time suggests Joanne went into the public toilets prior intending to buy ice creams. The police explained in one of their official press statements, "We have to be open-minded about whether Joanne did go into the Marquee or not? A place we do know Ice creams were on sale."

The search had been very high profile, but Joanne's disappearance remains as a suspected abduction at best! Joanne Verity, it seems, really has vanished without a trace! From information provided by the network provider for Joanne's mobile phone, the police learnt her last known location was at the Fête in Heydon village.

There have been many reports completed by various public and private law enforcement services. A significant finding from these led to an entry in the police record on Joanne's disappearance, of the whereabouts of every (bar one) known and suspected perpetrator of crimes against minors. In this record, every means, those who could have been in Norfolk on the day of the Fête. The omission is Oliver Stubs and he's been missing for longer than Joanne.

The truth is, no-one knows what happened!? Everyone involved with finding Joanne, from the Home Secretary to millions of public well-wishers, do hope Joanne is alive!

Nonetheless, given the current juncture of the investigation, regrettably, the softly spoken consensus is,"Lets hope Joanne proves to be a rare exception and is found safe!"

***

DC Sally Underwood's hand hovers above a handle of a door. She's thinking, Nothing heavy today, please!

As soon as Sally enters, a crescendo of whistles, wise-cracks and confetti shower upon her, so rendering any attempt to be inconspicuous fruitless.

Sally stands still because her colleagues are rushing toward her and soon assemble a human arch of affection. As Sally duly tip-toes along this isle she hears, 'Here comes the bride, all fat and wide ...,' bellow out in quite a good tune!

For the next five minutes the sole topic is the wedding and as a diversion tactic more than anything else, Sally hands a packet of photos to DC Bernice Buck who is instantly surrounded by nearly every member of the team.

Sally then switches a laptop on to read E-mails. There are 278 of them. Sally skims the in-box and very quickly spots one is red-flagged! In the Subject box, it states, "Strictly Confidential." I wonder what Sir Roger wants? she muses.

Excited, Sally opens it. "Sally, I understand you're back from holiday on July 16 which is next Monday I believe. Please come and see me in my office asap! It must be before 11.00am. Kind Regards, Sir Roger Bright. Detective Chief Inspector, MASH."

Prying eyes remain absorbed with Sally's photos, so she logs out and says, 'Will be back in a jiffy.' Her colleagues are goggling too much to have heard or care about where she might be going so soon? What does he want? Is it for a good or bad reason? Why bad? I've done nothing wrong, reasons Sally to herself

Sally soon reaches the reception desk on floor 7 and says to Sir Roger's PA, 'Good Morning Claudia.'

Claudia looks up. 'Oh, hello Sally. Did everything go to

plan?'

'Like a dream, thanks.'

'You look a wonderful colour.'

'Do you think so, thanks, Claudia.'

'So, is Mauritius the paradise they say it is?'

'Better.'

'Lucky you! So, how can I help?'

'I need to see Sir Roger, please. Is he in?'

'Yes,' Claudia confirms before pressing a button. 'Sir Roger, DC Underwood to see you. Is now convenient? Yes Sir Roger, I will.'

'Straight away Sally.'

'Great, thank you, Claudia.'

As Sally heads toward Sir Roger's office she hears Claudia ask, 'Sally; you're not leaving us are you?'

Sally looks back and says, 'No Claudia, why would I want to do that?'

Claudia is a bit embarrassed, so she just smiles and watches Sally knock and open Sir Roger's office door.

'Come in. Good of you to come so quickly, Sally. Please, take a seat.'

Sally chooses the middle of three empty chairs in front of a large desk.

'How are you, Sally? DI Oaks reminded me last week you were abroad, a wedding and a honeymoon in one I understand! Well, congratulations!'

Sir Roger gets up to offer his hand and Sally reciprocates. 'Thank you Guv.'

'Do we know the lucky man? I mean, is he in the force?'

'No Guv, she isn't.'

Sir Roger looks befuddled before he recalls the detail given by Oaks. 'Oh yes, of course. Forgive my mistake. Nice to have our first, ERM...' Sir Roger, unusual for him, is not sure quite what words to use and settles for, 'bride from a new age marriage!'

Although Sally believes Sir Roger isn't asking a question she gives a courteous reply. 'Yes, Guv. It's called a Civil Partnership Guv.'

'Does your husband, I mean partner work? Or, are you the bread-winner?'

'Sylvia is my wife as I am hers too and she is an Environmental officer for the County Council Guv.'

'Oh right, I mean good. Right, now then, to the business in hand! You joined us six months ago. Right?'

'Yes I did Guv.'

'Do you like working in the MASH Unit?'

'Yes Guv.'

'DI Oaks spoke very highly of you and shared he believes you to be a capable detective.'

'Thank you Guv. Detective Inspector Oaks is very kind.'

'And a shrewd judge of character too. Last week DI Oaks and I had a chat about an interesting letter sent recently to the Chief Constable. Have you met Frank Toddenham, Sally?'

'Not to speak to Guv. Only heard his speeches at corporate functions such as restructuring seminars, training courses and social events. Why do you ask, please Guv?'

'No particular reason other than wondering if you have, that's all. Frank opened the letter in question on Friday, July six. Alan, DI Oaks, called in sick last Wednesday and believed he might be off for a week or so. Said it's a severe bout of flu and he'll keep me informed. Therefore, we agreed to give you this assignment on your return,' and Sir Roger hands Sally the original copy of what is a hand-written letter.

Sally rises to her feet and accepts it, 'Thank you Guv.'

Sir Roger says, 'You will be only the fifth person to learn of the concerns expressed in the letter. It is also important to tell you, this assignment is at present very much on a, "Need to know basis". Am I clear?'

'I understand Guv,' replies Sally.

'If you will excuse me, Sally, I'll leave you to digest it. I'll be back shortly then we will discuss it.'

'I will, straight away Guv.'

Sally's calm persona includes a glint in her eyes. Whoa, they've given me lead responsibility for the first time! Sally wants to text Sylvia. Wisely, she thinks it would be best not too. Instead, she concentrates on the letter put in her charge.

By the time Sally is reading the letter for the fifth time, Sir Roger walks in.

Sir Roger says, 'Now then, I have asked Alex to join us.'

Sally responds with, 'Oh, hello Alex. Are you OK? ERM..., why the wheelchair?'

I park beside Sally and reply, 'Hi Sally, I've just heard something which warrants a congratulation, and I'm not referring just to your wedding. I'm fine, find walking, too painful sometimes.'

'Right, I see. And, thanks, Alex,' says Sally.

Sir Roger then says, 'The first thing I need to do Sally is, ask whether you are up to speed on the Joanne Verity investigation? Regrettably, more commonly referred to by the media as "The (Lost) Fêted Angel!"'

'I was an off-duty WPC at the time Joanne disappeared Guv. Although, actually Guv, I did attend the Fête. Since joining MASH, I have briefly read our summaries of unsolved crimes.'

'On WI duty and gaining top prize I understand,' compliments Sir Roger.

'Yes Guv,' replies Sally who is a little surprised and more than impressed.

Sir Roger smiles before saying, 'Well **if** what is in that letter is true, unless there is another girl in Norfolk who has vanished which we don't know about, it is possible the alleged perpetrator could be Joanne Verity's mother? I know Mrs Verity is unnamed in the letter. However, the sender's description of where the alleged unlawful activity might have taken place means, we might identify the snooped garden belongs to the Verity family home. If it transpires this is our finding then it will need delicate intervention, don't you think?'

'I see, yes Guv.'

'Do you think you can handle it, Sally?'

'Absolutely Guv.'

'Good. It is not as uncommon as you might think for members of the public to send letters of this type to the Chief Constable. What is unusual about this latest one is, the sender included within the address on the envelope, "To be opened by Addressee only. The sender is a Mrs Gillian White, and her husband's name is Harold. Mr White is registered for life as a Sex Offender and therefore managed by *MAPPA.

I have personally spoken with Sandra Ash who is Mr White's probation officer. I can confirm Mrs Ash emphasised how genuinely co-operative and committed Mrs White is about the MAPPA (Multi-Agency Public Protection Arrangements) plan. Like us, Mrs White is keen for our monitoring of her husband to be successful in its attempt to prevent him harming minors again. However, I did not reveal we had received this letter, to Sandra.

Taking account of Mrs Ash's opinion, I am confident Mrs White is sincere in her motive to inform us about concerns expressed in her letter. While I fully expect you could well discover her husband is in breach of his current probation order, the second concern expressed in the letter, I advise, requires us to be open-minded and circumspect. Even though I accept, from what Mrs White has written, there might well be an illicit liaison taking place?'

'Yes. I understand why Mrs ...'

Sir Roger holds a hand up.

'Please, I am interested in your opinion but without clarity of ages as well as the identity of those alleged to be involved, we cannot ignore this information!'

I see Guv.'

'So Sally, What do you make of the letter?'

'It's a good lead to start trying to establish some facts,' replies Sally.

'I agree. Alex, this seems a good moment for you to share information relevant to Sally undertaking this new investigation.'

'Certainly Guv. Where to start? Harold White is a dangerous and intelligent paedophile. His offence in nineteen ninety-six was being responsible for possessing obscene material in the form of photographs **he** took over fifty years. Extraordinarily, the legal process did not conclude in a court! Instead, the then Attorney General exercised a rarely used power to administer a sentence himself. As well as being registered as a Sex Offender, Mr White's sentence included a three-year probation order along with two years in custody, suspended for two years. For a different offence involving physical assault against a librarian in October two thousand and five, Mr White did answer to a Jury who found him guilty! He is currently eighteen months into a two-year probation order which again includes a custodial sentence, suspended for two years.

Two days before Christmas day in nineteen ninety-seven on Harold White's sixty-fourth birthday, the Local Safeguarding Children Board's predecessor, the Area Child Protection Committee, met to decide whether Mr White engaged in his sex offence activity, alone? The outcome was a unanimous vote that he did. Thus, the Board sanctioned full support for the existing plan set in place by members of MAPPA. Every year all the various MAPPA assessments' result in categorisation of Mr White, concerning measuring the risk of him re-offending, needing to be A plus! Any questions Sally, before I move onto Valerie Verity?'

'What reasons did the Attorney General give to justify actions taken?'

I reply, 'From reading the paperwork I admit I'm unclear. However, this happened a few years before I joined the team. Do you have any insight as to why Guv?'

Sir Roger replies, 'No. I tend to agree with you Alex having read White's file, too.'

'OK to go on Sally?' I ask.

'Sure.'

'Before concentrating on what might be specifically relevant to you Sally, I suggest it might be helpful also to read a full report I produced during the initial stages of our investigation into Joanne Verity's disappearance.'

'Thank you, Alex, I will.'

'To begin then, Valerie is bisexual. Clive accepts her sexuality. They explained they'd agreed with Clive's asking, that Valerie remained discreet for Joanne's sake and she continues to be faithful to their marriage. The prompt for such a disclosure derived from a question seeking an understanding of their decision to leave Germany and live in Norfolk? Both agreed on the imprint of a scar left from the incident when Clive discovered his wife in bed with a lover, laid too visible in their German home. Clive accepted a generous leave period to help them settle in as a family in two thousand and two, and then chose to leave the Army a year or so later.'

Sally says, 'Thanks, Alex. Guv, can I ask a question about something which confused me when I briefly read our file for Joanne?'

'Certainly Sally,' replies Sir Roger.

'It's Valerie talking about her estranged sister. How is it possible we couldn't find her? Or, was it because of the two sisters long estrangement and Valerie's reasons for not wanting us to make contact sufficient to eliminate Maxine Stewart from our enquiries?'

Sir Roger replies, 'No Sally, we did not make such a decision! There was no match countrywide with the date of birth and name given by Valerie. I admit though; it is baffling! I think that's about it for now. Or is there anything else Alex?'

'No Guv, other than stressing for a better understanding of context etc., it is worth reading all our files on our attempt to find Joanne Verity.'

'Absolutely,' agrees Sr Roger who then adds, 'Thanks for making time to meet us, Alex.'

'No problem Guv, Sally. Do you mind if I leave now please Guv? I have an appointment in Yarmouth to prepare for.'

'Of course,' says Sir Roger.

'Thanks. Good luck Sally,' I say and make my exit.

Sr Roger says, 'Sally, please report directly to me once your enquiries ascertain: What exactly is it we are looking into here? And Sally, until then, never hesitate to approach me if you need any advise or support.'

'Thank you Guv. I will.'

Sir Roger then says, 'In the letter, Mrs White gave us the phone number of a Day-Centre she attends. From a call made by DI Oaks at the time requested by Mrs White, he learnt she is only prepared to discuss her allegations further, face to face at the Day-Centre. The next day Mrs White confirmed directly to DI Oaks that two o'clock this afternoon is an excellent time to meet.

Mrs White also mentioned, Mr and Mrs Hartman accepted her invitation to be with her when we visit. While a bit maverick, evidently from the letter Mr Hartman is potentially a vital witness. So, I didn't decline her arrangements. Though, I did personally write to Mrs White explaining it will be you Sally, and not DI Oaks, who will visit her today. For speed and safety, I decided it would be best to make a detour home last Wednesday evening. So, I could post it through the Day-Centre's letter-box. Here is the address. I think it will be wise to take someone with you. So, I suggest DC Buck. Any further questions, Sally?'

'No Guv.'

'OK. Sally, I'd like to offer some advise, if that's OK with you?'

'Of course Guv, Yes, please do.'

'From experience Sally, this type of referral requires no flashing lights or swooping in with guns blazing! More a "Slowly slowly catchy monkey" approach. Depending on what facts you find, we will unearth a lot of harm or it will turn out to be the activities are quite the opposite!'

'Thank you Guv, I understand.'

'Good. Just two more things Sally. Always remember, we delve into people's lives to uphold the law! **And,** not for those into purchasing or selling voyeuristic tittle-tattle. Good luck Sally.'

Sir Roger stands to shake hands. 'Thank you Guv,' says Sally who then folds the letter before tucking it into her blouse pocket.

Sally then leaves Sir Roger's office a very happy and excited detective. Once out of Claudia's eyesight, Sally runs down three staircases and along what is a cruise ship style corridor. She then bursts into the MASH office. It is empty. Where have they all gone?

Catching her breath, Sally goes to her desk. She is glad to see the photos have been left tidily beside a sealed envelope with her name on it. On opening, she considers a welcome home card. "Missed you loads Sally, love Bernice" it tells her.

Sally refocuses and rereads the letter yet again. No matter how many times I read this, I don't have much to go on! Sally concludes.

Sally then spins her red office swivel chair 180 degrees to view carefully, for the first time, a ten-year-old framed photo hung on a wall. It is on permanent display at the insistence of successive Chief Constables. In the picture is Sir Roger receiving his Queen's Gallantry Medal at Buckingham Palace. Sally has learnt all about Sir Roger's brave action as does everyone who works at the station. But you never mention it. Commendable all round in my book Guv muses Sally.

Sally swivels to complete a circle and calls Bernice. 'Hi-ya, thanks for the card. Oh, cheers. Bernice, I'm also calling to say, and this is not a wind-up. No, promise. Well, the Guv has given **us** a high profile investigation to lead. Yep, so I need you to meet me here asap, please. Oh, wondering where you'd all gone. See you soon then.'

Sally starts writing a new episode on a police computer record in the name of Harold White. "16/07/2007 – SU – Letter received via the Guv. Instructed to investigate allegations made in a letter dated July 4, 2007. Further action required as follows:-

1) Check MPN history

2) Reread JV file

3) Discuss with BB

4) Interview GW at 14.00pm today

***

Sally is driving out of the station car park and says, 'Thank you again for the card Bernice.'

'You're more than welcome,' replies Bernice who then turns her head and sees Sally's bright green skirt has ridden upwards. 'You've got very brown,' Bernice adds admiring.

'The weather was glorious every day,' explains Sally as she adjusts the seat belt so that her skirt slides down a bit. 'Have you set the Sat Nav, please Bernice?'

'Yes. It says it will take us around twenty minutes. And it's only just gone one. Didn't you say we're not due till two?'

'That's right, so to show my appreciation for your kind gesture, I'm taking us somewhere nice for lunch. OK with you?' asks Sally.

'Cool. Where do you have in mind?'

'Somewhere as pretty as you,' replies Sally who is stunned by her candour.

'That is going to be difficult. Is there such a place?' asks Bernice.

Chuckling, Sally replies, 'Maybe that's for me to know and for you to find out Miss Modesty two thousand and seven!'

For fifteen minutes or so, their journey continues with only the sound of music.

Sally now pulls up and spook-ally the song playing on

"Heart FM" is, "Lay Down Sally" by Eric Clapton.

'Here we are!' exclaims Sally.

'There isn't anything here except countryside.'

'Very observant. Has anyone ever told you, Bernice, you'd make a great detective.'

'Ha ha,' retorts Bernice.

'Here you go,' says Sally, giving Bernice half of her sandwiches.

Both then get out of the car.

'It's such a lovely view isn't it?' suggests Sally.

'Yes. And, so is the countryside!' replies Bernice who then chuckles on noticing it is Sally blushing this time.

CHAPTER TWO

'Some bastard has attacked my Gillian,' shouts Harold White for the twentieth time. Only, this time he madly swirls two walking sticks in the air and above his head too. Two police constables are trying to console Harold. Thus far, all they've acquired is receipt of severe blows to their legs along with an invitation to "Fuck off."

PC Diderot gives up and looks again at the stomach-churning scene of Mrs White in an armchair. He's thinking, You poor lady. Obviously a stab into your heart. He then looks across at the fireplace again and hanging on the wall above is an impressive collection of Shinogi-Zukuri katana samurai swords. Each one is arched horizontally in a similar fashion to rows of seats in the upper circle of Norwich's Theatre Royal. Usually, there are five rows but the middle sword is missing and bloodstained.

PC Diderot is glad to be distracted by Adam, one of two paramedics who've just stopped trying to treat Gillian. Adam says, 'Mr White. You have a nasty cut. We need to get you to hospital. Are you going to let us help you into an ambulance?

Harold crashes onto his armchair as another two men enter the room. Harold then fumbles for his walking sticks and says, 'Oh no. Who the fuck are you?'

The man who replies is called PP by everyone, 'I'm DI Peter Parsons and this is DC Finley Billing. If I may observe Mr White, it has to be said, I've had friendlier greetings.'

'Hello Guv,' says the second constable, who then adds, 'Mr White is in shock and been stabbed too Guv.'

'I see. Forensics will be here soon, so best if you two start house to house right away. You too Finley, once we've had a good look around.'

PP then looks at Adam who responds, using non-verbal communication too, an answer which confirms Gillian White has died.

PP says, 'So, I finally meet the infamous Harold White. It is my understanding, Harold. You may have been the man who called nine nine nine. Did you?'

'Like I said to your plods. For Christ sake get poor Gillian out of here and get **me** to the hospital!'

White then hurls both sticks. One collides into a wall and the other smashes a TV screen.

***

Maxine Stewart is working from home today. Since starting at around 9 am she has only been disturbed once when a colleague phoned less than half an hour later. This conversation lasted 57 minutes. Just under an hour ago Maxine began a lunch-break to indulge in a rare treat of watching "Loose Women" in real time.

Up to twenty minutes ago, the four panellists concentrated discussion on the emotive link between experiments on animals and selling or buying products to aid human, "Health and Beauty."

All the talk of experimentation on animals triggered memories for Maxine about what happened when she first met Lord and Judge Reginald Chalice-Hermitage. His revelations educated her to learn the small print which established a lie to an 'organic' claim made by a trendy cosmetics company. All the same, it is even more interesting to know what led to Maxine meeting Reginald and what happened afterwards.

During the spring of two thousand and three, Reginald and his wife hosted an evening dinner party at their London residence in St. Johns Wood. Earlier that same day, Maxine, along with two colleagues from different sections within the County Council's Children's Services, travelled from Norfolk to attend a very hush-hush meeting in the House of Lords.

The purpose of the meeting was to obtain legal ratification for an adoption of a three-day-old baby. The proposed, approved adopters waited in a hotel nearby. Once the baby became theirs, they returned to their family home which was quite a distance from Big Ben.

The reason for so much secrecy was the baby's father was a son of another country's Ambassador. The mother, a fellow student at a University, said amongst considerable wishes and feelings, and I'm paraphrasing, the following:-

"The father should never know about the child because he would do everything to try and make all three of us live in his birth country. I can never accept and disagree with too many of this country's laws and customs about women and family lifestyle. I don't want to share my life with the father or raise my child alone. Particularly knowing, at any moment, there will be a high risk of losing my son or daughter by way of them being taken against my will to live in a country where the father will always have a home, including an unknown one probably. I don't believe in abortion."

Whatever the merits or otherwise? The mother's views and rights are ironic too because the father and grandfather of her child still speak quite openly about how much they enjoy so many freedoms' Britain offers to them.

Perhaps a more relevant and essential comment, stroke question, about the circumstances and issues of this adoption, is the one Maxine often shares when invited to co-facilitate training programmes. Namely, she asks as part of an imitative case study, "How does the outcome for the child fit with the principle enshrined in the Children's Act 1989 which advocates, "The best interests of the child are the paramount consideration?"

Maxine enjoyed the dinner party because a lot of discussions involved intriguing and amusing tales by Reginald. Most relating to events which have occurred within the process of deciding justice. By the time Maxine was ready to leave, her two colleagues had already gone. They wanted to see for themselves what the fuss is all about at String-fellows?!

Maxine was in the process of calling for a taxi when Reginald insisted he should give her a lift. After a brief tit for tat, including support from his wife, Maxine accepted the Judge's kind offer.

Maxine was not surprised when, on arriving at the hotel,

she watched a concierge drive Reginald's car to a VIP parking space. She was even less surprised when he exclaimed, "We are going to enjoy a nightcap." But, she was a bit surprised when, on joining her at a table for two with two large glasses of brandy, he soon made a call to his wife. He said, "Hello Darling. On my way home I've popped into the Club. Well, yes, you know me my cherub! Anyway, Zachariah is here, so as you can imagine the cards are already on the table. I know. And you too. See you in the morning."

Maxine is presently trying to re-engage with the slog of reading a defence manuscript. Giving full attention is difficult as she hears a report on the Anglia TV news lunchtime bulletin.

'Yes, that's right Jonathan. Although I need to stress, the police have not yet confirmed whether the death is suspicious or not? I have only just arrived in Thre3 Scor3, which is a tiny village just outside Norwich. The entrance to Rose Close, where the senior aged woman lived, has been cord-en off by the police. It is my understanding …'

Maxine pushes the evidence aside, leans forward open-mouthed and grasps her mobile. Then, without moving her shock filled eyes away from the screen, like a typist who looks up to chat with you while still composing, Maxine presses the right buttons for Valerie's land-line number to start ringing.

***

DC Finley Billing is engaged in a door-step conversation with a beautiful woman dressed only in a bathrobe. The woman is very drunk. What has been bordering on ridiculous is about to become farcical. The woman's phone is ringing and Finley watches as she bangs her head before grabbing the receiver from behind her front door. 'No I fucking ain't, so piss off,' she shouts and has no idea who she's said this too.

The woman tries to slam the receiver onto its cradle and on her fourth attempt, she crashes to the floor. She groans, 'Shit! It's OK officer. I'm not hurt.'

Finley wants to help but entering the house reminds him how he felt when as a boy he sneaked into a neighbours garden to pinch an apple from their impressive tree.

It takes nearly a minute for Finley to assist the woman back onto a settee. 'I think it might be best to call an ambulance Mrs...'

'No officer, please no,' she pleads.

Finley noted how frightened the woman's sunken, distant and lost even, eyes look. He then asks, 'Are you sure madam? Can I please just check there isn't a cut or any blood?

The woman drops her head and slurs, 'Yes. That's kind.'

Finley looks and says, 'Glad to say you've been lucky Madam.'

The woman lays down on the sofa and Finley asks, 'What is your name please Madam?'

There is no reply because the woman has closed her eyes and is passing into sleep. Finley's eyes oscillate, over the woman's now practically naked body, like wave ripples across the sand on the shore. Albeit, a lot more slowly.

Finley then scans the room. He observes the contrast between the cleanness of it except for empty wine bottles, cups and plates scattered on a coffee table. 'Finished here,' he tells himself.

Finley walks toward the front door and before adjusting the receiver he picks up a house key from the adobe coloured quarry tiled floor. He places the key on a small mahogany table. By doing so Finley catches sight of a high pile of unopened letters. He hurriedly flicks through them, retrieves a notepad and pen from his breast pocket and writes, "Mrs Valerie Verity, 5 Woodland Mews. VLP – 2 OOHH-13.41pm."

Pleased he has evidence of another enquiry, Finley moves onto the next house.

***

Having been met by apprehensive confusion at the Day-Centre,

Sally did not hesitate to come and see what has happened in Thre3 Scor3? Sally shows her ID to a PC keeping guard in front of the CRIME SCENE ribbon tapered across the entrance to Rose Close.

'Please don't tell me it's number eight,' asks Sally.

'Yes ma'am, it is! Old lady killed by sounds of it. Found by her husband.'

'Is the husband…?'

'He's just injured ma'am,' interrupts the PC completely unaware he is answering a different question to the one Sally was going to ask.

Sally and Bernice look at each other speechless, 'Who is the DI?' asks Sally.

'I don't know his name ma'am, sorry. Do you want me to let you pass ma'am?'

Sally scribbles a note on an unused party invitation card and says to the PC, 'Please give him this.'

'Yes, ma'am.'

Sally turns away and Bernice asks, 'Aren't we staying, Sally?'

'Think we're too late don't you? Come on; we'll be more use back at base, replies Sally.

Sally then throws a bunch of keys to Bernice. 'Do you mind driving please?' Sally asks.

'No problem,' replies Bernice who at the same time silently exclaimed, 'Surely you can you see in my eyes, it is obvious I will do anything for you, Sally!'

***

In the back of an ambulance, Gwen is doing a stout job attending to a very disturbed Harold White. 'How much longer Adam?' asks Gwen as she uses all her strength to prevent Harold bashing his head against a Scoop Stretcher.

'Leave me alone you stupid cow,' shouts Harold.

'Ten minutes tops. Do you want to swap?' replies Adam.

'Cheers Adam. I think it'll be OK now.'

Harold makes a loud grunt followed by a projectile of vomit right into Gwen's face. 'Shit,' she says.

Gwen regrets opening her mouth and with one hand she wipes some of it off.

'I said, leave me alone! You stupid fucking bitch!' shouts Harold.

He then wriggles his head free and smashes it against the stretcher again.

'What the hell is going on?' asks Adam.

'Keep driving Adam,' implores Gwen.

Gwen ignores her discomfort and anger and places both hands on her patient's head. 'Just get to A+E as soon as please Adam,' pleads Gwen.

Four minutes later Adam is outside A+E. If it had been a different circumstance, Adam and probably Gwen too, would see the funny side of how Gwen's appearance looks like great makeup for someone in a horror film.

Together, they lift out an uncooperative Harold and lay him on a trolley. Despite their patient thrashing his body, they run like crazy into A+E. The casualty team are waiting and a Senior Registrar says, 'On my three. One, two, three,' and Harold is now in a hospital bed.

'OK, Gwen. Go and get cleaned up. I'll take it from here,' orders Adam supportively.

Adam then says, 'This is Harold White. His BP is 186 over 80. He has stab wounds on the top of his head. He is in deep shock. He's witnessed his wife fatally injured in the same incident. Mr White has self-harmed during our journey here by banging his head against a stretcher. This has caused injuries to his left temple. Mr White has also been violently sick twice.'

Adam leaves and hears that weird grunt again. He looks back and Harold is half way to sitting upright as he gushes out another fountain of puke. All, unlucky to be near enough, are splattered with various amounts.

***

Clive Verity puts his car radio on to hear if there are any more revelations. 'You are listening to BBC Radio Norfolk and it is five-thirty precisely. Our main headline this evening is the sensational news of events going on in the Norfolk village of Thre3 Scor3. At lunchtime, a dead body of a woman, believed to be a pensioner, was discovered at a house in Rose Close. Then, a little later, in a Woods close to the village, police erected a tent around what is speculated to be the body of Joanne Verity. The girl who vanished at a Fête in Heydon three years ago. Chief Constable Frank Toddenham made a brief statement in a live broadcast we bought to you just a few minutes ago and this is a recording of what he said.'

"It is with deep regret I make this statement so early in our enquiries. I will personally investigate who is responsible for alerting the media without lawful authority to do so. I think it is important to remind everyone, under the new Justice Act two thousand and seven, such action is a severe criminal offence. I will only make or authorise a further statement when it is morally right to do so or it is in line with seeking justice.

I can confirm the death of a lady found in her own home is suspicious. This lady's husband was also a victim and is receiving appropriate medical attention. I can confirm it is our intention to ask this said man to help us with our enquiries when his health permits us to do so. I can corroborate skeleton remains recovered in the woods in Thre3 Scor3, are thought to be human.

But, we have not identified to whom they belong, not even if they are bones of an adult or minor. This means there should not be any further speculative or inaccurate reports. We have an open mind as to whether there is a link between the two incidents and unless we discover anything different, each is being responded to separately. That's all. Thank you for listening and I will not be taking any questions."

'For the latest situation, we can now go to our reporter in …'

Clive turns the radio off and says out loud, 'God, I still pray it's not Jo.'

Clive wonders if he should head to the police station but decides, No, Valerie comes first!

All of a sudden Clive senses painful knots in the pit of his stomach. He has experienced this more than once during each of the past three years. However, this time they're excruciatingly sharp!

***

Having powdered her nose, Bernice walks back into a MASH office where Sally sits alone.

'Ah, Bernice. We might as well call it a day. But, we are on standby. Sir Roger has just called to say he expects PP will be quite a while at the hospital. He also mentioned we might be needed to attend an E. n. E. M. A. meeting' says Sally.

'A what?' asks Bernice.

Sally replies, 'Sorry. Jargon for what is called an "Extraordinary Emergency Multi-Agency Strategy Meeting. Sir Roger explained, because of the nature of some information discovered only today, it is pointing very much toward a need for such a meeting. They are fairly rare events apparently."

'Wow. Did Sir Roger share any details,' asks Bernice.

'His, for example, was, we've discovered the head of Children's Services legal department, Maxine Stewart, is Joanne Verity's Aunty. Therefore no Subject of this meeting or any of their relatives will be informed about it until after it takes place, let alone invited! We need to double check our recording before going...'

Bernice interrupts, 'I've met Maxine, have you?

'Yes,' replies Sally.

Bernice then says, 'Shame! I was going to ask if you fancy a drink in the Cross Keys? Still, we could share a Clementine?'

'You don't give up do you,' replies Sally and is still smiling as she adds, 'I'm a married woman now you know!'

Bernice puts her face right in front of Sally's and looking into her eyes she whispers, 'Oh well, can't blame a nice girl like me for trying eh?'

Bernice pirouettes before slowly walking away.

'Hey. Wait for me,' says Sally as she grabs her handbag before giving chase.

***

On entering Draper Hill, Clive is pleased to see the police are blocking access to Woodland Mews. Clive is less than happy to also see a plethora of media personnel on each side of the road. Hope there is no stone hearted guttering type amongst you, muses Clive. Immediately this hope is dashed when from his lofty position, Clive sights a man in their back garden. This man is taking photographs through a bay window.

'I'm taking you out,' Clive exclaims out loud.

Clive reaches the blockade. 'Hello officer, I am Clive Verity. Here is the ID badge I use at work.'

PC Diderot checks it. 'Clear the way please.'

'Thank you,' says Clive.

'No problem Sir.'

Clive parks outside a neighbour's house and calmly walks to his home's side entrance. He unlocks the door of a utility room and walks through it. He then opens another door and as he steps out, Clive can see the invader still snapping.

'Hello, I'm Clive Verity. Would you like one of the two of us?' asks Clive who also offers his hand for a shake.

'Ah, from where did you come? You mean, you are The Fêted Angel's father! Wow!'

The alien then immediately starts flashing shots at Clive.

'Yes, I certainly am,' replies Clive who is now in front of the uninvited intruder. Clive offers his hand again, 'Hello, I'm Clive, how can I help you Mr?'

The encroacher puts his fire on hold and stretches out his

right hand to accept the shake. 'Griff...'

The reason for the pressman not completing his name is the impact of a fist hitting his midriff with immense force. Then, faster than a Muhammed Ali shuffle, Clive smashes his other fist flush onto the trespasser's jaw.

Griffin's descent is agonisingly slow and he involuntarily sprawls onto his hands and knees. Griffin is trying to speak but instead, he completes his fall by scraping his face against concrete slabs before dishevelling into a heap.

Clive stands astride and drags the skulker into the larger of his two sheds. From a shelf, Clive grabs the climbing rope and wraps it into the interloper's mouth. He then binds Griffin's hands and feet with spare lawn-mower cable and sits him upright against an efficient grass cutter.

Clive then removes a camera from around the neck of his captured "USP," as he calls them, and carries it outside. He turns and stares into eyes that have real fear in them now. These eyes watch Clive skilfully drop and trap the camera under a foot. And then, with one stomp, smash it into pieces!

Clive shuts the shed door and takes a short walk to their large conservatory. From here he enters a living room in which he is ninety-nine percent sure he will find Valerie on the settee.

Clive kneels beside his wife and then gently flicks wet strands of hair out of Valerie's sad eyes. Valerie is resting one side of her face on a pillow formed by her own hands. The tears trickling down cheeks though, belong to Clive.

'Val. It's me, sweetheart. Squeeze any finger if you can hear me.'

Valerie brushes a purple fingertip against her husband's hand and whispers, 'They've found Joanne.'

Clive moves to lay beside Valerie and they wrap their arms around one another. 'Sweetheart, it can still not be our Jo and.'

Clive stops to lick tears from his face and although the BBC News Channel has been on the whole time, it is only now Clive hears it.

'... are unconfirmed reports alleging skeleton remains found in a woods might well be Joanne Verity who went missing over three years ago.'

Strange thinks Clive. Val hates watching the news on TV. He searches for the remote and presses it off. 'Sweetheart, I'm back to stay!'

'Clive. I'm scared. I can feel it's Jo this time. I can't stay here, take me to the hospital, please Clive.'

Clive hugs Valerie.

Within seconds Clive hears another woman's voice. 'Sorry I was so long. Glad I went, I **had** left some files on the passenger seat. Oh, hello Mr Verity. I didn't realise you'd arrived.'

'Hi,' mimes Clive bending his head to see it is Valerie's, Community Nurse.

Clive gently extricates from his wife who is murmuring. 'It's OK Genevieve; Clive's here too now!'

Clive places a couple of cushions behind Valerie's head and she covers her face with both hands.

'I'll make us all a drink,' says Clive who stands before adding, 'Thank you so much for being here with Val. I just couldn't get here any earlier.'

'I need a hot brandy please if Genevieve is OK with breaking the rules?' asks Valerie whose speech is wispy and blurred.

'Yes, of course, it is,' says Genevieve sincerely while also thinking both parents have a look of fear. I fear for them too!

'Shall we have a chat in the kitchen Mrs, ERM... I am sorry. I'm brilliant with faces, names Crap!' says Clive.

'Treets, Miss Genevieve Treets. Thank you and yes, sounds a good idea.'

Genevieve follows Clive into the kitchen.

'Please, take this seat. What would you like? Tea? Coffee?' asks Clive.

'Coffee sounds nice. With milk only please,' replies Genevieve as she sits on a chair made of half Ash-wood and half wicker.

Genevieve then asks, 'May I call you Clive?'

'That is my name,' replies Clive warmly.

'I hope you don't think I'm forward Clive; it's just...'

'Please, go on.'

'As Valerie's Community Psychiatric Nurse, I suggest hospital is now what Valerie needs. More private and protective. I do hope you understand why I say this?'

Clive replies, 'You care too. Yes, I agree. Talking to Valerie may surprise you. I think she will be relieved to go.'

'Really? She's said so often how much she hated being in hospital following a need for urgent detoxification treatment.'

'Pretty certain. Obviously best you hear Val say the same thing to you, being an outsider as well. God, such a horrible word to use, sorry...'

'I understand Clive. Thanks, I will,' interjects Genevieve while accepting a mug of coffee.

'To give you both privacy, I'll take this opportunity to pop out for a few minutes to deal with the USP in my shed. OK with y...'

'You're what?' asks Genevieve whose facial expression displays a mixture of bewilderment, curiosity and to her surprise, concern even!

'When arriving here not long ago, I discovered an uninvited person hiding in our back garden taking photos of Val on the settee. I've tied him up in the shed, so I'm now going to hand him to the police.'

'You've done what?!!!' exclaims Genevieve, struggling to take it all in. 'And what do you mean by USP?' she asks.

Clive laughs and replies, 'My abbreviation for Uncaring Sick Pervert.'

Clive is pleased to see Genevieve fail to prevent a smile too.

'I see. Very interesting Clive,' Genevieve replies. She then takes hold of a mug full of hot brandy with a sprinkling of coffee stirred into it.

***

Maxine, Luke and Maxine's daughter Milena Trunch are sharing a meal together at home, albeit all watching transfixed to an extended edition of BBC Look East. Currently, a local news presenter is reporting live from Thre3 Scor3, '... and the latest confirmed report is that Mr Harold White, husband of the deceased, is being treated in the Royal Shakespeare Unit at Norfolk's largest Hospital just outside Norwich. The police have confirmed, as soon as Mr White is well enough, they hope he will help with their enquiries. The latest unconfirmed report is, the police wish to speak with the driver of a Navy Blue or Black van seen...'

'Do they think the old lady's husband did it mum?' asks Milena.

'No. What I mean is, the police aren't saying who murdered the poor old lady. It is standard practice to interview any witness.'

'Who may well be, just another victim,' interjects Luke.

'Will they interview neighbours mum?'

'I think you're wondering will they interview Aunt Val?'

'Yes.'

'They already have and she was very drunk I'm afraid. Val didn't say much on the phone and it is how she did speak that told me she was. I called Clive to check he was with Val. Clive said he'd spoken with Val's CPN. Fortunately, the CPN agreed to go and stay with Val till Clive could get away from work. Sod's law, Clive had to work in the Huntingdon office today.'

'What is a CPN mum?' asks Milena, despite pondering at the same time, But Aunt V hasn't been drunk for ages.

'A Community Psychiatric Nurse sweetheart.'

A mobile begins to vibrate, and soon its ringtone of a song called, "Losing My Religion" by REM, follows. Maxine reaches across Luke to pick it up.

'Hello. Oh! Hi-ya. Yes. Is Val OK? Oh, I see, and you mean

now? OK, where are you? I can hear voices and traffic. Oh, I see. Sure, see you there. Bye.'

'Clive said a Psychiatrist and Social Worker are on their way to assess whether Valerie needs to be in a hospital or not? Said, Val wants to go and she wants me to be at the hospital to help her settle in. Said I'd leave right away.'

'Can I come too please mum?'

'No,' say Maxine and Luke in unison.

Maxine explains why. 'Sweetheart, your Aunt Val needs to rest with privacy and quiet. Going to the hospital for your Aunt is a good thing! Aunt Val is not in any danger. Aunt Val needs time with people looking after her twenty-four seven. I promise, the moment it is a good time to visit Aunt Val, we will go together. OK?'

Milena nods and gives a reluctant smile. 'OK mum.'

'And anyway, it's the second night of the play and we enjoyed watching you last night. You were brilliant! And you've been going on and on about how much you are looking forward to a sleepover at Sophie's. If you want, I can call Sophie's mum to say I'll drop you off. OK?'

'No thanks mum. I need to get ready and I've got time to have a shower before they come.'

'Right, sounds a good plan,' agrees Maxine who then hugs Milena. 'Go and break your other leg tonight eh! Be good and see you tomorrow. Love you.'

'You to mum.'

Maxine then pecks Luke's cheek before saying, 'Will see you soon! I haven't forgotten our plan for ...'

Luke interjects, 'Oh, OK! Won't matter if it's another time. So, take as long as you need Max. Good luck.'

***

Geneviève left Valerie and Clive, once confirmation a Doctor and the emergency out of hours Duty Social Worker were on their way. Twenty or so minutes ago Maxine arrived. She is with both professionals in the kitchen. Maxine is the first to notice an ambulance backing up in Woodland Mews and hurries into the living room. 'It's here.'

'Right,' says Clive.

Maxine watches Clive kiss Valerie. 'I'll be following. Be brave sweetheart.'

'I want to take my handbag with me...' Valerie murmurs.

'Don't worry sis. I'll fetch it and bring it with us.'

'Make sure you do,' says Valerie.

Clive then stands very close to Maxine and says, 'Be best we follow in our cars.'

'Sure,' replies Maxine as she softly brushes a finger against her very secret love's arm. So secret, in fact, not even Clive knows this is the case.

To explain the context of Maxine's feelings is better realised by me going back in time again. For this and what are some other reasons too, the next chapter first tells you what happened on 2, 20 and 21 September 2002. Then secondly, what occurred less than two weeks ago on the fourth and fifth of July 2007.

Once again, what happens on each of these five days is, in the main, information learnt after the date on which this story ends.

CHAPTER THREE

September 2, 2002

'Val?'

'Yes, sweetheart.'

'Do you mind if I take Joanne to school? I've missed too many firsts in her life.'

'Oh how sweet,' says Valerie who then tweaks her husband's right cheek with her delicate and slender fingers. 'Of course, you can,' she adds.

'Ouch,' cries Clive hyperbolically and then retaliates by tickling his scantily dressed wife under her short silk bathrobe.

With both parents engaged in breakfast table 'playtime,' Joanne walks pass them to the fridge. She takes out a jar of blackcurrant jam in it and then begins to spread it onto a recently popped up slice of toast. Joanne smiles at the sound of her mother giggling and she turns her head, 'Morning Mum, morning Dad,' Joanne says brightly.

'Hi-ya sweetheart,' replies Clive who also winks at Joanne.

Clive is temporarily off his guard, and this enables Valerie another opportunity to breach her husband's defences. Albeit, the opposite cheek this time.

Joanne joins her parents at the table. 'Mum, does my uniform look OK?'

'A draw I think, and I'm sure if we'd gone into extra time, I'd have won,' says Clive as he raises his hands to signal full time.

Valerie retorts, 'In your dreams.'

Valerie then gently lifts her right hand to brush strands of hair out of her daughter's eye. Valerie says, 'You look, beautiful sweetheart,' which is something she says every day in one form or another. Valerie adds, 'Today you look smart too! Don't you think so Dad?'

'Very smart. Pity Mum and Dad had to go home yesterday,' says Clive.

Clive then dashes off his seat saying, 'Will be right back.'

Valerie and Joanne look at one another and shrug their shoulders.

'Where are you going...' asks Joanne who suddenly stops because Clive is back with a camera in hand. 'There. I'll take some photos when we get to the school. Mum and Dad will love to have one,' says Clive excitedly.

'OK,' says Joanne with a sigh and then adds, 'Seeing it's for Nana and Grandpa.'

Valerie interjects, 'Great idea Clive! And, a few for our family album too eh guys!'

Clive says, 'Of course' at the same time Joanne says, 'Here we go, snap snap snap.'

'ERM... Joanne?' asks Clive as he sits down again.

'Yes, Dad.'

'Would you mind if I take you to school? Mum and I have...'

'Yeah, I'd love you too, great. But, you're coming too aren't you Mum?' replies Joanne.

Valerie says, 'Not today sweetheart. Do you remember what you said so many times when we had breakfast in Germany?'

Joanne's face displays surprise, but she says, 'Yep.'

Joanne then reaches out to huddle with Valerie as emperor penguins do for one another during snow blizzards in the Antarctic. 'Thanks, Mum,' she says.

'What **did** you say?' asks Clive.

Joanne and Valerie look at one another and giggle. 'Doesn't matter Daddy. Will tell you on the way to school.'

Intrigued more than anything else Clive says, 'OK princess.'

'Are you excited?' asks Valerie.

Joanne's smile negates her reply, 'Bit nervous I guess Mum.'

'Of course, you are, that's only natural. Do you want me to do your hair?'

'No thanks Mum, I like it free,' Joanne replies before

crunching on her toast.

Valerie stands up and Clive spots his wife's follow me tilt of her head. He reacts accordingly. Valerie stops, and both lean against opposite walls in their hallway. She says, 'I'll see you later. I can now get my hair done. We've been invited to dinner with our neighbours tomorrow evening. As newcomers to the village only polite to go, don't you think? I'll be back about midday, maybe one.'

'Oh right, ERM ... Yes.'

Clive wants to say, Your hair looks great! You only went last week. Instead, determined to remain focused on Joanne, he chooses to be neutral. 'OK sweetheart. I look forward to seeing the improvement.'

'Cheeky bugger,' retorts Valerie and they then both re-enter the kitchen.

'Are you ready Joanne?' asks Clive.

Joanne hurriedly pushes the last of the crust and crumbs into her mouth which is followed by a gulp of some tea. 'Yep,' she splutters.

Joanne wipes off the seeping tea and accepts her father's offer to hold hands. 'Shall we walk princess?'

'Yes, Dad. And can we say hello to the horses on the way please?'

Clive opens the back door.

'Hey, hold on you two,' says Valerie who then hands Joanne a new school bag.

'Thanks, Mum.'

'And take these,' says Valerie.

'Wow. Great. Nice one Mum,' Joanne says before she accepts the fresh carrots. They then share a hug. 'Have a great Day Jo,' Valerie whispers.

'I will. Won't I Dad?'

'Definitely princess, definitely,' repeats Clive and once again he holds hands with Joanne. They then begin the mile or so walk to the school.

Valerie follows them until she reaches the end of a porch. She watches them disappear when turning onto Woodland Mews Lane. Valerie then rushes upstairs into the bathroom. She immediately turns on the shower and then looks into a mirror above the wash basin.

'Shite,' she bemoans on seeing confirmation of a spot in an infant stage of development. It is protruding from the middle of her forehead. She removes some cotton wool from a pretty yellow and blue patterned bowl on the windowsill and squeezes the unwanted addition, 'Of all days,' Valerie verbalises to the face in the mirror.

Moments later, Valerie steps into the shower. A mighty fall of hot water soon combines with shampoo. Valerie glances at the clock above the bathroom cabinet. It displays 08.30am, and Valerie has an 'appointment' at 10.00am.

***

As Valerie exits the shower, outside school gates, Clive pecks Joanne's forehead. He then crouches so they are face to face. 'If you don't like this school princess or England even, please tell me. I promise I'll then talk to mum about returning to Germany. OK?'

Joanne squeezes her father's right hand. 'Thanks, Dad,' she says, and they walk through the gates and onto the tarmac covered playground.

It is not long before they approach the halfway point marked by a red chalked circle used for Hockey and football matches. Joanne stops walking. She looks up at Clive. Clive cannot but help notice the eyes looking at him sparkle brighter than any star. 'What is it, princess?' Clive asks.

'I do not care most of the others are with their Mums because I have the best and bravest Dad in the world,' says Joanne.

Clive gently ruffles his fingers through Joanne's hair and says, 'Thank you, princess. Such a nice thing to say.'

'And Daddy, me and Mum were giggling cuz I used to say it

would be great to have breakfast with you too, and then sometimes you take me to school.'

'Ah, I see. Well, I had a similar wish too, Jo. So, today special for both of us eh princess!'

'Yes, Daddy.'

Clive can now see a reflection of himself in Joanne's eyes. Just like he used to do when his mother smiled at him. 'God, you know what Joanne? You look so much like Nana Verity when she was your age.'

'Do I?'

'Yes,' confirms Clive.

They start walking again. Soon reaching the tail end of a queue to await a welcome by the Head Teacher. For some in this line, it is their first day at a new school. For Joanne, there is the added ingredient it is the first taste of English Education.

Clive looks all around, and many of the mothers take the opportunity to offer their new peer a,"Welcome to our clan," gesture. Clive acknowledges each one with a courteous smile. He appears to be unaware most of the tribe are also signalling, in respective ways, their approval of this particularly handsome new member.

At the head end of the queue a mother hurriedly, albeit reasonably gently, barges out against the incoming traffic. After taking a few steps, Maxine Stewart stumbles against Clive. 'Sorry, in a rush. Big day at work. It is my daughter's first day here, so had to come,' Maxine gabbles.

'Snap. It is my daughter's first day too,' Clive replies resting a hand on Joanne's shoulder. 'This is Joanne.'

'Hello, nice to meet you, Joanne.'

'Hello.'

'Sorry, must go, I really can't be late, bye,' says Maxine.

Maxine then runs toward her car. Clive and Joanne look at each other and shortly hear from a distance, 'Really am sorry for being so clumsy. Nice meeting you and hope to again. Bye,' shouts Maxine waving.

Clive and Joanne reciprocate with hesitant waves back.

Maxine then says to herself, 'Where has that sex on legs been hiding?'

It is a fact, neither Clive nor Maxine recognised the other. It is also a fact Maxine and the woman to whom Clive is married, are estranged sisters!

The rare occasions Maxine had a chance to get a peep of Valerie's, "To old for my girl boyfriend," happened fourteen years ago. These attempts involved looking out of her bedroom window to watch Valerie return home late at night in Clive's car.

Two things happened each time. Clive remained in his car with its headlights on, and Maxine quickly returned to her bed because their mother opened the front door to march out and shout her, disapproval sums up the words she used!

***

Joanne is outside. She is sitting on a bottom step of five that lead to one of the fire exit doors of the large Assembly Hall. Joanne opens her pink lunch-box and bites into her cheese and tomato sandwich. Joanne then hears, 'Can I join you, please? My name is Lilly. What is yours?'

Joanne looks up with her cheeks bulging and sees Lilly's friendly face. Joanne swallows hurriedly and replies, 'Sure,' and then slides along to make space. 'My name's Joanne. Is this your first day too, Lilly?'

'Yes, bit scary isn't it!' says Lilly.

'Yes. Would you like one of these?' asks Joanne.

'No thanks. Got my own here,' says Lilly and the two girls share a smile.

'I was behind you in the queue this morning with my Mum. Do you live with just your Dad then?' asks Lilly.

'No, with Mum too. She had an important meeting to go to this morning,' replies Joanne who feels a need to explain her mother's absence. She then adds, 'We came to England in June. We used to live in Germany because my Dad is in the Army. He's going back soon. He has too because it's his job. Do you have any brothers or sisters?'

'One of each and I'm the eldest. Do you?' asks Lilly.

'No. Just us three. Well actually, it's mostly two.'

'Why did you leave Germany?' asks Lilly.

'Mum's idea.'

'How long did you live in Germany Joanne? Was it exciting to live there?'

Joanne replies, 'I was born there actually. Mum and Dad are both English, and because the land where the Army base is, is British it means I'm only English too. Yes, it was exciting, and I miss my friends. What about your Dad? What is his job?'

Lilly hesitates, and Joanne senses her new friend starting to look a bit embarrassed. Joanne gently places her left hand on Lilly's right one, 'It's OK, you don't have to tell me anything, and if you do, I promise I won't tease you. I'm not like that,' states Joanne.

Lilly replies, 'Thanks. My Mum says she doesn't know where my father is and even if she did I'm better off without him. It's hard though because my brother sees his and my sister sees hers at least once a week.'

'Wow, I bet. Has your Mum looked to find him?' asks Joanne.

'No, says she will tell me about Dad when I'm old enough to understand.'

'Oh,' replies Joanne who hesitates before adding, 'I'd hate not seeing my Dad. Tell you what Lilly. Next time Dad takes me out somewhere exciting for the day, you can come too. He's great fun. OK?'

'That would be great,' says Lilly before adding, 'Thank you for not teasing me.'

Lilly then hugs Joanne and says, 'So what does your Dad do in the Army?'

'He's a soldier. I know he does lots of other secret things too.'

'Has he told you about any? Or have you heard him telling your Mum?' Lilly asks excitedly.

'Bits. They both tell me I must never tell anyone else,' replies Joanne.

'How amazing,' exclaims Lilly.

'Does your Mum work?' Joanne asks.

'Yes. Mum designs and makes dresses for weddings and christenings.'

'Wow that's clever,' says Joanne as she accepts Lilly's offer of a penguin biscuit. 'I'd love to see them one day and thank you, Lilly.'

'You will Joanne, I promise! Do you have a mobile phone?' asks Lilly.

'Yes.'

Lilly says, 'My number is a nought followed by nine sevens and then two.'

Joanne retrieves a phone from her leather school bag. Lilly watches her compose and send a message. It says, 'Hello to my nice new friend Lilly. Luv J. xx.'

Joanne continues to stare into the face of her phone and soon hears Bleep Bleep. She opens the text and reads, 'U2.Ly. X'

A shadow then creeps eerily over the two girls and in unison they look up and assume standing in front of them is one of the prefects of the school. 'Hello, my name is Milena. Are you both new too?' and the intruder's delivery is genuinely warm and friendly.

Joanne and Lilly glance at one another. 'Yes. I'm Lilly, and this is Joanne. Would you like to join us?' and both girls make space for Milena to snuggle between them.

Milena accepts their invitation and then moves her head side to side like many spectators do to watch tennis at Wimbledon as she says, 'Thanks, guys. Love your bag, Lilly!

'Thanks, my Mum made it for me,' says Lilly as she hands the bag to Milena.

'That's cool, it's stunning. Love all the colours. Your mum is...'

Fate then, dictates all three girls are now finally enjoying their first day at their new school.

***

September 20, 2002

'Time for bed young lady,' says Valerie and Joanne can hear this time her mother means it.

'OK, Mum. I'm just going to ask Dad something first. You go back on Sunday, don't you

Dad?'

'Yes. Afraid so princess.'

'So tomorrow is your whole last day at home for ages, so can we please go somewhere nice?'

'Where do you want to go princess?'

'London please Daddy,' shouts Joanne who is jogging on the spot.

'London it is then.'

'Oh nice one Dad,' says Joanne before using a finger to stroke her top lip. She then adds, 'I don't mean to be rude Mum. I do mean just me and Dad. Please can I, we? You see, my friend Lilly hasn't ...'

'It's OK Jo. I remember you telling us. Of course, you can,' replies Valerie.

With excitement brimming toward overspill Joanne hugs Valerie. 'Thanks, Mum. Lilly will be happy too,' she says.

'Could be a bit short notice Val?'

'True. What is Miss Thompson's home number, Jo?'

'It's three, three, eight, four, three, seven Mum.'

Valerie then dials and listens to four rings. 'Hi Helen, it's

Valerie Verity here. I'm fine thanks. And you? Sorry to ask this late ...'

'Up to bed princess. You are getting up early. Best go and get some more beauty sleep. OK!' says Clive.

'Cool. Goodnight Dad and thanks.'

Joanne then hurries out of the room and before she reaches the stairs begins composing a text to her best friend.

'... that's wonderful Helen. Sure. I'll let Clive know that. Bye.'

'Are you OK with this Val?' asks Clive.

'Yes. Jo is going to miss you as much as I am. Besides, Lilly is a lovely friend, and they'll enjoy having you to themselves.'

Clive knows his return to Germany is difficult for all of them and attempts making light of it. 'Time will fly past. Before we know it, I'll be back, and you'll be wishing I wasn't under your feet or cramping your style.'

Valerie replies with a chuckle, 'You know, you might be right! You also know Jo, and I will count down to the day you're due home again.'

Clive then joins Valerie on the sofa. They nestle into one another. After an hour Valerie is struggling to stay awake, so Clive switches off the TV.

As Clive returns to the sofa, Valerie smiles at him because she's thinking, 'You are about to hold me in an over the threshold lift and carry me to our bed on which we will make love until at least when the sun rises.'

Valerie is not wrong.

***

'Wakey Wakey. It's a beautiful morning Jo,' says Valerie opening Joanne's bright orange bedroom curtains.

With eyes still shut and head now under bedclothes, Joanne mumbles, 'What time is it mum?'

'Quarter to six and a brew is boiling. What would you like

for breakfast? How does a pancake with syrup and Jam sound?' suggests Valerie.

'Yes please, Mum.'

Joanne then peers over her duvet just in time to see her mother disappear.

Valerie skips to descend the stairs and is merrily singing a song. Joanne starts singing it too as she begins the daily routine of showering and deciding what to wear?

***

'Ready Dad.'

'Hokey Cokey princess. Just need to finish checking the oil and water.'

'Can I sit in the front please Dad?' and answering her question before Clive does, Joanne hops in.

'Sure, and put the seat belt on please Jo.'

Clive then shuts the bonnet. 'Have a good day Val.'

'Will try too,' says Valerie standing on the front doorstep in her favourite bathrobe. Valerie blows a kiss to both and says, 'You too. Take care and have fun!'

Joanne jostles her head out of a window and says, 'We will. Bye. See you tonight mum, love you.'

Valerie and Joanne wave until the car exits Woodland Mews. Joanne then hastily sifts through some CD's and places a, "Now That's What I Call Music," album into the player. She sets the volume high.

***

Joanne's exhibiting a most beautiful broad smile which is quite an assertion given it's happening in what is the mother county of many a beautiful Broad. Joanne sees a sign confirming they are on Bishybarnabee Way which is where Lilly lives.

'What number is it Jo?'

'There isn't any number Dad. The cottage is called Sangria

Creek. It's here. On the left.'

'Right,' says Clive who pulls up and then makes a comment most visitors say when seeing Sangria Creek for the first time. 'Wow. What a fantastic home.'

'It's great! Isn't it Dad?'

Joanne bursts out of the car and runs up to what is the original wooden front door. She taps it with a black wrought iron Gargoyle knocker.

Helen answers, 'Hello Joanne. How are you?'

'Very well thank you, Miss Thompson.'

'Good good. Lilly? They are here,' shouts Helen politely.

'Hello, I'm Clive. Nice to meet you, Helen,' says Clive who is now right behind Joanne.

'Likewise Clive! It's nice to put a face to someone I've heard so much about.'

Clive and Helen shake hands over Joanne's head, and Helen observes silently, 'Now I know where Jo's stunning hair comes from.'

Clive says, 'Thank you for agreeing to such short notice. Are you sure it's not inconvenient because …'

'Hi-ya Jo,' Lilly says merrily. Lilly then squeezes past her mother and hugs her friend. 'Thank you so much for keeping your promise! You're the best friend ever! I can't believe I'm going to see London. It's exciting!'

'That was a bit rude Lilly. How about saying hello to Joanne's father, Mr Verity. And, thanking him too.'

Both girls have an arm around one another with beaming faces looking at Clive. Lilly says, 'Hello Mr Verity and thank you so much for taking us to London.'

'No problem, you are very welcome Lilly.'

Helen then says, 'Now, I think you were asking me something, Clive?'

'ERM … yes. My plan is for us to explore some famous sites in London. Should be a real adventure.'

'Sounds wonderful,' Helen agrees.

'We hope to fit in Buckingham Palace, a Museum, a ride on the Eye and maybe a picnic in a park. I'll try not to be back too late. Before nine OK with you Helen?'

'Yes, and thank you for including Lilly, it's very kind and please thank Valerie again for me won't you?'

'Yes, of course. Here is my number. Text me, and I'll then be able to let you know we arrived safe and should it look like we're running a little late I can let you know.'

Helen is smitten. And, is doing her best not to show it. 'Absolutely! Good thinking,' she says quite seriously. Helen accepts the folded piece of paper before sliding it into a hip pocket.

'Right, guess we need to get going. You just can't predict what's happening on the M twenty-five,' says Clive.

Dancing like supporters on the North Bank after a Thierry Henry goal, Lilly and Joanne chant, 'Here we go, here we go, here...'

By the time they are on the A11, all three are singing "Angel" at the top of their voices. However, Clive is simultaneously doing some reflection. It's great that at last, I can show Joanne where I was born and raised. I think Joanne will love the surprise!

***

It is nearly quarter to ten, and Clive drives into Highbury Grove. 'Where are we Dad?' asks Joanne rubbing her eyes.

'A place called Highbury in North London princess and any second now I'll be turning into Highbury Hill.'

'Nana and Granddad live on Highbury Hill don't they Dad?'

'Yep. And what did I often promise you in Germany?'

'To show me Nana's house one day. And it is the house in which you were born. And because it's number eleven, eleven is your favourite number.'

'Good girl,' says Clive gobsmacked at so many cars parked

on the road he enjoyed playing on when growing up.

'Wow, wicked Dad! Do they know we're coming?'

'Yes, they do princess.'

Unknown to both, Clive's father stops peeping through a net curtain and alerts everyone to his son's arrival.

Joanne gently nudges a sleepy Lilly. 'Lilly, we're at my Nana's house. You need to wake up because ...'

'Ah, found a space,' says Clive and it takes a matter of thirty seconds or so for all three to be walking toward number eleven.

Joanne looks up at her father with her eyes full of excitement. She says, 'Brilliant Dad.'

Clive does not answer. Instead, he affectionately ruffles the top of Joanne's head and looks to his left. 'Are you OK Lilly?'

Lilly replies, 'Yes thank you, Mr Verity. It's great being in London.'

'My name is Clive, so no more of the Mr Verity. Agreed?'

Lilly smiles. 'Agreed Mr ... Clive,' and both girls giggle.

They are now two houses away from number eleven, and Clive notices the front door is slightly open. 'Wait here please girls.'

The girls watch Clive climb three steps to the front door. He rests a hand gently on it.

'Hello? Anyone home?'

In a flash, Shaz pulls on the door. Squashed in the hallway, a large group of children and adults instantly cheer and chant. 'We want Joanne, we want Joanne; we wa...'

In shock, Clive steps back, still not entirely taking in what is happening. Joanne shrieks excitedly as she runs and swivels around her father and into her grandmother's open arms. 'Nana!'

'What the ...,' Clive asks laughing.

Shaz answers. 'When Valerie phoned your mum to say you were on your way, we all thought this is an excellent way for everyone to welcome Joanne into the fold at long last! Poole and his motley crew are here too.'

'I heard that.'

'Fantastic!,' says Clive.

Remembering Lilly, Clive walks back to the gate. 'Come on Lilly, and I'll introduce you to my family and friends.'

Everyone in number eleven leaves the house just under an hour later. In an inter-changeable convoy, they all visit the National History Museum, have a ride on the Millennium Eye and have their photos taken with a guard outside Buckingham Palace. Around four o'clock they all share four family size buckets of Kentucky Fried Chicken in Regents Park.

***

'Thanks, Jo, and you too Clive. I've had a wonderful time. It was brilliant mum! We went everywhere and I met Jo's Grandma and pa. Jo's pleased they said they're going to leave London and move to Norfolk. Aren't you Jo?'

'Sure am,' agrees Joanne who then hugs Lilly as she adds, 'I'm glad you came to Lilly, and you can come next time can't she Dad?'

'If there is a next time. I expect Mr Verity is a very busy man,' suggests Helen.

'Clive is my name, Helen. I'm sure there will be another time, perhaps we can all go? I'm sure I speak for Valerie too when I say you'd all be welcome to join us.'

'Thank you, Clive. An offer we are almost certain to accept one day and thanks again for taking care of Lilly.'

'No problem Helen. Come on Jo.'

Jo says, 'Goodbye Lilly. Goodbye Helen.'

***

The last stretch of the journey home involves a lot of narrow lanes with sharp bends. Clive is about to negotiate the final one when in the corner of his eye he reads a sign for Rose Close. On impulse, Clive turns into it and parks outside the home of Harold White's neighbour.

'Come on Jo, just want to check on Eddie. Do you remember? The man I told you was going to a hospital to have a hip replacement?'

'OK, dad.'

'I just need to give him a little something to aid his recovery. It's in the boot.'

'What is it, dad?'

'Some of those ciggies from Germany that you hate the smell of so much.'

'Oh, Dad. You can't give cigarettes to someone who isn't well!'

'Eddie will appreciate them. Come on.'

They reach the front door, and Harold answers their knock. He thinks he's hiding his surprise at seeing who is standing in his arched porch-way. Clive also heeds the stylish suit worn by Harold.

'Hope you don't mind Eddie? I know it's gone eight and I can see we're interrupting. I wanted to check how your operation went. I go back tomorrow, and I thought you'd like these.'

Clive hands over his gift and Harold just about manages to stop himself saying, 'But I don't smoke.'

Instead, after momentarily diverting his eyes to the girl standing shyly by her Dad, Harold answers. 'Thank you for these. It went as well as can be expected, and it is very kind of you to enquire, very kind. And this is Joanne I presume?'

Harold places the cigarettes on a shelf in the porch.

'Yes. Joanne, say hello to Eddie.'

'Hello, Mr Eddie. It is nice to meet you, and I hope you are getting better?'

Harold stretches out his arm to shake hands with Joanne. 'Nice to meet you and I am making good progress. Thank you for asking. I would invite you both in, but we're in the middle of hosting a dinner party. Perhaps another time?'

'We'd like that wouldn't we princess!'

'Yes,' says Joanne and she folds her arms while gently swaying side to side.

'Splendid!' exclaims Harold. 'Good luck Clive and keep safe.'

'Dad will Mr Eddie because he's the best.'

They all laugh, and after both visitors shake Harold's hand again, they turn to leave. Joanne is behind her Dad, and she gives a quick glance back. Harold waves and with his other hand blows a kiss. Joanne responds by putting into practice the Royal salute learnt earlier today outside Buckingham Palace.

Harold waits for them to exit the Close and walks the short distance to the bins. He throws the cigarettes into a green one. He then returns inside, and as he shuts the door his wife calls out, 'Who was it, Harold?'

'Morons.'

'Who are Morons?'

'I said Mormons dear, not Morons,' replies Harold with a chortle.

***

July 4, 2007

Luke Stewart admires the view out of his kitchen window. He's beguiled by a rising sun diverging fantastic shades of orange and red. Lighting up a sky which is set to become a bright Indian ocean blue. A kettle whistling breaks Luke's languid gaze. He makes two mugs of tea and carries them to a bedroom where Maxine lays asleep. He softly places one cup in front of a bedside clock displaying 05.37am.

Luke tip-toes to the other side of the room and rests his mug on a scarlet coloured carpeted floor. Quietly, he opens a curtain-less sliding door and positions an armchair so he can look out at their colourful non-overlooked garden. He sits and sips his tea and whispers, 'It **really** should be a lovely day.'

***

Four hours later in a neighbouring village of Thre3 Scor3, a council mini-bus parks outside the house where Gillian White lives. Gillian is the last pick up on account of living nearest to the mini-buses final destination which is a private Day-Centre.

Gillian prefers to be called Jill and the mini-bus driver Bethany was told this nearly a year ago. Jill is slowly pushing herself up the front garden path, and Bethany says, 'Hello Gillian. How are you today?'

'I'm very well, thank you, Beverley,' replies Jill.

Ah, poor lady, hope I don't get dementia at Gillian's age, Bethany muses once again.

Jill has some uncomfortable health difficulties. Dementia is not one of them. Once Jill's chair is securely placed, she says brightly, 'Good morning Mr Jacobs. Good to see you're still with us. Have you been away somewhere nice?'

'Yes. My daughter invited me to stay with her for a couple of weeks,' Mr Jacobs replies.

'Grandchildren?' Jill asks.

'Yes. Three of the little darlings.'

'How lovely! Where do they live?'

'Budleigh Salterton. Do you know it? It's in Devon, on the coast,' answers Mr Jacobs.

'Oh yes, it's lovely, isn't it? I went there once during a lovely weekend in Exmouth. Such a pretty county!' says Jill.

'It is that Jill. And, how are you keeping?' Mr Jacobs asks.

'Good, thank you. Although, not sleeping too well. So, a bit tired,' replies Jill.

'When I can't sleep I find brandy with hot milk does wonders,' Mr Jacobs advises.

'Or a Salted Caramel Vodka,' suggests Jill with a smile.

'Put your seat belt on please Mr Jacobs,' asks Bethany and like a schoolboy on an outing he turns to face the front and refastens his belt.

Bethany then starts the last leg of this morning's journey. Within a few seconds, Jill looks out a window and begins to do something she's done quite a lot since her widowed cousin Maggie died fourteen months ago. Jill's thinking about her bitter-sweet time in Scotland in the early 1970's. It was there Jill lived with Maggie's family when she left her marriage for what didn't turn out to be on a permanent basis.

Such a pretty cottage just outside a lovely wee village overlooking a not so wee Loch. What a breathtaking view. The Loch surrounded by magnificent mountains. The only change to the landscape over thousands of years is the village itself. Why did I ever listen to my parents? They lived in Bermuda. And Harold? It took him eighteen months to ask after me, and even then he tricked Maggie to meet him in Edinburgh. Who am I kidding? I know why! Guilt! Oh, Maggie, I miss you so much. You understood. You helped me cope and remain sane.

Jill twists to look out a different window without any break in her ponder. And Bernard, wherever are you? I expect you returned to South Africa eventually, though you may, of course, have gone straight from Scotland soon after sending me your Dear John letter. Whether my child is also yours or Toms, you left me pregnant believing you are the baby's father. No matter how much I've tried to understand, I find it hard to accept you've never asked about us? Especially our child!

Jill bows her head. Oh, Tom, I am sorry for always keeping you my secret. I guess modern science can now prove you.

Jill's eyes are filling up and absent-mindedly staring at a newspaper on her lap.

'Are you all right Gillian?' asks Bethany while resting a hand on Jill's shoulder.

'Oh, are we here? Must have dozed off,' says Jill.

'Are you unwell Gillian? Do you want me to take you back home? It isn't... '

'No. Thank you for offering Beverley. It's just; I'm a bit tired, that's all.'

'OK. As long as you're sure?' asks Bethany.

'I am,' replies Jill.

Unusually Joy, the manager of the Day-Centre, has come outside to greet the arrival of those in the mini-bus and says, 'Good morning Jill. You're a dark horse, aren't you! If I had known a tall, dark-haired handsome man would be standing in my office today, waiting to see you, I might well have been fussier with my make up this morning.'

***

In Woodland Mews, a peaceful silence in Thre3Scor3 is broke by the familiar tune of rap-a-tap-tap knocking on wood. Valerie thinks this sound is part of a dream. Only after a second encore does she struggle off a settee she slept on last night. Valerie is naked. Needing to use the cast iron doorknob as a prop to stay upright, Valerie fumbles as she opens the door.

'Hi Aunt V.'

'Hello, Milena. Is it Wednesday already?' replies Valerie.

'Of course, it is Aunt V. Would you prefer I don't come in today?' asks Milena.

Valerie gestures impatiently and Milena steps into a large farmhouse style kitchen. The heavy wooden door shudders as it's unintentionally slammed shut. Valerie's head has to then absorb a thumping like a punching bag when pounded by a boxer.

'Blimey girl!' Valerie complains.

'Sorry Aunt V. Have you been drinking? Oh Aunt V, you...'

'Great skirt, very short mind. It suits you,' interrupts Aunt V who wants to brush aside what was, even for Valerie, massive consumption of wine.

'Thank you, Aunt V. I'm glad you like it.'

'Coffee?' asks Valerie.

Milena nods, 'Want me to help?'

'No thanks.'

'OK. Where shall I wait for you, Aunt V?'

'The garden was nice last time. The sun-beds are already out,' replies Valerie.

'OK.'

Milena skips to and out of the back door. She reaches two sun-beds positioned side by side and lays on the one nearest to her. Milena stretches both legs and uses a toe to shake off a shoe one at a time. She then flicks her long hair off her neck and positions her entwined hands on her belly button as if in prayer. Milena closes her eyes. 'Lovely,' she says quietly as the warmth of the mid-morning sun begins to soak in.

Eventually, Valerie is carrying a tray. On it is a plate covered with two-toned milk chocolate fingers and to full mugs. One with coffee and the other Baileys Irish Cream. She stops to perch the tray on a sill of a window in the large utility room.

Valerie then muses at the sight of a red blanket of hair glowing in the sun as it drapes and loll-ops over the head of the lounger. How wonderful! Your beautiful hair moves like a closed curtain flapping in a soft breeze in front of an open bedroom window on a warm summer night. Valerie then lifts the tray and steps outside for the first time in a week.

Milena, with eyes closed, listens to Valerie put the tray on a table which stands at the foot of each sun-bed. Valerie then stumbles, and a mug falls onto the grass. 'Whoops,' she says.

Milena opens her eyes and asks, 'Are you all right Aunt V?'

'Fine, thank you! I'll make you another in a Mo...'

'No need. I'm not thirsty, to tell the truth,' Milena interjects reassuringly.

'You sure Hun?'

'Yep,' confirms Milena.

Valerie drinks a fair bit of her coffee before resting the mug on the grass. Albeit, it's nestling like the "Leaning Tower of Pisa."

In silence, Valerie gently places a hand on Milena's praying ones. Aunt and niece slowly lift a finger searching to touch the other. Before long, two sets of five fingers entwine and not for the first time Milena asks her Auntie, 'Where is Jo, Valerie?'

***

Three hours ago Maxine phoned in sick after needing to use the bathroom. She then returned to bed for more sleep. Now, Maxine opens her eyes for the fourth time in ten minutes. She's looking at a full mug of cold tea. All of a sudden, Maxine remembers! Thoughts and anxiety engulf her. I'm sure Luke said, it really should be a lovely day. Didn't he? Why today? Does it involve me or someone else? If so, who is she? What does she look and is she younger?

Maxine sits up and rests both of her hands on the quilt beside a thigh. She whispers, 'It's simple really, isn't it? I don't know the answers!'

Maxine lays down again and stares into a large oval shaped mirror on the ceiling. Tears are tears rolling down each cheek, and soon, as is frequent when upset, Maxine thinks about Valerie and right now decides to join the mirror in some reflecting!

Six months into our reunion things were going so well. Dam us hosting that 'Old Year's Night' party. Ironic or what! Cuz, one of the thrills for me, was to use the party to celebrate our six months of reunion. Instead, incredibly, it tore us apart again. I know my response to your offer to help with preparations was as subtle as a snake with a rat in its mouth. But, your chronic drinking meant you simply couldn't! Sorry, sis, I reacted too much as good lawyers do. Say it how it is or how they want others to see it! God, I was a fool. You were, are heartbroken for Christ's sake! And, nearly everyone expects Joanne's dead. Add to this, Clive moving out too, for reasons I still cannot quite fathom? I know you say you agree with Clive, "It's for the best." But, is it temporary? Whatever, it's another loss, and it's obvious you love and miss him. Yes, sis, you had every right to throw me out! But why have you ignored all my attempts to say sorry? I can't believe there is no contact again! God, sis, I wish I'd known it was Clive I bumped into at St.

Clotho school. We'd have reunited sooner, and Joanne would have been with Milena and me instead of at that bloody Fête and Christ Sis! He's too good to lose! Not to mention, waste!

Maxine shuts her eyes to avoid the sight of her face smothered with guilt. She then says out loud, 'Clive is right! The way to sort things is face to face. I'm coming to see you, Val, today!'

Maxine glances at a clock. It reads 11.34am.

***

Clive inhales smoke from a just lit cigarette and is in a thoughtful mood. Thankfully, inside my car, I'm allowed. For how long though eh? How kind of them! No doubt, one day this will be illegal too! I get the right bits of the new law. But, don't understand why every public place? Pubs are a cracking example! Why can't it be legal to permit bars to be owned and run with a "Yes Smoking" sign? Easy, this way there is choice, tolerance and equality. Nanny state? Definitely. Dictatorship? Probably. And, to think the passing of this dirty law was lobbied for by people seen as PC Do-Gooders?

Clive smirks, but it soon recedes. And, as if that is not enough piss to receive, our country's lawmakers exclude themselves from this law! Instead, they are free to choose not to smoke indoors when at work! On a purely voluntary basis, you understand? Come on, wake up! This law is dangerous! Our 'volunteers' have tested how they can take even more control of you. I mean, it won't stop with the no-smoking in public places issue. Will it!

Clive bangs a fist against the steering wheel. Words from a book he studied at school come to the forefront of his mind. How does it go? I think it's, "All animals are equal but some more equal than others."

'Selfish hypocrites and control freaks,' Clive murmurs while extinguishing his cigarette.

Clive then retrieves his phone from a trouser pocket. He wants to check a text, sent by a mate who is affectionately known as Ripper. Jack acquired his nickname from an extraordinary ability to slice clothes off someone with three swift swipes of his bayonet, without even a speck of blood spilt!

Clive stares at the text gathering some thoughts. You turn Ripper down! How else can they pay for alterations needed to their house? He fights for his country and comes home with both arms, legs and an ear blown off, not to mention also losing sight in one eye, and you turn him down? It's wrong they might have to take their children out of a school in which both are doing well!

Clive can't stop a picture; he will carry forever, coming into sharp focus again. It is Ripper in bits at a battlefront they fought together on, in Afghanistan. How the fuck did you survive at all mate?

To stave off tears, Clive rereads Ripper's message. "The lady from the council explained the financial rules mean because I receive a war pension, I'm over the threshold to qualify for a grant. How can we afford the thirty thousand or so pounds they agree it will cost for Zara, the kids and I to stay in our home? Are they mad mate? The equity in our house is in the minus box, and even if there was any, how could we afford any increase in our mortgage? The war pension helps mate. It's not enough though, to cover all other outgoings too. Get a job. Any ideas who will employ me?

Apparently, we are, the fashionable word is, eligible to move into a council or social housing bungalow but none of us wants to leave our home! OK, if it wasn't practically possible to alter our house, fair enough! But, as the helpful lady from the council agreed, it can be mate! She said the budget holder decides that we don't meet the criteria. Then the rules are wrong, right mate! If I can't qualify, who the fuck does? Humiliating it is mate! I hated needing to apply anyhow! Is the service for them? Pricks eh! LMFHO!"

Clive chuckles and puts his phone in the glove compartment. I understand why you hate charity mate. But, I will speak with someone I know who fundraises for the British Legion and is pally with a local MP. Whatever mate, we'll find the money somehow! I know you'll put yourself in Residential if it is the only way to prevent Zara and the kids not having to leave your family home. One way or another Ripper I'll.

Luke taps a window, startling Clive. Clive gets out. 'Hello Luke, how are you?'

'OK, thanks. You?'

'Good,' says Clive noticing sweat all along Luke's forehead.

'How is Valerie?' asks Luke.

'Do I Care?' replies Clive mischievously.

Luke is not sure what to say, 'So, this evening still OK for you Clive?'

Clive detects Luke is nervous. He's seen similar when in the company of some enemy Officers he engaged in classified undercover operations. Clive hates the physical stuff so will try and avoid it if possible! However, Clive is determined to do whatever it takes to snare Luke and Maxine.

'Definitely. Do you still want to meet at mine?' asks Clive for clarification.

'Yes, is about six OK?'

'Yep, I take it you know where I live Luke?'

'Yes.'

'Right, see you later then,' says Clive before leaping into his car.

As Clive soars off to buy some stamps before lunch break ends, Luke still asks, 'What tipple would you like me to bring?'

***

Maxine chose to enjoy a scenic walk from her home to a nearby village where her sister lives. At present, she steps out of a field onto a trodden made path that leads to an entrance of a pretty woodland. There is a strong smell of lavender in the air as Maxine meanders between healthy tall trees. Then, in the distance on the other side of the wood Maxine thinks she can see Milena. Maxine leans to her right and left a few times to avoid branches, and although not seeing anyone, she calls out, 'Is that you Milena? Hello, it's me, Mum!'

There is no response. Maxine carries on forward, pondering. If it was you, Milena, why aren't you at school? I assume you've visited Val. Perhaps I'm mistaken. Val will tell me.

Maxine has two hundred yards to reach one of a few exits from the woodland. She is currently passing a thick fallen trunk of a once glorious Oak tree which is laying on the opposite side of a human-made pathway. Hidden behind it, is Milena whose waiting to hear the click of a kissing gate.

Milena's heart is racing fast. I think mum saw me! And where is she going? Aunt Val's? Why today? When did they make up?

'At last,' whispers Milena who then peeps over the trunk. All clear means Milena gets to her feet and uses both hands to brush debris off her clothes. Oh my god, I've dived onto a dead rat! Ignoring her disgust, Milena opens a phone James Hawker bought her and decides to write him a message, 'Hi Jimmy, I'm on my way over. Need some advice. X.'

***

Milena is outside Hawker's flat as he is not at home. And so, she sends him another text. The irony is, only a matter of a few hundred yards from where Milena began her journey to see Hawker, he was and still is in the home of his friend Harold White.

'Who is that?' asks White snappily.

Damn, thinks Hawker. Instead of answering, Hawker hands White an SD memory card and says with a grin similar to the one used by a scary character in the film "Chitty-Chitty-Bang-Bang,"'It's a good one.'

White turns his TV on and slots the card into it. He presses play and gets back into bed. 'Thanks, James. So, who sent the text?' White asks again, though more warmly this time.

Hawker replies with a lie because Milena is his secret and he wants to keep her just to himself, 'Just a silly girl who's got a crush on me.'

Hawker deletes Milena's message and switches his phone off. 'It's time to buy a new one,' he reminds himself.

'Sounds like you're in there, eh boy!' White retorts.

'Not bothered,' says Hawker as he adjusts some clothing while watching the TV before adding, 'Concentrate on the video Harold.'

Hawker then begins to think about the moment he first laid eyes on Milena. There you were, in the woods. You were sobbing, and I comforted you. If it weren't for you being in school uniform, I would not have believed your next birthday would make you a teenager. I thought all my birthdays came, right then! You're the most beautiful creature I have ever seen. You.

Hawker is interrupted by White saying, 'Great girl in this one James but...'

White stops because he can see the film is close to its first pivotal moment which he wants to enjoy.

***

For at least a minute, Maxine has stood motionless outside her sister's front door. She now decides to push a doorbell gently, and without knowing it, her heart is thumping just as her daughter's had done a few minutes earlier.

Valerie is on her settee. She is wearing her birth-suit having just had a shower. On a nearby tenure, marble coffee table is a half empty or is it half full bottle of brandy? Valerie nearly ignores the bell but believing Milena has forgotten something, she sort of puts a robe around her before shuffling to the door. Through a frosted pane, Valerie can recognise the person standing on the other side. With a combination of shock and excitement rushing through her, she is glad for now her visitor cannot see either. Painfully slow, Valerie opens the door.

Wary of what reception she might receive, Maxine takes a couple of steps back. Her first thought is, Amazing! With all your problems how can you look that good? I have no idea! Maxine then says sheepishly, "Hello Val. Nice to see you.'

Valerie looks into Maxine's eyes and says, 'You too sis. Would you like to come in?'

'If you're sure?'

'I'm not,' replies Valerie with a chuckle that turns into a cough. 'But you are very welcome,' she splutters.

Maxine enters what is for Valerie, the only place in the world, the universe even, in which she has frequently and sometimes still does obliterate everything!

'Would you like some lunch, Max?' asks Valerie.

'Sounds great. I'm starving. Had no breakfast.'

'A bit of salad with some wine OK?'

Maxine hesitates. 'Yes, please. That would be lovely,' she lies.

'Please, make yourself at home.'

'Thanks. In the living room OK?'

'Of course.'

Maxine enters her favourite room in this house. She settles into an armchair after picking up the latest copy of Cosmopolitan laying on a leather cushion. On the front cover is a piece of yellow sticky note paper and she reads it. "Hope you enjoy these. Don't need them back. Regards, Genevieve."

Maxine wonders, Whose Genevieve? and she searches for the problem page.

Five minutes later Valerie comes in and places a tray on the coffee table. 'Help yourself,' she says.

'Thanks, it looks tasty,' replies Maxine and both sisters give a friendly smile.

'So, why have you come today?' asks Valerie more jovially than she feels.

'I miss you, and us.'

'Do you?'

'Yes, truly.'

'I miss you too.'

'Oh Val, I am sorry! I shouldn't have judged and deserted you. We've lost each other once, never again, please? I can't imagine how much pain you must feel. Please, accept my apology and understand my motive was, no is, totally around you staying, well...'

'It's OK sis; you care I know! I do understand because I'd also find it hard to watch someone I love, well, you know.'

Consumed with relief, Maxine offers both of her hands, and soon there are four interlocking tenderly. And, conversation flows.

***

Luke pulls up outside what used to be the house belonging to Clive's parents. Sadly, both died within eight months of each other during 2005.

Luke checks his mobile and opens the one unread text. 'Val needs me so am staying over 2nite. Will call u l8r.'

In haste, Luke digests the text. Maxine hasn't seen Valerie for months. I wonder what happened? I look forward to finding out.

Luke checks the clock, and it flicks onto 18.24pm. He then grabs a sports bag and says, 'Shit, I'm late. Time to go where the unknown awaits.'

Clive opens the door with just a towel wrapped around the waist. 'Just had a shower. Do you want to come in?' asks Clive cheerfully.

Luke accepts the invitation.

'Drink?' asks Clive.

'Yes please and sorry I'm late. Please use this,' replies Luke handing Clive a bottle of red wine.

'Sure. Thank you,' says Clive before adding, 'Please take a seat in here.'

Clive points in the opposite direction to where he's heading which is the kitchen.

Luke observes this house is dull compared to the much bolder design in Woodland Mews. It is far too modern, minimalist even for me, he decides.

Luke opts to sit on one of two armchairs that are positioned facing each other. Between them is a short-legged square table. Luke is not alone long.

'So, why are you here Luke?' asks Clive handing Luke a large glass of wine before sitting in the empty armchair.

Luke gulps more than sips and is struggling a bit to untangle his thoughts. 'To explore,' replies Luke in a barely audible murmur.

'Explore what?' asks Clive confidently.

'Cliché I know, my feminine side perhaps?'

Clive responds with, 'Do you think all men have a feminine side? Or, for that matter do all women have a masculine side too?'

'Well, no I, yes they, no,' replies Luke.

'Interesting, nor do I. So, tell me, do you have a feminine side?' asks Clive.

'Well, I'm not sure...'

Clive interrupts, 'How does it feel being in the company of a man who only has to remove a towel to be naked?'

Clive bends forward to pick up his glass.

Luke mimes, 'OK.'

'So, what do you want? Any fantasy?' asks Clive as he leans back, drinks some wine and crosses his legs.

'Luke nearly chokes on his wine before saying, 'I need to change first. Where...'

'Sure', Clive deliberately interrupts Luke again, and he is enjoying his prey dangling like a puppet on strings.

Clive then adds, 'The bedroom is second on the right after going straight on at the top of the stairs. There is a long mirror you will probably appreciate on the inside of both wardrobe doors.'

'Wow! It's just...'

'I know what I want Luke. I thought you did too! But...'

'No, you're right. I mean, I do. I'll go upstairs,' Luke confirms.

Luke lifts his bag and carries it across his chest. As he enters a hallway, he says, 'Will call you when I'm ready.'

Clive replies, 'OK.'

Clive then opens a wooden box on the table in front of him. From it, he takes a rolled joint. After lighting up, Clive downs his wine in one and says quietly, 'Piece of cake.'

***

Milena is at home laying on a sofa and is watching her favourite evening soap. Her concentration is intense because of Carla, who looks so much like her mum, is about to answer a business partner's proposition that they mix work with pleasure?
Milena is also rummaging inside a large packet of twig-lets and is not sure if the ringtone she can hear is Carla's phone or her own?

Carla and Liam are now engaged in a passionate kiss, wooing Milena to say out loud, 'Wow! Liam is cool!'

Straight-away the tune synonymous with this drama starts to play, signalling another batch of adverts is about to begin. Milena is disappointed, but at least this distraction means she realises there is a need to answer her phone.

'Hi, Mum. Yes, I did. Is Aunt Val OK Mum? Oh, I see. Good. Send her my love. Since about two, lots of study time on a Wednesday remember. Yes, and popped in to see Aunt Val on my way home. I'm doing a Sociology assignment on addiction. No, he isn't. His sports bag isn't in the utility room, so obviously playing squash. Mum, I am sixteen you know! I cooked a pizza. Right, he knows. I'll ask him to bring back a caramel Mcfluffy too then. Bye Mum. Love you too.'

Milena delicately fills her mouth with twig-let scraps and

the familiar tune starts again. Wow! 'They've been kissing for ages,' comments Milena.

Once this episode ends, Milena begins to search other channels. Before too long the words become a blur due to her tired eyes. She settles for Discovery showing the release of orphaned elephants into the wild.

Milena's pose on the sofa is similar to a nude sculpture of a Roman Goddess! Suchlike, millions of people, admire in many cities across the world. Content with developments in her favourite soap, charmed by the elephants in play and excited by the prospect of some rare time with just Luke, Milena shuts her eyes. See if you can resist me tonight! She muses.

***

Luke whispers to Lucy in the mirror, 'I am at last in your shoes,' and then calls, 'Clive, you can come up now.'

Lucy's facing a closed bedroom door and feels her heart beating faster than the speed of light. In an attempt to calm it down Lucy completes a few seven eleven breaths. Then tardily, Clive opens the door.

'Hello, I'm Lucy,' and immediately Clive's nakedness disconcerts Luke.

Clive does not say anything and takes steps until standing right in front of Lucy – 'No, I don't want to,' Luke cries out before running out of the room.

Clive smiles and thinks, Yes, great result! He then turns off a rolling camera and calmly calls out with a laugh, 'Luke you can't run out in those clothes.'

Clive strolls to the top of the stairs in time to see Luke suddenly come to a halt three steps from the bottom. Luke reluctantly completes an about turn. 'Sorry Clive, I think it's just the dressing up I like.'

'No need to say sorry Luke. It's fine. I understand I think!'

***

Valerie is in a much needed deep sleep and next to her, is Maxine, wide awake. The time shown by the digital clock on the bedroom TV is 21.06. The land-line phone then begins to ring.

Maxine rushes to what every member of the Verity family call, "Our Games Room." Reacting with so much haste means, as Maxine answers she nearly drops the receiver.

'Hello, Mrs Verity's residence. Yes, Clive, it is. Val's asleep, don't want to wake her. No, only a couple of bottles in the bin. No, honestly, no need she's fine. Well, that's just it. Out of the blue Val called asking to see me. Wanted to patch things up. Yes, it is. Yes and I cooked us a decent meal. Sure. Funny you should call because I need to talk with you. Can't talk about it here. Can't come now, promised Val I'd stay for breakfast. GP? Are you alright? Oh, I see. Will try anyway and hopefully catch you before you leave. Bye. You too.'

Maxine pauses outside Valerie's bedroom and is a little relieved to hear light snoring.

***

Luke concludes some self-analysis with, At least I now know it's the clothes and not men I need. He then picks up freshly cooked fish and chips and steps out of his car. Luke notes the only light shining inside his house is from a Plasma TV. He deftly turns a key and is a little surprised not to hear Milena call out.

Luke pops his head into the living room. A Sleeping Beauty is what comes to mind. With the whiff of Cod piercing his nostrils, Luke surreptitiously leaves undetected and heads to the kitchen. He unwraps his dinner and begins to eat a chip at a time with fingers. In an attempt to block out this evening's events, Luke relives a more successful jump he made nine days ago. Arguably, his "Chair," in Grand National parlance.

Has to be the boldest decision of my life. Helen is a talented woman because it fits perfectly. I knew there was a chance of rejection and it was a certainty Maxine would be shocked! Such a fantastic relief she accepts it all. I think she was most put out by me keeping it from her for far too long!

Luke stretches to get a fork, and his thoughts evolve to Milena. Seems only yesterday, not two years ago, when I first saw you naked. You arrived home from school and took a shower straight away. Where was Maxine? Oh yes, a three-day convention in London. I remember I was still preparing us a Salmon salad when you came downstairs wearing only a towel. We talked and laughed as we ate, and then suddenly you leapt up to rush for some water saying, "Blimey Luke that chilli in the rice is mega hot."

Unbelievable! Because it was when you turned the tap off you seemed to realise the towel was laying in a bundle across your feet. I still can't believe, instead of feeling embarrassed like I was, you flirted with me, tried to seduce me even. I admit you looked fantastic, easily the body of a beautiful young woman. But, of course, you were most definitely a girl! Need some brown.

'Hi-ya, did you win?' asks Milena excitedly.

A chip misses Luke's mouth as his eyes see a naked Milena walking until half covered by a chair stood at the opposite side of the table. 'Win?' replies Luke.

'You've been playing squash haven't you?'

'Oh yes. No. Dennis beat me for a change.'

'Did you get me a Mcfluffy?' asks Milena who notices a frown, so she adds, 'I sent you a text after mum let me know she's staying with Aunt Val tonight.'

'No, sorry. Had my phone off,' Luke explains.

Milena ambles toward Luke.

'Put some clothes on Milena,' demands Luke who then springs off his seat to fetch some sauce.

'Must I?'

'Yes, unless you are going straight to bed.'

'On my own?'

'Yes.'

'You don't mean ...'

And so, this latest battle between one Tempted and a young Enchantress commences. In truth, this time neither are sure whether they will be a victor or defeated?

***

July 5

Ignorant of the fact, of course, Maxine parks in the same spot her husband used just under fifteen hours ago. She knocks unaware Clive already knows she's arrived. He was on the lookout in a bedroom above a garage.

Maxine knocks again. Still no answer. She then looks through a kitchen and living room window. 'Where is my phone?'

Maxine scampers to retrieve her mobile from the car and calls Clive. All she hears is an invitation to leave a message. She tries the house phone. An answering machine comes on. She calls the mobile again. 'Hi, it's me. I've arrived and guess you've already left for the Surgery. Hope you're OK. Speak to you soon. Bye.'

Clive waits until Maxine drives away. He changes his clothes and heads toward the kitchen. He puts a Tia Maria Tea, a cream bun and his ipod with speakers attached, onto a tray and walks into his back garden.

Clive is in a Tuxedo and bow-tie. He soon reaches a cast iron bench on which his guest is sitting in the middle, Wigwam style. 'There you are my lady,' says Clive.

'Thank you, Parker, most kind.'

'You're welcome my lady.'

Clive removes his top hat to take a bow. He then switches the ipod on. 'Anything else you require? Me, lady!'

'I want, you!'

Ecstatic the song playing is, "Chasing Cars" by Snow Patrol, Helen grasps the bow-tie and adds, 'You remembered! Thank you!'

CHAPTER FOUR

Returning to the evening of July 16, 2007

If there is one person who can be described, with accuracy assured, as someone who does not live his life, "Like a hamster in a small wheel," it is Luke Stewart!

About half an hour after Milena left to perform in the play, Luke began transforming to Lucy.

Lucy is wearing her favourite dress made by Helen Thompson. Its colour is an effervescent scarlet, and the style would blend well at a ball. It is sleeveless, and she is wearing long black leather gloves. On her legs are fishnet stockings, also black and to complete the alteration, Lucy has tastefully applied a wig and make-up too.

Lucy is on a sofa watching the ITN News. She lights a cigarette and takes a sip of a Gin and tonic from a large glass. This pleasurable state of expectancy is interrupted by the sound of a text. She opens it. 'On my way home. Val is comfortable in the hospital. Do you want anything from the chippy?'

'No thanks,' Lucy replies.

Lucy turns off the TV and puts music on and soon, "Undiscovered" by James Morrison starts to play through speakers located in an attic bedroom. She then fills a glass with Maxine's favourite wine before climbing their lighthouse shaped staircase.

Four minutes later Maxine walks through the front door and says brightly, 'Hi-ya.'

'Hi. I'm up here,' replies Lucy.

'OK. Be with you in a Mo,' says Maxine before fetching a plate to share chips on.

***

Harold White is in police custody. He is masticating over today's extraordinary events; You're no fool, DI Parsons. Me being in here and not sectioned in a hospital is proof of that! But, you seem to believe I killed Gillian? So, you're not a total non-fool! I expected to be a suspect, but it's looking like you're using this crazy situation to pin something big on me! Everything was going well until you nestled in! But, you won't, can't even, win! I have an Ace to use! Yes Maxi, you have a lot more to lose! Thanks to James bold efforts today, I don't't!

***

The E. n. E. M. A. meeting started at 12.15am. Currently, Mrs Hicks is talking and being honest I'm thinking about revelations shared earlier when Debbie, a Social Work Manager, spoke. She said, "Thank you Chair. I need to begin this report with some context. There are more than one historical, social work episodes with more than one subject on our agenda tonight. Second and by no means least, I must stress some information only discovered within the last twelve hours!

To be informative as possible, I needed to decide which path to take you along? Rightly or wrongly, Valerie Verity and Maxine Stewart are sisters! However, by adoption to a couple named David and Henrietta Hurst who thus became their lawful mother and father. Each adopted on the same day. This day also being when each sister was born. Even so, they do not share any birth parent. Thankfully, the extraordinary circumstances of how this happened have not been legal for quite a few years, well decades! The trigger for finding out Valerie and Maxine were adopted derived from one of some routine checks we make for such a meeting we have tonight.

The specific check leading us to what, really was, at first an 'incidental' search is corroboration of their date of birth. I will share more detail about this a little later. What I will say now is, this means for the first time since Joanne went missing we not only have learnt Joanne and Milena are cousins. But also, it is Maxine Stewart, our head of children legal services, who is the estranged sister Valerie spoke about to the police, back in two thousand and four! And whom the police, or nobody else for that matter, were able to identify until less than a dozen hours ago! You see, up to this discovery, no one had any reason to doubt Valerie would not know her sister's correct birthday!

We do have the name of Valerie Verity's birth mother and sadly insufficient history for Maxine. Nevertheless, we **do** know Maxine is adopted because her birth certificate, like Valerie's, betokens each was arranged in a concealed manner by way of actions of a GP. Detection and verification were supplied only yesterday by a Registrar at the Offices for Births, Deaths, Marriages and Civil Partnerships in Kings Lynn.

You may be interested to know it is the responsibility of Registrar's to deny any happy would be newlywed permission to marry if it was detected certificates led to an adoption trail indicating an incestuous union! Such a decision sometimes explained to a prospective newlywed who was unaware of their adoptive heritage!

I suggest, more relevant for the respective mothers of the two minor Subjects' we are discussing tonight, such practice puts a messy spanner in the works for the likes of us! Well, anyone attempting to interpret the identity of someone's natured and nurtured influences! Don't you?!

Valerie and Maxine have separate sets of unrelated birth parents. Challengingly, we have only found out the identity of one of the four. Amongst Norfolk's official medical records and inside its archive files folder we found a scanned copy of a single piece of headed paper. It is dated the sixth of June nineteen seventy-two. All that is written on it is "TA-Successful caesarean delivery. Too young to raise children. Adoption immediate. GP present. Heritage-NFN. No Further Action Required. ME."

On the said day all other caesarean sections in Norfolk involved women aged over sixteen. The name of the GP present who signed Maxine's birth certificate is a Logan Baird who was also David and Henrietta Hurst's GP.

Dr Baird passed away quite a few years ago. By scanning all his records we discovered he had a brother called Frazer who was also a GP. Frazer practised in their native Scotland.

Oh, and regrettably Frazer is deceased too.

Now Valerie. It is in Scotland where we found a scanned copy of a patient file in no name. It is labelled with just the initials JS. There is only one document within it. The content of this document is a key piece of a jigsaw which shows Mrs Gillian Joy White, AKA Jill Spears, the eldest Subject of the three on our agenda tonight, is Valerie Verity's birth mother and therefore through a blood line is maternal grandmother of Joanne Verity. Whom, as I think you all know, is the girl who the police think they might well have found after three years being missing!"

At this moment there were gasps, open mouths, some heads turning left or right and words suchlike, "What the...?" All, creating a dissonance similar to what you hear when witnessing a murmuration of Starling birds.

Debbie continued with, "Also dated sixth of the sixth nineteen seventy-two, the notes on this document read, "Jill held her baby for five hours post giving successful birth and then handed Perla to me. Both mother and baby well. Maggie, with help from a friend, travelled by car through the night straight to Norfolk with Perla in her arms. Birth Certificate fully completed. FB."

For very different reasons then and with contrasting journeys, two newborn girls arrive on their birthday at the home of Mr and Mrs Hurst. For this otherwise happily married couple it created the family life they'd yearned so long for! Well actually, it states in their Adoption Assessment, "Seconds after Henrietta accepted David's proposal of marriage," apparently. So, I imagine after so much pain these two girls were a wonderful twin gift!

Gillian White wanted to find her daughter. On the twenty-first September nineteen eighty-nine, she kept an appointment made with a Duty Worker in our then Adoption Department. Mr White did not attend and during the discussion, Gillian explained, "Although I was married to Harold White before and after I had my baby girl, he is definitely not the father. He will only find out if he is alive when I find Perla."

The outcome of Mrs White's visit to us was; we were unable to find any documentation nationwide which substantiates an adoption of her daughter? Even if we had, we could not have shared any information to Mrs White without Valerie's consent.

Nevertheless, I do think it is appropriate to say what action we did take! Our Duty Worker that day wrote, "I am touched by Gillian's story. Mrs White accepted my advice to compose a letter which we will keep safe, just in case 'Perla' ever came looking for her."

It is only yesterday, following a request from the police for us to organise searches of our multi-disciplinary databases, we opened the letter Gillian wrote to Perla. The letter is signed JS and so making a triple link between this letter, the GP patient file and initials used as part of the signature on the letter tonight's Chair received a week or so ago. Valerie has never contacted us. Remember though, it is possible Valerie and or Maxine has never found out they were adopted!

Yesterday, I personally spoke with a senior partner in the firm of solicitors for whom Maxine began her professional working career. To summarise, he mentioned there was an unusual anomaly that occurred during the process of hiring Maxine. On an application form Maxine gave her date of birth as six six seventy-two. After Maxine was interviewed and offered a trainee-ship she needed to give proof of identity. Of which one is a birth certificate. I was advised Maxine appeared genuinely shocked to have a need to try and explain why the date on her certificate was third of October nineteen seventy-two?

The explanation given to me is, "Maxine and her mother spoke to us together. Mrs Hurst admitted Maxine was born on October third but because she and her husband had adopted Valerie a matter of a few months earlier they decided to let the girls grow up believing they are non identical twins."

The senior partner concluded by stating, "Whilst it was of course an irregular development to deal with: Following our said meeting we rightly saw this as an innocent untruth and honest mistake by Maxine. After all, we had viewed Maxine's legitimate birth certificate which did confirm   who she was!"

Obviously these revelations prompt more questions needing answers which I'm sure we will discuss and debate during the second phase of this meeting. This said, I think it is appropriate to mention two things now. First, Maxine applied to be a trainee solicitor after Valerie left home and was then ostracised by her family. Second, the senior partner explained during their meeting just referred too, it became clear Maxine had never seen or asked to see her birth certificate before applying to join them.

I have reached a point now, where I think it gets even more interesting! We have found social services files relating to Maxine and Valerie's parents. You see, Henrietta and David Hurst did also formally complete an application process which approved them to be Adopters.

However, Mr and Mrs Hurst were later removed from our pool of Approved Adopters. In fact, in the file, it states, it was Mr and Mrs Hurst who initiated this process! They sent a letter of resignation to be considered by an Adoption Panel who then formally sanctioned de-registration to be carried out. Which it was.

In their resignation letter dated April twenty-six nineteen seventy-two it reads, 'Two weeks ago I, we received confirmation I am three to four months pregnant. A miracle beyond our wildest dreams!"

Conscious Renee Yeastfield from St Clotho school has shared a full report about 'Child Welfare Support' provided to Milena Trunch, I want to emphasise something. All social work intervention in two thousand and three occurred on a basis it was sought or agreed to by Maxine Stewart and Milena. Everyone involved recognised the challenges with parenting Milena whose physiology has been exceptionally advanced from when aged just eight!

Because Milena confided, to her mother, she had a sexual relationship with two peers of the same gender during the eighteen months prior to Maxine Stewart seeking support, we and the police interviewed Milena under usual protection procedures. It is important to note, legally we didn't have to! Milena chose not to elaborate and refused to give names. Thus, no further action could be taken by the police!

There were no social work records of Joanne Verity until routine liaison between the police and ourselves following the awful discovery of her ab..., disappearance."

'Whoops, concentrate Alex,' I tell myself.

Thank you, Mrs Hicks and I'm sure all information being shared is valuable to all of us. Now then, oh yes, Mitchell Jud please,' says Frank.

'Hello, I was on duty the day Milena and Mr and Mrs Stewart kept an appointment which Maxine arranged with Connexions. It took place on June twenty-five two thousand and three. The purpose of the referral was to explore how Milena could be assisted with finding a suitable interest outside of school?

Milena was interested in the arts, particularly Amateur Dramatics. In fact, it was Milena who mentioned she'd heard about a society in Little Snoring called, The Thespian Players. I remember Milena also saying she hoped to be an actress and a painter one day. We liaised with the said society run by a Mrs Beryl Lattimer and advised the Stewart family it has a reputation of being a prestigious and popular organisation. And, Mrs Lattimer mentioned more than once, "We have a Lord and Judge as our patron." The distance of eighteen miles from the family home did not prevent all three expressing a keenness to give it a try.

A few months later during a brief meeting with Milena, she told me, "Yes, I did join and it's brill thanks. There are loads of great people and we have loads of fun." This concurred with the feedback I already had from Mrs Lattimer who stated, "Milena has settled in very well." Hence, no other contact needed or requested.'

Frank says, 'Thank you, Mr Jud. Sadie Wood next, please.'

'On fourteenth June this year, I received a referral to our

Care and Repair Team from an Occupational Therapist. I arranged my first visit for Monday twenty-fifth June.

Mrs White was warm and friendly and certainly understood why I had come. It was evident after fifteen minutes or so, Gillian was going to decline assistance. Well, to put this more accurately, it was obvious Mr White chose to impose barriers and dominate the discussion.

To be honest, and I am, Mr White was irritable, rude, dismissive and patronising toward Mrs White. So, in a polite, professional and diplomatic way, I told him this! I reminded him the purpose for a shower is to meet the needs of his wife. Therefore, I suggested to Mr White, if he wanted to remain a constructive part of our conversation he should allow his wife to answer questions for herself. He went silent and after two minutes sulking and during which he was ignored, he left the room and I believe went upstairs.

My conversation with Jill lasted a further two and a half hours. Admittedly, we became frequently sidetracked from the business at hand. Jill did not say yes to help, but she did agree to take more time and think about the pros and cons. We agreed to meet again on Friday last at the Day-Centre. Mrs White said it will be a lovely day for me to visit because that day she'll be celebrating her birthday.

When I arrived at the Centre, Mrs White greeted me with a huge smile and kept telling anyone who would listen how kind I am. Introducing me as the daughter she never had and how much she would like to meet my mother to tell her how lucky she is to have a daughter like me.

From this, I knew Mrs White was not going to say she has changed her mind. I think it might be useful to try and summarise some of what Jill said by way of an explanation.

"He wouldn't like it, my dear. I know you mean well and it's ever so kind of you, it really is. Spend the money on those that really need it dear. Samantha, my nurse, helps me wash etc. I know you think I need it and perhaps you're right! I understand it might take a while dear and Dr Craig told me I've only got a year, maybe two years tops. I'm not sure if I'll get long enough to enjoy it."

I left only when Jill accepted my business card and assured me should she ever change her mind, she will contact me. No more, chairperson.'

The room is loud with silence again and as if sensing everyone's emotional exhaustion, Frank says, 'Thank you Mrs Wood. Time for another break. Please return in fifteen minutes.'

Samantha Mee, who was Gillian White's District Nurse, is the first to get off her chair and is crying before she reaches the door.

Everyone leaves the room this time. I wait to be last out and then drive into a lift. I put a stick in my mouth and use the hook on one end to push the down button. Eventually, the lift door opens and unlike everyone else I go outside through the main reception's automated front door.

Pleased there is no one about, I turn right and right again until I am halfway down one side of the office building. Using the same hook I used in the lift, I unzip my fly and soon some pebbles covering the first row of bricks laid above ground, are dampened. I am thinking, if someone catches me pissing up against a wall, at least I can honestly defend my action by stating there is not a toilet in the building someone using a chair with wheels can access.

Ready to leave undetected, I head back and suddenly say out loud, 'Shit.'

To go inside you have to use a keypad to enter the code to unlock the door. But, it's too high, even using my stick. I'm so used to being at work wearing my legs and therefore able to press a code with my nose, I had not worried at all about not being able to get back in.

I turn round and place a packet of cigarettes on the ground. I am about to open it with some toes when I hear a familiar voice. 'I guessed you might need to come out here,' says Claudia laughing.

While scooping up my vice, I spin 180 degrees and I say, 'Oh nice one Claudia and thank you. Have you had a smoke yet? My shout.'

'Thanks, Alex. Already had one. Besides, 'Todders' has asked me to get back before the rest of you. I've already given everyone a copy of the report you asked me to photocopy. See you in a Mo.'

'Thanks for that,' I reply and then add, 'Claudia, please hold on for a moment. I have a question to ask you.'

Claudia steps back outside. With a smile, she says, 'I am taking the minutes remember, mustn't be late. What is it you're bursting to ask me then?'

'Why is 'Todders' chairing this meeting? I'm sure Melanie was next on the rota.'

Claudia replies, 'She is, I mean was. Frank was insistent he should do this one. This

is a very unusual act of chivalry on his part because he's always been so irritable and contemptible whenever he's been summonsed to Chair one.'

'Exactly, I remember you telling me that before,' I reply.

'Anyway, never mind that. What do you think so far? It's better than fiction in there, isn't it?! I mean, it's hard to get one's head around that concealed adoption stuff Debbie mentioned, don't you think?! It would matter to me if I didn't know I was adopted! How about you Alex?' asks Claudia.

'Yes, it would Claudia. But maybe it's true sometimes, that "Ignorance is bliss?"'

'I see where you're coming from. If me though, I would want to know, no matter when! Must dash, see you in a Mo.'

Before continuing with where I went after following Claudia back inside. I think it's useful to shred some insight as to, why Valerie Verity was put to one side by her parents? Information which is recorded in official documents.

"Valerie's mother, Henrietta Hurst, was unofficially adopted herself in 1946 when aged sixteen months. Her birth parent's names were Henry and Maxine Kepler. On the night both died, Henrietta was being looked after by her grandmother Florence Kepler. Florence also lived in the family home. It was soon after Henrietta's ninth birthday that Florence explained how her only child, Henry, and his wife Maxine died.

Henry and Maxine lived in Rothbury, Northumberland. A small town in the heart of the County with the proud reputation as England's oldest Kingdom. A few miles outside the town stood Kemsley Paper Mill which was owned by the successful Bowater group. To earn more money, for what was then seen as treats, both of Henrietta's parents occasionally worked a bit of overtime on the same shift.

On the evening of 27 August 1946, the mill caught fire. In total thirty-three workers died that night! Tragically, despite Henry and Maxine being rescued alive and taken to Hospital, each inhaled too much toxic fumes to survive.

A second severe loss for Henrietta came when she was fourteen. Her grandmother died of a sudden and massive heart attack. With no other living relative, Henrietta was placed, by the equivalent of today's Children's Services, in a residential setting. In here she was taken care of by the Sisters of St. Agnes nunnery in a beautiful village near Rothbury, called Holystone.

Henrietta did not resent this enforced and significant change to her life. She said, amongst a lot of things, "It made me continue to feel safe, able to find peace of mind, enjoy genuine friendship, love and security. But, best of all by miles will always be, it is while living at St. Agnes I met David, the love of my life."

David was an only son and had triplet older sisters who all died before he was born three years after them. David's parents were titled and called Leslie and Barbara Hurst. They were affectionately referred to, by those close to them, as Lord Les and Lady Barb.

David was raised in a family home called Crag-side House set in a glorious landscape of rolling hills full of meadows crammed with flowers displaying every colour imaginable.

David was 21 and Henrietta 18 when they first met at the annual Northumberland villages' carnival. David was judging the best float competition and Henrietta was that year's Miss Northumberland for the third year running.

Henrietta and David were smitten and before either of them celebrated another birthday they were married. Soon after the luxurious wedding, David was offered a retainers jockey contract with one of "The Sport of Kings" most successful racehorse trainers. They left Northumberland and moved into Paddock View, a beautiful Georgian Mansion House half a mile from Newmarket's July racecourse.

Within two years, Henrietta fell in love with a petite thatched cottage commanding views of the North sea beyond Holkham Beach Bay. Despite the commuting, both were thrilled to make this their family home.

For the next seven years, everything was positive except for one thing. Henrietta discovered she could not conceive. David was totally supportive of their application to become adoptive parents. They were approved in May 1970. Two years later and no child needing adoption ever matched with them, as you've heard, they sent their resignation letter. Setting off the process for completion of their de-registration.

Another sauce are GP records. By the time Maxine and Valerie reached school age, in a GP file on Mr Hurst it is written David said, "Hettie borders on being obsessive about our girls! While she is a wonderful mother, in relation to each girl, I do think she can be somewhat possessive, controlling even sometimes."

Many years later in the same file, David said, "For Henrietta, she can't forgive Valerie for what she sees as betrayal and abandonment of our love and happy family life. I miss Valerie and love her deeply."

Claudia climbs the stairs. I pass the lift, take a right and then left turn and am pleased to see the exit doors are wide open. Just before going outside, I stop and place my gold coloured box on the flat surface of the "Push Bar To Open" rail. I then bend forward and using my mouth, retrieve a single cigarette holding it between my lips. I knock the packet onto the floor, grab it in a foot and finally go outside again.

I approach other smokers standing under what is already known by its nickname of, "The naughty crèche."

I welcome the coolness of a fairly nippy breeze, park and look up to admire the clarity and brightness of the Hercules constellation. Amongst those inhaling away is Sadie Wood, and I ask Sadie if she would help me light up? Sadie gladly does so.

'Thank you, Sadie isn't it? ' I ask.

'Yes, and you're very welcome Alexander.'

'Please, Alex. Pardon the expression, Sadie. Is this your first EnEMA?'

'At night, yes Alex,' and we both smile.

I then say, 'I won't be surprised if we're still here come breakfast time. If we are, I would highly recommend heading straight to a nearby old-fashioned café. They do a cracking Rosie Lee and full English!'

Sadie asks, 'Why do you say old-fashioned?'

'The bacon is smothered in fat and the owner doesn't give a stuff if anyone smokes in there,' I reply and we both laugh.

'Blimey, get that. But to say old-fashioned seems strange for a law which only came in sixteen days ago,' says Sadie.

I enjoy Sadie's radiant smile and to myself, I say, 'Wow! Your face is brighter than an exploding supernova.'

I then reply out loud, 'True Sadie. Still...'

'All things considered, quite a momentous day on the legal front concerning adjustments' to our rights,' interjects Genevieve Tweets who is rolling up her cigarette. She adds, 'What, with the new Justice Act coming into force on the same day!'

Sadie agrees, 'Certainly was. I don't know what you both think? I'm still gob-smacked...'

Two cigarettes later Gênevieve, Sadie and I are back in the committee room where there are various conversations taking place. All suddenly stop as Frank enters and takes his seat nearly ten minutes late.

'Before resuming with Mr Forrester, I need to explain Mrs Mee is too upset to return. Dr Patel has kindly offered to stay with Samantha until both hopefully rejoin us soon. Alex, are you ready?'

'Thank you. Yes, I am Guv. Where to begin? So much startling information in one meeting. I will follow the order of our subjects' as listed on tonight's agenda.

Hearing tonight that Gillian White is Valerie Verity's birth mother, and grandmother of Joanne renders me speechless at present, to be honest! Hopefully, I'll be able to offer some considered thoughts after our open discussion a little later.

In front of you is a copy of my summary and conclusion in a report completed in July two thousand and four. I haven't heard anything to alter my view that neither Clive nor Valerie Verity are responsible for what has or might have happened to Joanne?

Earlier, DI Parsons advised us forensics may well confirm the skeletal remains found in a woods yesterday do belong to Joanne. This is very sad to hear. For everyone here not party to involvement in two thousand and four, I will repeat some of what I shared then.

By way of a telephone interview with General Smart, I learnt about a distressing incident in the Verity family home in Germany. It happened around four in the afternoon on Christmas Eve two thousand and one. Namely, Clive came home unexpectedly for Christmas to find Valerie in bed with a lover who, Valerie told Clive, was a reservist on a four-week training deployment.

Clive explained he thought it would be a nice surprise for Joanne too, who was expecting her mother to pick her up from a friend's parent's house at six in the evening where she'd stayed for a sleepover.

Tonight's significant additional information from General Smart that Luke Stewart, in his role as an Army Reservist, was on the base too at this time is fascinating. Though I suggest, not itself conclusive, it was indeed Mr Stewart scarping away?

When I spoke with Clive about my conversation with his commanding officer, the breach of confidence made him angry.'

I briefly glimpse at General Smart whose head is bowed.

'It did not take Clive long to become calm and composed again. So much so, he revealed something he didn't confide to General Smart. Namely, the man was indeed clutching clothes when running. But, they were unquestionably women's clothes.

Clive also shared he believes Valerie when she explained it was an 'accident' meeting with "Deirdre" in a unisex gay bar. So, to cut to the chase, over time Clive accepted Valerie is bi-sexual and Valerie agreed to his asking, that she remained discreet for Joanne's sake as well as his. To quote Clive, "The most important thing is Valerie continues to be faithful to our marriage."

I suggest if Valerie had shared with you, Miss Treets, that Clive knows about her sexuality and say you discussed this with Clive, for whatever reason, then Clive would know she'd broken their promise to each other. Valerie wants you to believe Clive must not know.

I interviewed Valerie Verity five days after Joanne disappeared. Sadly, from how others describe Mrs Verity tonight, it seems she has altered beyond all my recognition. There is also a lot of antithetical information shared tonight, compared with two thousand and four. So, I think it is important to repeat what Valerie Verity said about her parents' and sister back then.

Valerie told me they disowned her for choosing to marry Clive. She had tried to maintain contact and a year or so after Joanne was born she gave up! Valerie admitted this still hurts and found the rejection of Joanne unforgivable. On returning to England, Valerie said she looked for her parents only to discover they had both died. For Valerie, Maxine choosing not to tell about the latter was another unforgivable act by her sister. And a further reason, I presume, why Valerie was adamant there had not been any contact with Maxine since living with Clive in Germany.'

I pause.

'I would also like to express how sad I am about what's happened to Gillian White to..., sorry, yesterday.

Since two thousand and one, I have been a member of MAPPA. Therefore, I've contributed to all but one of Harold White's annual reviews.

I concur with what Kerry and, his probation officer, Sandy have already highlighted. Namely, my judgement too is Harold White poses a high risk of re-offending. I also think it is necessary to emphasise, since her husband's assault against a librarian, Mrs White was consistent in her determination to assist MAPPA with implementing a plan to minimise this risk. A plan realistic and humanly possible under the law, of course!

When MAPPA next review Mr White, it will be different in that our assessment will incorporate addressing recent new laws in the Justice Act!

Bare with me, please. I'm going to refer again to my involvement three years ago.

Valerie Verity did not comment whatsoever about being adopted, let alone a Mrs Gillian White. After all, why would she have done? As far as Valerie knew, and might still believe for that matter, and as everyone else did until yesterday, Valerie's parents' are Henrietta and David Hurst!

Milena Trunch is someone I have not heard anything about until today. Valerie and Milena's sexuality might be an indicator of an inappropriate relationship? Though I accept the statements made by Leon and Patricia Hartman are accurate in their identification of Milena, it is important to stress the descriptive word used was embrace.

Secondly, while the minor adult feature is a concern, if found to be a truth, it is important to remember it is possible Valerie nor Milena know about their legally manufactured family tie. Also, assuming the Hartman statements are factually correct then evidently Valerie and Milena know one another. However, this does not automatically mean we can be sure Maxine and Valerie have found each other again too?

With the latter in mind, and with your permission Guv, please can Claudia share some relevant information I asked her to gather for this meeting?'

'Oh, yes. Splendid! How avant-garde. Are you OK with this Claudia?'

'Yes, Frank. I'll get you back for this Mr Forrester,' says Claudia failing not to smile.

'Please, call me Alex.'

'Don't push it!Right. At four thirty yesterday afternoon, Mr Forrester contacted me to say he's out of the office for the rest of the day and Sir Roger had contacted him about various developments going on.

Mr Forrester, then asked if I would do a search on our database of the police officer's written accounts of interviews with each pupil at St. Clotho school in two thousand and four.

I put Milena and Joanne's names and the word cousin in the search box. The one match is the record of a WPC Emily Boddy who recorded her interview with Milena Trunch. There is not anything to suggest Milena knew Joanne to be her cousin. There are; however, comments corroborating what Renee from the school shared earlier that she is sure neither girl did anything to indicate they knew they were related. Me done.'

'Thank you, Claudia. Excellent!' says Frank.

I then say, 'Yes, thank you from me too Claudia. If I had not heard about Valerie Verity's very different lifestyle and behaviours tonight, if pressed for an opinion, I would say with certainty Valerie would not seek relationships with minors. At the risk of sounding contradictory, despite Valerie's current persona, I still do think this is probably the case.

I begin my conclusion, I'm afraid, by advising there are now more questions that need to be asked and answered to attempt a substantive generic diagnosis. I do though want to offer two key factors which should be included in our impending 'what next' discussion?

First, Harold White is no fool, the opposite in fact. I would take very seriously what he's told Sally and Peter about Maxine Stewart. I am specifically referring to the fact that she was his solicitor when he avoided public prosecution back in ninety-six.

The second is more a short list of What Ifs? I think we need to address their respective hypotheses to decide if any of them are relevant to understanding, who might be responsible or not for at least some if not all the alleged or inferred crimes we are discussing tonight?

What if Valerie and or Maxine now both know their truer ancestry and or are in contact?

On the assumption they have had contact, What if either Clive and Valerie Verity and or Maxine now know the officer Valerie was with on that Christmas Eve, is Luke Stewart?'

A final important consideration is, has Harold White's hatred of law enforcers in his life in any capacity, and the prospect of being found in breach of his probation order, enough motive to murder, his informant wife? I think it is probable as much as it's improbable. Finished Guv.'

Frank feels the whiff of an uncomfortable silence gripping everyone in the room. He scribes an asterisk beside both Stewart names. He then says, 'Thank you all and before...'

'Excuse me Guv,' interrupts Sir Roger lifting his hand how he was taught to do at school.

'Sorry, Rog... Sir Roger. Please, do carry on.'

'Thank you, Frank. I think it is essential to inform everyone what the official status has been concerning the investigation into Joanne Verity's disappearance. It remains open, though, I admit, it was severely scaled down!

At no time has either parent been seen by the police as an official suspect. In fact, our procedural actions meant we were able to eliminate them. It is because of very recent events and enquiries why we are having this meeting tonight.

In particular two significant factors. The first is learning unthinkable, seems more appropriate than unknown, the identity of some extended family members. The second is finding what are almost certainly skeleton remains of a child so near to the scene of the murder of Gillian White. That's it Guv.'

'Thank you, Sir Roger. Most useful and now, reminding you the questions we need to answer are laid out on a sheet of paper attached to each agenda, I invite questions and discussion. Please...'

One of two resident layperson members present, is the first to put a hand up and Frank then says instead, "Please, Eva, Lady Chalice-Hermitage, do begin.'

'And so believe me, the mother of all such discussions, starts in earnest!'

CHAPTER FIVE

When the E. n. E. M. A. meeting began, everyone at it was unaware Milena was in a car with James Hawker. The first journey in this chapter is what happened between Hawker and Milena through this same night?

As Hawker exits the grounds of Little Snoring village Hall, he asks Milena, 'What did you say to Sophie and her mother then?'

'Told them because my Aunt is in the hospital I wanted to be at home, and I had called mum who agreed to pick me up. Had to cuz we were staying at Sophie's granny's house tonight which is not far from here. I've already replied to a text from Sophie saying I'm already home.'

Hawker turns his head to see Milena smiling at him. He then gives a rare sincere compliment. 'You were perfect tonight. I think it is one of the best best productions ever done by the Thespian Players. Choose a CD to play if you like? They are in the same place as my other car.'

'OK. And by the way Jimmy, why are you using this car? It's so old and uncomfortable. Do you want one of your favourites on then?'

'No. Your choice' replies Hawker in an unfamiliar generous tone.

Whichever one I grab first, Milena decides. Not looking to check the content of her lucky dip, she slides a CD in. Then turns the volume up a bit and the first track starts. Milena is a little disappointed it is not one of her CD's. But, she likes to hear what music Jimmy loves.

Hawker is glad for music too. He is thinking about his current position very carefully! Why has Gillian been murdered! Out of nowhere! Staggering! By whom? And, Harold is as flummoxed as me!

It was risky Harold! But you are right! The girl needed to move. Ten seconds earlier and everything would still be sweet as a nut. Damn that bloody dog! Harold will be seriously pissed off the pigs are questioning him. Better finding the girl in the woods than in his shed though. Still near his home, sure! Pure coincidence doesn't prove anything! Don't panic Harold; we have a good plan. It should work. If it doesn't, at the end of the day I can fall back on the truth! You might well have not killed your wife, but you did the girl mate! Now to convince Milena, it is time to fulfil her dream of living in New Zealand!

The owner of the dog who fought Hawker for possession of a tarpaulin is a woman who lives in a village called Barnham Broom. Her name is Gemma Moss. In Miss Moss's statement to the police she included, "When I caught up with my dogs in the woods, Butch was barking like crazy, at Zeus! Zeus was tearing at, you know, how awful! It is then; I heard a car head off at speed! Sorry, I didn't see the vehicle or the person driving."

Hawker's wrists are tense as he grips the wheel and is shaking a bit too. Milena notices and asks 'What's wrong Jimmy?'

Hawker absent mindedly replies, 'Harold bloody Wh...' and shuts up.

'Who?'

'Shut up Milena. I'm thinking.'

Milena responds childlike by turning up the volume very high. Hawker increases speed, and suddenly Milena switches the music off.

'This isn't the right way home Jimmy.'

'I know.'

'Why? Where are we going?'

'How does that promise of New Zealand sound to you?'

'Really? But why now?'

"You trust me don't you?'

'Yes Jimmy, you know I do. It's just I've got no clothes, and there are mum and Luke! They need to know! And what about our passports?' she asks with faint protest.

'I'll buy you loads of clothes. I have money. Oh, and **we** are a family now, OK! We can tell them when we've found a place to live. OK! As for passports, I went home during Act Two and packed everything we need.'

'How much money do we have?' Milena then asks inappropriately.

'Enough to make our dream come true that's for sure. Oh yes, and I've destroyed our phones. Not a problem because until we buy new ones, I can use this one. It will do till then.'

'But when I mentioned it...'

'Had to be done. Don't want anyone stopping our dream, do we! Do you remember conversations we've had about what to do if ever caught together?'

'Yes, and you said when I was sixteen you...'

'That's still true Milena. Now we must wait till we're out of this country. So, until then, although nothing should go wrong, if it does, never admit knowing me before you were sixteen, never! Otherwise, we're both be in serious trouble! OK?'

'Yes, but...'

'No-one will approve of us here! Crazy because now you can give legal consent. So remember, don't worry or panic if the pigs arrest me. They've got nothing else on me, and I'll be back home within days, maybe hours. I promise! I'll then contact you. Understand?'

'Yes, Jimmy. I'll never betray you, we love each other,' says Milena quietly.

'Yes we do,' says Hawker as he gives Milena's bare thigh a gentle squeeze.

'Which airport are we flying from?'

'Amsterdam. I'm driving to Harwich. Should make a ferry that leaves just after four.'

'Mum says you need a special visa to live in New Zealand. How did you get ours?'

'All in hand. Trust me,' replies Hawker as he puts the music back on, loud!

***

Hawker parks outside a Little Chef just off the A14. 'Come on, you need to get out of those clothes, and we can get something to eat and drink while we're here. Can't be longer than half an hour mind. OK!'

'Sure. Thanks, Jimmy.'

'There are toilets you can change in just inside the entrance. You go ahead Milena, and I'll follow you in soon. Here is a suitcase with some clothes you left at mine. Or do you want your overnight bag?'

'No, the suitcase is cool. Nice one Jimmy,' replies Milena as she grabs it and jogs away.

Hawker opens the boot to check he has everything he needs. They'll never find my hideout, and there isn't anything in my flat. So, there are just two leads for the pigs to link me to Harold. His call yesterday to a mobile that's now smashed to smithereens and fingerprints in his house. We have an answer for both! Great, everything covered! Well, except this car has no tax or insurance. Will be bloody unlucky to get stopped at this hour. Of course, the pigs will find it abandoned. By the time they discover it belongs to Ollie, we'll be long gone!

Milena opens the suitcase and sees a couple of dresses in it. Immediately an infusion of a sense of reality engulfs her. Milena stares into a mirror and starts to cry and shiver.

'Jimmy will understand and take me back home,' she says naively.

Milena then hastily takes everything off, bar underwear, and chooses the blue dress. She then throws her Bunny girl waitress costume into the suitcase. By the time she's clothed again, Milena has stopped crying. She then uses toilet paper to tidy her face, especially the smudged mascara giving two black eyes look.

***

Thinking courageously to say something is one thing! Doing is quite another!

Milena failed to share her thoughts throughout their entire time in the restaurant. A mixture of not wanting to let Hawker down and fear! A fear Hawker will react the same way as when she previously suggested they tell her mum of their plans to live in New Zealand.

They have been on the road for five minutes and not only is Milena very scared again, she feels sick. With a need to defeat both she gingerly summons up the courage to ask, 'Please Jimmy, pull the car in!'

Hawker laughs. 'Must be kidding! No can do!'

With no control, Milena throws up all over the gear stick and Hawker's trousers. His reaction ends with skidding to a stop on a hard shoulder.

Milena then hurls out the car. Her knees hit the ground, and at the same time the grass bank is showered with puke, and she's gasping for breath.

Hawker gets out the car and stands behind Milena, watching with rage and anger!

He begins to weigh up his options. To get rid of you now is my most risky option! Not far behind is leaving you here! Or, shall I keep you with me? No, maybe take you home? Harold always says the riskiest option is the most likely to succeed! Perhaps not this time?

Hawker decides to give himself a bit more time to choose. He calmly opens the car's left rear door.

'Get into the car,' he orders.

Wiping her mouth with both arms and terrified, Milena complies.

'No, not the front seat,' shouts Hawker who then takes hold of Milena's shoulders and spins her around. He then pushes her in until her head clunks against the opposite rear door.

Hawker undoes his fly.

'No Jimmy!! I'm sorry,' Milena shrieks!

'Shut up,' retorts Hawker as he parts Milena's clamped knees and rips off a thong.

Milena kicks out. 'Please, Jimmy – No!'

Hawker, with his knees on the edge of the back seat and his face over Milena's, repeats, 'Shut up.'

'I'm really...'

Hawker then thumps Milena hard in the belly.

Milena's defences crumble, sanctioning Hawker to leap onto and into his helpless victim. Recovery of some breath, allows Milena to start shrieking again. Sadly, all subsequent groans and whimpers gradually reside until eventually, they fade into silence. A silence which was broken fifteen seconds or so later by the swoosh of a lorry rushing past from the opposite direction on the other side of a central reservation.

***

A very different car journey is currently being made by Andy Rioch, who is the County Council's top IT person. He is not concentrating on his driving. His mind is preoccupied with exploring reasons for literally being woken in the middle of the night! By a phone call from, no less, the Chief Executive of the County Council!

"Andy you must come into work immediately. We need you too," are the sum of the Chief's words by way of an explanation.

A CD is playing in Andy's car. It is by, The Dire Straits and currently a brilliant guitar solo in the song, "Sultans of Swing," is blaring loud!

With so much distraction it is perhaps no surprise Andy has no idea the traffic lights are red as he turns right off Dereham Road. Like nearly every road in the city, Grapes Hill does not have another vehicle on it. From the top of the Hill Andy turns left, and fortunately, every traffic light along Queens Road is green. At the last set, he goes left, and it's not long before he's on Martineau Lane which is the address for County Hall.

Andy arrives at the barrier manned by a security guard who comments, 'Must be big to get one of us dragged out at this ungodly hour eh! Still, I mustn't complain I'm getting treble pay.'

Andy hands over his ID.

'That's great. OK. There you go,' says the guard and the barrier gate tilts upward.

On parking, Andy recognises the only cars present. One belongs to the Chief Executive; the second by the Director of Children's Services and the final one to Head of Public Relations and The Media.

Andy Rioch is excited. Determined to look cool, Andy swipes his ID badge and ambles through a revolving door. He heads straight to his two-man one-woman welcoming committee who are at a reception desk drinking horrible dispenser tea.

'Hello Andy,' says Melanie Furze who is Director of Children's Services. 'So good of you to come at this ridiculous hour. Can I get you a drink?'

'No thanks,' says Andy who then sits on a seat left for him.

'Am I right to assume Andy, you do recognise my colleagues William Williams and Nicolas Tingle?'

'Yes, Melanie.'

'Good. 'I'm sure you have already surmised, it must be a grave matter to need you here right now! I speak for all three of us when I say we are genuinely appreciative.

I shall now get straight to the point. Sorry, before I do, I must explain you are going to be instructed to undertake a highly irregular task that ultimately I have given consent too. It is an urgent and essential component of a child protection and murder enquiry. Therefore, you must keep the knowledge of your actions and findings totally confidential and report them only to me.'

'I see,' says Andy.

'We need you to search the First Care computer records a Maxine Stewart has accessed from the first day employed by us. We are particularly interested in five names. These are Joanne Verity, Milena Trunch, Valerie Verity, Gillian White and Harold White.

Maxine Stewart usually arrives at work at around eight

thirty-am. Arrangements are in place to meet Mrs Stewart on her arrival, and she won't be permitted to go to her office. When you have completed the task, I want you to call me personally. My mobile number is on here too,' says Melanie handing Andy a folded A4 sheet of paper.

'Once you have the findings please discuss them with me, straight away! Any questions Andy?'

'No. None Melanie.'

CHAPTER SIX

'...and now we have decided what actions to take, I once again offer a big thank you for all your contributions, patience, dedication and endurance. And, more importantly, pat yourselves on the back for achieving our objectives!

Before we all leave, I remind people to exit from the same door you came in. Sorry Alex, you still need to use the main entrance. That's it. Thank you, everyone.'

On each side of the table, preparations are being made to go home, and I attempt to get Frank's attention. I say, 'Excuse me Frank, have you a couple of minutes please?'

Frank raises a hand of acknowledgement and semi shouts, 'I do need to brief those upstairs, so to speak. So, can it wait?'

I reply, 'No, just want to say your helpful explanation on how I get out Guv reminds me, is there any progress on an agreement being reached to make the fire escape and toilets accessible in here, like they are in the building we use on the other side of this Business Park?'

'Still, with the Planning Department I'm afraid, and despite the powers, I do have I can't magic away red tape,' Frank explains before offering a shrug of his shoulders!

I respond with, 'Thank you for the update Guv. Easy to remember! During eighteen months there is no change. Right?'

Frank pushes both hands against the table, and once upright I watch our Chief Constable give a signal to three other detectives to follow him for a debrief.

I muse, For all the skills Frank does posses, I assume he has not detected there is a question mark at the end of the word Right. Why not be honest? Even if it means the reality is, "No one gives enough shit! Including me!"

I exchange we got it right smile with Claudia for a prediction she made in one of the breaks. Which was, "At the end, Simon Graham, from Education, will be the first to leave the room."

There are now just six people left.

'Alex, is the taxi on its way? asks Claudia.

Not sure what time I'd be returning home means I haven't booked one. To make sure Claudia doesn't delay going to get some much-needed sleep I reply, 'Yes, it is thank you, Claudia. Safe journey home.'

'And you, see you tomorrow,' Claudia says and then disappears with her hand already fumbling in her handbag for cigarettes.

The first of only a matter of a few uncomfortable seconds pass. Surprised Sadie Wood seems to be one of four women exchanging debrief pleasantries, I am stunned to then suddenly hear, 'Is that promise of breakfast genuine then? I'm gasping for a cup of tea.'

'Oh. Yes. The Old fashioned café?'

'Yep. Sounds good to me!' replies Sadie. She then adds, 'Goodbye ladies, nice to meet you.'

With no interrupting this particular inner circle's conversation it seems, Sadie turns away and follows me to the lift. I am still listening.

'At last. I was beginning to wonder when we will be on our own?' Says Debbie Eagle in what both Karen Trinket and Kerry Cozen think is an unnecessary bitchy tone. Neither of them makes a challenge preferring to concentrate on finding out why Debbie asked them to stay behind a little longer?

'I shall come straight to the point. I am concerned about the decision not to proceed immediately with a forty-seven investigation into the allegation of sexual abuse against Milena.'

Karen shrugs her shoulders and is about to respond when Kerry beats her to it. 'To be frank with you Debbie, I cannot agree! Although, I do naturally believe an investigation is required sooner rather than later. Valerie and her husband need time to hear about their tragic, no devastating loss first.'

A little relieved Kerry has taken the lead and pleased they think along similar lines, Karen supports by sharing her opinion. 'I agree with Kerry, Debbie.'

'But it's not confirmed it is Joanne they've found.'

Karen and Debbie frown their disquiet, prompting Debbie to add, 'OK, sorry, I accept it will be.'

'It is...'

The lift door closes.

***

A minute or so later, I am tangled in a revolving door and applying maximum power and speed, in reverse! It seems to work because the chair flings backwards. However, the joystick is out of my control due to a shudder of my body. My spin and skidding end because one of my chair's handles smash into the glass of a fire bell. The bell instantly rings out its ear-piercing shrill. With Sadie laughing, I quickly get out of reverse and bolt free through a now permanently open, not to mention, damaged door, as fast as I can!

'Alex, shouldn't you stay and explain,' Sadie conveys still laughing.

'No, will phone Sir Roger from the café,' I reply.

I stop to wait for Sadie. I then say, 'We won't get breakfast till lunchtime if I stay now and fill in accident reports etc. Plus, I think we've done enough 'beyond normal duties stuff' for one day, eh?'

'You sure Alex? Sadie asks.

'Yes.'

We head toward the café, and soon I notice a lone reporter perched on the bonnet of a car with the Eastern Press logo splashed all over it.

I pull up, and so Sadie stops too. 'Has the exhaust blown?' she asks.

'No, nothing like that,' I reply chuckling.'

'Why have we stopped?'

I explain, 'Don't look, please. Have you spotted a pressman

too?'

'No,' is the reply and I think it takes the unnatural application of disinterest by Sadie not to have at least a peep.

I say, 'If he engages us do you want us to be Forrester or Wood? Or assuming we are of similar age and you are looking easily no more than the early thirties, my younger sister is an option too.'

'Flattery will get you everywhere,' says Sadie with a laugh. She then adds, 'Now I know you're pulling my leg,' and Sadie looks over a shoulder. She then says, 'Oh you're not joking,' and then looks at me again before adding, 'Sorry.'

'No problem. So which one?'

'Mr and Mrs Forrester-Wood sounds noble, cool even, don't you think?' replies Sadie.'

'Well yes,' and we both laugh. I then say, 'Shall we continue Mrs Forrester-Wood?' and I gesture, "After you," with a foot.

'Yep,' replies Sadie as she places her left hand on the right armrest of my rider.

Soon, we are passing the lone reporter whose managed to detect where to try and gain an exclusive. I offer a silent acknowledgement of admiration. I then recognise the journalist and ponder, from his demeanour, it seems he doesn't reciprocate this!

***

In the old-fashioned café, Sadie and I are the only customers. Sadie is already on the second pot of tea. Till now, our conversation has been dominated by what was shared during the night and to a much lesser extent on things that were not. I have phoned Sir Roger as promised.

'Very unusual décor in here isn't it. Feels like we're sitting on a game board for draughts or chess. Seats are lovely and comfortable though. Look, amazing! There is a different picture embroidered on each cushion?'

'Yes. Homemade too. The cushions I mean. Would you

prefer a game of Draughts or Chess?' I ask.

'Right, I get it now. I think my answer has to be chess if we are to play a game in here.'

I reply, 'I favour chess. More moves to enjoy.'

Sadie refrains from responding because we hear Sizzler say, 'There you go Alex,' as he places the largest fry-up Sadie has ever seen in front of me.

'Thank you Sizzler. Sizzler, this is Sadie Wood and Sadie this is Nelson, known to friends as Sizzler.'

'How do you do, nice to meet you Sizzler,' says Sadie and they shake hands.

'You too Madam,' replies Sizzler before going back to the kitchen.

'Did Sizzler do the embroidery for the cushions?'

'No, his wife, Claire did.'

'Very clever. And I've just counted the are thirty-two tables in here. Very cool.'

Sizzler returns, 'And this is for you Madam, and as a new customer I've added an extra egg and rasher, and only Alex will pay for his breakfast. Do either of you want another drink?'

'Another pot of tea would be nice please and thank you. Are you sure? I don't understand?' asks Sadie.

'Certainly madam. It is our custom for all first-time guests accompanied with a regular. What about you Alex. Another coffee?'

'No thanks.'

'Claire,' calls Sizzler. 'Another pot of tea for Sadie please.'

'Coming up.'

'Bonn Appetite to the both of you,' says Sizzler who then spots a regular customer has walked in, prompting him to leave us.

Sadie leans over her breakfast and whispers, 'I'll never manage all this Mr Forrester.'

I smile and reply, 'Do you have a dog Mrs Wood?'

'Yes, why?'

'So do I. Her name is Bridie, and she's a cross. Her mother is a Boxer and her dad an Alsatian.'

'Unusual, how old is she?'

'Three and what is your dog's name?'

'Polly and she's a greyhound. She's eight now, bless her.'

'Well, if you don't want everything on your plate just ask Sizzler for a doggy bag and he'll be only too pleased as he loves dogs too. I'm sure Polly will be happy too won't she?'

'Yes she will,' replies Sadie.

Claire rests a fresh pot of tea on the table.

I say, 'Thank you. Is your mother still recovering well Claire?'

'Yes, she is and nice of you to remember and ask.'

'Don't be daft, and after what we've listened to all night, it's refreshing to hear something good happening to someone.Oh, I am sorry. Claire, this is Sadie Wood, Mrs Wood, Claire.'

'Nice to meet you,' says Claire as she offers her hand to Sadie.

'Likewise. I adore your cushions. You're very clever.'

'Thank you. Is there anything else you need?'

I say, 'No thanks.'

'Nor me. More than enough and very tasty.'

Claire gives a brief friendly laugh before explaining, 'Nothing to do with me! I hate cooking!'

'Snap,' replies Sadie.

'Enjoy your breakfasts,' says Claire.

As we tuck in earnest, Sadie asks, 'You want to know something strange Mr Forrester?'

'Strangely, yes.'

'That reporter we passed. I'm pretty sure I've met him.'

'A friend?'

Sadie hesitates with a puzzled frown, 'No. Do you know

anything about the Rowland case?'

'A bit, why?'

'Last time I saw him was after a Rowland case conference. He kept on harassing me for information and followed me home the cheeky bastard.'

'He didn't hurt you did he?'

'Not physically no. Persistence is scary after six hours though. You just want him to go home and get a life.'

'What happened?'

'I phoned a police officer I'd met at the conference, and she arranged for the creep to leave me alone. Bernice Buck is the officer's name, and she reckons she'd probably wouldn't have succeeded if there had been a gang of reporters camping outside my house. What's more, that reporter ruined loads of flowers and plants and never apologised once or offer to replace them.'

'Out of order, lest he should have done. You are not alone, not that makes it better of course. Some colleagues have told me similar tales.'

'Can't say I'm surprised,' says Sadie who downs utensils beside Polly's treat.

'Do you enjoy your job Mrs Wood?'

'My name's Sadie.'

'Sadie, do you enjoy your work?'

'The hours can be unsociable sometimes,' Sadie answers laughing.

'Care and Repair officer is a new one on me.'

'Really? I 'd love to be a detective.'

'So you can arrest and throw everything, including a kitchen sink at that reporter eh.'

Sadie says, 'Too right! I'd like to thank you for suggesting breakfast here Mr Alexander Forrester. Do you often invite strangers to join you?'

'Mr is more than sufficient by the way and to answer your

question, all the time Sadie,' I lie.

'Really? You are pulling my leg, right?'

'Ab...,' I begin to reply.

But Sadie adds, 'Is it just women?'

I completed my answer. '...solutely.'

'What?' voices Sadie with concern.

'I mean, yes absolutely, I'm pulling your leg.'

Sadie smiles and says, 'That's good.'

'Sadie, may I say something riskily honest?'

'Is it flattering?'

'Yes.'

'Then no.'

'OK.'

'But I don't mind you being an exception.'

'You sure?'

'No,' replies Sadie with a chuckle.

'Forgive my honesty, but I can't help myself not to say, you have wonderful eyes, Sadie and an even brighter smile. No bullshit, I've been drawn to you from the first time we met. It...'

'We've only met tonight Alex. Wh...'

I interrupt, 'I have been wondering if you didn't remember. It was at the tail end of this summer's County Council's annual staff pi..., party. We were both waiting outside for a taxi to go home. You were somewhat tipsy and merry and kept missing your cigarette when trying to light it. I offered you the one I was smoking so you could use it to light your own. We chatted and laughed for over half an hour or so I think. And, when you waved goodbye as your taxi sped away, it took a while for the warmth of your company and yet also the hollow feeling of thinking, I'll probably never see you again, to go. Might sound soft but genuinely true. Ho..'

Sadie leans forward, 'I do remember now. I wouldn't believe you were a cop, would I? Cuz you said you were after I admitted getting cheap baccy. Thought you were winding me up.'

'Yep, it was funny, I think we even did the 'No your not, and yes I am routine' in between our laughter.

'For what it's worth I did tell a girlfriend who asked me how that night out went, that nothing to remember other than having a giggle with a nice man when waiting to go home. We laughed because I admitted I don't think we even exchanged names, did we?'

I smile and reply, 'Yes we did just before you dive-bombed into the back seat.'

'I can't remember that at all. Worrying eh, being in such a state. How embarrassing,' says Sadie with a glint in her grin.

'You promptly sat up and wound down the window to wave and say, thanks for the light. We laughed, and you looked happy as you too quickly went out of my sight.'

Sadie looks straight into my eyes as she says, 'Thank you for the compliments, and Mr Forrester would you have shared them if you knew I am spoken for or am married?'

'No. Are you?'

'No. Divorced four years ago. We have two daughters. Are you?'

'No.'

'Have you been married Alex?

'Yes. For five years.'

'What happened? I know I'm nosy, but I mean well,' replies Sadie with a gorgeous smile.

'Sure,' and I smile back before adding, 'She fell in love with someone else.'

'Children?'

'No, been divorced since I was aged twenty-six. May I give you my number, please Sadie?'

'You may but why do I need to ring you? I'm with you now. What would you say?'

'I'd like us to see one another again if you feel the same?'

'Yes, I do Alex.'

'Would you like a cigarette Sadie?' I ask as I lift my left foot across the table and release a lit cigarette from between my toes into an ashtray.

'Thank you. How did you do that? Asks Sadie who then bends her head to peep under the table for a clue.

Sitting upright again, Sadie smiles while taking hold of her cigarette. 'So good after a meal isn't it?'

'Absolutely. Are you from Norfolk?' I ask.

'No. Rutland. Have you heard of it?'

'Smallest county in the country, near Leicestershire. I love Pork Pie, don't you?'

Sadie smiles, 'I do actually. So, you from around there too, surely not?'

'Born on an island. Do you want to hazard a guess which one in this world it is?'

'OK. Somewhere exotic, I think. I'll go for a British or ex British colony. I say Seychelles.'

'Nearly, Minster on the Isle of Sheppey.'

'Never heard of it, where in gods name is it?'

'Kent.'

Sadie laughs and then says, 'You had me thinking sand, sea and sunshine,' expresses Sadie before resting her cigarette in the ashtray and reaching down to pick up her handbag.

I watch as Sadie fumbles with both hands and an unopened letter, a pen and lighter fall out onto the table. 'It's here somewhere,' says Sadie.

Eventually, Sadie's left-hand escapes the bag and in it is her card. Which she places on the table as she says, 'I work very near the sea. Tomorrow I finish at five. I'd like it very much if you do call to say you're able to meet there, say five five-thirtyish?'

'Wonderful,' I reply and am pleased to see Sadie works in Cromer where there is a train station.

I then ask, 'Sadie, would you please push your card closer to me so I can try and slip it into my shirt pocket.

'There you go.'

'Thanks. Do you live in Cromer too...'

CHAPTER SEVEN

With both hands rubbing tired eyes, Sally says, 'I cannot believe we have been ordered to interview Valerie Verity first!'

PP is driving, and a hundred yards in front is a sign indicating the hospital is four miles away. He is also running on reserve fuel, so to speak but senses Sally needs to talk. 'You think Harold White did it, don't you? PP eventually asks.

'Yes, I do. Don't you?'

'No,' replies PP.

'Why? Who do you think is the killer?'

'Of Joanne or Mrs White?'

'Both,' Sally lies.

'Clive Verity for...'

'You think **Clive Verity?** Are you serious?' Sally interrupts. She then looks at PP and sees his huge grin and adds, 'You bastard.' but fails to stop a brief bout of laughter.

'What you haven't given me a chance to say is, I do think it could be Clive killed Mrs White to frame Maxine Stewart be...'

'Sorry to butt in. That's absurd!'

'Is it?'

'How on earth do you reach such a conclusion?'

'Are you interested to know?' asks PP as he steers the car into a lay-by.

'Yes. Sorry, I am. It's just never occurred to me that Clive Verity might be that involved. What is his motive?'

PP replies, 'To kill two birds with one stone. Would you agree with the high profile investigation and media publicity to find Joanne makes it probable Maxine Stewart recognises her sister is the missing girl's mother and attempts to find Valerie?'

'OK. Yes.'

'Therefore, assuming they are in contact, do you agree it is reasonable to suppose Clive Verity and Luke Stewart have met too?'

'And so Clive might now know as well as Valerie, Luke **is** the officer who surely did run from their house in Germany?' interjects Sally.

'Yes.'

Sally is silent for a few seconds. 'OK. Surely, if Clive Verity wanted to hurt anyone, it would be Luke Stewart?'

'Instinctively you might see it that way. Look at it from each Verity's point of view. Valerie Verity has years of separation from her sister, and through the horror of losing her daughter, she is reunited with Maxine, only to find Maxine's husband is the lover with whom Clive found her. If nothing else, if you accept contact between the two couples has happened, I think it is reasonable to assume you would agree Clive has learned that Luke has been in the Territorial Army for years?'

'Yes. Fair enough,' says Sally.

'What Alex confirmed is, Clive, admitted it was a male carrying women's clothing. I'd put money on Clive probing to see if there is any evidence of some interesting dirt to dig up amongst what is the rock of Luke, so to speak. It's also possible, Valerie and Luke have met. Needing them, I suggest, to decide if Valerie should even confess to Clive? Or, equally, it might be they've tried to keep their secret just that!

Sally says, 'Wow. There are big ifs in there though. And how would Clive find out? And besides, remember killing Mrs White is killing his wife's mother,' Sally reasons.

'The latter is easy to answer. No-one, let alone Clive or Valerie, knew about this tie until less than eighteen hours ago.'

'Yes. OK. Good point,' replies Sally with a casualness doing an injustice to her real status. Which is, she responded thoughtfully.

Sally then sprouts a few more questions. 'You still don't know how Clive discovered Luke's into cross-dressing? Why he'd choose to hurt Maxine so much and most of all why murder an innocent old Lady?'

PP lights up a cigarette, and they both open a door. PP then places a cassette into the car stereo and says, 'My answer to your first question is I don't know, but as I just said, I'd wager he has.

The motive to use Maxine is to hurt Luke and them too. I think when talking with Clive Verity, he will reveal he also holds a lot of contempt for Maxine as-well.'

'What facts do you have to think that?'

Maxine Stewart was a junior solicitor in the firm which defended Harold White in nineteen ninety-six. You aired this fact yourself during the meeting. Secondly, when questioned as part of the investigation into his daughter's disappearance, all the interviews with Clive Verity are on tape. During the second interview, Clive chose to have a solicitor present. It is a fact his solicitor is heard saying something pertinent.

Before I play it, it is important to remember at the time of the investigation into Joanne's 'abduction,' some of the information shared last night means, the official consensus was Valerie and the then unidentifiable Maxine, were not in contact! It's all on here,' suggests PP as he switches on the tape. The preliminaries confirm who is present and for the first time, Sally listens to what Clive's solicitor said.

"Look, before we start I must protest on behalf of my client. He, we accept it is standard practice to interview parents of a missing child, but my client has asked for representation. Unbelievably, on the basis, he fears he is now a suspect. The fact Mr Verity was on top of Shining Tor, in the peak district, at the time of his daughter disappearing makes this ridiculous! Even more so, when you know, there is a convicted RSO who lives in the same village! As if that is not enough, the Council's head of the Children's legal department knows what a dangerous and disgusting man White is, because she used to be part of a team which defended him. Damn it!"

Sally is stunned. 'Can I have a cigarette please?' is all she can say.

'You don't smoke,' retorts PP with a smile. He then turns off the tape.

'I do now. Why aren't we, you not taking the tape to Sir Roger?'

'Sir Roger is aware of their content but as you've been so right to emphasise you cannot deal with Ifs and Buts. It is a fact Clive Verity heard this. It does not prove he has acted upon the information. I think in time, you will see he has,' asserts PP.

Before Sally speaks, PP gets in first to share what he believes is another crucial observation. 'Remember Sally, Clive Verity is a trained killing machine, and the stabbing of Mrs White involved a clinical insertion into her heart. I'd put money on the weapon having Maxine Stewart's finger-prints on it.'

'Why would anyone credit Maxine's motive for needing to murder Mrs White,' Sally asks sensing a crack in PP's thought.

'To prevent Mrs White's informant actions causing Maxine's role in assisting Harold White to maintain his freedom and anonymity becoming, public knowledge through White's discrediting of Maxine. Or more accurately, Valerie finding out about Maxine's role!

I fully appreciate we do not precisely understand the nature of the relationships between everyone discussed last night. I just find it difficult to accept there is not anything significant amongst them. Especially the relationship between the Lawyer and SAS assassin!'

Sally says, 'Wow, when you put it like that! My head's spinning again. Why...'

PP interrupts, 'A PC McDermott took guard duty into Woodland Mews and thereby Rose Close from five-pm till midnight yesterday. He told me this morning he's sure Maxine Stewart was in the Verity's house when an ambulance came to take Valerie to hospital. He explained, Clive was with him when Maxine arrived, and Clive told him it was OK to let her through.

Trevor is PC's name. Trevor said he recognised this was, "The head legal bod from the County Council" as she co-ran a course he'd attended as part of his post-graduation training.

Trevor told me he looked up handouts etc. related to the course and showed me Maxine Stewart was indeed the name one of the facilitators. Trevor also confirmed what Genevieve Treets told us about her visit there yesterday. Finally, as you know, we are still waiting for AFC Computer LTD to inform us when Clive arrived at their office in Huntingdon yesterday morning and of course when he left?'

'Good God! I agree that does change our understanding somewhat. But why didn't we look into Maxine Stewart at the time of the interview with Clive Verity?'

PP switches the tape back on, and Sally listens to the DI's reply which answers her question.

"I fully appreciate the frustration we all share with Mr White. Nevertheless, I do not accept the slur on Mrs Stewart's integrity. In this country, everyone has an entitlement to legal representation, and the fact is, Mrs Stewart was simply doing her duty as an employee of a firm who was acting on behalf of Mr White."

PP turns the tape off again. 'If that interview happened today I suggest we'd react with a bit more thought, wouldn't we?'

'Well. Yes, I do. Is it rather than Clive Verity framing Maxine, she has done it?'

'It is possible. If Maxine has though, why spare Harold White his life?'

'OK. You said you think Clive Verity believes Harold White murdered Joanne, so why did he not frame Maxine with killing Harold White as opposed to his wife?'

Sally's heart is thumping fast and hard. She examines her colleagues face for what she is sure will be a sign confirming she has just offered the flaw in PP's theory.

'My first response is to correct you. What I said was, it is likely Clive Verity believes this is a strong probability too. Secondly, given Clive Verity learnt from the interviews that White is an RSO, therefore by association, a suspect, the DI on the tape told me they rightly had a duty to share with Clive and his Solicitor, the evidence of Mr and Mrs White being in the hospital on the day of the fête. My belief is, Clive wrongly had contempt for White's wife as well as Maxine for being party to protecting someone he has never been able to rule out as a suspect. For Clive, I suggest it was and still is too coincidental to have someone like White as a village neighbour without believing he might well somehow be involved?

I am also aware one of the interviews on tape was halted and concluded another day. Clive Verity was unable to stop crying when he realised Harold White is the same person he believed to be a friend called Eddie. You see, Clive's friendship with Eddie, meant White also befriended Joanne and Valerie.

I accept I do not know if what I'm about to say is a fact. But, I'm somewhat confident if Clive confided to you why he moved out of his family home he would explain as well as difficulties associated with Valerie's drinking, it is due more to the guilt that it is he who involved White in their lives.

Clive knows he would be top suspect if anything untoward happens to White and most important of all, until yesterday, **no-one**, including Clive and Valerie, had no official reason to believe Joanne's missing person status needed to change to that of a murder enquiry. Which cruelly led to all involved, no matter how unlikely, to hope one day Joanne will be found alive.'

Sally pauses to gather her thoughts and then makes a friendly challenge. 'How much would you risk?'

'Risk? What do you mean?'

'How much are you prepared to bet? I say Harold White has done both.'

PP smiles. 'Oh, I see. Is fifty OK with you?'

'You're on,' states Sally offering her hand.

PP accepts while musing, You are an attractive woman. He then says, 'What a terrible waste!'

'What is?'

'Throwing your money away,' lies PP unashamedly.

'We'll see! Don't you think it is too soon to go and see Valerie? The poor woman is in turmoil,' Sally reasons.

'It is Clive Verity we are going to see. The strategy decision is not to interview Valerie until medical opinion advises us she is well enough.'

Sally stays silent. Although she still thinks she's right, Sally is not as confident as she was when their conversation began.

PP then revs the engine a split second before Sally's mobile plays her favourite song and she looks down and sees it is BB calling.

'Hi, Bernice. Really! That's good news. What now? But. OK. Will do. Bye.'

'Results are in on the samurai sword. Bernice also said Sir Roger orders us back to the station right away.'

'Nice one eh Sally? No doubt another piece of the jigsaw has been put in its correct place,' PP predicts.

As PP then does a U-turn, he says, 'There will be more than the update on the sword, Sally.'

'Bernice didn't mention anything else.'

'Sir Roger wouldn't call us in unless there is something more significant, trust me, Sally.'

'Makes sense I guess. Can I have another cigarette please.'

'Sure. Promise though, not to tell Sylvia it is me that led you ash-tray.'

'Promise,' replies Sally laughing.

CHAPTER EIGHT

Maxine locks her car and heads toward the sizeable entrance into County Hall. She soon passes through a large revolving door. In one hand is a briefcase and with the other, she swipes her ID card. The barrier does not open. Maxine tries again with the same outcome.

'Good Morning Maxine,' says Melanie with false cheerfulness.

Maxine does a double take and sees it **is** Melanie Furze who is greeting her from inside.

'Oh. Hello Melanie. Are you going out anywhere interesting today? Have a problem getting in. I think it's my badge,' says Maxine with a chuckle.

'No. I'm not going out. I'm here to meet you. I need to discuss an important matter with you.'

Melanie nods to Christopher who is head of security, and he releases the barrier's lock.

'Oh OK. Sounds exciting,' says Maxine.

'I think it is best to use my office,' Melanie advises.

'Fine. Are you al-right Melanie?' asks Maxine.

'Yes, let us just wait till we sit down please Maxine.'

The two women soon enter a lift with Christopher. 'Morning Christopher. Can I give you this to check out please?' asks Maxine before adding, 'I think it might be faulty.'

'I'll get it fixed or replaced with a new one Mrs Stewart.'

'Thank you.'

They reach floor nineteen and Melanie leads the way to her office. Christopher, as prearranged, waits near the lift.

On entering, Melanie offers her colleague one of two armchairs facing each other: with a low glass diamond shaped coffee table between them. Maxine chooses the chair which allows you to look out of a vast window: at a view imitative of a Constable painting!

Melanie places two unsealed envelopes on the coffee table and sits opposite Maxine, so obscuring the picture a bit.

'Breathtaking view you enjoy, isn't it Melanie?' asks Maxine.

'Yes, it is. After four years I never tire of it. Sometimes when I need to reflect, I sit where you are. Every time I look there is something I've not noticed before. You're right; it is beautiful!'

Maxine's eyes catch sight of her name on each envelope: due to the table's shelf underneath literally mirroring its surface on the top. Although extremely curious, Maxine resists her instinct to seek clarification. She senses Melanie is a bit nervous so decides to wait and see why?

There is a knock on the door, and Melanie's PA walks in with some tea and biscuits.

'Thank you, Katie,' says Melanie.

'Black or white Maxine?' asks Katie.

'Milk and two sugars please.'

'No calls to be put through until further notice, please Katie?'

'No problem Melanie,' replies Katie before leaving.

Melanie's intends to keep this as brief as possible and formally starts with, 'It is my responsibility to inform you, Maxine, you are being suspended from undertaking your employment duties for the County Council. You will remain on full pay. The...'

'What? What's go...'

'Please Maxine, let me explain first?'

Maxine slowly uncrosses her legs. She then shuffles to the front edge of her seat, rests an elbow on each knee and then touches each cheek of her face with the palm of a hand. By now Maxine's eyes are exhibiting her courtroom glare as she says to her boss, 'I'm all ears, Mel.'

'Information has been brought to my attention which seriously places you and the County Council in an untenable position! Information which requires the police and us to complete our separate investigation. At this moment in time, I am unable to expand further but can stress, to date, no one has accused you of anything. The need to suspend you is equally for your benefit as well as ours. The outcome of each investigation will determine if and or when you can resume your duties?

On the table, I have two sets of papers and whichever you choose requires your signature. This one permits you to remain on full pay under the auspice you are on indefinite leave, and this one is the formal suspension.

An essential condition of both is, you do not have any illegal contact by any method with any employee of this County Council! Including those employed by organisations we own and have service level agreements or contractual links.

If we discover you do have said contact, then your employment contract with us will be terminated immediately. Under your full pension rights respected along with receiving in full three months notice pay as is your entitlement under the terms of your contract.

I sincerely hope you agree to sign one of these because if you choose not too, then the Council will be forced to act as I just described, now!

I am acutely aware this is a shock to you and no doubt leaves you with many feelings and questions. I must stress I am unable to answer any in respect of either investigation. Naturally, you may want to receive advice from your union representative. He is waiting outside my office. Do you wish to speak with him?'

Maxine is still staring into her friend's eyes, and she slowly crosses her legs again: and a rush of anger is consuming her entire body. Drawing on the experience of such combat in courts, Maxine says, 'There is a third option you know Melanie. I can resign. I won't choose to do this so I will sign the first option, please. Garden leave is its official unofficial pet name, I believe! Quite apt as my commitment to my job means: I do not enjoy my garden nearly as much as I'd like to!'

Maxine turns over both documents and then reads and

signs where appropriate. Maxine then slides them to Melanie who, after countersigning, gently pushes one back.

Maxine picks it up, folds it and then places it into her inside jacket pocket. She then rises to her feet and with briefcase in hand slowly leaves the room. With an astounding demonstration of keeping one's dignity, Maxine accepts Christopher's company while ignoring the union chief steward's offer of advice.

On reaching the ground floor, Maxine and Christopher walk side by side all the way to her car. Christopher then dutifully watches until Maxine drives out of the Council's grounds. In his left hand, he's still clutching Maxine's unbroken ID badge.

***

Clive is at home in Woodland Mews. He is tidying the living room and is about to carry a black bin liner over each shoulder into the back garden. Soon, Clive re-enters the living room and begins to search through their CD collection. He retrieves, "Dark side of the moon," by Pink Floyd. He presses play and puts the volume at maximum.

Clive goes upstairs to change and shower. His emotions are chaotic and racing. At least I've had a chance to clean up a bit. Will help when you come home. Fucking hell Val! How can I tell you Sir Roger has just confirmed our worst nightmare? We can make sure Jo rests in peace now though and...'

Thirty or so minutes later, dressed in a shirt and pair of jeans he'd forgotten he had, Clive enters the living room again. He empties the remainder of a large bottle of Vodka into his glass. He then sits on a settee and takes another swift, albeit, galactic gulp! Clive's whole body stiffens and with his chest and stomach crushed by the tightness of his breathing, Clive's guilt is overwhelming. But, most painful of all are a flurry of shooting pains conducting from his brain. They are exploding against all parts of his body like a torpedo does, once it smashes into its target!

Clive leans into the softness of a cushion and looks at his

favourite photo of Valerie which stands on the mantelpiece opposite him. I remember how I, we felt when I took that picture, Val. An incredible sunset was shining on the most see through ocean water I have ever seen! And, even though you are barefoot on the most golden sand, it is you Val who is the most beautiful attribute in the photo!

Clive sits upright. He is in a trance-like state now, and his face and neck are contorting; "Incredible hulk" style! His veins look as though they are about to burst as he cries out, 'Who am I hunting, Jo?'

Clive grabs his glass and consumes the remaining vodka. By doing so, Clive begins listening to the music. The first words he hears are, "There's someone in my head but it's not me."

***

Sally and PP enter Norfolk Police HQ in Wymondham. In a cross parent tone, Bernice says, 'What's kept you? Come on; Sir Roger is waiting for us.'

All three walk briskly and when near to Sir Roger's office Sally notes Claudia has been more fortunate and ordered to go home for some well-earned sleep.

PP knocks and starts opening the door.

'Come in.'

All three then take their seat along with some other invitees who've waited patiently for their arrival. PP sits next to Finley and also present are Melanie Furze, myself, Andy Rioch and Todd Lever who is a forensic pathologist.

Sir Roger moves from behind his desk and by doing so changes what was a human horseshoe into an oval. In the middle stands a ball-shaped base which supports a relatively small square flat table-top. We've created Saturn, I muse.

Sir Roger then speaks first.

'I would like to start by saying, for many of us here; sleep must seem like something we used to do. I want to commend your dedication to duty. I have called us here because there are critical developments to share. Ones which will influence how we proceed with both investigations. Todd, can you please update us with your findings?'

'Yes, certainly. The samurai sword used to kill Mrs White, provide two further facts. All blood on the sword is Gillian White's and the only fingerprints on it are Harold White's. As you are probably all aware, the murder weapon is one of five owned by Mr White. We checked for prints on the remaining four. None found or, for that matter, had any bloodstain.

The wound and splash pattern of blood is consistent with a single thrust into Gillian White's heart. Time of death is fifteen-minute leeway each side of ten-am yesterday.

In all, we took eight sets of fingerprints from the home of Mr and Mrs White. Two are the White's themselves, and a Mrs Ash, Mee, Wood, Candlish and Clinch have been contacted to arrange what we expect identification of five more. Our remaining print, when searching our biometric databases, match with someone called James Hawker. Finley will give more details shortly.'

Todd pauses and appears to be hesitant before saying, 'What word to use? A bundle found in a woods near Woodland Mews, in patent terms, is remains of a human skeleton cloaked securely in a blue tarpaulin cloth. It is with grave sorrow I confirm by way of dental records these bones belong to Joanne Verity. Decomposition phase indicates Joanne died between two and a half to three years ago. The cause of death appears to be strangulation.

Somewhat surprisingly I think, the only other item found in the tarpaulin is a mobile phone. The single fingerprint found on materials that made up the bundle on both the outside and inside was on the mobile phone. Therefore, my professional judgement is, it is reasonable to conclude this print is Joanne Verity's.

From the Sim card, we checked the content of texts and voice-mails. The last text is from Ly, and I think it's right to read it as, "where r u Jo? r u OK? call me." Then a plus sign is used with the rest saying "Miss u loads. luv Ly.xx."

It was sent on thirty-first January two thousand and five. There are two hundred and ninety-two same messages amongst the rest that proceed this one. We know Ly was a best friend of Joanne and her name is Lilly Thompson.

Will inform you when we have anything further to report.'

The room is full with silence, and apologetically Sir Roger breaks it.

'I do understand confirmation Joanne Verity has lost her life is difficult to hear. Without wanting to sound sanctimonious in any way whatsoever, I would like to remind you, our feelings are not anything compared to those of her parents!

I informed Clive Verity less than three-quarters of an hour ago. I support his request to be the person who tells Valerie Verity. Under the new J Act, we have to respect victim's wishes about how the rest of the world hears such awful personal news. Therefore, our Chief Constable will confirm the identity of Joanne at a press conference at six-pm today. So giving Clive time to let loved ones know first.

I also sanctioned Clive's request to inform his wife's sister, Maxine Stewart. Thus, we can now be confident Valerie and Maxine are in contact. Clive explained it was Maxine who approached first eighteen months or so ago. I did not mention our meeting last night or discuss anything about it. It's not the right time! Furthermore, it is hopefully useful to remember. The reasons stated by the Chair of last nights meeting as to why we made a legal decision not to inform or invite any family member, still stand! Naturally, in due course, we have too!'

Sir Roger stops.

'Bernice, would you like a moment?' Sir Roger asks.

'No Sir, just so sad. Thanks for the offer though Sir. I'm fine.'

'OK. Right, Mr Rioch. Please, can we have your findings?

'Certainly. I was briefed to search Maxine Stewart's PC to

ascertain whether she has any history of access to specific files and folders relating to five named people.

For Joanne Verity, no deviance of access at all.

In respect of Harold White, only professionally legitimate access concerning a MAPPA Plan.

There is no such explanation for the record of a meeting between a duty post-Adoption Social Worker and Maxine's parents. Mr and Mrs Hurst sought cooperation from Social Services to stop their other daughter, Valerie, eloping to Germany with a man they insisted was too old for her! Valerie was sixteen.'

Nor is it clear why, a week ago today, Maxine accessed Mrs White's Adult Social Services record?

Last, there is also evidence that on one occasion Mrs Stewart accessed her own daughter's Children's Services file. I surmise she did so to see the recording, given it is Mrs Stewart, and staff at Milena's school, who were responsible for a joint referral in the first place.

If it is of any assistance, I have copies of each record's date-stamp profile. These tell you how often and when Mrs Stewart accessed them? I have to be honest and say any employee could use another's computer. To do this, they would require knowledge of another's unique password. I advise this is extremely improbable. However, nonetheless is possible!

I have already shared my findings with Ms Furze who I think wants to discuss some additional matters with you.'

Melanie says warmly, 'Thank you, Andy, for your speedy, thorough and accurate hard work. And yes, I do need to share the outcome of a meeting I had with Maxine Stewart which ended less than two hours ago.

Mrs Stewart has signed an agreement not to have any communication with any other employee of the County Council. She is officially on indefinite leave pending the outcome of our enquiries. I have not explained as to why? Other than, we are acting upon information received. Mrs Stewart did not ask me any questions whatsoever and left with no incident.'

'Thank you, Melanie. Now you please, DC Billing.'

Finley shuffles his notebook. 'Let's see. James Hawker's date of birth is eleven eleven sixty-eight, and he lives at two hundred and three A, School Lane, Little Melton, Norfolk. As the crow flies, it is one and a half miles tops between his address and Woodland Mews.

James Hawker is a freelance photographer who has resided at his current address since nineteen ninety-three and had no conviction history at all! The reason for finding Hawker's fingerprint on our records is, that on fourteenth December nineteen eighty-eight James Hawker was arrested and charged, along with his parents and elder sister, for causing a breach of the peace. Their arrests were one of quite a few other CND activists demonstrating outside the Sizewell Nuclear Power Station in Suffolk. Charges dropped nine months later. That's all Sir.'

Sir Roger then looks at me.

'Do you have any thoughts to share Alex?'

'Yes, Guv. I suggest we question this James Hawker next. Concerning both crimes Guv! Do you agree with me, Peter and Sally?'

'And Maxine Stewart too!' replies Sally.

I say, 'Perhaps Hawker first? Then Valerie Verity before Maxine Stewart, Guv.'

'Why?' asks PP.

'Before giving my answer Peter, I need to explain the context of my resistance.

I am not of the opinion we discount Maxine Stewart as a suspect for Mrs White's murder for reasons we have already discussed in the strategy meeting.

If my memory serves me right, we also identified a motive can be made for Luke Stewart, Valerie Verity even, and of course the more realistic possibility of Clive Verity.'

Sally fails to prevent a slight smile.

I continue, 'At the end of the E. n. E. M. A. meeting we

decided the next person to interview is Valerie Verity because of the concerns Sally is investigating.

I still agree with this decision. Only, even if Valerie Verity is well enough to be interviewed right now, I would support James Hawker being our priority. My reason is Sir Roger, concerning Joanne Verity, I rate suspicion of family members behind a convicted RSO and a discovery of a possible accomplice?'

Sir Roger comments, 'I agree. I call this meeting to an end. Peter and Sally go home and get some much-needed sleep before you interview Hawker, and no doubt White again, tomorrow.

Do not worry about the time we have. Under section two A of the J Act, we have grounds to keep them in custody without charge till after their alleged victims' respective funerals if we wanted too. I don't anticipate we will, only it means we do have time.

Finley and Bernice, please arrest James Hawker right away and get a warrant so you and a forensic team can search his home too.

***

Maxine, immersed in a book, is wearing a tee shirt with an elephant printed on the front and back, white shorts and laying in an orange helicopter hammock purchased in the Range.

Within easy reach of her right hand are a bottle and glass. Outside on the gravelled front drive, Milena's relief at being home is replaced by a tint of anxiety at seeing both her mother and Luke's car.

Milena puts her sleepover bag on the front doorstep and walks down the right side of the house toward a gate giving access to the back garden. She looks through a tiny hole in the gate and is surprised to see her mother is drinking wine this early in the day. Milena returns to the front door and goes in.

Maxine is oblivious to Milena getting a glass from a cupboard before then sitting at the kitchen table. Milena muses, I'm so glad you understand I just got scared Jimmy and it's great you agree to give me a few days to tell Mum about New Zealand. Did want to get my A' Level Art but you say now or never? So, never it can't be!

Milena decides to join Maxine and heads toward and then through their conservatory.

'Hi Mum, are you not well today?' asks Milena cheerfully.

Maxine is so engrossed she jumps and nearly tips out of the hammock.

'Blimey Milena, you nearly gave me a heart attack girl. Never mind me! Why aren't you at school?'

Milena is sat on one of six silver coloured meshed chairs and put her empty glass on the opposite side of the bottle.

'To be honest, Mum, I'm tired. I told school nurse I was feeling a bit sick so she agreed it was best I went home. How is Aunt Val?'

'Clive text earlier to say Aunt Val had a good night.'

Maxine puts her book down. She then precariously clambers out of the hammock and into a chair on the other side of what is a glass topped table.

'Can we visit today, please Mum?'

'I honestly don't know sweetheart. I'll speak to Clive and see what he thinks. Probably today will be a bit too soon. How did last night's performance go?'

'Perfect thanks, Mum. Sophie and her mum say hello.'

'That's nice.'

'Can I have some wine please, Mum? And where is Luke? Why isn't he at work too?'

'Luke's grandmother had a nasty fall last night. He said he could do with a day off, so because Elaine needs help to get checked over at A+E, Luke phoned into work saying he's sick. Which aptly leads me to, wine not a good idea for someone feeling sick, don't you think?'

Maxine grins before pouring a pub's short style amount in the glass. 'There you go.'

'Thanks. Is Nanny Elaine seriously hurt mum?'

'Luke just text to say the doctor's verdict is more shaken than stirred!'

'That's good.'

'I'm glad you're home Milena. I need to discuss something important with you. While reading, I did wonder about coming to take you out of school, actually.'

'What? You mean Aunt Val isn't OK?'

'I've already said how Aunt Val is.'

'Is it about, why you aren't at work today.'

'Not exactly. You know there was something horrible found in the woods near to the home of the murdered lady yesterday?'

'Yes.'

'Reports on television and radio keep saying Joanne might...'

'Oh no Mum. Please say it isn't,' cries out Milena as she rushes and crashes onto her mother's lap.

Maxine comforts by holding Milena tight and kissing her forehead. 'I know it's terrible and I've told you because I fear it will prove to be Jo this time,' whispers Maxine.

Milena is crying, and Maxine gives comfort by stroking under a ruffled short sleeve top. She then notices what looks like a small reddish bruise.

CHAPTER NINE

Wendy's wait for an answer ends, 'Hello. It's Dr. Caspar. Valerie needs you here straight away Mr Verity. No. Yes. Right. Drive carefully.'

Wendy looks at Gerry, who is a promising Junior Registrar, and he says, 'You are doing the right thing Wendy.'

'Thanks. Clive will be here soon. So, not a word Gerry. If anyone deserves a chance for a personal and private goodbye, it is Clive Verity! I'll wait here. Best you go Gerry to meet Clive outside and try to bring him directly here.'

Wendy checks her watch. It is 10.28am.

'Will do,' says Gerry exiting the staff room with Wendy right behind him.

Wendy then heads into Valerie's room where Amanda is dutifully watching over.

'Nurse Gallop, Valerie's husband will be here soon. No-one else must come in before he, we do. Thank god most patients are out on a day trip eh!'

'Yes Dr. Caspar, and I haven't touched a thing.'

Amanda and Wendy look at the syringe on the bed which Valerie used to stop her pain.

'I just want Clive to see Mrs Verity before the awful hullabaloo begins once we report this...' Wendy was going to say suicide but instead says, 'Valerie's death. And whatever reaction there is from the police etc. I will take full responsibility and any flack if needed. I promise Amanda!'

'I understand and, if you don't mind me saying, I agree with your decision. I admire your bravery too!'

'Thank you.'

Wendy jogs into her empty office. Her mind is streaming with thoughts and right now and by far most regular is, Where did you get it from?

Gerry stops Clive just outside the main entrance. 'Hello Mr Verity, I'm Gerry, Dr Caspar's junior registrar.'

'Is my Val all right? What's happened?'

'Dr. Caspar is on the ward. I will take you to her. She will answer all your questions.'

Clive starts running. Gerry keeps up and manages to get onto a flight of stairs ahead. Gerry turns left at the top and slowing down for a few strides then takes a right.

Clive accelerates past and is soon banging on the doors with both hands. He turns his head shouting, 'Let me in now for Christ's sake!'

Wendy rushes to help Gerry. The sight of Clive stops Wendy in her tracks. He has each arm upright with both hands and his face also pressing hard against the door's central pane of glass.

Wendy moves forward and finds it difficult to witness Clive's eyes pleading to her, 'Please tell me Valerie hasn't gone.'

From Wendy's expression, Clive knows his worse fear has happened. He drops to his knees and his finger nails slowly scratch the glass to such a pitch, Wendy's teeth grate.

Clive's hands eventually separate from the glass and he falls onto his back sobbing. 'No, not Valerie too,' Clive cries out loud and repetitively.

Wendy opens the doors. As she then gets on her knees to comfort Clive, Wendy whispers, 'Gerry, please make us all some tea.'

***

Wendy enters Valerie's room with Clive right behind and he's shivering more than shaking.

On reaching the side of the bed Clive says, 'Val looks too peaceful to be dead.'

'I am sorry Clive,' says Wendy while lightly gripping his hand. She then adds, 'Amanda, can you help Natasha with Mr Johansen please. Thanks for your help and support.'

Clive passes Amanda as he walks to the other side of the

bed.

'Take as long as you need Clive.'

Clive looks up. 'I really appreciate this Wendy! Thank you.'

'Like I said, take as long as you need,' says Wendy before leaving.

Clive straddles a seat and then takes hold of Val's cold right hand. Pouring through his brain are numerous memories and they flash in his mind as quick as they then vanish. Clive then spots a piece of paper Wendy had mentioned. It has his name on it and is laying on a pillow beside Valerie's head. Clive reaches across and delicately unfolds the paper wearing a pair of pink Schottlander Nitrile Gloves. 'Definitely Val's writing,' he tells himself.

He begins to read.

Clive, Please forgive me. I have been in love with you since we first met. You are a fighter, my hero. I just can't fight any more. You know we both know, at last our Jo has been found. I am so sorry and thank you for being you. Please understand I now need to be with Jo. Whenever it is your time to join us, we will reunite for eternity. Please try and be happy till then. I Luv U Clive and Love Me always. Me. XXX

Please tell Sis and Milena I love them! And, because I know you will need to know, I kept the syringe hidden in my handbag. Truly Sorry. Try and smile with me whenever you hear our song. x

***

Clive Verity's mind is in disarray and yet somehow he finds himself parked outside the Stewart's house. Unable to get out he murmurs out loud, 'Neither of my girls would be dead if it wasn't for the bloody Stewarts! But, Val adored her sister so there are more important things to deal with now.'

Clive selects Luke's mobile number and it's soon answered.

'Its me. I'm outside you're house,' says Clive crying.

Luke and Maxine rush out of the house. Luke opens a door and Clive is banging his head against the steering wheel.

'Hey, come on Clive,' says Luke as he places an arm around him. 'Come on mate lets get you inside.'

Luke looks at Maxine and says, 'Get the bloody kettle on! I've got this under control. Poor man is upset enough without you staring daggers at him.'

Maxine reasons in silence. I don't mean to stare. It's just I think I know why Clive is so upset. Maxine is now feeling cold and is shaking a little as she follows Luke and a stumbling Clive into the house.

Clive and Luke sit on a sofa and after getting something medicinal to go in a glass, Maxine joins them. Milena then runs downstairs to see what's going on.

'Mum? What's happened to Clive?'

'Sit down please Milena,' Luke advises.

Seeing what a traumatic state Clive is in, Milena does and watches open mouthed as Clive downs a large brandy. Clive then fumbles up his left sleeve for what is a crumpled photocopy of Valerie's letter which he hands to Luke.

Luke reads the first three sentences and passes it to Maxine. Milena moves to stand over her mother's shoulder and it isn't long before both burst into floods of tears.

Then, Milena screams and runs to the front door.

Maxine shouts, 'No,' and hurtles after her.

'Maxine!' cries Luke and quickly catches up to hold both.

'Where are you going Milena?' demands Luke.

'To see Aunt V. Who else you dipstick,' Milena shouts angrily. She wanted to say, 'My best friend Jimmy. I want Jimmy to be with me at the hospital.'

'We can't go now sweetheart,' says Maxine.

Milena worms free and storms upstairs and on entering her bedroom thrashes its door shut! Milena is struggling to breath and is crying. Joanne and Aunt Val! Why? Feeling totally confused and alone, Milena then mimes more than whispers amongst a snivel, 'Where are you Dad?'

Milena cannot understand why her father's face is in the forefront of her mind. For, what is the first time since he said goodbye on that dreadful day at Heathrow airport.

Why did you leave me Dad? You always called me your beautiful princess. Why did you say Dad is a bad man mum? Dad liked me. I know he did because we did nice things together and he was always telling me how much he loved me and told me he is the father of the most beautiful daughter in the world!

Milena stares into her dressing table mirror. She is no longer crying and she tells herself out loud, 'I will find you Dad.'

***

On that upsetting day for Milena and her father, Toby Trunch flew from Heathrow direct to Australia. He accepted the offer of a permanent position within a team of lawyers who represented the Australian government. Toby did so, not expecting it would result in the end of his marriage with Maxine. Perhaps, there are clues to understanding why this happened in the contribution given at the E. n. E. M. A. meeting by Karen Trinket, who manages Norfolk's Family Conciliation Service. Known as CAFCASS for short.

Karen said, 'Thank you Frank. All of my contact with Toby and the then Maxine Trunch was via email. Toby contacted us first and I personally dealt with his request. At this time, as you've heard, he was living in Australia.

Mr Trunch used to work for their Government as a legal advisor to a Minister responsible for The Social Justice Department. From a covert enquiry made yesterday, I am able to confirm Toby Trunch is now an Australian citizen living in Perth. He is employed by his adoptive country as an ambassador with the United Nations.

Toby's first email is dated sixth of October nineteen ninety-nine. He wrote to ask us to try and open dialogue with Maxine about his right to have contact with Milena! Or put another way, Toby expressed his heartbreak at Maxine's unlawful refusal to let him have contact with Milena.

After making applicable checks on all information provided by Mr Trunch as evidence he had made reasonable attempts to try and achieve contact with Milena, I wrote to Maxine. It was Maxine who confirmed they agreed to use CAFCASS. And I quote her. "Neither of us want to wash our linen in public."

It is important to add that both agreed I could forward their respective responses along with any advise I felt was appropriate to the wishes and feelings they expressed. Therefore, dialogue began when I simply forwarded Toby's first email onto Maxine.

Maxine replied with a significant attachment. It was a two minute video of Milena explaining to her father why she does not want to ever see him again. On a number of occasions during the video Milena says, "You should never have left us Daddy."

At this time, Milena was eight years old and Maxine agreed for me to speak with her daughter at St. Clotho Junior school. I did so with a teacher present for all but ten minutes of a meeting that lasted just over three quarters of an hour. I concluded there was not any sinister factor or pressure influencing Milena's decision. Milena also understood she has the right to change her mind but was adamant she never would.

In line with our three way agreement, I forwarded the attachment sent by Maxine onto Toby. I included details of my actions and analysis of them. A week later Toby replied and thanked me for my assistance. He expressed his sadness about deciding not to pursue access and added he hoped letting fate take its natural course will mean, one day, Milena will change her mind. I passed this onto Maxine and we have not had any form of contact with either parent since."

Right now, Toby is temporarily living at The Old Mill

Cottage in Snape village, Suffolk. He has been for nearly three months now. Toby Trunch currently works for The Australian Government within DFAT which stands for Department of Foreign Affairs and Trade. One annual duty is to head Australia's representatives at the UNFCCC conference. (United Nations Framework Convention on Climate Change).

This year's "Conference of the Parties" as it is known, is being held in Bali, Indonesia from 3 to 14 December. The honour of the opening speech has been given to Toby Trunch by way of recognising his outstanding contribution toward trying to achieve the ultimate convention objective which is to, "stabilize greenhouse gas concentrations in the atmosphere at a level that would prevent dangerous anthropogenic (human induced) interference with the climate system."

The specific theme Toby is recognised for, is his contribution in the reduction of emissions caused by deforestation and forest degradation.

Toby was delighted his employers agreed to pay for him to rent a cottage in England while he researches and produces his speech. He openly explained having time in England will give him an opportunity to attempt reconciliation with his daughter, Milena.

Toby was equally candid with his employers that a possible consequence of a successful reunion could mean his current project will be his last. Whatever does transpire, Toby assured his boss, he will only attempt to find Milena after his speech stroke report is completed. Toby is due to return home on 30 September 2007.

Toby has found it very difficult to stick with his self imposed deadline. So, is proud to date he hasn't made any attempt to find Milena whatsoever. His only ventures outside of the village have been walks, cycle rides and boat trips beside and or on the river Alde.

Other more frequent places Toby has visited are the Golden Key Pub and Café 1885. It is the owner of the latter which Toby has taken, amongst the many attractions in Snape and the surrounding area, the most shine too!

The proprietor of Café 1885 is Louise. Louise is a tall slim woman who sadly became sole owner of the café when also becoming a comparatively young widow three years ago.

Louise lives with her two sons aged six and eight in a spacious four bedroom flat above the café. Louise is proud of how both boys are progressing given the heartbreak they all felt, still feel about losing their father so tragically early. Louise would be the first to tell you her son's stability owes a great deal to the dual rocks in the shape of the children's paternal grandparents who live nearby in Saxmundham. It is rare if the boys don't sleepover in Saxmundham at least once a week.

When Toby woke this morning his first thought was how much he's looking forward to visiting Louise this evening. All day he's felt excitement of anticipating what Louise and he both see as possibly, or is it hopefully, a first sleepover?

CHAPTER TEN

Hawker was arrested today at 11.23am. Until he's questioned sometime tomorrow, somehow each detective involved engages in their respective home lives.

PP is fully dressed and asleep on his marital bed. Harriet, their youngest, has crept into the bedroom ignoring what her mother had told her quite a few times, "No Harriet. Daddy is tired." Harriet is beaming for getting this far and makes a run for it.

Successful, Harriet's momentum means both of her hands claw hold of the bed cover, and she crawls until her kicking little legs land on the softness of wool. PP has awoken but pretends not to be. Harriet gets to her feet giggling and jumps on the mattress before dive-bombing onto her father's belly.

'Hi-ya Daddy, got yea got yea,' shrieks Harriet before then bouncing and giggling.

PP grabs Harriet under her arms, and she displays shock until she is looking right over her Daddies face. Her expression transforms into to a magical smile.

'Hi-ya princess,' and with sound effects, PP swishes Harriet around in his hands and adds, 'You are flying like an eagle. Whoosh!'

Trying not to laugh Harriet's mum says, 'Sorry love, just, so keen to see you.'

'Look, mummy, I'm flying like an eagle,' and she giggles again.'

'No worries Nicola. How are you?' Asks PP before bringing in the eagle to land on his chest. Nicola then lays next to her husband and replies. 'Good. We all are.'

Nicola and PP kiss and then Nicola says, 'It's great to see you, stranger. Cup of tea?'

'Yes please,' both reply in unison and all three laugh.

While Nicola leaves, Harriet wriggles free from her father's close grip and shouts, 'Bet you won't find me,' and she scurries out of sight.

'Bet I do,' says PP in his best "Tell them about the honey mummy" imitative voice.

PP then takes off his tie and rearranges his rumpled clothes a bit before following down the stairs.

***

Harriet hasn't touched her drink so engrossed is she in today's episode of Tele-Tubbies. Nicola and PP have their arms around one another's shoulder and are on a sofa at the opposite end of the room.

'We've had a letter from Martin's school today,' says Nicola who takes it out of her Jean pocket and hands it to PP.

With no clue to his thoughts as he reads it, Nicola brushes a tear or two from her eyes. On finishing the sensitively written contents, PP looks into Nicola's wet sentiment and hugs her.

'If Martin is OK with the idea then I think we should be too. What do you think?'

Nicola cannot answer; instead, she lays her head against Peter's broad chest and with his strong arms wrapped around her, she cries uncontrollably. PP offers various words of reassurance but at the same time is thinking, 'Work demands are not good for my family. I wish and want to say; I'll change jobs. The reality is there are commitments, and it takes time to develop a plan B.'

PP disentangles from Nicola and looks at her, 'But, there is a promise I, we can keep!

'Promise? What do you mean?' asks Nicola.

'Once Martin is well enough, we're going to Brazil! PP states with conviction.'

'What? Brazil?'

'Martin's told me many times if he there is one place he'd choose to see more than any other in this world, it is to see England play Brazil at the Maracana football stadium in Rio de Janeiro. If I had the power to guarantee England really could be there, then it would happen. What we bloody well can do though, is take him to see a match there.'

'Sounds thrilling. Why not the new Wembley? A lot more practical and less expensive' reasons Nicola who is no longer crying.

'Because I know, he'd love it!'

'Yes, he would. We all would. OK. Why not? Although, isn't it famous for its beaches too?' asks Nicola with a grin.

'Yep, and beautiful...'

Nicola gives PP a friendly single finger poke into his rib, 'Don't even think it, OK!'

'Who? Me? Never!'

***

Harriet is asleep, and Nicola is on her laptop researching flights to Brazil. PP is soaking in a much-needed bath and planning the itinerary for when Martin visits Brazil. His thoughts punctuated by intermittent pulses of realism telling him; time might be too tight? However, not even PP's sense of reality contemplated even a fraction of what happens!

The head of care at the residential school Martin is a border at, shared in his letter that some pupils frequently ask if they could visit Martin at home? PP decided to speak with Martin when he came home from the hospital on Thursday 19 July 2007.

Two days later father and son enjoyed going to London to watch Norwich City beat Arsenal 1-5 in a pre-season friendly at the Emirates Stadium. On their return journey, they had a bite to eat in a McDonalds. During which PP told Martin about his mates wanting to see him. Martin said yes with a smile his Dad will never forget!

Martin had not seen his mates since the school Christmas party in mid-December 2006. The visit took place on Wednesday 24th July which was two days before the school broke up for the summer holiday.

Nicola, PP, Martin and Harriet decorated their large L shaped living room into a setting befit for a party atmosphere. Even Martin's bed which PP had carried downstairs before he'd left for work, was tastefully decorated! Primarily by his excited young sister.

Martin's friends arrived just before four o'clock. PP had promised to be home by five. Nicola, heard the beeping sound of a vehicle reversing into their driveway, and went outside to greet Martin's friends. She was unaware the same number the school bus holds which is twelve could have been filled twice more with peers who wanted to see Martin.

With Harriet beside her mum, they watched as the bus emptied. Some walked independently and had no arms. One jumped off the lift landing on his arms as he had no legs. Some wore artificial limbs and or used crutches.

Harriet giggled and thought how much fun it is having Martin's friends visit their house. With two guests who use wheelchairs safely down, Nicola helped the driver fold the lift and close the doors.

Inside, Martin was already in fits of laughter, and he did not notice, at first, his Dad had kept his promise not to be late. Soon, lots of food and drink was available, and the laughter made Nicola and PP the happiest they'd felt since Martin had been home. Some of the banter was a bit raw for Harriet's ears, but both parents hoped she was at an age, she was pretending she understood.

The party ended at eight o'clock, and the driver was very apologetic they had to go so soon. Martin's best friend, Trinky being his nickname, was the last to say bye. He had so much to say, and yet he didn't air anything because he'd noticed Martin finding it difficult to say goodbye to anyone. So, when it was Trinky's turn, he kept things brief.

'See you in September mate. OK!' he said'

'Sure, can't wait,' was Martin's reply and then both gave the other a hesitant smile.

Three days later, Martin died peacefully in his sleep at

home. The cause was Duchene Muscular Dystrophy which progressed to a point whereby Martin's body was unable to fight off the mildest of chest infections or even a common cold! Martin was twelve years old and, when told, friends cried. Some cry later than others.

***

'Finley,' calls his mother, 'Finley? Where are you?'

'Here mum, what's up?'

Finley is buttoning his shirt on joining Hazel who is in her favourite armchair in her best-loved room in the house. The empty armchair beside her offers more warmth and comfort because she can still see Finley's father who died eleven years ago.

'Are you meeting Kristina tonight?' asks Hazel.

'Yes. Why?'

'Will you give this to Rosa for me please?'

Hazel hands her son a beautiful tapestry which she made. It is a decorous portrayal of the cottage in which Kristina has always lived.

'It is Rosa's birthday tomorrow. Have you remembered?'

'Yes, I have Mum, and I have a card and some flowers, and...'

'Huh' interrupts Hazel. 'You never buy me flowers and yet someone who is not even officially you're mother-in-law until next year gets the red carpet treatment!'

'Actually, it's more the red Rosa treatment mum!'

Finley is still grinning as he bends to kiss his mother goodbye. Hazel turns her head in mock hurt, and she lies, 'I prefer chrysanthemums anyway.'

'See you soon mum.'

Finley soon opens the front door. He picks up the flowers and leaves. Hazel, resumes reading a novel to see if her amateur sleuth skills have detected correctly, who done What?

Two hours sleep has refreshed Finley more than he'd expected. In truth, Finley is still high from arresting James Hawker earlier today. So much so, presently, Finley recalls something he said to BB when she gave him a lift home from the station afterwards. Fantastic two days. Why I joined. Doesn't Hawker look so normal? Can we be sure he's the right man?

Finley then absent-mindfully starts to cross the A148 from Sharrington Road to Field Dalling Road. He has no idea the pedestrian traffic light is red. It is only the shrill of tyres skidding that alerts him to dive, so avoiding instant death under an enormous lorry.

Finley's dive changes to a roll, and he lands on his backside. He's sitting upright watching a lorry smash into railings and come to a crashing halt.

Finley stares at the lorry driver opening his door and scrambles quickly to his feet. If the driver knew the "Nutter" crossing the road is a police officer, he would probably be surprised by the swiftness Finley disappeared out of sight.

Left in the middle of the road is a bunch of flowers, a card and brown paper bag with the tapestry safe inside it. The lorry driver decides to retrieve them. By the time he's using his mobile to report the accident, there is a substantial traffic jam in both directions.

Finley bangs on a front door. Kristina answers and says, 'Oh my god. You look whiter than snow. What's happened?'

Finley rushes past Kristina.

'Finley,' cries Kristina and she runs after him. She finds him standing in the kitchen. Finley opens his arms, and they hug tight.

'That was too close Kris. I nearly died then and there!'

'Die! How? What's happened?' and Kristina steps back and puts both hands gently on his shocked face.

'Shall I call nine nine nine? Is someone after you?'

'No! I mean, no need, it's nothing like that. Nearly got myself run over, that's all. Loo...'

'That's all! Nearly run over! Oh, thank god you weren't.'

'Look, I've stopped shaking. Let's get a drink, and I'll tell you exactly what happened. It was my fault, Kristina! Just not concentrating. Mind on work. Honestly, it was me...'

'Stop. Let's get them drinks. What do you want?'

'OK. But I cannot leave it long before phoning our local station to explain the crash was all my fault.'

'Sure. Vodka, Whiskey, Be...'

'I'll have a large bloody Mary please,' replies Finley who sits on one of two high wooden stools positioned alongside a breakfast bar.

'I can let you get away with getting my name wrong. To call me large, well no desserts for you tonight.'

Kristina then stretches to reach the Tabasco sauce from the top shelf of a high cupboard. Finley is staring in the direction of Kristina's Kylie-like bottom but not at it as such. He is further distracted on hearing Rosa say merrily, 'I'm home, sweetheart. Have you had a good day at work?'

'Hi, mum. We're in the kitchen. Do you fancy a cuppa?'

Rosa delays answering until, with a Lathams bags in each hand, she reaches the arch brick entrance. 'Yes, please. Coffee for me sweet...'

Rosa stops because "My gorgeous" future son-in-law, who automatically stands whenever Rosa comes into a room, needs to be kissed! 'Oh how nice to see you, Finley. Kristina's been telling me how busy you are. Have you caught the nasty criminals yet?'

Finley knows Rosa thinks his job is like Starkey and Hutch. Full of thrill rides chasing robbers from other people's homes or banks. Today, there is no made up extras to make Mrs Thorpe laugh. His reply is honest. 'Yes. Just need to prove their guilt in a court now. How are you, Mrs Thorpe?'

'I'm very well thank you and how many times do I have to tell you, you're practically family now, my mother named me Rosalind, Rosa to friends.'

'Yes, Mrs Thorpe. Sorry, Ros...'

'Leave him alone mother. Finley just had a nasty shock. Silly bugger nearly got run over!'

'That's awful, how?'

'I'm waiting to hear too. So, shall we swap rooms first? The sofas a lot more comfortable,' suggests Kristina as she offers a hand to Finley.

'How exciting,' comments Rosa and she follows in tow.

***

Rosa is nearest the fireplace.

'You are a lucky lad young Finley. Of course, what matters is you are still with us! But, you know don't you, it was a ridiculous thing to do!'

Rosa sips the last of her coffee. She then adds, 'I don't know about you two? I can do with another brew. Kristina sweetheart. Would you please do the honours. You make tea so well.'

'Flattery doesn't work with mum. Have you lost your legs?'

'Haha. Sorry sweetheart. Just feeling thirsty. Per...'

'I'll get you both one,' says Finley but as he rises, both women say, 'No,' with so much conviction that despite their different tones, Finley does as he's told.

'Have you been shopping, Rosa?' asks Finley.

'No dear, I wish! I've spent most of my time at a ghastly parish council meeting. They are frightfully boring so luckily only happen four times a year.'

'Mother loves it, Finley. Don't be fooled. Mum revels in the opportunity to get the latest gossip and scandal! Don't you mum?'

'Who? Me? Honestly sweetheart. How shallow of you. You could arrest my beautiful daughter for slander I dare say, detective? I can assure you I am very discreet,' says Rosa smiling at Finley.

Finley says, 'Are you? I mean, yes you could. I can take a formal statement if you want to press charges.'

'Hey, cheeky sod. You're supposed to be on my side,' says Kristina.

'Oh Kristina, did you see my note with a message from your manager at work? They want you to cover staff shortages for tonight's shift.'

'Yes. Thanks, Mum,' and then facing Finley, Kristina adds, 'Sorry babes. Double pay though! All help for the honeymoon eh?'

'Cool. I'll go home and fetch the car and give you a lift to the hospital.'

'Oh thank you. My hero. It's OK. No need. Amanda has been roped in too and is picking me up around ten. Which means we've got time for a drink and a bite to eat in the local, shall we go? You coming to mum?'

'No. Thank you for including me, sweetheart. I will have a bath and have a nice brew ready for when you get back. And seeing you are such a heroine willing to rescue other people's problems, there could well be that last piece of cake as an extra treat to go with your tea. Don't worry Finley. I'm sure I can rustle up something for you too.'

'See you later mum.'

'Have a nice time and Kristina?'

'Yes, mum.'

'Take charge when crossing any footpath let alone a road.'

'I will mum.'

'Bye Mrs Thorpe.'

It is after they exit the front drive Finley remembers, Shit! The presents! Mum will be furious! He then says, 'Best we walk via the scene of the accident. I can then give my statement. Sorry Kris, hopefully, should still have plenty of time.'

Rosa reaches for the TV remote laid on a small Ivory coffee table snuggled against her armchair. Rosa always tries to watch Emmerdale. So, at first, is disappointed to see Anglia

News are overrunning. A matter of a few seconds pass and Rosa's emotions alter somewhat after digesting Joanne Verity has at last been found!

***

Sally's betrothed is putting the finishing touches to sowing on twenty tee shirts being worn at a hen party tonight. The meetup time is 8 pm and as Sylvia uses her teeth to tare the last unwanted thread of cotton, she glances at the oven clock and sees it's just gone seven. Sylvia puts her tee shirt on and goes upstairs.

'Sally love,' says Sylvia gently nudging her wife's bare shoulder. 'I've made you a coffee.'

Sally barely opens her eyes but says, 'Nice one Sylv. Thanks.'

'If you need to rest more, we don't have to go.'

'No way. Should be a fun night out!'

'OK. I'll drive.'

'No need Sylv. With all the overtime we can afford a cab,' replies Sally who then gently pulls on an arm belonging to Sylvia.

'We need to get ready otherwise we'll be late. Though, bit miffed cuz I've got a stinking headache,' says Sylvia.

'Poor you. Not one of your migraines I hope,' Sally sympathises.

***

Sally and Sylvia are twenty minutes late when the taxi pulls up outside the Apostolis Greek restaurant. Affectionately known as the Goddess! They walk in holding hands, and Sally is surprised to see Bernice amongst the twenty look-a-likes. Though, less surprised one of the two empty seats is next to her.

Sally takes her expected place. Reluctantly, Sylvia settles for the seat on the far end and opposite side of what is one table made with four placed together.

***

Forty minutes into the celebratory shared meal, Sylvia excuses herself and heads into the ladies room. The evening entertainment is a Greek version of three singing and guitar playing amigos. They walk across from another table and stand behind Sally and Bernice. Sensing their presence and not noticing Sylvia has left the room, Sally turns her head. She can see three ridiculously happy smiling faces. Without waiting for their leader to ask. Sally makes a request. "Forever and ever," by Demise Roussos, please?'

Soon, all twenty-two diners soon stop chatting and eating because the band are making it clear they are singing for BB and Sally. Bernice and Sally have an arm around one another and are swaying side to side in an embrace. This playing along is then reciprocated by everyone in the restaurant, actually, making a similar motion. Albeit, most have their hands above their head.

Bernice then gives Sally a gentle squeeze and whispers discreetly into her right ear, 'You look lovely.'

'Thank you,' replies Sally.

Sally's breast feels receipt of a text. Sally checks the message. It says, 'Gone home. Taxi already on the way. It is a migraine I'm afraid. Sorry. X Have a gd time. Cu l8r + LUV U. Sylv XX.'

'God, its great to have brilliant eyesight,' observes Bernice to herself.

***

Sir Roger has not managed a wink of sleep. Before getting home, he met with Finley and Bernice following a successful arrest of Hawker. Sir Roger then personally completed the necessary communication to secure Hawker in a rarely used custody cell in the basement at HQ. It was while engaged in this task Sir Roger was shocked from hearing the tragic news of Valerie Verity's suicide? Todd Lever also advised Sir Roger, the pathologist who attended the scene said. "I'm 99.99% recurring, it is suicide!"

Sir Roger then spoke with Dr Caspar. Not only does he learn Clive was too late to speak with Valerie about Joanne, but also, when Clive left the hospital he said he needed to let Valerie's sister know of both tragedies.

Sir Roger also updated Sally, Peter, Finley and Bernice about the latest turn of events before finally ordering the DS dispatched to the scene at the hospital, to meet with him at 5 pm. The outcome of their discussion was Sir Roger transferred responsibility for looking into Valerie's death directly to himself! In response to the DS surprise as opposed to protesting, Sir Roger explained "It is a temporary arrangement because the DI which will permanently take over tomorrow needs to get some sleep tonight."

Finally, Sir Roger informed the Chief Constable about everything, so enabling Frank to alter his statement for the scheduled press conference.

When Sir Roger arrived home, he discovered his wife Sheila was pulling her hair out! She was busy preparing a dinner party for six people. Sir Roger had utterly forgotten it was their turn to host what is a bi-monthly event. It is in sorts a 'work dinner' get together. The three ladies dining are Norfolk's three trustees of a branch of what is a national charity which supports Victims' of Crime.

At the table with Sheila and Sir Roger are, Mrs Cynthia Rochester with her husband Richard, and Lady Eva Chalice-Hermitage is sitting next to Reginald.

'Have you had a chance to get some sleep Sir Roger,' asks Eva sympathetically.

'No Eva, hope you have?'

'Yes thank you. I'm sure we wouldn't have minded cancelling. You mu...'

'Rubbish cherub! It would mean missing out on asking Rog, what did the latest ghastly enema dig up then? Must be juicy given the inconvenient time, eh Rog?'

Sir Roger has never taken to Reginald. He wants to ignore the question, but Sheila would not want her fellow trustee Eva, made upset. Eventually, Sir Roger gathers the most economical answer his tired brain can muster. 'It was very productive Reggie and not inconvenient at all!'

'Sir Roger, are you enjoying your meal? asks Cynthia who has learnt to know when tension is raising its confrontational head.

'Delicious and splendidly presented Cynthia, as usual.'

Sheila smiles at her husband's compliment.

'I agree,' echoes Cynthia who always manages to hide her jealousness of Sheila.

Reginald returns to probing Sir Roger. 'Do you talk with Sheila about cases in which you are involved? Or are you like Eva and I, maintain adherence to the laws of confidentiality and all that?'

Eva glances sweetly at Sir Roger, and Sheila's smile recedes, albeit briefly. Sir Roger is delighted to have another opportunity to address Lord Chalice-Hermitage as Reggie; as the Judge hates this particular version of his name!

'Reggie, I am of the opinion. No, I correct myself. I am certain Reggie, each person in this room carries out their duties and responsibilities in the same way you describe how you do.'

'Here here,' mumbles Richard cheerfully as some gravy creeps in a straight line through the centre of the valley in his chin.

It is everyone witnessing this dribble that conceals a second reason for their good humour. Namely, the only person around the table not smiling is the Judge.

***

Half an hour later everyone has finished the main course.

'Is everyone ready for dessert? And don't worry I only helped with the main course,' jokes Sir Roger.

'What is it, Sheila?' asks Eva.

'Chocolate Fudge Cake.'

'Homemade though,' Richard exclaims in unison with his clapping, and Sheila muses, Thank you, Dickey, for another display of admiration.

Sir Roger is already on his way to fetch the cake, so he misses Sheila's face slowly blushing.

Sheila moves off her seat, but Cynthia says, 'No Sheila, you've worked hard enough! I will assist Roger.'

Reluctant to do so, Sheila sits back down. 'Thank you,' she says out of politeness.

Once out of sight Cynthia approaches her prey with deftness a cat catching a rat would be proud. Sir Roger has his back to Cynthia and is bending forward to slice the cake into equal portions.

I'm not going to let this opportunity go by, Cynthia decides.

CHAPTER ELEVEN

I am looking at a dashboard of a black and white Mini Cooper S Cabriolet. Its roof is open, and it's in a car park used by Council employees in their Cromer office. I note it is 17.06pm and as I spin round, I enjoy another draw on a cigarette to counter some butterflies in my belly.

I hear Sadie's voice, 'Hi-ya, hope you haven't been waiting long?'

'Only about three hours, so not too bad. How are you, Sadie?'

'Wow, hope I'm worth it. I'm good thanks. You?'

'You are! You had a busy day at work?'

'Well, same as every day I guess. You know, I've made the world a better place and apart from this, not too busy thank you. What about you?'

'I have no doubt you do! As for me, I'm not sure if I can say better. Hopefully, a little safer.'

'Have you slept since our all night-er? I had to go to Wymondham to give my fingerprint before I got to my bed.'

'I know and yes I have thanks. Had to wait till late afternoon before getting home.'

'Really? Oh of course. I am sorry. I was shocked and sad when I heard Frank's statement on the telly. Horrific for Clive Verity. And you've met Valerie too. Are you OK?'

'I agree, awful for Clive. Shall we try and forget work and take a stroll along the prom? Ice cream on the pier perhaps?'

'Sounds nice.'

'Have you ever been a passenger on a motorbike, Sadie?'

'Actually no. Dangerous things if you ask me.'

'It is downhill most of the way from here. Would you like to hitch a ride with me?'

'OK. Where do I, sit?'

'You don't. You stand behind me and balance on the curb

climbers.'

'How? Do I hold on?'

'Yes. To me or the armrests. I've got a bag hanging over the back of my mean machine. Feel free to put your handbag etc. in it. It zips up too.'

'Thank you,' says Sadie who walks behind me to unload her arms. She then adds, 'This should be fun. Bit risky too! Hell, who cares? Let's live for the day eh!'

'Sounds good to me!'

Sadie follows instructions and encouragement until she is safely on board.

'How fast can this go?' Sadie asks with her face now very close to mine.

'About sixty to eighty depending on gradient and condition of terrain.'

'What!'

'Inches per hour that is. Are you ready?'

Tightening her grip, Sadie says, 'Yep.'

I switch the power on with a big toe, turn the speed setting to maximum, hold the joystick with my left foot and push it forward. Acceleration is instant. I then take a sharp left onto a steep path which leads directly to the town's long seaside promenade.

Sadie seems to be enjoying the mild breeze blowing through her long hair. She says, 'I love the smell of the sea, don't you?'

'Yes,' I reply.

Sadie decides to move a hand one at a time from an armrest to each of my shoulders. If you ever hear me sing you would be in no doubt; I can't! For a change, my latest attempt appears to bode well. Sadie is duetting with my very out of tune rendition of Bruce Springsteen's "Born to Run."

Before long we reach the top of West Cliff which leads you onto the 'Esplanade' as the locals call it. 'Hold on tight Sadie,' I suggest.

Walking in the opposite direction are two retired couples' who split to cheer and clap as I and a waving Sadie race through.

With the pier now in site Sadie says, 'Lovely that the sea looks blue for a change.'

'Certainly is. I will pull up outside the entrance to the pier. The wooden flooring is a bit bumpy. Or do you fancy living dangerously and maybe falling off?'

Laughing, Sadie says, 'Go the whole hog and throw me over the side why don't you! Don't stop though. Let's go for it!'

'Never say I don't do as told. Hold tight.'

Sadie rattles and bounces but does stay on board until we stop next to an outside table belonging to a café bar. The bar fronts Cromer's famous seaside pavilion theatre.

'Thanks for the lift. That was great,' says Sadie who then gets on her feet and retrieves her handbag.

'Nicest passenger I've ever had. Enjoyed it too.'

'I'll get us a drink and ice cream. What do you fancy, Alex?'

'Ninety-nine and a cappuccino, please Sadie.'

'Any particular flavour?'

'Vanilla or strawberry thanks.'

'Right you are. See you in a bit.'

I nudge my mobile which is in a breast pocket against the edge of the table until it pops onto it. With my lips and tongue, I push the phone's flap up. From the same pocket, a metal straw fell out too and with it, I open a text from PP.

"Hello Alex. Awful news about Mrs Verity isn't it! We are interviewing James Hawker at 7 pm. I know you took Toil this afternoon and sorry, but I would appreciate you being in the VIP box please."

***

Hawker and his solicitor sit facing a one-way mirror. Hawker's cursing, chastising himself even, for deciding to return home.

Another five minutes and I'd been on my way again. Well, at least it was not Ollie's car on my driveway. Realistically, all they have is one STD card with a bit of dodgy porn on it. Even if they decide to charge, unlikely as that is! If found guilty, it will be my first conviction! Should mean worst case scenario is free within a year, eighteen months top. More likely to be a non-custodial sentence anyway, I reckon!

Until recently Hawker's prediction would warrant being a reasonable assumption. His confidence suggests he is not aware of more detailed small print, so to speak, outlined within the new JA legislation!

Neither Sally or PP share Hawker's limited knowledge as they enter interrogation room number three. A room dimly lit with its four walls painted a raspberry red. The only contrast is metal grey on the room's door and flaxen shaded table and chairs made from wood. Sally and PP are soon sitting with their backs to Finley, Bernice, Sir Roger and Frank who are watching from the transparent side of the mirror.

'It's like being in a cinema,' says Finley rubbing his hands together as the recording begins.

'It is also a good opportunity to listen and learn DC Billing,' comments Frank.'

I tap the door of the VIP box, and Frank lets me in. 'Thank you,' I whisper.

Claudia has already draped a tiny two-way microphone behind my left ear, and Sir Roger moves from his position between Bernice and Finley gesturing me to take this place instead.

'... and also present is DI Peter Parsons. Mr Hawker, do you understand you are still under caution?'

'Yes.'

'Do you know a man called Harold White?'

'Yes, he's a friend.'

'Have you ever been to Mr White's house?'

'Yes.'

'Did you meet Mr White at his home on Monday sixteen July two thousand and seven?'

'No.'

'When was the last time you visited Mr White's house?'

'Probably, a week last Wednesday. Why do you ask?'

'Do you know Mrs Gillian White?'

'I know of her of course. I wouldn't say I know her.'

'Can you please give your whereabouts on Monday last between nine O five-am and midday.'

'I left my home at around eight thirty and drove to a village hall in Little Snoring. I am responsible for setting up the props when the Thespian Players are performing. Monday was our second night of a play called Heroes. It is...'

'What time did you arrive at the village hall?' interrupts Sally.

'About nine fifteen, you can check with Beryl who is our president, she let me in.'

'When did you leave the village hall that day?'

'I came home about four-pm, showered, eat and changed before heading back to Little Snoring to do my bit for the show. I'm glad to say it's greatly received.'

'Can anyone vouch you were at the village hall the entire time between nine fifteen-am and midday?'

'Beryl was there until around ten. She returned with her husband around one-pm I believe.'

'Did Harold White call you at all yesterday?'

'Yes, he did, just after Beryl left actually. The poor fellow found his wife murdered in their own home. He was clearly in shock, and one needs comfort from friends at such times.'

'Is it not the case Mr Hawker, that immediately after Harold White phoned you on Monday last you, in fact, left the village hall to visit him at eight Rose Close?'

'No, I told you. Harold needed to speak with a friend. I offered to come over. He insisted all he wanted was for someone to know he fears the police will arrest him. He wanted a friend to know he didn't murder his wife! Oh yes, and just before Beryl left, as I've said around ten, she introduced me to a man she'd arranged to help me with the two-person task of erecting a massive mural used in the play. His name is Isaac, and I don't know his surname. I assume Beryl does because I think she mentioned getting contact details for Isaac by way of word of mouth. Hopefully, Beryl can assist you. Obviously, from your line of questioning, I detect you need to know my whereabouts are kosher. I'm sure this Isaac fellow will corroborate everything. He stayed in the hall with me until around twelve thirty, maybe twelve forty-five. I know it wasn't long after he'd left, Beryl returned with Clifford.'

PP asks. 'Now, we move onto our search of your flat at two hundred and three A School Lane, Little Melton. It is your home isn't it Mr Hawker?'

'Yes.'

'Do you recognise this Mr Hawker?'

PP places a single STD Memory card on the table. 'I am showing Mr Hawker exhibit K Three Five One.'

'Yes, you, of course, found it in my flat and to be specific in a draw of my TV cabinet.'

'Yes, we did. Does it belong to you, Mr Hawker?'

'No, in truth.'

'How did you come by it, Mr Hawker?'

'Found it three weeks ago when rummaging through an unofficial rubbish tip on a neglected industrial estate in Wheaton. The pit is only five miles from Little Melton, and I often pop there. You'd be amazed what some people throw away.'

'Have you seen what is on the card Mr Hawker?'

'Only a bit, not my cup of tea. Better luck next time hopefully.'

'So why keep it?'

'I have deliberated whether to hand it into the police but

feared interrogation. You know, about why I had it? Probably would have taken the risk sometime shortly, so quite useful you have it now isn't it? Hope you find the filmmaker, eh!

'We know what model of camera was used to take what's on this particular STD card. Be sure if we find one belonging to anyone we suspect to be responsible for its creation, I will personally let you know, Mr Hawker!'

PP pauses.

'Meanwhile, shortly we will charge you with possession of unlawful pornography.'

'How? It's not mine and I told you I intended to show my find to the police! Can they do this?' asks Hawker looking at his solicitor.

'Since first July this year James they can. If this is the only charge, you are entitled to be released on bail.'

'That's something I guess. Am still surprised though!'

'Mr Hawker, have you lent this STD card to Harold White at any time?'

'No, why would I?'

'How long have you been friends with Harold White?

'I've known Harold since I joined The Thespian Players fourteen years ago.'

'Are you aware Harold White is a registered sex offender, Mr Hawker? For crimes against minors!'

'What? Harold? Hard to believe, so, **no,** I didn't know!'

'Like, I assume, you weren't arrested for breach of the peace? asks PP who then stares out Hawker whose self-satisfaction and arrogance did, recede a bit at this moment.

'Do you recognise the person in this photo, Mr Hawker?'

'It's the girl in posters and flyers who went missing a few years ago, isn't it?

'Yes, it is. Do you know the girl's name?'

'I know her first name is Joanna.'

'Have you ever met Joanne? Joanne Verity is the girl's full

name, Mr Hawker?'

'No, why would I have done?'

'We found Joanne Verity's skeleton remains in woods behind Rose Close on Monday last. When you visited Harold White on this day did you arrive via this woods?'

'I didn't visit Harold on the day you are referring too and in answer to your question! Whenever I do visit Harold I arrive in my car!'

'We have a witness statement which says yesterday at around eleven fifty-am in the said woods, she found one of her dogs trying to rip open a tarpaulin in which Joanne's remains were wrapped and bound. Our witness says, soon after separating Joanne and her dog she heard what she describes as a car "hurtling away at speed."

Mr Hawker, it is you who was disturbed by our witnesses dog isn't it?'

'No. How can it have been? I've already told you my whereabouts yesterday!'

'Can you please tell us what you did on July third two thousand and four Mr Hawker?'

'I do not intend to appear unhelpful. It is usual for me to struggle to remember what I did just weeks ago so my honest answer about a day three years ago is, I don't remember. Sorry.'

'Do you keep a diary?'

'No.'

'An electric one?'

'No.'

'Pretty unusual for someone who makes his living as a self employed freelance photographer? Wouldn't you agree?' asks PP.

'Yes, I agree! But, officer, there is a clue to how I live my life in the job title! It's the word, **free!**'

'Thank you, Mr Hawker, I think we will stop this interview,' and PP's right-hand moves toward the tape recorder.

'Just a moment please DI Parsons,' says Sally with real authority and with a signal to everyone to remain in their seat. Sally does not care how long things take!

'DI Parsons, please hand me exhibit K Three Five Two.'

PP retrieves from the floor a sizeable rustic lattice patterned pirate treasure chest trinket box. He places it in front of Sally.

The curiosity on the solicitor's face is acute, and Sally uses the chest's leather handle to open the box tardily. She then takes a lucky dip and grabs an ID badge not intertwined with another. Without saying anything, Sally offers it to Hawker!

'For the benefit of the tape, I am showing Mr Hawker one of thirty-eight items that make up exhibit K Three Five Two. We found it yesterday during a search of suspects home. Remind me, Mr Hawker, what is your profession please?'

'Do you have difficulty hearing? You already know what it is!'

Hawker then throws back the badge identifying him as a hospital porter. It skims the table and bounces onto Sally's lap. Hawker is thinking, Shit!

'Have you ever been employed as a plumber doing boiler installations, Mr Hawker?' Sally asks ignoring Hawker's response.

'No comment.'

'Have you ever been a courier driver, Mr Hawker?'

'No comment.'

'Have you ever been a roofer, Mr Hawker?'

'No comment.'

From a breast pocket, Sally pulls out a badge she'd taken from the chest before entering the interrogation room.

'Have you ever been a policeman, Mr Hawker?' Sally asks with her eyes depicting a tiger stalking its prey!

'No comment.'

Sally clutches three badges like a fan and waves them in

front of her face.

'Impressive aren't they! We found them in your flat. Why do you have thirty-eight of these, Mr Hawker?

'No comment.'

'Is it presumptuous of me to detect you're parents named you Master Jack?' asks Sally staring right through Hawker's lying eyes.

'No comment,' says Hawker calmly.

All cards, having been put on the table so to speak, are retrieved by PP. Except for the one of the policeman.

Sally rests it face up and says curtly, 'You can keep this one a little longer PC Plonker. It is nineteen twenty-four-pm, and I am concluding this interview.'

***

'Hello Claudia,' says Sally.

'Glad to see you made it in today,' I joke.

Claudia pulls a face and responds with her usual friendliness, 'How did you manage without me?'

'Well, of course!' sallies Sally with a chuckle.

'Shall I come back later to finish tidying up, Sir Roger?'

'Yes please, Claudia. That won't be this evening. Get yourself home. Thank you for staying as late as you have. I appreciate it.'

'If you're sure Sir Roger, then thank you. Goodnight everyone. Good luck!'

A chorus of 'Goodnight' is returned.

'Please, all take a seat,' and before anyone settles Sir Roger continues, 'Well, where do we go now? Describing Hawker as cool is a bloody understatement! Mind you, for once I enjoyed hearing, "No Comment!" Talking of which, does anyone want to make one?'

Everyone looks at Sir Roger with each hoping they manage not to speak first.

'We might yet get a break from Todd and his team,' says PP in a positive tone.

'True. I have just had a brief conversation with our Chief Constable in which Frank made it clear, no matter what we think unless any evidence materialises we will have to release Hawker with no charge! Except for possession, and failing to report to police the existence, of illegal pornography.

I'm still gutted and amazed we didn't discover any IT communication paraphernalia other than a land-line in his flat.'

'We did find a couple of cameras Guv,' says PP.

'Not an incriminating one Peter. As Frank also stressed, a source of evidence might come to light from our next interview with Harold White. He might contradict or discredit something we've just heard from Hawker?'

'Sir,' says Bernice.

'Please, do ask away Bernice,' replies Sir Roger.

'We do have evidence White is responsible for the murder of his wife, don't we?'

'It's certainly looking that way, Bernice. I suggest we meet here at midday tomorrow and evaluate again. Peter and Sally, I anticipate, after we've met tomorrow, you two will interview White again. Before then, I want both of you to speak to Beryl Lattimer and this Isaac chap to check if Hawker's alibis are kosher. Fin...'

'Sorry to interrupt Sir. It...' says PP'.

'I know very well who this Isaac might be. There are other men with the same Christian name,' counters Sir Roger.

'Yes, Sir.'

'Finley, check every name on Hawker's ID badges against names we recorded as attendees of the Fête in Heydon three years ago.

Bernice, check the name of every owner and tenant of every garage, lock up – Call them what you want! Look in Norfolk, Suffolk and Cambridgeshire. Damn it! Add Essex and

Lincolnshire too! Remember, there are thirty-nine names to check! Help each other when you can and start right away, please. If you discover any match, contact either Peter, Sally or myself. No matter, what time of day it is!'

'So, that's the long and short of it I'm afraid. Alibis of all who've been identified as suspects at some point check out, cross-referencing of names fruitless and no more findings of note from Forensics.'

Sir Roger then leans against the back of his green captain's tub leather swivel chair, exhibiting a facial expression of resignation.

'Is one alibi Isaac Stubs Sir?' asks PP.

'Yes, it is Peter. His only ever arrest never mind conviction is that six months in prison for contempt of court. Of course, assuming the CPS do agree White to be charged, in court a defence counsel might yet go on to demonstrate Stubs is not a worthy witness! Nonetheless, in my opinion, and one shared by the Chief Constable, it is Beryl Lattimer confirming she did arrange with Stubs to help Hawker, that gives credence to this alibi.

I'm afraid, no matter what any of us involved thinks or feels about who murdered Joanne! There is a complete lack of proof Hawker was at the White's house on Monday last. Hopefully, all is not lost! We can charge Hawker with two breaches of Section five of the J Act which clarifies what obscene publication offences are. And, we do have evidence White murdered his wife! We still need to interview White again to get his take on the friendship between him and Hawker. As Frank said, our two suspects stories may not tally. Any other questions before...'

'Yes, Guv. Sorry didn't realise...'

'It's OK Peter. Carry on.'

'Do you think it's improbable for a defence counsel, to demonstrate there is reasonable doubt White killed his wife, Guv?'

'Fair question Peter. I will do my best to try and explain why I think the answer is yes! First, the only fingerprints on the weapon used to commit the murder belong to Harold White.

Two, forensics corroborate Harold White's agreement with us there is not anything to indicate any use of forced entry into his house!

Three, before hearing Gillian scream, Harold White also accepts there was not any knock on a door or window. Nor any sound of either a front or back doorbell or a phone ringing!

Four, Gillian never owned a mobile and five, she was found dead in her armchair which had its back facing the front window of their living room. Which rules out an expected or unexpected visitor making their presence known by whatever alternative means you can imagine?

The next factor is interesting because although we all suspect it is near as sure as one can be, Hawker did visit eight Rose Close on Monday last! Hawker's alibis, including White's, in addition to forensic outcomes, means we can't prove he did visit on this day!

We have thoroughly searched the nearby woods which is a comparatively small one. Not a sausage!

We also know an early morning monitoring visit by White's probation officer did not include leaving a front door key under a plant pot which was itself unusual as on all other occasions when visiting at this time, Sandy has confirmed, she put Gillian White's house keys in the said place.

Sandy Ash also mentioned a potential explanation for the said change to pattern of behaviour? Namely, Gillian explained to Sandy the nurse wasn't arriving till later. Due, to Mrs White visiting the Day-Centre in the afternoon as opposed to the usual occurrence of the mini-bus picking her up around nine-thirty AM.

When Sandy left this same morning she confirms, all swords were in their usual place on a wall above the fireplace.

We found the said key laying in its usual place on a hallway shelf inside, what I have to say is, the most beautiful shell I've ever seen! Gillian's District nurse has shared with us, that Gillian told her, this shell is a keepsake from Laig Bay on the Isle of Eigg. It was a gift from someone when she lived in

Scotland.

There is no evidence of robbery being a motive and to think theft you have to accept someone did get in! Whatever way is hard to hypothesise isn't it? For reasons I've just outlined!'

Sir Roger stops juggling what is a pelican's foot shell from one hand to the other. Instead, he stretches an arm, so his hand releases the shell to stand on his desk.

He then continues. 'We have looked at family members, friends or anyone in Gillian's life to explore identifying someone other than Harold White who might have a motive? I have no intention at all to repeat what were quite a few possibilities! Not least because all alibis considered show us they were elsewhere at the time of Gillian death. White has three siblings alive, and they live in America, Argentina and Barbados respectively. Each state they haven't spoken to their brother for over forty years.

We have spoken to every member of the Octagon photography club. None stated socialising with White outside club related activities. None expressed anything which would concern us. All remarked White is the most knowledgeable and gifted member of the club. Each one also mentioned White particularly enjoyed their fortnightly trips to historic sites or places of interest in Norfolk and Suffolk. As far as we know, White has no other known friend other than Hawker. Hawker is not a member of the Octagon Club.

All this plus some new information I will share shortly means I am confident evidence points to White and will prove it is he who acted upon his motive to kill his wife! White's primal need being he will do anything to avoid incarceration! For any of his crimes this is, be they known, alleged or suspected!'

Everyone else in the room remains silent as they watch Sir Roger retrieve two envelopes off his desk. With his head down he takes out a letter and swivels back to face Finley again who is directly opposite him.

'The first letter is to DI Oaks and the other to me. Both are from Gillian White. This one is dated tenth July two thousand and seven and arrived on my desk on the same day this second one did.

It reads, "Dear Alan Oaks-Detective Inspector, Following our telephone conversation yesterday, I am writing to thank you for arranging our meeting to discuss concerns I expressed in my letter to your Chief Constable. I am nervous about attending this meeting for worry of my husbands reaction to probable further action you take afterwards. Not to mention, should he get wind of it before Monday? I am writing to confirm I have every intention to make the appointment along with my friends Mr and Mrs Hartman. Yours sincerely, Jill White."

The second is dated thirteen July two thousand and seven and didn't arrive via The Royal Mail service. It was given to me four days later by Mrs Sadie Wood when she came in to give her fingerprint.

Mrs Wood explained Gillian asked her to post this letter just before Mrs Wood left at the end of a meeting with Gillian. Some of you probably remember Mrs Wood mentioned visiting the Centre on the day Gillian celebrated her birthday with a party there.

Mrs Wood told me when she accepted this letter she didn't even think to look at who the recipient was. Mrs Wood put it straight into a sleeve in her handbag and over the weekend completely forgot about it!

It reads, "Dear Sir Roger Bright-Detective Chief Inspector, Thank you for informing me so promptly my meeting next Monday is now to be with a DC Sally Underwood. Unfortunately, the manager of the Day-Centre took it upon herself to deliver your letter yesterday via the centre's Mini-Bus driver whose name is Bethany. As luck would have it, Bethany knocked the door, and Harold answered. Before letting Bethany in to hand me your letter she said, "Hello Mr White, sorry to disturb you. I have a letter for Gillian found this morning at the Centre. It sates police are senders on the back; we thought it best for Gillian receive it soon as possible. May I come in please to hand it to her?"

Harold insisted I opened it in front of just him of course. Harold is furious and threatening to harm me if I continue with my arrangement to discuss further the concerns I reported to your Chief Constable. I have heard such a rant from Harold many times before, and while it is unpleasant and alarming, I hold my own. Though, this time he said more than once, "If you don't, I'll Shut you up for good!"

I have written this letter to state I have every intention of meeting DC Underwood on Monday next, and I am now comforted by knowing I have explained what would be the only event, other than me dying from natural causes, that will stop me keeping this appointment!!! Yours sincerely, Jill White."

Sir Roger folds the letter and swiftly observes from right to left each member of his team. 'Any comments, questions?'

None aired and for a short while, it is quiet.

Until, Sir Roger continues, 'Everything I'm about to share, any of you can quote me as saying, I said it is, "On the record!" However, I expect each of you only to do so in line with your duties or responsibilities and when the law needs you too!

You might find it odd I start by saying, well-done everyone! Why? Because I think we all feel a failure and yet I believe we have solved both 'Who Done It' elements of our investigations. We can only prove one of them! Though, the solution of the wicked abduction and murder of Joanne Verity remains a priority!

We will be advising the public should a lead occur which proves White and Hawker did not commit their barbaric crimes against Joanne, then this would mean our sincere belief they are responsible was wrong! However, we will add we expect if there is a lead in the future which does help us solve the identity of the perpetrators, this will prove we are right!

The sad reality we face in the short term is, unless either premiss happens, resuming with our duties is likely to be an emotional challenge! More importantly a **lot** more so, for our victims' loved ones as they attempt to 'get on' with their lives!

The Chief Constable has been authorised by the Home Secretary to make a formal statement at a press conference arranged for nine-am tomorrow. Frank will say, in his own way, what I have just shared with you. Only, with one significant addition! Frank will make it very clear the police are not expecting a need to look for any other suspects in pursuit of bringing to justice those responsible for what happened to Joanne Verity!

I know you all like to rib me about my use of quotes and I enjoy the banter. So, just in case you thought I was going to let you down, here is my latest offer. Someone once said, "*SUCCESS IS NOT FINAL, FAILURE* is not fatal: it is the courage to continue that counts."

***

'How is it going Alex?' asks Sir Roger having just entered the VIP box once more.

'They're doing well. Near to ending questions about Joanne. I'm afraid no contradictions from White, Guv.'

Sir Roger stands beside me, and we both listen.

'...and before DI Parsons discusses the progress of our investigation into the murder of your wife, Mr White, I have a final question which requires a yes or no answer, please?

Am I right in understanding you deny any involvement whatsoever in the abduction and murder of Joanne Verity?'

'Yes.'

'Thank you for your cooperation,' says PP and he opens a Viking office depot cut flush folder and takes from it a copy of Gillian White's letter to Sir Roger.

'For the benefit of the tape, I am about to hand Mr White exhibit K Three Five Three. Can you please read this,' asks PP who is surprised by White's eagerness to take a look.

'Do you recognise the handwriting Mr White?'

White doesn't look up or stop reading as he answers, 'It's obviously Gillian's.'

Mrs Mary Oswald, White's reluctant solicitor, is watching Harold read the letter and notices both fists clenching tighter and tighter.

PP and Sally are watching closely too, and the atmosphere in the room is much like waiting for an inevitable explosion you get once a fuse is lit to a firework.

White, slams both fists on the table. His tone is calm. 'I didn't kill Gillian.'

'Do you deny Mrs White's allegation that you threatened to shut her up for good?'

'I've already told you I admit to being angry she'd contacted you and yes, we quarrelled! I admit saying to Gillian if she met with your slut sidekick then when she returned home, she would find out she will never be able to enter our home again. That would have shut her up.'

'Not necessarily for good, which is what Gillian said she feared and I put it to you, Mr White, she did so with good reason, didn't she?'

'Are you, both of you, really as thick as you look! It won't work. No. I'll make sure it doesn't.'

Everyone watching is amazed White then begins to laugh, and it's definitely at PP and Sally.

'Do you wish to say anything further about the letter Mr White?' asks Sally and White halters his laughing briefly to reply. 'No.'

PP interjects, 'OK. I must inform you Mr White, DC Underwood and I will now take you upstairs to our custody You will be charged for the murder of Gillian White and placed on remand in prison, I mean, Justice Centre to await trial. No doubt you will instruct your solicitor to apply for bail. The interview is now ending at fourteen O nine-pm.'

'Hold on! You're insane! I didn't murder Gillian. It's a fucking stitch up! Have you questioned Maxi Hurst?' demands White staring into PP's eyes.

'Assuming you're referring to Maxine Stewart? Personally? No.'

'I have Mr White,' says Sally.

White then shifts his gaze, and says, 'Alibi obviously and

from your delivery, it's equally obvious she's said nothing so calling my bluff too! You, sidekick, and you're so called superior for that matter, are not worthy of hearing first what I have on Maxi Hurst. You can tell her I will revel in disclosing everything if, as I'm now realising might be happening, I am taken to court.'

White then looks at his solicitor. 'For Christ's sake do something to challenge this farce! Surely I can get bail?'

Mary replies, 'I will make an application immediately Harold. Hopefully be heard in court sometime tomorrow?'

In unison, Sally and PP take hold of an arm each and carefully force lift White to his feet.

'Get off me, you morons!'

White's resistance is futile! As they make their way out of the room, it is evident White's resolve remains intact as he incessantly rants, 'You numb-skulls are going to look so stupid in court!'

In truth, he's using a considerable number of other words too which are more akin to the hotness you get in a red giant star as oppose to sounding blue!

***

Sally is smiling as she walks along a corridor on a floor of Wymondham Police Station she has never been on before. The passageway is lit up by a row of fluorescent cat eye tubes on the ceiling along with its canary yellow painted walls.

Sally feels right about the interview of White earlier this afternoon. She is also looking forward to seeing Alex Forrester in his office. Or to be more precise, curious to see inside it for the first time. Just hope he hasn't gone home yet, Sally muses and after two more strides, she knocks on a half-open door.

I say, 'Come in,' and Sally pops her head, a shoulder and one arm into view.

'Hi, Alex. Is it a convenient time to have a quick chat, please? If I'm interrupting anything, it can wait.'

'Now is fine Sally. Please take a seat.'

Sally chooses the one on the other side of a low circular coffee table. It is in a corner where two vast walls to ceiling windows meet at a right angle.

'What a lovely naturally lit office you have Alex. How much did it cost to persuade Sir Rog to allocate you this room then?'

'Caught him on a good day I guess. Though mentioning I was inspired to try and join the police by a documentary telling the story of why he was awarded his medal: Might well have helped a bit too?'

'I don't have you down as a creep, so nice try Alex. No way is any of that true! Seriously though, was it simply a lucky inheritance?'

I laugh and reply, 'Well, it was of sorts. It was Sir Roger's office. On my first day here, he mentioned that once I got the all-clear for the post, he and Frank agreed for Sir Roger to move out of what was then his office into here. The thinking behind it was Sir Roger's room had most space and therefore better for a person who uses a chair with wheels.

I asked Sir Roger if he had a preference between the two rooms? He admitted, while bearing no hard feelings at all, he'd not have chosen to move otherwise.

I advised Sir Roger the layout of his new office is ideal because it's more compact. After a few weeks, Sir Roger said he felt OK to accept his old office again. Naturally, I didn't mention either the light or view just happen to be brilliant too!'

'Naturally.'

'You said you have something to discuss Sally. Hope I can be of assistance.'

'Yes, I want to thank you for the support you gave me when interviewing White earlier today. It helped.'

'Thank you. Genuinely no need. It's part of my job description you know.'

'That as maybe. It doesn't necessarily follow a person in a post can do the job. You are the most non-patronising man I've ever met, so please accept my thanks.'

'Well, seeing you put it like that, thank you, Sally. Oh, and congratulations on the strong possibility of scooping all the winnings of our betting pool.'

'Bit premature as the last word I had from PP on the subject was, there is no winner!'

'Yes, PP shared his take in things. Thinks the bet is null and void because only one murder has resulted in a charge. Given today's outcome, I suggested he should morally pay up. I reasoned that given White is directly responsible for his wife's death and officially we are not looking for anyone other than Hawker and White for the murder of Joanne; this makes you the winner! Right?'

Sally laughs and replies, 'Bet he loved that!'

'He grunted, "No chance," I think. Is there anything else I can help with Sally?'

'Yes, please. Is now OK to have a read of, I think you called it a BPF?'

'Now is fine. I appreciate it's late in the working day, so tomorrow is no problem either, Sally?'

'My wife is working late tonight so now is a good time. Of course, if you are about to go then yes, tomorrow morning is great too.'

I go to a row of draws laying on the floor side by side. They cover the entire length of a wall's skirting board. I lift up the lid of a draw labelled miscellaneous and grab the loose sheets of paper on top of a pile of folders. 'There you are Sally.'

'Thanks, Alex. Is sitting here OK?'

'Sure.'

'Why do you keep these in your miscellaneous cabinet Alex?'

'The BPF is my creation. I find it helpful because of its clarity, and it's useful to expand on. For instance when a full departmental profile report is requested or needed by Sir Roger. Or, for a court, for example.'

'I see.'

'Don't mind if I carry on with a few bits do you? I'm planning on leaving about six, so plenty of time.'

'Great and of course not. Oh Alex, before I start reading. Something eerie and yet consoling happened to me during the interview with White. A line of a song on one of my mum's favourite albums kept popping into my head. It goes, "I'm sinking in the Quicksand of my thought, And I ain't got the power anymore." It's by Da...'

'Bowie,' I interject.

'Yes,' says Sally with a wry smile. She then adds chuckling, 'I forget your an oldie.'

'Cheeky or what? All the same, what you just shared is fascinating Sally. And, I like Bowie too.'

'Ditto,' replies Sally.

'At the other end of the room are tea and cake facilities. Can I tempt you with any of them Sally?'

'No but thanks for the offer.'

Sally then looks down and starts reading.

"Background Profile Fact-sheet – Harold White – DOB – 24/12/33

Heritage

Born and raised in Norfolk. Throughout entire childhood and beyond university years subject lived in the same family home which was Hoveton Hall near Wroxham. Subject's father was a member of parliament from 1922 to 1964 and Home Secretary from 1935 to 1945 and for a second time from 1951 to 1964.

The subject was one of six siblings and second eldest of two sons so did not inherit Hoveton Hall when his father died in 1982. Subject's mother died in 1979, and his two youngest sisters killed during a bombing raid in Norwich in 1942.

No contact for over forty years between subject and his three siblings still alive. All live abroad.

Education

Subject attended Greecham private school from aged 5yrs and boarded weekdays from aged 11yrs to 18yrs. He dropped out of Oxford University after two years of a four-year degree course in Economics.

Career

Subject has never worked. Lived off a lifetime allowance provided through special banking arrangements made by his father, and also his quarter of inheritance money along with a similar share from the sale of Hoveton Hall by his brother in 1971.

Significant Relationships

Subject married in 1964. No children.

Used to be a friend (Socialite Buddy) of Jeremy Dillinger – who was rightly arrested in 1981 yet not charged as a suspect in a double murder committed in 1953.

Recent E.n.E.M.A. reveals subject's wife left him for eighteen months during 1970/71.

Interests

Listed in Who's Who in 1961 where it quotes Subject's interests as dinner and dance parties, fast cars, Tennis, Amateur Dramatics and Photography.

The subject was a subscripted member of P.I.E. (Paedophile Information Exchange) This lobbyist organisation operated from the early1970's until it was shut down and made illegal in 1984.

Amongst material found in Subject's possession in 1996 were some copies of two newsletter publication produced by P.I.E. called "Magpie" and "One Night Bangs."

Previous convictions

Three-year probation order in 1996 for possession of illegal pornographic photographs pertaining to minors and were taken over a span of fifty years.

The subject also listed as a Registered Sex Offender in 1996 and on 1 July 2007 status of 'Lifer' was added to his registration.

A second three-year probation order in 2005 for common assault against a librarian who confronted Subject about a pornographic picture found stuck in a book he was returning.

Current professional involvement

Subject reviewed by MAPPA annually and is currently classified as a high risk to re-offend.

Mrs Sandy Ash is his current allocated Probation Officer.

Involvement with Statutory Child Protection Agencies

As a Minor – None found.

As an Adult – Please cross reference Previous Conviction in 1996.

Also in 1996, an adult female made a historical allegation of serious sexual assault against her by Subject when she was aged eight. A charge made and then dropped by the CPS. On the grounds of alleged victim's learning disability made her evidence unreliable.

Health and Treatment

In Recovery from Alcohol and Prescription Drugs dependency since 1976.

Hip replacement in 2002.

Attended counselling sessions as directed by a condition of the probation order in 1996. Chooses to decline any other ongoing support offered after that.

Intellectual Capacity

Subject able to understand differences between right and wrong, consent and force and yes and no.

Reason for current police investigations

Charged with murder of his spouse.

Helping police with their enquiries into abduction and murder of a female aged 14yrs."

Sally puts BPF about White on the coffee table. She briefly glances at me as I talk on the phone. She then starts to read about Subject two.

"Background Profile Fact-sheet – James Hawker – DOB – 11/11/68

Heritage

Born and raised in Northern Ireland. Throughout entire childhood and while at University of East Anglia subject lived in the same family home which was above a Post Office Shop.

Subject's parents both continue to work as co-managers of a shop to this day.

The subject moved officially from his family home to his current address in 1993.

Subject has an elder sister.

Education

Attended Christian Primary School and then St. Lootiers's College from aged 11yrs to18yrs. Completed a first honours degree in English Literature at UEA in1989.

Career

The subject was an unofficial apprentice from 1990 to 1993 for his paternal uncle who ran and owned a camera shop in Coshen which also had a photography portrait studio attached to premises.

The subject became a freelance photographer and chose to move back to Norfolk to begin this venture. This continues to be his occupation.

Significant Relationships

Not Known. The subject is single and never married.

Friends with an RSO whose name is Harold White-aged 71yrs.

Interests

Photography and member of an Amateur Dramatics Society. Multi Alias'. Good at disguises.

Previous convictions

None.

Current professional involvement

None.

Involvement with Statutory Child and/or Adult Protection Agencies

As a Minor – None.

As an Adult – None.

Health

No issues.

Intellectual Capacity

Subject understands the meaning of and differences between right and wrong, consent and force and yes and no.

Reason for current police investigations

Subject's fingerprint found at the murder scene of an adult female. Record of fingerprint held from an arrest outside Sizewell Nuclear plant in 1988. The subject was protesting with his parent's and elder sister when they joined other CND demonstrators while on an annual family holiday to Orford.

The subject also helping police with their enquiries into abduction and murder of 14-year-old child - female.

Charged with possession of an illegal pornographic film pertaining to sex between adults and minors stored on an STD card."

Sally looks up. 'May I ask you a question or two please, Alex?'

'Sure.'

'Who was this Jeremy...'

'Dillinger.'

'Yes him. Who was he accused of killing?'

'Two women at a party celebrating the Queens Coronation in 1953. I know it may be hard to believe, was even before my time! The party host was a cabinet Minister's Permanent Under Secretary, whatever that means? And...'

Sally laughs as I continue, '...Jeremy Dillinger was arrested for their murder after White's father admitted in his autobiography the man convicted for the said murders was innocent and should not have hanged. The name of the innocent man was John Hambleton who was the Permanent Under Secretary's son.

'I see. And what is a Socialite?'

I laugh, 'Well I call them groupies for people famous because of power, money or entertainment skills. Or of course any combination of the three!'

'I hadn't cottoned till now how well connected White is. Are you still undecided about whether White killed Gillian or not?'

'No, it seems his fear of being locked up has proven to be his strongest. My niggle is, White would have known murder of his wife in their home would inevitably involve contact with persons in authority. So, I accept the evidence now indicates White is the culprit! But, it is this element of contradiction to a powerful characteristic action of his which causes me to waver a bit still.'

CHAPTER THIRTEEN

So far, Harold White's 21st day in a cell is much the same as the previous twenty. White is laying on his back with eyes open and his brain perpetually ticking things over. Sometimes, I learnt, he even talks stuff out load! Suddenly, White hears the sound of a key to his cell. Then, a Warder proclaims, 'Your visitor has arrived, Mr White.'

White doesn't speak, he just calmly gets to his feet, tucks his shirt in and chooses not to change his slippers for shoes.

The Warder and White walk down one of quite a few similar corridors within the new Norfolk Justice Centre. All hallways darkened by walls coloured a lamp black grey. Maxine is in 'D' Wing's visitor room adjacent to the Warder's work station.

The visitor room is small and bereft of furnishings apart from its mustard coloured carpet floor tiles. There are also two black skyline chairs positioned for Maxine and her designated chaperone which Frank insisted on providing.

Maxine is visiting because the Chief Constable and Sir Roger advised Clive Verity, that given the CPS have agreed to prosecute White for the murder of his wife, it is inappropriate to allow Clive, the victim's son-in-law, to do so! However, both Senior Officers did agree Clive does have the right to ask a person of his choice to represent him instead. Clive was gutted to be prohibited but displayed certain grace and understanding in his acceptance of their decision.

Maxine and DC Billing are staring at the prisoner's seat positioned no more than five yards in front of them. Instinctively, both look right on hearing White entering with a Warder cuffed to him on both sides. They walk until White is standing with his back facing the front of a sturdy built chair crafted from Oakwood.

The male Warder says, 'Mrs Stewart, it is my duty to advise you, we will leave the room while you speak with Mr White. We will be watching on our monitoring screen without listening.

However, if required, we can come to your rescue very quickly. Would you prefer we secure Mr White to the chair?'

'Never mind what she wants, since when has it been allowed for you morons to treat remand prisoners like this! I demand a solicitor be brought here right now!'

Maxine replies, 'Yes, please. But, I want to reassure you both, I already feel safe.'

The female Warder releases her hand from a cuff and asks, 'Please sit down Mr White.'

White glares with disdain as he says. 'I have changed my mind. I no longer agree to receive my visitor.'

While the male Warder detaches himself from a cuff too, he asks his colleague, 'Can you please repeat what you asked Mr White to do, Warder Miles?'

'Please sit down Mr White.'

'Are you fucking deaf. I told you I'm out of here! Get...'

The male Warder intervenes. 'You sit down by yourself within five seconds, or we will force you to be cooperative. One, two, thr...'

White complies while Maxine smiles.

'Thank you. Mr White, I have been authorised by Chief Constable Frank Toddenham to inform you, in the event of you changing your mind, your visitor today must be provided with an opportunity to try and discuss the reasons for her visit. The matters are moral issues so do not constitute a need to adhere to your request for a solicitor. We will now strap your hands and feet to the chair and clamp a helmet on your head.'

With amazement twinkling in her eyes, Maxine watches the vision of White become akin to a person with the mixture of rigidity displayed by a monarch crowned and a pilot fastened into his seat during a descent he knows will end in a crash!

'Hokey Cokey. Jean and I will now leave the room, Madam.'

'Thank you,' replies Maxine while she and White stare right into each other's eyes.

'You fucking bitch!'

'Do you know why I am here Harold?'

'I'm pretty certain I know why you are Maxi. Who are you?'

To White's annoyance Maxine answers and of course he is not aware of the agreement made with Clive, which is, only Maxine will talk.

'I am here Harold on behalf of Clive Verity to ask you not to attend your wife's funeral, please?'

Ignoring Maxine, White repeats a revamped version of his previous question. 'She has explained why she's come. So, why have you?'

'Harold, I shan't beat around the bush, 'Do you...'

'Hold your horses, Miss Hurst. I know you have the bottle. But, we, as in you and me, know the real reason you sent a request to visit me, don't we?'

Maxine does understand why White would presume he knows. It is to her credit this didn't cause her to decline Clive's asking.

'It is not why I am here Harold, and my name is Mrs Stewart.'

'It was Miss Hurst when we first met! For the benefit of the muted in our midst, I'm happy for you Miss Hurst, to choose which one of us explains the circumstances, so over to you.'

'Harold, it isn't why I am here. So, I am not going to play.'

Maxine knows White is and she's resigned to her companion hearing the ugliest event in her life.

'OK. You were how old when we first met?'

Maxine doesn't answer.

'I'll remind you Maxi, sweet sixteen. Unusual location wasn't it! A car crash on Park Road near The Victoria Pub in my favourite coastal village of Holkham. Now then, who caused the crash?'

Silence.

'What's more interesting is, whose car were you driving?'

Silence.

'The answer is, Maxi was driving her parents' car, as they were staying with friends for a night in Newmarket. It was her mother's car to be precise.'

White moves his gaze from Finley to Maxine and continues, 'You know what Miss Hurst, I am no doctor but I'm pretty sure the trigger for Gillian's later health problems was you smashing side on into the bonnet of our stationary car that night.

Gillian and I had spent a lovely day with two friends on Holkham nudist beach and just finished dining and wining in the Vic. Instead of getting out of your mother's car to see how we were, you revved up the engine and sped away. Excellent credentials for a want-to-be lawyer, I think not!

You had no idea our friends saw it all happen. We all helped Gillian into my friend's car and then Sidney, and I set off to catch you up. We made you stop in a lay-by on the A149. Remind me, you were heading in the direction of Kings Lynn weren't you?'

Silence.

'I imagine your friend here is expecting to hear something along the lines of police and ambulance were then called etc. etc. Only, as you know, that isn't what happened at all, is it?'

Silence.

'Sidney's wife drove, at Gillian's insistence, in the direction of Wells-next-the-Sea to go straight home. Fortunately, it seemed then, none of us was seriously hurt. When Sidney and I joined you in your mother's car, you sobbed and pleaded for us not to tell the police. Why? Your ambition to be a lawyer. You knew a criminal record would put pay to that! Not to mention, also the fear of experiencing the wroth of your parents!

One way or another, all three of us were in a bit of a pickle weren't we?! So, how was it best to resolve a tricky situation with an outcome to satisfy all three of us? Still, we came up with a solution didn't we, Maxi!'

Silence.

'Have you guessed what Maxi agreed too yet, mute?'

'It's me you're talking with Harold. So, if you are going to continue with the worse I suggest it's pointless because it makes no difference to why you are sitting there and me here!'

'You are good Maxine, I even admire you, to be honest. Very clever and convincing. I know I didn't kill Gillian. I told them brainless detectives this from the start! When first interviewed, I even fed them a lead to seriously look at my educated belief in all probability it's you who is responsible for setting me up! In fact, it didn't take long before I started believing you did do it!'

Silence.

'Gillian's unexpected presence put pay to your original plan. I believe...'

Maxine interrupts, 'How would I, anyone gain entry? Even you agree there was no force entry!'

Harold laughs before retorting with, 'Have you forgotten what you did when we met that second time? A week or so after our memorable first encounter, eh! You see Maxi, I still: No, I'll save this for the judge!

For now and getting back to when you interrupted, I believe your initial intention was just me? I think this because you could not have known Gillian was going to her Centre later than usual on that Monday!

Furthermore, my solicitor has documented evidence from three senior police officers. Whereby, each one categorically states details of Gillian's letter to the Chief Constable and subsequent action taken did not get discussed with anyone else outside their circle. Until this is, they ordered detective Sally slut sidekick to nose in! At a similar time to when you killed my wife! And so changing your plan to framing me, right?'

Silence.

'I think my other assumption is more than reasonable, too! Gillian's presence meant you lost the element of surprise to take me off guard literally!'

White deliberately spits onto the floor a sizeable droplet of phloem which lands approximately three inches away from Maxine's shoes. He then says, 'Gillian didn't deserve to be slaughtered, you bitch!'

Maxine is sweating as if in a sauna but sticks her right arm out horizontally and gestures a palm of reassurance to the Warders. Maxine is also maintaining eye contact with White and decides to wait.

'Now, your work links you with the police a lot more than your previous employer, doesn't it! I admit I cannot be certain which of the three spoke to you about the letter or know exactly when and in what context this happened? Or, even their reason for doing so? But, I want you to know, I know you must have got wind of the letter because, apart from me, you are the only person who could suffer if Gillian continued, how shall I put it? Encouraging police to dig further! The difference from nineteen ninety-six to now is, as you know very well too Maxi, we were then on the same side! Tell me, was it difficult to lie when the police questioned you as of course, I knew they'd have too?'

Maxine is still trying to deal with being reminded of what happened to end their second meeting. But, you'd never know this from how she replies with, 'You're right, they have. There were not many questions to answer because I have an honest alibi for the timespan during which you, not me, murdered Gillian!'

'Well, naturally you have an alibi. I am confident when a jury, a Judge and therefore the world hear about our antics in Holkham there will be at worse, a retrial? But, a more probable outcome would also be the best outcome! Which is, a new trial with you charged with murdering my Gillian!'

Silence.

'As you also know Maxi, there is a lot more detail I haven't reminisced about yet isn't there? And, to the mute brain here, you will have to wait until I'm cross-examined in court to hear the rest! You are lucky though Miss Hurst. To cope with the aftermath, you can draw on your previous experience of being a victim of a drama in court! Albeit, it was a very different kind. Clever of that Stubs fellow wasn't it! I am looking forward to it already!!'

'Harold, do you still intend to attend your wife's funeral

which will be part of a joint ceremony with Joanne Verity and her mother, whose name is Valerie?'

'I have no idea why he's doing a joint funeral. What have they got to do with Gillian, apart from being neighbours?'

'You don't know?' asks Maxine.

'Don't let me down Maxi. Come on, are you saying you believe the mumbo-jumbo about Gillian being the mother of, what name did you say?'

'Valerie.'

'Maxi, I used to think you were a remarkable woman with beauty and a brain! Not anymore. They, by whom I mean the police, do-gooders and media moguls, have seduced Clive, a war hero, to engage in an occasion that makes them all feel better. There is no other reason. Why can't you see, any link to Gillian is a deliberate spread of romantic but fabricated conspiracy rumours! Reported, mostly by the press and fed to them by the police and you too probably. Wake up, Miss Hurst. Gillian was unable to have children! I even told my solicitor it's a waste of time getting a second opinion from a quack! Because I know the upset of us not being able to conceive means Gillian would never have given her child away! All part of the conspiracy to try and nail me for something I didn't do because, as the Chief Constable stated to the world, they can't get me for something they claim I did do! Outrageous! Not only is it untrue I've killed Gill..., anyone as it happens! But, it is crookedly arrogant too!'

'I want you to know Harold; I advised Clive I am sure you won't change your mind. So, on behalf of Clive I ask, will you please reconsider and not attend the funeral ceremony?'

'If you explain to me, Miss Hurst, why this Clive Verity chose you to represent him I might then be able to give you, for old times sake, due consideration?'

'Clive Verity is my brother-in-law which obviously means he married my sister,' replies Maxine who is thrilled to see genuine surprise expressed in White's eyes.

'So, you see Harold; my motive is threefold and simple to understand. Clive nor I want you anywhere near Valerie and of course their daughter Joanne. The remaining reason is the most important because we both believe Valerie too, would not want you to be there!'

'I'm charged with killing my wife, not this Joanne girl. After giving due consideration my answer is, your question is unimportant. My solicitor assures me I have the right to choose whether or not to attend my wife's funeral? The fact Clive is choosing to have a three in one supported by the law is an outcome I had no influence over, let alone agree on!

Now I am fully aware of why you and Clive do not want me present; I respectively advise it is worth remembering two facts when examining your motives. I am not guilty, and not tried yet! I don't want to talk with you anymore! So, my last comment, to use your own words, is also easy to understand. If Clive allows Gillian to have a separate funeral then he wouldn't need to see me, and instead ask you to do so, would he?'

Maxine stands and says, 'Harold, I'm here only because Clive would have come. I even advised Clive if he had been granted permission it will be a total waste of time. I'm glad he hasn't felt the pain your attitude would have given him. You see Harold, Clive believes good is in everyone. I know from my work this is not true!

Therefore Harold, all I can tell Clive is that you fully understand the hurt your presence will cause and I am confident you will attend.'

Maxine hesitates before continuing. 'I am also certain Harold, those who care about Clive and the three deceased will show impeccable dignity and respect throughout the whole service. No matter, who is there!'

Finley follows Maxine's lead of turning her back on White. Then, immediately Maxine spins round again, 'Oh yes. One last thing. Given the facts, others may be surprised by your refusal not to attend. For me, it will be easy to explain as I already knew you're a piece of human shit!'

When his visitors are about to exit the room, White chirps, 'Maxi, as you leave you do not know if I will attend or not, do you? And I'm sure even your muted numbskull will tell you I am right!'

CHAPTER FOURTEEN

August 14, 2007

Clive has not long stopped crying and is checking himself in a mirror at Woodland Mews. He places a comb and a clump of tissue paper into an inside breast pocket.

'It is time to go now Clive,' shouts Maxine politely from her position at the foot of a staircase.

'On my way,' replies Clive softly and he soon reaches the top of the flight.

Maxine says, 'You look fantastic! Valerie and Joanne will be so pleased you are in uniform again.'

Clive starts to descend, 'Thank you, Maxine. I feel a bit stronger now too.'

Maxine ascends, and soon they lock arms, 'Are you sure you're ready Clive?'

'Yes, let's go.'

As they walk toward an open front door, dominant in their view is a giant hearse and shadows signalling it is a warm sunny summer day.

The hearse was specially built and laid out to accommodate Valerie, Joanne and Jill. Clive kisses Maxine on a cheek and steps in to sit on a double seat beside Joanne's coffin. He then rests his right hand on Joanne's favourite photo of the three of them. It was taken by a stranger during a short cycling holiday in The Black Forest.

Maxine joins Luke and Milena in a limousine waiting on Woodland Mews Lane.

Carole, today's Director, is in front of the hearse looking very dapper in her skirt suit, waistcoat and black top hat which has a matching coloured chiffon dangling tidily against the back of her neck.

Carole is clasping a pair of black leather gloves between her hands. She glances briefly behind to check everyone is ready and then takes her first stride forward.

The chauffeur carefully follows his Director as they take their place at the front of the cortège. Not for the first time, a bearer sitting behind Clive marvels at the pavement on each side of the Lane jam-packed with residents from Thre3 Scor3 and its four neighbouring villages.

Carole comes to a halt in an atmosphere which you would hear a pin drop if one fell! She then gets into the hearse and the cortège, consisting of a hearse, limousine and six civilian cars is now ready to proceed.

From Woodland Mews, the hearse leads them onto Marlingford Road which in turn takes them to a quintessentially ancient Norfolk village called Bawburgh. Clive was tipped off by Leon Hartman that nearly all villagers in this vicinity planned to pay their respects. Even so, he is genuinely amazed to see an unbroken human chain of good wishers on both sides of this road too. There are so many it is enough to warrant deployment of police officers to keep their route clear.

Many in the crowd wear attire as if they are going on to attend the chapel service. The majority, along with all police officers, remove head ware to bow as the hearse passes. Some are shedding tears too.

This public display of respect continues during the entire crawl through Bawburgh, and if anything, now they are veering off New Road onto Chapel Break Road, the numbers have swollen further. Two hundred yards farther on the left is Bishybarnabee Way. Clive notices Helen and Lilly Thompson amongst those at the front of the crowd.

'Director, please may we stop?' he asks.

'Yes, Mr Verity.'

The chauffeur then responds accordingly to Carole's nod.

'Thank you.'

Clive steps out, 'Helen, Did you and Lilly not get my invitation?'

'Yes, we did Clive. It's just; There are blocks to all roads. The police say the crowds are like this all the way to the church.'

'Really? Wow. Right, join us.'

'No, but that's kind. Thank you for offering Clive,' replies Helen.

'Come on Mum,' says Lilly while taking hold of her mother's hand.

Clive grasps Helen's other hand, and before she knows it, Clive leads their climb in. Lilly sits next to the bearer, and her mother slides in against Clive while she whispers, 'Thank you, Clive. You look fantastic!'

***

Before the cortège left Woodland Mews, Harold White was handcuffed to a SERCO prison escort and led into the back of a white MPV vehicle. They began their journey just under twenty minutes ago.

White smiles. Another fifteen minutes or so and I will see Maxi again, he muses.

All of a sudden, White and a Warder shake as the wheels of the van crunch over a large stone boulder. It is one of many used in the hapless task of trying to protect the shoreline of Happisburgh village from being lost to the North Sea.

'What the hells going on Bill,' shouts Ben.

Ben then helps to pull their prisoner back onto his seat, while Bill gets out.

'Are you hurt Mr White?' asks Ben.

'No and get your hand off me...'

'Sorry about that guys,' says Bill opening the van before adding, 'Good news is, no puncture! So, getting back won't be a problem.'

White cannot believe Bill looks so cheerful and retorts, 'What do you mean, we haven't arrived yet, you moron! Don't just stand there man; I don't want to be late! It's my wife getting cremated for Christ's sake...'

'Would you like a cigarette while we wait, Ben? There is a bench look. With a nice view of the sea too.'

'Sounds good Bill, yes please.'

Ben stands to force White to follow him out.

'Oh, I get it. You morons have been told to explain the van broke down and by the time it was fixed the funeral would've long ended.'

Bill, who is a friend of PP, replies, 'You're right Mr White. Keep walking Mr White. I'll give you the details once we've settled.'

'Morons,' White exclaims.

Within seconds White finds himself sandwiched on the bench and Bill cuffs himself to their prisoner too. Bill then dexterously uses one hand to remove two cigarettes from a packet resting on his thigh. Likewise, Ben gets a lighter from a trouser pocket and lights both cigarettes now hanging between Bill's lips.

Both escorts then place their smoke between two fingers. The uncomfortable consequence for White is, every time Bill and Ben take a puff in tandem, each of White's arms jets up akin to that of a person in plaster following treatment for a double fracture.

Bill then says, 'Where was I? Oh yes, in an hour or so Mr White, I will contact a vehicle recovery service run by a Ned Proctor. His garage is about a mile from here, not far from the Lighthouse Inn near Walcott. Have you ever eaten there Mr White? Excellent selection of guest beers!'

Bill and Ben inhale and then exhale into White's face.

'You two are so well named. As brainless as the original Flowerpot men,' ridicules White who knows the protest is futile.

'And you are perfect to be our, 'Little Weed,' quips Ben.

Bill then resumes information sharing with White, 'When Ned leaves, he will write an official receipt for the cost of successfully fixing what will be a serious mechanical fault. In...'

'Naturally,' interjects White.

'In fact, so serious Mr White, it will verify to anyone in

authority who might ask and I'm pretty certain no-one will, that it was simply out of our control and unavoidable you missed your wife's funeral.'

'Numskulls,' White groans with his head staring at his feet.

Both escorts enjoy another drag. White coughs, and it sounds profound. He now has a ball of mucus on his tongue. He separates it in his teeth, and pee shoots the front half onto the bridge of Bill's nose and rotates his head to fire the remainder, accurately, into Ben's lug-hole.

***

The cortège arrives in front of Colney Chapel's very wide porch entrance. The latter decorated with numerous flowers with colours that match those on the inside too. Helen and Lilly follow Clive out, and Clive shakes Reverend Julian Islington's hand, 'Thank you for all your support in the conduction of this funeral today.'

'It is the least we could do Mr Verity, and I'm certain it is God's will too.'

Maxine, Luke and Milena are beside Clive, and the Reverend shakes hands with each. They all then take their respective positions amongst twelve other bearers. Julian and Carole exchange pleasantries as they witness the procession assembling. Carole then lines up a few yards behind Julian, and an organist starts to play, "Chi Mai," which prompts the procession to begin moving forward.

The first coffin to pass the first members (Frank and some of his employees all dressed in civilian clothes) of a strictly invited congregation is the one in which Jill is laid to rest. Luke is one of her two middle placed bearers. Joanne follows, and Milena is a bearer at the front, and then Valerie with Clive and Maxine bearing at opposite ends.

A significant number of tears are evident by the time two mothers and two daughters are in front of the chapel's altar. All four family bearers take their seat in the front row, and Julian formally begins the service.

'Welcome to our chapel to celebrate the lives of Joanne, Valerie and Jill. We will begin with a hymn that was a favourite of Joanne Verity, "Morning has Broken."

At once, the organ bursts into life, "Morning has broken, like the first morning Blackbird has spoken, like the first bird."

Praise for the singing, praise for the morning, praise for the springing fresh from the word..."

'Please sit down' asks Julian who then walks into and up the pulpit.

Julian starts his short and prepared 'Mardle' about the lives of all three deceased. Clive can hear Julian's voice just not his words. Clive is sat with each of his hands covering one of his knees and is looking at the altar with his mind very much elsewhere.

'If I only knew before what I know now, none of you would be dead. Please try and forgive each other, if not me, for our Jo's sake. She needs you to look after her now. Oh, princess, you weren't an apple in your mother's and my eyes, you were, are and always will be our bloody great bowl full of every fruit there is!'

Tears are streaming down Clive's face, and in comfort, Maxine gently squeezes his left hand and Lilly his right.

Julian is concluding the Mardle, '...and with God's help bring them together in an afterlife as it should have been here on Earth. Let us pray.'

"How lovely is your dwelling place, O LORD of hosts!

My soul longs, yes, faints for the courts of the LORD; my heart and flesh sing for joy

to the living God.

Even the sparrow finds a home, and the swallow a nest for herself, where she may lay her young, at your altars, O LORD of hosts, my King and my God.

Blessed are those who dwell in your house, ever singing your praise!"

'Please now join in with the Lords Prayer.'

"Our father, who art in heaven, hallowed be thy Name, thy kingdom comes, thy will be done, on earth as it is in heaven. Give us this day our daily bread. And forgive us our trespasses, as we forgive those who trespass against us. And lead us not into temptation, but deliver us from evil. For thine is the kingdom, and the power, and the glory, forever and ever. Amen."

'We will now sing our second hymn chosen by Jill Spears who most of you know as Mrs Gillian White. It is called, "Blowin' In The Wind."

Everyone who can then stands.

"How many roads must a man walk down.

Before you call him a man?

How many seas must a white dove sail

Before she sleeps in the sand?..."

'Thank you; please be seated. Clive Verity will shortly say a few words. So, I am taking this opportunity to ask you, immediately after Clive returns to his seat, to please stand and we will sing our final hymn, Lord of the Dance, chosen on behalf of Valerie Verity.

While we do so, our three sisters will take a journey which will end later today with a scattering of their ashes at our nearby woodland Memorial Park. Once the procession exits our chapel, you are all welcome to make your way to our adjoining community hall. In there, will be ladies from the Women's Institute who have kindly prepared to serve refreshments.

'Clive,' says Julian who also gestures a cordial invite.

Instinctively, Clive springs to attention and strides forward. His pace is deliberate, slow and cumbersome. He faces everyone and is fighting against tears, determined to deliver his tribute.

'Words are not my thing, as many of you know well! Here and now, I'm glad for an opportunity to utter a few.

To Joanne, our princess. I, we love you and I am sorry.

To Jill, may you blow in the wind in peace, forever!

To my Val, when it is my time to leave this crazy world, I agree with you! We three will be eternally reunited. Until then I will miss you and never stop loving you both.'

With every eye in the chapel fixated on him, Clive removes an I-phone and a small amplifier from his right breast pocket. In deathly silence, Clive connects the two before placing them side by side on a grey stone floor. He presses play and their 'our' song, "Like a Virgin," begins. After Madonna's voice fades, we hear "Immortality" sung by Celine Dion & The Bee Gees and then "Angel" sung by Shaggy.

***

The last song tipped the balance for Lilly, and she's still crying now she and her mother enter the community hall. Lilly is clinging to Helen and privately wondering, I'm not sure if I want to go to the Memorial Park.

This emotional challenge is soon deflected a little by Janet Strumpshaw, 'Lilly, would you like a cherry bun and an orange juice?'

'Yes please,' Lilly murmurs barely audible.

Helen looks around. Clive is on the other side of the hall, and their eyes meet.

'You OK,' mimes Clive.

While Helen replies with a nod and each gives a resigned smile, both women who were offering their condolences to Clive twist to see whose caught his attention?

To the far right of Clive is one of quite a few dispersed groups of mourners engaged in conversation. From left to right are Finley, Sally, PP, Sir Roger and Bernice. Frank gave his apologies explaining, "A three-line whip to attend a work function in City Hall, I'm afraid!"

Clive excuses himself from the company of Rosa Thorpe and Lady Anne Ellen and heads toward the police team. Soon, he is within earshot, and Sir Roger is talking.

'You have done a remarkable job! A credit to the force and

yourselves. Well...'

'Excuse me, DI Parsons, may I join you for a brief moment?' asks Clive.

PP turns round, and his colleagues form a circle around him and Clive.

'Hello, Clive. Please call me Peter.'

'Peter, I want to offer my sincere condolences to you and your wife and given this recent loss, it is most generous of you to come.'

'Not at all. Thank you, and I will pass your sentiments onto Nicola.'

'Thank you too for making appropriate arrangements for one of the more distasteful challenges this funeral presented,' says Clive now very conscious PP's colleagues are openly listening. Clive then adds, 'To all of you, thank you for all your hard work and commitment.'

PP looks direct into Clive's tired eyes, 'I'm certain I speak for each colleague by saying you're more than welcome. Also, your bravery is commendable and an inspiration!'

'Here here,' Sir Roger says.

Clive shakes each officer's hand and then turns to see where I am so he can express his same thanks to me. He scans the room three times before he reminds himself. Of course, Mr Forrester said he would try and wear his legs today.

So, Clive scans as he had just a few seconds ago and spots me perched on the hall's stage talking with Sadie and Ripper. Also with me is Ripper's wife Zara, and two women Clive does not recognise and whose names are Sandra Ash and Samantha Mee.

***

Clive is with Julian in Colney chapel's tiny office. Julian is holding a larger than usual urn made from pure gold and designed for each of the three deceased to be scattered together.

The Government's Home Secretary funded the urn by law. Which is, the Judiciary Victim's Department advises the Home Secretary about what a next of kin's wishes are with regard to any special assistance required for arrangements of a funeral for someone deemed a victim of a crime recognised as premeditated murder!

Any such next of kin have a free choice whether to apply for such funding and it is means tested. Clive is a legitimate next of kin for each of today's victims following a judgement made by Crystal Frampton QC.

In a jacket pocket, Clive already has two gold locket's paid for by money raised in a collection Claudia instigated at police HQ in Wymondham. This total increased with a generous cheque from The British Legion. All the money donated voluntarily, goes into a specific time-limited official 'Residents of Britain' fund.

Julian believes he must say something along with handing Clive the urn. But for the first time, even after seeking God's help, he cannot find words. Clive takes joint hold of the urn and bursts into tears. Not like he did earlier today. Clive is crying bucket loads! He's struggling to breathe even and rests his head on his now crossed arms spread next to the jar on the table between them. Julian gently grips Clive's head.

'God have mercy on your soul Clive. Letting it out is good,' he says softly.

Clive sits up, snivels and wipes his eyes dry. 'Thank you, Julian, and to both, let's hope so eh!'

Clive then clutches his precious pot of gold.

'Shall we rejoin those waiting to go with you to Colney Wood Memorial Park?' asks Julian.

'Yes.'

Both men gather respective headgear and leave to take their seat in a large people mover driven by Luke.

To get to the Memorial Park necessitates travelling on the Watton Road until reaching a busy roundabout which also gives access to the even more hectic A47 which is known locally as Norfolk's M25.

Once again, Clive is genuinely humble and amazed at the number of people in unbroken lines on each side of both of these said roads. He also notices access is blocked onto the A11, the nearest Norfolk has to a motorway!

What Clive does not find out until tomorrow is, many lining every road within sight of him and their police escort have travelled from all over Britain to pay their respect. In fact, he also discovers some mourners came from other countries to arrive in Britain for just the same reason.

Luke is about to veer toward the large black wrought iron gates which signify entrance into Colney Wood Burial site. As Luke makes this manoeuvre, Clive silently expresses, 'I am so pleased the media do seem to be using any tool of their trade, none whatsoever!'

Julian steps out of the car and unlocks the gates. There is no-one else in the Memorial Park. The crowd concentrated outside the Park's entrance keep their promise to now lead the dissipation of what has become a human chain meandering every which direction across four square miles of the south-western border of Norwich.

Luke drives in behind Julian whose Clergy stole is flapping slightly in a gentle mid-evening breeze. Soon, in complete silence, everyone gathers near to Julian who then leads them further into the woods. Their destination is a site called Bluebell Rise, and it is here where Jill stated she wants the scattering of her ashes to take place when she made a "Pre-need" purchase five years ago.

***

'That was very moving Reverend Islington, thank you,' says Clive who then strides forward until he is centrally positioned between two tall trees which he could touch with each set of fingertips if he so desired to stretch each arm out. He removes the urn's lid and crouches to lay it amongst grass and wild bluebells. Slowly, Clive rises until he's holding the urn high above his head thus enabling sun rays to make it sparkle.

For what feels like an age for those watching and yet is only a matter of a few seconds later, with all the considerable power he can muster, Clive empties the urn akin to that of a fire-fighter throwing water out of a bucket in an attempt to dampen the top of a twenty-foot flame.

Everyone behind Clive joins him in looking up at an ash-cloud swirl and rain between the same two trees so temporarily blocking out a clear reddish-orange dusk sky.

***

Over the next half an hour, under Clive's wish, everyone else left except for Ripper. An hour later Sadie, Zara and I return. In less than five minutes we see Clive pushing his best mate toward us. Ripper is holding the urn between his chin and short leg.

Zara gets out from a rear passenger seat and assists Clive to help Ripper. Zara then sits in the middle of the back seat before Clive climbs in beside her. A police motorcyclist then closes the door before getting on his bike to complete his final escort duty of today. During the ensuing journey, there is no conversation in the car other than those heard on Radio Five Live.

Sadie pulls up in Woodland Mews and those who can give a wave to the police escort as he spins 180 degrees before accelerating away.

'Thank you for everything you've done for today and please keep in touch eh!' says Clive while Zara and Ripper begin to get out.

Sadie, who is helping Zara, says, 'You're most welcome.'

Clive opens his door, and I turn my head before saying, 'Clive, I hope you don't mind if I just mention something before you go?

'Go on.'

'Shortly you will receive an invitation from a Victim Support Liaison Officer offering you an opportunity to discuss some options, you may or may not want to take up? If you think Sadie and or I can be of any assistance after such a discussion, please do not hesitate to ask. Perhaps we could talk over a pint?'

'Thanks, Mr Forrester, I will if I need to,' replies Clive as he gets out with the urn wrapped tightly against his heart.

Sadie looks pleased to see what are more friends of Clive who travelled up from London outside his open front door. Sadie though, cannot prevent a micro waterfall of tears trickling down both sides of her face as Clive is comforted by a lifelong friend whose name is Shaz.

***

Toby and Louise are on a settee in the flat above Café 1885. They are watching a video made on, inevitably I suggest, a mobile phone belonging to a lawbreaker whose motive was probably cultured by financial or fifteen minutes of fame needs, tastes and desires? Their watching footage of a broadcast on a late night edition of BBC Look East.

Toby suddenly sits on the edge on hearing a reporter's sentence end "Milena Trunch is a bearer for her cousin Joanne Verity and Maxine Stewart is doing the same for her sister, Valerie Verity."

Toby says, "Stone a crows Louise, that is my Milena and her mother! Incred...'

'You sure Toby?' interjects Louise.

Toby starts pacing to and fro in front of Louise. Both of his hands comb through his hair in every direction, and he replies, 'Yes. No doubt at all! What the hell has been going on?'

CHAPTER FIFTEEN

14 February 2008

I have been up since 3 am. I'm watching a third and final recording of "MOTD" showing highlights of fixtures played on February 9 and 10. I glance at a clock and muse, Blimey, it's nearly 6. Today is going to be more eventful than I could ever imagine possible!

I slide onto an arm of a settee and do a brief 'bum in mid-air' leap onto a manual rider. I push until I reach my bedroom and take a peep. Sadie looks asleep.

'Sadie. Sorry sweetheart, we need to get up. A taxi booked for seven.'

Sadie lifts her head with her eyes pretty much still closed. 'Ten more minutes,' she declares as she grabs a sheet and covers herself tent style.

'Sure. I'll put the kettle on.'

I go to the kitchen and pick up a stick to press an on switch. Unaware Sadie has crept up behind me; she makes me jump by tickling both sides of my belly. 'That will teach you for disturbing my sleep,' Sadie says laughing. She then asks, 'Come on then; the big mystery day has arrived. Tell me where are we going?'

'What and ruin it being a surprise!'

'Will I like it?'

'No.'

'What do I need to wear?'

'We can go as we are if you like?'

'Ha-ha. OK. Smart? Casual? Not knowing means I have both in my lovely new Tripp suitcase. Proper bargain I'll let you know! Reduced from hundred and forty to thirty-two in Debenhams.'

'A real deal! You look great whatever you wear! Casual today and I can confirm we are away until Sunday evening.'

'Passport?'

'No. Pot of tea?'

***

Sadie is curled up asleep with her head resting on my lap. I have rarely been able to sleep in a car, and I smile on seeing a sign expressing, "Welcome To The Wye Valley. An Area Of Outstanding Natural Beauty!"

I ask the taxi driver, 'Fancy a bit of lunch Marcel before we reach Symonds Yat? On me. Feel sorry for you. You've got to do five hours back!'

'Thanks, Alex. Sounds a good idea. I'll pay for myself mind. It's part of the job. Thanks for the offer though.'

'Rubbish! That's exactly why you're not paying!'

***

'What a lovely pub. Food looked yummy. Was it as tasty as it looked Marcel?' asks Sadie.

'Yes. Very.'

'Thought so, pity Captain Spoilsport here insisted on rationing us to a drink only. Made me feel hungry too. Sadist, don't you think Marcel?'

'Yes, Sadie,' says Marcel as he starts to drive the final short leg of our journey by exiting the grounds of the fourteenth century built Kings Head.

'Want to know where we are going now?' I ask Sadie.

'Might help if I do, now we've reached Ross-on-Wye,' interjects Marcel.

Sadie quips, 'Nice one!'

'Postcode is H R 9 6 J L. When we are heading toward Goodrich, there will be a lane on the right with a sign for Symonds Yat East and Yat Rock. This lane is an unnamed road and not much further along will be a sign on the left saying, "Welcome to Forest View Guest House."

I then look at Sadie, 'Our home for the weekend and set in a landscape which is in my top three of the most beautiful places I've ever seen! Its location is in the heart of an area known as the Wye Gorge.'

***

'Marcel, it's OK to go straight through the front drive and bear right until we reach a small tarmacked area for parking. The owner thinks it will be easier for a rider.'

'Wow, what a lovely view of the river,' exclaims Sadie who then grabs hold of my head, turns it to face her and gives me a real smacker of a kiss. 'You're right, and it's like you, beautiful!' she says.

'Glad you like it.'

'I'll help you with the chair Alex,' says Marcel.

Sadie then gives me a brief hug with a peck on the cheek before exhibiting a magical smile and says, 'Well done. I'll take the power chair and luggage in.'

'No need,' I say, but Sadie is already out of the car.

I decide to wait until I'm out too, to explain why it is best to leave the power chair in a nearby parking space with our luggage on its seat?

***

Marcel is sat on a broad wicker hamper chest which itself rests against a big ancient Oak tree. He's sipping a cup of tea from one of five flasks Marcel's girlfriend made to help me prepare for today.

Marcel says, 'Right, need to head off and thanks for the tea. You certainly have a fantastic picnic on that table. So, both of you, enjoy!'

'Are you sure we can't tempt you to have any nibbles, Marcel?' asks Sadie.

'No problem Marcel. You're very welcome,' I add.

'Thanks, guys. Need to get home. Gemma will be up to her neck in it, what with three kids and now for a few days four dogs to keep an eye out. See you Sunday. Is between midday and one-pm to early Alex?'

'Not for me. You OK with that Sadie?'

'Sure. Sounds perfect.'

Marcel leaves, and immediately Sadie gets off her chair and walks behind me. She gently pushes my rider away from the table before then straddling across my lap. Followed by motioning her face toward mine. She says, 'Now for a proper kiss.'

***

'Is the owner OK with us doing this?' asks Sadie spreading jam on a home-made cheese scone.

'Yes. I checked it out when booking. I explained I had something special to announce. That I wanted to do so during a picnic with a person who is, if anything, more beautiful than this stunning square acre garden. Pleased to say it's worked out well.'

'Announce? Special? What is it?' asks Sadie's with eyes wide open they're threatening to pop out!

'All in good time. I'm not teasing. Please nudge my ipod a bit nearer to me?' I ask, desperate not to let my excitement get the better of me.

'Want me to attach the speaker too, Alex?'

'Yes please, Sadie.'

I choose a song written by Mike Batt called, "Nine Million Bicycles," and set it on repeat.

'There are a few clues to hear from this song first,' I say calmly.

'OK,' replies Sadie quietly and she listens. We both do.

"There are nine million bicycles in Beijing

That's a fact,

217

It's a thing we can't deny

Like the fact that I will love you till I die..."

Sadie wipes a tear from both her eyes. She says, 'For once I don't know what to...'

The sound of a text from my phone interrupts her.

Sadie reaches into my jacket pocket and places a phone on the table. I open the lid. 'Yep. It's arrived I think? It's from Sally.'

'It's OK Alex. I'm as keen as you to know, what is the jury's verdict?!'

I pick up a spoon again and say, 'Here goes.'

Sadie just cannot contain herself and rushes to peep from beside my shoulder.

We read, 'Hi Alex. I thought u were winding me up about not being in court today! So, as promised, I'm letting u know the outcome. I've just come outside. The atmosphere in the court is electric, and out here it's pandemonium. In court, Maxine Stewart fainted when the foreman of the jury announced their majority verdict. AV u said something suchlike, "Spit it out Sally," yet? LOL! White found guilty of premeditated murder. Life behind bars without parole. The first inmate in a JC D Wing in the country! Judge also announced, "Nature of crime meets criteria for a 'Loved one' of the victim to apply for a sentence to be considered to include a death penalty option." No privileges except reading books. Social isolation except for daily exercise in the central courtyard if prisoner requests this. Latter reviewed if prisoner admits his guilt. Great eh? No doubt on his way to the JC as we speak. What a result! We're all mtg up at the Fat Cat around 6. Hope u come! Which, reminds me! Where r u? Lol.'

'Holy shit,' says Sadie who then puts an arm around me and says, 'I think deep down I thought White's character assassination of Maxine Stewart would cause the jury to be undecided, making the outcome at least a retrial.'

I don't look up or say anything. I type,' Wow. Thanks 4 message Sally. Sounds ur having quite a day 2. Sorry, 2 say I can't make tonight. I'm with Sadie in Gloucestershire. Well done. U always said White did both! Enjoy the pub. Will see you on Monday.'

'What do you mean by both Alex?' Sadie asks while she sits down beside me on a quest aluminium folding chair.

I switch off my phone.

'Truth is Sadie, I'm permitted to say we, as in the police, are more than suspicious White and Hawker are responsible for what happened to Joanne Verity. Did you hear the official status of this investigation announced by the Chief Constable on the telly?

'Yes,' replies Sadie.

'So, answering your question, Sally was consistent in her belief White murdered his wife and Joanne too. She had a bet with DI Parsons who thought Clive Verity and White would be the respective killers. I was congratulating her for winning.'

Sadie turns the ipod off and sits on my lap again. She hugs me gently, and with her lips practically kissing my left ear she whispers, 'Where was your money speculating? And what's in the box with pink ribbons around it?'

'Murders first?'

'Yes.'

My heart is thumping just a bit too fast for my health, yet, somehow I am can appear all together as I begin my reply. 'I opted out of the bet because I knew Harold White would become **the** suspect. Half the betting pool was a donation to the National 'For support to Victims' of Crimes charity.' So, I got ribbed for betting on Luke Stewart being the culprit of both crimes.'

Sadie leans backwards. Perplexed and not quite sure she heard correctly, she asks, 'Alex? Did you say you knew? What do you mean?'

'Before answering I must say if you consider what you are about to hear is unacceptable that while losing you and us will be heartbreaking. If we are to continue sharing our lives with one another, you have to know my truth!'

'You're scaring me now Alex.'

'I'm sorry. That's the last thing I would knowingly do.'

'OK. I trust you so I'll listen.'

'Thanks. How best to start? In a bag under the table is a tape recorder with a cassette in it. Would you please lift it onto the table for me, Sadie?'

'Sure,' replies Sadie who then asks, 'Do you want me to press play.'

'Not quite yet, please. I cannot assume your response to what I'm about to reveal. It is for this reason I want to express two heartfelt, albeit conflicting sentiments before I do. I brought you here to show you my new, if you like, get away from it all home is how I currently see it!

One of two items in the box is a twin set of keys to Forest View guest house. It has not been lived in since a dear Auntie died over a year ago. In Auntie Rochelle's Will, there was confirmation what she'd told me years ago; Forest view is mine.

Auntie Rochelle also decreed Forest View will cease trading as a B and B upon her death. In effect, those that worked here lost their livelihoods. Unsurprisingly to me, Auntie Rochelle ensured each employee received a generous redundancy package which consisted of a lump sum at least equivalent to three years wages.

'Blimey. I mean that's amazing. Very sweet and generous. Sounds a nice lady and that you were fond of her,' interjects Sadie.

'Yes I was, still am!'

Sadie says, 'Alex, are you asking for us to live together, here?'

Sadie stretches and waves her arms in every which direction.

'Yes and no. What I mean is, continue living and working in Norfolk and do whatever **we** choose with Forest View. Move into my bungalow in Norwich and shortly make us joint owners of Forest View. As the saying goes, "What we make of it is then down to us!"

Sadie is shredding a tear or two, laughing and smiling all at the same time. She says, 'Holy swept. Yes, I think. I mean, yes. I'd love us too.'

Beaming I say, "Fan – Bloody – Tastic!'

Sadie puts a hand on each side of my face and moves forward until our lips touch to share a belonging and passionate kiss.

***

'Didn't you say something about a conflicting sentiment too,' asks Sadie.

I wish I were in a dream I could wake up from, but I reply, 'Yes. Shortly I will play the tape. Please try not to say anything until it ends. My conflict is I want you to truly believe I fully understand I accept you might choose to end us. If this is what happens, I will never think badly of you, and I have no doubt I will always be in love with you!'

'I'm...'

'Please Sadie. When you're ready?'

'OK. Sorry. I'm ready.'

I pick up a knife and press play.

"Why do you want today's conversation recorded Jill? I only do this when interviewing you for MAPPA reports because it's more practical than scribbling notes.'

'Good point Mr Forrester. For the benefit of the tape, today is fourth July two thousand and seven. In my hand is today's Daily Express Newspaper and the headline on the front page is "FIND THE DOCTORS OF DEATH."

My full name is Gillian Joy White. My maiden name was Spears. I was born on thirteenth July nineteen forty-six, and I am one hundred percent of sound mind!

Previously, I have only met with Mr Forrester on a purely professional basis as required by law and specifically by way of his role as a member of MAPPA. Other meetings also occurred during two police investigations into crimes alleged to be committed by my husband, Harold White. Today's meeting is taking place at my request in a small staff room at the day-centre I attend. It is ten-thirty-am.

I will now answer your question succinctly, Mr Forrester. In the future, you may want a record of today's conversation to assist you. In fact, if ever it is necessary to achieve this, with all my heart I want it to succeed!'

'Wow. I'm intrigued, to say the least!'

'It is tricky to know how to start. Please bear with me. Do you recognise the person in this photo?'

Silence.

'Yes, I think I do? Why would you have a photograph of this person? Do you...'

'What is the person's name please, Mr Forrester?'

'Valerie Verity.'

'Now read what is on the back of the photo?'

Silence.

'I think I'm getting it? It's not Valerie; it's you! Date reads thirtieth July nineteen sixty-six. In colour too. Incredible! I ...'

'Yes, it is me, Mr Forrester. It shows how much my health, and age a little I guess, has affected my appearance somewhat, eh? Don't answer!'

'But why...'

'I am Valerie Verity's birth mother and therefore am Joanne...'

'What? When did...? How long have...?'

'Sorry to interrupt you, Mr Forrester. Can I please propose for my confiding in you to have a purpose, please let me explain my story first? Then I will discuss, answer questions and negotiate what action if any, you and or I will take. Deal?'

'Yes. OK. Sensible. Deal.'

'Thank you. To my shame Mr Forrester, I gave my daughter and only child up for adoption. I named Valerie, Perla. Harold is not her father, and she was born in Scotland. To this day, Harold does not know about my having a child at all!'

'What? How...'

'It's OK. I understand you will react. Nevertheless, please may I explain my story first?'

'Sure. Sorry.'

'I have chosen to tell you because I like and trust you. And, therefore will at least give due consideration which is, in truth, all I can expect to ask! Even if the outcome means subsequent choices, you make foil my wishes and feelings.

'Thank you. I can choose to leave now. I don't want to though.'

'Good. My second bombshell is my husband is responsible for murdering Joanne Verity. 'As you know...'

'Hold...'

'Please Mr...'

'OK. Sorry.'

'As you know I have cancer. And, advised a year or so ago I have two years tops, to live. The truth is, for a few weeks now, most days are difficult, so I now think my curtain has begun to come down on me. I don't have much time left. I messed up for Valerie when alive, so I'm determined to do right for her daughter through my death.

Mr Forrester, a friend, someone I've known for many years and I can honestly say, I trust with my life, told me something recently which led me to decide it is now the right time to start implementing my plan. Hence I will be sending a letter addressed to your Chief Constable. I have it with me. Look, all signed, sealed and ready to deliver into a red pillar-box.

It is this same friend who sowed a seed, as it were, for the formulation of my plan. Though, I prefer to call it my wish! But, my friend is not responsible for the idea it now includes causing my death and, as you would expect from a true friend, did all that is acceptable to persuade me to alter it. But, being a true friend has also acknowledged it is my choice to make!'

Silence.

'Talking with you now is placing one of a few cogs I need in my wheel to continue going in the right direction! Another reason for why now, is the bonus of the Justice Act enforced three days ago!

Oh and yes, should I forget to mention later, my said friend does not know I'm meeting you. I figured you have the right to give your consent or not, to me informing him or her?

It is correct to acknowledge without help from my said friend my wish could not happen. Soon I hope the world will discover my husband murders me. In short, Mr Forrester, I want my death to look like murder when in fact it will be 'Assisted Suicide.'

'Look, may...'

'Therefore, I intend to frame Harold for a murder he would not have done because of another he has done! Believe me, Mr Forrester, Harold murdered my granddaughter, Joanne Verity!'

Silence.

'I'll see if I can get some tissues.'

'Thank you, Mr Forrester. No need to look for some. Have one up my sleeve.'

'If you don't mind me saying Jill, you certainly do!'

Silence.

'Is that a smile? Jill, are you OK?'

'It's a lot to take in isn't it?'

'Understatement of the... I've ever heard actually!'

'I am confident my wish will result in the police charging Harold and the CPS prosecuting him. I cannot be sure what each member of any jury, not to mention the Judge will decide but I rate my chance of success very high!

'Obviously, you also want to know why I am so confident of my blood tie with Valerie and Joanne. But first Mr Forrester, I will share why Harold is guilty of murdering Joanne. For both it is my goal to be as sure as it is possible to be, you reach decisions about how you respond in the knowledge you understand why they are true?

You might remember I attend this day-centre alternate Mondays as well as every Wednesday. When Bethany arrived to bring me here on what was Monday twenty-second January this year, I explained I was not feeling well.

I enjoy my time here, Mr Forrester. I feel alive when here and in good company! Reminds me of a favourite café I used to visit regularly, usually on a Tuesday afternoon. There is a clue to other reasons why in the name. It's called The Sanctuary Café!

So, as you can now probably gather, I must have been unwell to cancel my visit! As you also know, I sleep downstairs, and after I shut the door, I went to bed with only my coat and scarf took off.

I woke around one-pm and could hear Harold talking to another man. Sorry, never even seen him, let alone know his name? They were in the living room which is on the opposite side of our hallway. From my unwitting eavesdropping, I figured they were having a bit of lunch. Their subsequent conversation meant it became obvious Harold had no idea I didn't go onto the mini-bus.

Seldom does Harold change his morning routine? He gets up and comes downstairs between five and six. Then after making breakfast for us, he went upstairs till lunchtime. Every Sunday is the exception as on these mornings Harold always attends to his beloved samurai swords!

Silence.

'Jill...'

'No. I have to finish Mr Forrester. You see, Harold's friend then said something which sent shivers down my spine! He said, "My hands might be clumsy, but least they haven't murdered anyone, eh Harold! Also, bit rich being moaned at by the fool clumsy enough to strangle our Fêted Angel! Far too early!"'

'Oh no...'

Jill re-interjects, 'Harold went ballistic verbally! I was

terrified and convinced he would march into every room in the house. Thankfully, instead, he ushered his friend out the front door and after the most extended ten minutes imaginable I heard Harold go back upstairs.

As far as he knew, when I opened and shut our front door around four o'clock and shouted "Hello," I was returning from a day at this centre. Having to wait till then meant for at least two hours I laid in bed with wet clothes.'

'This is awful Jill...'

'I can't disagree with that! I have no doubt we will discuss the many What about, Ifs and Buts later? For me, **the** issue is, they did the horrendous crime! You know as well as I do any investigation stemming from a 'She said, He said' statement from **me:** will not prove their guilt in a court of law! And, that's assuming the improbable 'IF' of the CPS agreeing to prosecute in the first place!

In fact, I strongly advise, the opposite will happen! Confronting them will make them more guarded, and I think we can agree, given the police have no lead in three years, the two poor excuses for a human being have already demonstrated how brilliant they are at covering their tracks! Would you like another coffee, Mr Forrester?'

'No thanks. Do you Jill?'

'No. Probably will before the question and answer session begins.'

'Sure.'

'What would happen if I had chosen to tell you about Harold's chat with his friend without mentioning my wish? I'm sure we can agree you would update whoever is in charge of investigating Joanne's, disappearance, is still, as we sit here right now, it's official status isn't it?'

'Yes, it is Jill.'

Silence.

'And, this detective through no fault of their own will, I stress again, achieve, pardon my French, sweet FA concerning to justice!'

Silence.

'Therefore, in the context of this same scenario, if you **do let me** fulfil my wish and later on there is a need to question murder over assisted suicide? Then, logically this would lead to an endeavour which tries to unearth the identity of the person assisting me! I'm convinced if anyone can do this successfully, it will probably be you, Mr Forrester!'

Silence.

'I would like to remind you where I, and Harold, were on the day Joanne was reported missing. I was seriously ill in hospital and admitted three days earlier. From this moment I was in and out of consciousness so many times over the next few months, even my consultant lost count.

For the first two weeks, Harold never left my side except for having to go home on the first Monday after Joanne disappeared. As you know, so that the police could search our home and no doubt question Harold. A perfectly reasonable action for the police to take, given the nature of Harold's convictions. And of course, to us living so nearby to the Verity family home.

The outcome of this line of inquiry was the same as every other lead, resulting in still not having any concrete idea of Joanne's whereabouts at all! I predict by now every fish and chip shop in the country are using sheets of paper that don't have reports about Joanne as yesterday's news!

It took eighteen months before I came home from the hospital via nearly a year in a rehabilitation unit near Wisbech. From the time of my return until what happened on January twenty-second, I took an interest about Joanne in a manner mostly; I think it's reasonable to suggest, like millions of people did and hopefully still do when there are scarce newsworthy reports related to the police completing their search for Joanne.

I say for the most part because, I admit, I was also relieved to know it was impossible for Harold to have attended the fête. Equally, to hear the outcome of a thorough search of our home and questioning of Harold was, and to quote the then lead investigator, who told me, "We are pretty sure your husband isn't involved."

Therefore, since I've heard the awful truth straight from the horse's mouth nearly, my brain and body have struggled to keep up with many emotions and thoughts. Not least, what do I do with their revelation?

I spent the first month or so reading and watching yesterday's news. There are very few pictures of either Joanne's father or Valerie. There was one photograph which fleetingly drew my attention, but it was a chance meeting on March six when everything changed!

'I met, well to be truthful, met is not the right word. I saw Valerie in the waiting room of what is our mutual GP Surgery. Honestly, after only seconds, did I start taking in my thought of, 'Wow, I used to look like you! Crazy, I know, and of course, muddled up with my excitement were all the natural emotions of telling yourself, 'Can't be? Surely not?'

I deliberately positioned myself beside Valerie and prompted polite conversation. You're an intelligent person, and I confidently predict you don't think I then did like you'd find in a Hollywood, tear jerker! You know, the mother sees long lost daughter in the waiting room reading a Norfolk Life magazine and says, "Hi, I've got a photo of me which I'm pretty sure tells me you are my daughter! Whom, as soon as you were born, I gave away to be adopted. Adopted by, "A very respectable couple who live in Norfolk." I didn't mean too, sorry, fancy coming round for a get to know one another chat with a bite to eat?" Am I right?'

Silence.

'Instead, after five minutes or so Valerie's **full** name was called out followed by, 'You can't do that in here! To which Valerie said, 'Think they're talking to me. Better go. Nice to chat with you. Take care, Bye.'

Valerie then stood up and left. "Bye, I said."

I then looked at the empty chair in which Valerie **Verity** had sat! Still digesting the identity of the 'stranger' in the midst, as it were, I was also replaying how Valerie told me she just walked in requesting some help with a wound on her forearm. How she'd accidentally cut herself when trying to make a sandwich. She then openly said with a chuckle, "My fault, pissed as a fart."

In this bag, Mr Forrester is a glove. As you see, it has blood on it, and I've kept in a forensic friendly state. I have never handled Valerie's glove without wearing a pair of my own. For fear of contamination, naturally!

Whilst we had chatted, my beautiful sad-eyed daughter took a glove off her left hand so she could light up a cigarette. Tells you how drunk Valerie was eh! She was reprimanded but sweetly accepted this. Best jump the queue trick I think I've seen!

I stared at the glove she'd left behind for what were seconds but seemed like a lifetime to me. I grabbed the glove and went without keeping my appointment.

I am going to give you this bag which has a couple of other useful bits of a source to gain evidence. Evidence which I am certain will prove Valerie is my Perla! I will put this photo in here too as both evidence and a personal keepsake from me to you.'

'I think...'

'I have nearly finished Mr Forrester. Thank you for your patience. I am perfectly aware of the selfish components of my disclosers to you, here today. You must believe me when I say, should you decide to prevent my wish from happening, I will respect, though not agree with your decision. Be sure to believe I also recognise the dilemmas you face, your integrity as a professional law enforcing officer and not forgetting, of course, the risks you take should you agree to remain silent?

It is why I convey with genuine warmth, please try and forgive me. As the saying goes, you only live once, so given my health, I'm going for a jackpot!

You see, a significant reason for choosing to tell you is, I hope one day you are able to let Valerie, maybe Clive too, listen to our recording of this conversation.

I'm not going to reveal details of how I will die or exactly when? I think this means you may be more natural in responding, should you remain silent? And, more importantly, I will also not reveal the identity of my said friend thus taking this with me when I start my journey into what's beyond life on our blue planet? Also, be in no doubt we have put in place a robust protection plan should such a need be required?

Lastly, never underestimate how hard it is to live so close to Valerie having made a decision never to try reunification. It is the world not knowing our connection which is so vital for my wish to come true!

But, there is a paradox which has given me a small crumb in my cake, as it were. My cousin Maggie and her husband who was a GP and arranged Valerie's adoption assured me her adoptive family lived in Norfolk. The decision to return to my marriage made it **convenient** to live in this county too. My wish then was finding each other. Well as you've just heard, at least this has happened of sorts.

I will put the recording of our conversation in this bag for you too when we've finished."

I stop the tape and Sadie's still holding my hand and says, 'Oh my god Alex. That's not the end though is it?'

'No. For now, arguably forever, you don't need to hear the rest to understand what has happened.'

'I think Jill was remarkable and I get what she did. Do you have any idea who is the friend she spoke about, Alex?'

'I would be lying if I said I hadn't given any thought to that. Later on the tape you can hear me comment, advise, and 'counsel' Mrs White. Call it, whatever you want? To sum up, I expressed my concern that for anyone, it is, a big ask and failed to persuade Jill the alternative could bring justice!'

'Sure. I get that too. I know the truth so might as well tell me who, eh Alex?'

"OK. But Sadie, it is only a thought which I hope you are the first and last person I will need to discuss it with.'

'Go on, Alex,' says Sadie.

'Do you remember from that never to be forgotten all night-er we met at, a mentioning of a Mr and Mrs Hartman each making a statement saying it is Leon Hartman who recognised Milena Trunch as the 'girl' with Valerie when Harold was 'Peeping Tom' again?'

'Vaguely, I think.'

'The 'Peeping Tom' activity is also what Jill referred to in her letter to the Chief Constable.'

Yep, remember now,' comments Sadie.

'And, how the Hartman's explained their sixteen-year old daughter was a pupil at St. Clotho school and used to be good friends with Milena?'

'Yes,' replies Sadie.

'Well, it is my understanding Patricia Hartman, and Jill were friends for over twenty years or so. That's all. I have no intention to delve any further! Admittedly, a lot less so, I've also considered Jill's long-time District Nurse, Samantha Mee.'

Sadie says, 'Could be I suppose, fits, doesn't it! Well both do, I guess.'

I reply, 'Sadie, I've already stressed I don't know who? Do I!'

'No. Sorry. One more question. Did you consent to Jill telling her friend about talking to you?'

'I advised Jill, that is her call. I explained her friend knowing or not, would not make a difference to my consideration of how I would respond? Jill agreed she would let me know if she did and similarly I promised to give her notice should I choose to foil her wish! Sad to say our conversation on the tape is the last one we had!'

Sadie squeezes me tight, albeit tenderly, and I whisper, 'Have I lost you?'

'Never, no! Never!'

We listen to the silence and then from a distance hear the voice of one of two men in a canoe paddling against the flow of the river. Sadie then rubs her nose against mine and says,

'Besides, I haven't found out what else you've got me in that pretty box yet.'

'It's got a bit chilly. Would you prefer to move inside?' I ask.

'No thanks. It's lovely out here. I will go and get my coat though. Are you OK with just your jacket, Alex?'

'Fine thanks. I'll light us both a cigarette. God knows I need one!'

***

Sadie says, 'Phew! Shall I open another bottle of wine? Is a bottle of Sangria this time OK, please?'

'Yes, great! You'll be relieved to hear the second preamble is somewhat lighter.'

'Can't lie. That sounds good,' says Sadie as she grabs a bottle from the blue cooler box under our camper style dining table.

I begin, 'From aged anywhere between eight to eleven, I've had a recurring dream. It is impossible to say how many times, and it has been infrequent. I remember when I was around eighteen and at college, I described this dream in a short story I wrote for an A' level assignment.

The dream begins with me sitting alone in a fishing boat similar to that of an Orkney Long-liner.'

Sadie scoffs a laugh, 'It's the thought of you with a fisherman's hat on.'

'I know. I'd look ridiculous, wouldn't I! Anyway, in my dream, the boat drifts and steers itself forward toward at what I first think is a footbridge. The clouds are black and spawning out the torrential rain. At the same time, a gale force wind is swiping painfully into my face. Remarkably, despite this combination, the boat remains calm and illogically on a straight course?

It is only when underneath the footbridge I realise I have sailed into total darkness. In the distance, I can see a tiny ray of light, so I figure I'm taking a journey in a long tunnel.

I have no idea how long the tunnel is, and in the dream, it feels like the journey is incomprehensibly quick? I feel relief and surprise as I leave the tunnel because although I can still hear the horrendous strength of the weather behind me, miraculously I am soaked in warmth from burning hot sun and I look up into a cloudless sky.

I countenance all around me and on each bank of the river I see an array of trees and wildflowers in full bloom. The trees encroach over the shimmering river and by doing so create an arch above me. I note the path of the stream ahead swerves right and it is as the boat begins to make this turn I always wake up. Every time I do, I try to make sense of it? Please now look behind you and tell me what you can see?'

Sadie, surprised by the sudden ending does as I ask. After a few seconds she answers, 'I see a narrow part of the river, and it has pretty flowers and trees on both sides. The trees hang over from both bank edges and meet in the middle to form an arch. I can see through the arch and note the river changes direction by flowing to the left.'

Sadie turns to face me again, and I say, 'Sadie, you are the meaning, and destiny of my dream!'

Sadie is blushing and says, 'I love you, Alex!'

'I love you too! You can open the box now.'

Excited, Sadie places both hands on the lid. 'You sure?' she asks.

'Rarely been as certain about anything in my whole life,' I reply.

Sadie carefully unties the pink ribbons and then slowly lifts the lid. Inside the box, Sadie sees a set of keys on top of another smaller box. Attached to the keys is a label tag made of leather. Scripted on it is, "Forest View Guest House." Sadie lifts the keys and lays them on the picnic table and says, 'Thank you, though we need to talk a bit more about this later.'

I smile and mime, 'OK.'

Sadie lifts the smaller box at the same time as placing the bigger one on the grass beside her. So thereby, resting this second box on her lap. Sadie opens it and sees the third box, but this looks very different. It is a light pink heart-shaped Pandora Valentine's jewellery box. It is complete with the brand, "PANDORA – Unforgettable Moments" on its top surface. Attached to it is a small heart key ring which is part of a the zip that opens the box.

Sadie begins to unzip and soon sees a Pandora two-tone charm bracelet. Carefully picking it up, Sadie exclaims, 'Holy mackerel, thank you so much, Alex. It is lovely!'

Sadie then tries it on. Beaming, she says, 'Fits perfect. So, this is the reason why you were interested to know the difference in centre meters between the thickness of our arms and hands. Cool, you bugger.'

'You really like it then Sadie?' I ask.

Sadie replies, 'I love it,' and we share a thank you kiss.

Sadie then sits back down and while taking a closer look at her present observes out loud, 'Oh, there is already a charm on here. Did it come with this included,' she asks.

I reply, 'No. It is a love and guidance pendent given to me when I left school. Not a childhood sweetheart though, promise.'

'I'm intrigued. Who was she, assuming it was a she?' Sadie asks.

'Yes it was, her name was Miss Spires. Miss Spires was the first person and member of staff to meet me with my parents when they handed me into the care of Chailey Heritage. The residential home and school I told you I lived in from aged three months to when I left sixteen years later.'

'Wow. Why do you think she gave you this. Not that she shouldn't have, it's just...'

I interrupt,' It's OK Sadie, I understand what you mean. Ultimately, only Miss Spires, who sadly passed away quite a while ago, can answer your question with accuracy assured. All I can suggest is, even in so-called normal family life, there are many parents, aunts, uncles, grandparents etc. etc. who, while they would be hard pushed to admit it, have favourite offspring, descendants or siblings.

The only other possible clues I can offer are, I was once asked as part of a group exercise on a work-related training course to identify the person who had the most influence on my childhood upbringing? Most replied mum, dad, or both as they couldn't split them. Everyone present though did give a blood relative. Except for me, that is.

I replied Miss Spires, and Jill was her Christian name. I did so because by then, well before then, I understood Jill was the first person I felt loved me for who I was: no matter what labels were put on me. I am far from unique because everyone is! However, not many children who lived in the home, percentage-wise, were a baby bundle placed in your arms the first time you met them!

There is also a third fact which I understand can be interpreted different ways, including her feelings for me, did not have anything to do with Miss Spires never having a child of her own.'

Sadie holds my hand, kisses me and then says, 'I didn't think I would like receiving this any more than I just did. I was wrong. Thank you, Alex. From my heart!'

'You're most welcome. It's nice to see it shown off again,' I reply.

I then add, 'Miss Spires took the pendant from a chain around her neck. She did so during the moments we said goodbye on my last day at school. If I had known then what I now know about life, I would have asked Miss Spires, how did she come to wear it? I'm no expert, but it seems old to me.'

Sadie smiles and replaces the Valentine jewellery box into the box on the ground.

***

Earlier this evening Sadie said, "When I was putting all the boxes together again, in my mind's eye was the picture of Joanne's smile on a 'Missing Person' poster eclipsing that of a trapped White. Who would care Alex? I don't, and I'm far from being alone, don't you think?"

***

I am getting ready for bed and Sadie bursts into the bathroom holding a Ross Gazette newspaper and shrieks frenetically, 'Oh my god, you fool!!! I've just read about all crimes you can get the treatment White got handed in court today!'

I am on the toilet and I fear the worse outcome again! Still, I reason to myself, was going to bring the subject up tomorrow anyway. Best time as any.

I watch Sadie open to page two with her lips quivering as she speaks, 'It says here, the last one on the list. It states, never mind what it.'

Sadie suddenly stops. Her stare is piercing my eyes looking at hers, and it is heartbreaking. Sadie then asks, 'What if Clive chooses...?'

The remainder of our conversation is long and emotional for both of us!

CHAPTER SIXTEEN

Still February 14, 2008

Oliver Stubs *alias* Robert Hardeen steps into an open-air restaurant connected to his favourite hotel in Serrekunda, Gambia. He heads to a corner at a familiar table for two. Like every night, since he arrived on February 5, 2008, Hardeen is waiting to eat alone.

The cheeks of Hardeen's bottom are still getting comfortable against the hardness of the wooden seat when the chief waiter signals Sunlit to attend Mr Robert.

'What would you like to drink Mr Robert, please?' asks Sunlit softly.

'A Bloody Mary please,' replies Hardeen while looking into Sunlit's beautiful black eyes.

'I know how Mr Robert likes it, yes?'

'You most definitely do Sunlit. How is your family?'

'They are all well thank you, Mr Robert. Mr Robert like something else? To eat?'

'A salad and fruit platter please Sunlit. I need to be fit.'

'Fit? Mr Robert help me understand please.'

'Something you are Sunlit,' replies Hardeen whose eyes are admiring Sunlit's pert bosoms cradled in a waitress uniform.

Sunlit replies, 'Sorry please, I don't understand.'

Worried her bosses may be watching; Sunlit hastily adds, 'I go now and get your order, Mr Robert. Thank you.'

Hardeen smiles and hands Sunlit the menu. He watches her almost trotting toward the restaurant's bar.

Sunlit is sixteen years old and the eldest child of seven. Therefore, she has a big responsibility to help provide for the family, along with her widowed mother. In contrast, Sunlit is the hotel's youngest employee and has been ever since Hardeen first visited three years ago. All the staff at the hotel use the nickname Jesus when talking amongst themselves about Mr

Robert.

With Sunlit out of his sight, Hardeen uses a hand to brush some thick black hair off his bearded cheeks. He then glances at people sitting at other dining tables in the restaurant. Each guest is silhouetted by the onset of dusk as it gathers pace. Thus soon, there will be a clear star littered black sky.

Hardeen is nearly halfway to completing his scan when he unexpectedly stops. A striking woman whom he's never seen before is sitting at a table at the other end of the restaurant.

Rosa Thorpe arrived on holiday in the early hours of today, and she is staying at the hotel for three weeks. Rosa is presently lamenting, How marvellous to return! Away at last from the stress in England.

Hardeen's scrutiny of Rosa intensifies as he muses, It's been a long time since I've enjoyed sex with a white gi..., well actually, a woman even longer! You look pretty, slim, classy, refined and a challenge that should be fun.

Rosa senses she is countenanced and once again lifts her eyes to peer over the top of a menu board held in her left hand. What a handsome man is her first observation. A mixture of Kris Kristofferson and in that suit John Travolta.

The inevitable then happens. The two stranger's eyes lock, and Hardeen smiles. He then gestures an invite to Rosa offering the empty seat opposite him.

Initially, Rosa's body language indicates she will decline the kind, generous, intriguing and welcoming offer, but curiosity wins. She leans to pick up her favourite handbag off a concrete paved floor.

Rosa then places the bag across her bare knees and puts her cigarettes and lighter back into it. She stands and puts the strap of her bag over her right shoulder. With her left hand, she pulls down both sides of her purple fluted sleeve lace skater dress. Now composed, Rosa starts walking toward Hardeen's table.

What a body, Hardeen is thinking, and he stands in preparation to greet his guest.

Rosa reaches the table, 'May I?'

'Yes. Of course.'

They shake hands, 'Hello my name is Rosalind, Rosa to friends.'

'Hello Rosa, I'm Robert. Robert Hardeen.'

Pleased to meet you, Robert.'

Hardeen swiftly moves to pull a chair out from under the table.

'Thank you for inviting me Robert,' says Rosa turning her head to smile at Hardeen as she takes her place at the table.

'An absolute pleasure,' responds Hardeen as he retakes his seat opposite Rosa. He then asks, 'Are you holidaying alone or on a business trip, perhaps?'

'Without question a holiday Robert. I arrived this afternoon for a guaranteed three blissful weeks. So...'

'Sounds like to me, you've been before then. Sorry for interrupting.'

'That's OK. Yes, five years ago with my husband. We treated ourselves to a second honeymoon to celebrate our twentieth wedding anniversary. Sadly, William died nearly seven months later. He had been poorly for quite a while so anticipated. We came in February because our anniversary is on the 19th. We renewed our vows in a ceremony just over there actually.'

Rosa points to a gap between an outside bar and a block of luxury holiday lets.

Hardeen looks too, and both admire a brightly lit orange sky symbolising the sun has just set, and he hears Rosa add, 'Just us, a local Catholic priest and two witnesses on the beach. We then hosted a cocktail party right here for everyone staying and working in this wonderful hotel. I promised William I would come back here for our twenty-fifth and I'm so glad I have. Such precious memories for us here.'

'I'm sorry about your husband; it must be very hard, especially with him being, and you looking, so young.'

'Flattery will get you everywhere,' replies Rosa with a facial expression hinting at thanks for the compliment and also bit too smooth.

'Excuse me, Mr Robert. Here is Bloody Mary Mr Robert please,' interrupts Sunlit who then moves the glass from a tray onto the table.

Thank you, Sunlit. What is your poison, Rosa? On me,' says Hardeen.

'A large glass of Hotel California's best Red wine please Sunlit.'

'Yes, Madam. I get for you now.'

Rosa rests her elbows on the table with her hands clasped, 'William was forty-five when he died and I am now forty-five. We have one daughter whose name is Kristina, and she gets married in July this year on her father's birthday. Which is very sweet, don't you think?'

'I do. Yes,' agrees Hardeen before asking, 'Are your daughter and son-in-law to be, here on holiday with you?'

Rosa chuckles, Kristina has long passed the time an enjoyable holiday necessitates being with her mother. No, I'm entirely alone. What about you Robert? Are you on holiday? What is your story?

Saved by the bell seems apt because before Hardeen starts a reply, Sunlit says, 'Red wine for you madam. Thank you.'

'Wonderful,' says Rosa helping herself.

'Yes Madam,' says Sunlit who turns to leave.

Hardeen then asks, 'Sunlit, please cancel my salad and I will let you know when we'd like to order some food please.'

'Yes Mr Robert,' replies Sunlit walking away and thinking a chance to earn a bit extra tonight is not possible.

'So, are you on holiday Robert?'

'Yes, Came here in two thousand and six for the first time and enjoyed it so much, I now make it an annual treat.'

'Where do you live in Britain?' asks Rosa.

Hardeen smiles, 'I haven't lived there for a long time. I was aged six when my parents left Sleaford, and we emigrated to Canada. I now live in Vietnam and have done so for fifteen years.'

'How interesting,' says Rosa sincerely before commenting, 'I'm from Norfolk, so my roots are not too far from your own. Why Vietnam?'

'My wife was from Vietnam, and we met when we were students at the University of British Columbia,' replies Hardeen matter of factly.

'I've visited Vancouver, a gem of a city to live, in my view! Oh, do excuse me, Robert, did you say was?' asks Rosa hesitantly.

'Yes. My wife was only twenty-seven when she died.'

'Oh, how awful! ERM... How tragic and so young too. What happened? No, sorry, Robert. If you'd rather not talk about it, I'd understand.'

'Thank you, Rosa. But it's OK. And after all, you have been open about your sadness. I also feel comfortable enough to be equally candid,' replies Hardeen while retrieving a cigarette from a packet in his shirt breast pocket.

Hardeen then says, 'I note you smoke Rosa. Would you like to try one of Gambia's finest? I think they're a lovely cigarette.'

Well, given such a glowing recommendation, yes I will, thank you, Robert.'

Hardeen assists with the lighting up and continues his story with Rosa. Who, through no fault of her own is oblivious to a fact that she is looking into as the title of a song by that great band The Eagles declares, "Lyin Eyes!" With the addition, they also belong to a 'Viet-con' of sorts!

'Qu 'y and I were enjoying a weekend exploring beautiful Mangrove swamps on a small boat. For lunch, on a Saturday we moored against a bank edge and sat on land to dine with our two male tour guides. We'd not long finished eating when one of our guides started to clear the plates away. With no warning at all, he then held a gun to my head. His partner in crime grabbed my wife and dragged her about two hundred yards. I could not see Qu 'y, but I could hear everything as the bastard, well you know.

I don't know how long I listened, yet it felt hours. All of Qu'y's screams and cries for help gradually lessened in frequency until the two men swapped places. More screams and shouts until this time silence.

Then suddenly, with the gun still stamping my scalp I was ordered to the spot where Qu 'y lay de..., perhaps I should stop,' suggests Hardeen, sensing Rosa's understandable display of shock of horror.

'Thank you, and I am sorry. Awful feels such an inadequate word to use. But, if you're OK to continue I would like to hear.'

Hardeen stubs out his cigarette with a hand that is shaking before saying, 'Naturally I was convinced I would then get killed too. But to my amazement, they robbed us of everything we had and spat on me before leaving on their boat laughing. We were, literally cast aside.

I learnt in a hard way the desire in Vietnam, to solve this type of crime is not pursued as in England for example. The Canadian Government were very supportive and determined to achieve justice. But, as far as I know, Qu 'y's killers remain unidentified and free.'

Rosa, in truth, is feeling a little overwhelmed and nauseous even. She panics inside, What to say? I had not expected to hear such a cause for Qu 'y's death. It's awful, no. It's horrendous, cruel, nasty, disgusting, wicked, barbaric, and twisted. You poor man. But none of these is in her response, 'So, you are how old now?'

'I'm Forty-One,' replies Hardeen as he feels the warmth of Rosa's hand resting on his.

Hardeen waves at Sunlit and then says to Rosa, 'Choice, is, of course, yours. But I sense we'd both perhaps like something light. Soup and a mushroom and onion omelette is probably a sensible option. What do you think Rosa?'

'Sounds perfect!'

Rosa moves her chair, so she is at a right angle to Robert, 'You know Robert, it is truly appalling what you and your wife were forced to suffer. My heart goes out to you.'

'Your kind sentiment is appreciated. I want you to understand it is such a difficult experience to live with and share. Over time I've realised, whenever it appears I have met a new friend it is better to mention it early. So, you can understand why I spend some days like a depressive recluse. The memory of that hateful day continues to play havoc with sleeping too.'

'I'm not surprised,' says Rosa sympathetically.

'Would you like to see a picture of Qu 'y?'

'Sure.'

Hardeen retrieves a wallet and hands a photo to Rosa.

'Wow, you look different don't you, and Qu 'y is beautiful.'

'Yes, she was. Hope I haven't changed for the worse?' asks Hardeen chuckling.

'Well, you look like a good maturing wine from here,' replies Rosa shyly.

'Mutuality, it seems, is firing across our table,' suggests Hardeen before saying, 'Thank you.'

'You're more than welcome Robert.'

'Can I be open with you Rosa?'

'Yes. Of course, you can. Ask me absolutely anything!'

'Do you know why I invited you to join me?'

***

Rosa and Hardeen left their dining table to go to bed around 4.30am, and Rosa then took a shower. After which, to her surprise felt kinda awake. So, by 5.15am Rosa was sat in the open air restaurant again and she is enjoying a Brandy cappuccino as she reads a book. At 7.30am Rosa stood on the shore with tequila in hand to celebrate the sunrise.

It is now almost precisely 9.15am, and Rosa is back at her

table. Rosa is wearing a pair of Prada sunglasses, a lilac woollen shawl which is draped around her neck and over each shoulder. Rosa crochet this herself, and it compliments well with a lavender comfort bra top and short white skirt worn over a bikini.

Rosa is reading chapter 16, 'Hello Rosa; you're an early bird too eh!' says Hardeen jovially.

'Oh, you startled me a little, good morning Robert. I didn't go to bed. Came straight back to savour all this.'

Rosa's arms are wide open. She then adds, 'I haven't had breakfast yet. It would be nice if you'd like to join me?'

'I'd like that very much,' Hardeen replies.

'Good. You wait here, and I will serve you up a nice breakfast. Any particular allergies or dislike I need to account for?' asks Rosa.

Hardeen chuckles, 'I don't mind helping you know, but I can hear you want to. So, answer to both is no. Except, I don't like scented or aromatic tea.'

'Right, see you soon.'

'OK.'

***

Rosa rests a large tray assorted with breakfast delights onto the centre of their table. Hardeen exclaims, 'That simply looks delicious, thank you, Rosa.'

'No problem. Spotted British papers have arrived. Just nipping back to grab the Independent,' says Rosa as she hurriedly walks away.

Of course, loaded on the overnight flight from London, muses Hardeen.

Hardeen then takes two pieces of toast and spreads butter and apricot jam on both. Before long Hardeen is about to take the first bite when Rosa says, 'Made it.'

Hardeen's reply is slow because he can see a picture of Harold White behind imprinted fake 'jail bars' with a headline underneath. "WHITE FOUND GUILTY OF MURDERING HIS WIFE – SENTENCED FOR LIFE – WHAT WILL NEXT OF KIN DECIDE?" But eventually, he does say, 'What! I mean, well done you.'

CHAPTER SEVENTEEN

February 28, 2008

Toby Trunch is a delighted man, or more accurately, father. Toby is in a Myer run coffee bar inside their largest department store in Perth, Australia.

'Look Dad! What do you think? Aren't they great! Says Milena while cat-walking her multicolour nails in front of Toby's face.

Toby replies, 'Yes princess! They look fantastic! You will be the bell of the Valentine Ball, assuming the college doesn't have another fire on its grounds this Saturday too?'

'Don't be silly Dad, that won't happen again,' says Milena as she crash lands on a chair still admiring her outstretched fingers.

'Mum Skype me while Trisha did me nails Dad. Mum says hi. She phoned to wish me well at the Ball, again, and wanted to know if I've chosen to change what I will wear?'

'That's nice. Are your Mum and Luke OK?' asks Toby.

'They're fine. Mum said they had booked a trip to Amsterdam in May which is cool isn't...'

Toby interjects, 'Yes. Though, they're going to that summit in Strasbourg in May too aren't they?'

'Yep. Mum said they thought it was a good time to fit in the sights of Amsterdam! Then they are getting a train to the conference thing or whatever it's called. What is it, Dad?'

'It's a meeting where all EU MPs from all member countries are meeting to decide if Britain's new Justice Act law means they should expel them or not from the union?'

'What's wrong with us having such a law?' asks Milena.

'A good question Milena. What indeed!' replies Toby.

'Seriously Dad, why might they expel us?'

'OK. The EU does not agree with any death sentence option because this contradicts a fundamental right of every human being which is a right to live. The Justice Act includes a clause allowing victims of certain types of premeditated murder to seek a panel of three Judges from the Hose of Lords to consider changing a life sentence to a death sentence. It...'

Milena interrupts, 'But victims are dead Dad, so how can they...'

Toby interjects again, 'In this piece of legislation Milena, Victims' also includes any significant Next of Kin or identified important loved one. In the case of Joanne's maternal grandmother, for example, Clive has the right to seek this change.'

'Do you think Clive will Dad?

'Your Mum told me, Clive's wishes will be heard and considered as part of Harold White's appeal later this year. Obviously, if White's appeal, which has to be within six months of his conviction date, is successful, then whatever is Clive's wish becomes null and void.'

'Do you think Harold will be let off?' asks Milena.

'Probably not but best never to assume,' Toby replies.

'Hope not Dad,' says Milena.

'I'd be surprised if he his princess, try not to worry too much. I'm...'

'Dad?'

'Yes princess.'

'Can I have a coke please Dad,' asks Milena with her bright eyes, undoubtedly it appears, continuing to melt Toby's fatherly love and heart.

***

DC Sally Underwood bangs louder on my office door than I think she intended. And, she sort of stumbles entering.

'Hi Sally,' I say laughing before then asking, 'Are you OK?'

Sally fumbles to close the door, sits on a chair adjacent to my desk and breathlessly asks, 'Have you heard about

Hawker?'

'Don't think so, what about him?'

'He's dead Alex. PP says by all odds foul play involved.'

'Wow! When?'

'About two hours ago. In the boot of a car left near an unofficial rubbish tip on a neglected industrial estate in Wheaton. Pretty apt don't you think!' says Sally with feeling.

'How did he die,' I ask.

'Don't know details. PP's sent a message and is still at the scene. I came straight here to tell you. Amazing stuff eh!'

Sally's excitement is tangible as she adds, 'You said you thought Hawker is at risk from a vigilante attack.'

I'm still taking in the news, and I reply, 'Sounds like it is too early to be sure that is what's happened, Sally. Be very interesting to hear what has though and even more intriguing how the investigation into Hawker's death conducts, don't you think?'

Sally briefly looks perplexed, and then a penny drops, 'Yes, it certainly will be.'

'Sally, hope it's OK to ask, how are things with Sylvia?'

'No change. Which is better than worse,' suggests Sally.

'I am sorry Sally, ' I reply and I admit I'm also thinking, It's hard to understand how exactly things can get worse?

***

The venue for the delayed Valentine Ball is the Curtin theatre used by students at the John Curtin College of the Arts on Ellen Street in Fremantle. Toby was able to use his contacts within the Australian Government to secure a place for Milena on a Visual Arts program.

Milena is currently resting from a bout of some serious dance banging to a song called "Sandstorm" by Darude. She's sitting at a table amongst many college peers and friends. Directly beside her is Brett who has been besotted by Milena since day one. To date, Milena has batted off all invitations, and not just those from Brett.

Brett leans his face close to Milena's ear. The first consequence is his nostrils are irritated by loose ends laying amongst Milena's very stunning red hair. He asks, 'Nearly everyone in the class has agreed to move onto my place when this ends. My parents are on vacation in Hobart. You'll come too, won't you Milena?'

Milena stands and turns to face Brett. She then retrieves her phone from her cupped bosom and replies loudly, 'Maybe. What's your address, please? Dad is picking me up.'

'Six-nine six Hamilton Hill. It's walking distance from here,' replies an expectant Brett.

'Will let you know later,' says Milena whose already begun a text to Toby letting him know the new pick up point but with no change to arranged time.

Milena then says, 'Now going to dance with Kelly. Isn't she just great! She has got it all!'

***

It is also around ten o'clock in the Gambia, but of course, it's AM. Rosa and Hardeen nestle in bed like inseparable spoons.

'I can't believe it is my last weekend already,' Rosa sighs.

Hardeen hesitates before answering, 'Doesn't have to be,' he suggests softly.

Rosa replies, 'I wish,' with a chuckle.

Hardeen gently lifts Rosa's arms and spins 180 degrees before putting her arms back around him. Hardeen places a hand on each cheek of Rosa's face and gives a gentle kiss on her lips. 'What I mean is, can I come and see you soon, in Norfolk? I've fallen for you, Rosa. Hook, line and sinker.'

Rosa is speechless. So, Hardeen expands, 'Of course, I'd have to go back to Vietnam to organise a few things. Ask Phuc, my shop manager, to run things on his own for a while. If we feel the same in a few months, maybe a bit longer, then I can go back again just to tidy things up or maybe even sell my business there? What do you think?'

Rosa wipes away tears of joy which are blurring her vision and replies, 'Sounds wonderful.'

***

Milena is sitting next to Kelly on a six-seater settee in house number Six-nine six. They are giggling at everything after sharing, what was for both, a first green smoke. Made outrageously strong by Brett.

The living room is crowded with students and vibrating to the sound of "Airborne." Kelly and Milena help each other up, and then they start to dance. It does not take long for an audience to encircle around them.

Brett enters the room with a bottle of Dogbolter in one hand and a newly lit joint in his other. He is immediately spellbound by what is now a show more akin to a frenzied lesbian striptease dance. Brett transcends the circle for a close up of Milena and Kelly practically swallowing each other's tongue.

Brett steps nearer with intent to writhe dance behind Milena. But, with no warning, Brett is pushed to the ground by Toby who then uses both arms to come between the passion gently. He then sweeps Milena off her feet and swiftly carries her out of the house.

Brett's face is bleeding and pierced by landing on the end of a sharp high heel. Kelly, who is looking at Brett's face, is screaming hysterically along with shouts from others suchlike, 'Has someone called triple zero! What the fucks going on! Get Brett onto his back. We need some towels, a sheet!'

CHAPTER EIGHTEEN

Hardeen bends to kiss Rosa,'Will be back by eight at the latest. Sorry to leave you on your own all day but every Monday...'

'It's OK Robert; I think it's great how you help out and sponsor Sunlit's family. Hope you have a nice day.'

'Are you sure you won't join me, Rosa?'

'What, and miss out on my last pampering day, or more importantly, my yoga class run by the gorgeous Jato?' says Rosa with a bright grin.

'Enjoy your day Rosa. Look forward to hearing all about it at dinner tonight. I've reserved our table already. Bye,' replies Hardeen.

Hardeen is soon passing the hotel's kitchen which is a shortcut to its car park. 'Have a nice day Mr Robert,' says Head Chef Isatou who then adds to Sunlit, 'And you too Sunlit. Make sure you thank Mr Hardeen. He is a good man for taking you home. See you altine. fo tuma doo.'

'hoa. Ndeyjoor. val ning bara. fo tuma doo oncle.'

'Bye Isa,' says Hardeen with a wave.

Hardeen and Sunlit hurriedly get in a car hired at Banjul international airport for the duration of 'Mr Robert's' vacation.

***

The only car that can be seen for miles in any direction, on a barely visible dirt track road, is a blue Toyota Tarcel. At the wheel is Hardeen who earlier on, enjoyed a treat from his passenger while also driving along. Presently, they are approaching the rural village of Kunkujang.

Kunkujang is where Sanji lives with her seven children. Their house is a narrow rectangular single floor dwelling. It has a perimeter wall all around it, and this is about fifty yards away from the home. Within this area are ten children, six sheep, six goats, ten chickens and Sanji talking with her sister and brother-in-law.

Inside the home is Hawa helping her younger sister Alanso wash her hair. They are using a water-filled steel bucket, soap and a loofah made from the dried fibres of the baobab tree. It is also in this room where the whole family use what is called a pit latrine or squat toilet.

Hardeen pulls up beside the outer wall of Sanji's house. He then reaches for three large bags of goodies and already Sanji's eldest son, and two siblings are running toward the car, 'i be nooding Sunlit. Hello Mr Robert,' all three shout excitedly.

Hardeen puts the bags on the ground and squats with opening arms. All five share a hug. 'Nice to see you again Mr Robert,' says Sanji who has walked across from inside the wall.

'Hello Sanji, you look very well,' says Hardeen.

'You well to Mr Robert? Come in please,' invites Sanji as she shakes Hardeen's hand.

Everyone then hears Sunlit yell repeatedly as she runs inside to find her two sisters, 'i be nooding Hawa. be munto Hawa? Alanso?

***

In the centre of the room where Sanji's family socialise is a Wolof, one-pot. It is full with some Benachin, Jollof rice, and home-grown vegetables. Today though, inside the pot are also onions, mushrooms, a tomato pasta sauce and some meat. Meat is such a rare treat and was cooked by Sanji's family in honour of as well as a thank you to their special guest.

All nine diners are ringed around their feast and sitting wigwam style. Hardeen is between Sanji and Sunlit. Sanji ends a prayer and then points at Hardeen saying, 'Please Mr Robert, Domo.'

Hardeen uses fingers to scoop from the Da and then opens his mouth to accept the food. Everyone waits until he swallows before they engage in a courteous free for all.

***

Hawa is crying. Saying goodbye to her mother, brothers and sisters are understandably overwhelming. Nevertheless, Mawa is also excited and looking forward to starting her first week working at Hotel California. Mawa wants to help her family as her eldest sister does. Mawa also feels grown up and can't wait to see what's beyond Kunkujang.

Sanji gives Mawa a last hug and looks to the floor as Sunlit takes Mawa's hand and they walk out of the home and toward the car.

Hardeen gets out and helps put Mawa's bag in the boot. He then watches Sunlit make sure Mawa is safely in the front passenger seat before taking steps to sit beside her.

'Bye Sunlit,' says Hardeen.

Sunlit kisses Mawa and says, 'fo tuma doo, Mawa,' tenderly.

Sunlit then skips around to Hardeen's window. 'Bye Mr Robert. Thank you. Good luck in England Mr Robert.'

Hardeen starts the engine, 'Be back soon Sunlit. Take care,' Hardeen replies with a minimum of warmth.

All of Mawa's siblings watch Hardeen reverse before all six wave shouting, 'fo fuma doo, Mawa.'

They keep shouting, "Goodbye Mawa," as they run behind the car until it is no longer visible.

Mawa's journey to Serrekunda took Hardeen an hour longer than Sunlit's ride home. The reason is not anything to do with going slower, roadworks, diversions, traffic jams, an accident, comfort breaks, getting lost or malfunction of the vehicle.

CHAPTER NINETEEN

March 5, 2008

Sally and her wife's parents are having breakfast together at the Sorrento hotel in Cambridge. None feel able to eat much, settling for toast and a lot of tea. In less than half an hour they have an appointment with the head neurological consultant at Addenbrooks Hospital.

'I'll drive,' offers Sally and Mrs Jeannie Windshield bursts into tears.

'Thank you,' says Phil Windshield comforting his wife.

'I don't think I can go, Sally. Sorry,' says Jeannie.

'I understand,' says Sally sympathetically.

'Come on Jeannie, lets just pop back to our room and see how you feel after freshening up,' suggests Phil trying desperately not to feel so gut-wrenchingly helpless. He then adds, 'Sally, if we're not in reception in fifteen minutes go ahead without us. I'll do my best that you don't face this meeting on your own. I promise.'

'Sure,' says Sally sincerely and she watches Sylvia's mum and dad leave the dining room. Sally then heads outside for a fresh air walk while she waits. I now wish I'd let you be here with me, laments Sally about Bernice's offer to give support.

Sylvia is in, what the medics call, "A state of Brain stem death." Meaning, Sylvia has permanently lost the potential for consciousness and the capacity to breathe. Today, Sylvia's significant loved ones will decide whether to agree with the head consultant, that now is the right time, sadly, to disconnect the ventilator?

In early December last year, Sylvia was involved in a ten car smash-up caused by a lorry jackknifing in fog on the notorious A47 bypass in Norfolk.

Tim Burton is the name of the consultant Sally is meeting. Tim is at a table in the staff canteen checking his to-do list. He has already been on duty since 7.00am. Tim ticks his next job:

Sylvia Windshield.

Tim glances at his watch, then takes a final swig of tea and heads to the visitor's room on Emirates Ward. Waiting for him are Karinsa who is the Ward Sister, Mr and Mrs Windshield, Sally and Bernice. Bernice waited from 8.00am in the hospital's primary reception figuring Sally would come through that way.

All, except Jeannie, react to a door opening, 'Sorry, I'm a little late. I simply had to have a drop of tea,' explains Tim.

Tim then acknowledges his colleague and shakes hands with everyone else thanking them for coming. He pulls a chair a little closer to the centre of the room and sits facing a human horseshoe.

'Three of the four of you know I am Tim, but sorry madam I do not know your name?'

'BB, ERM..., Bernice Buck. I'm a friend and colleague of Sally.'

'Very considerate. OK...'

Jeannie bursts into tears and while her husband consoles her she splutters some words quietly, 'I'm sorry Doctor. But please don't ask me to say yes.'

Tim looks at Phil first and then Sally, 'I understand Mrs Windshield and I won't.'

'Thank you, Doctor,' says Jeannie trying hard to arrest her crying.

'We can discuss what's best to do for Sylvia for as long as you need. Though, I do not want to prolong this upsetting situation unnecessarily. Sally, do you have any questions?'

'Is the diagnosis you explained last Friday one hundred percent permanent?

'Yes Sally, I'm really sorry to say, I'm afraid, barring a miracle, it is.'

Sally asks, 'Phil, do you want to say anything?'

'Yes. Doctor, we love Sylvia, our only child, more than any word can ever convey. Sylvia adored Sally, and their wedding is one of the happiest and proudest days of our lives. Sally has insisted Jeannie, and I's wishes should prevail above hers, despite the law! But the truth is we agree! Don't we Sally?'

'Yes. But Phil and Jeannie want to say goodbye first, and only I will stay with Sylvia during...'

Sally can't finish and buries her face into Bernice's arms.

'Karinsa, can you please stay with Sylvia's family while I go and see Dr Gunawardena.'

'Yes, of course, Tim.'

'Thank you,' says Tim and he stands up before adding, 'I sincerely believe your decision is the right one and I admire and commend your courage. I'll be back soon.'

After the five seconds or so it takes for Tim to exit, Karinsa is the only person in the room not crying uncontrollably. Nevertheless, Karinsa does have moist eyes as she frantically tries to decide how best to console them all?

CHAPTER TWENTY

April 22, 2008

I am sharing a meal at home in Norwich. The chef though is Kam, and it is rare we eat together. Kam has the most beautiful eyes I think I will ever see. Not anything complicated or hidden. Naturally, a sincere compliment to someone who has become a friend as well as an employee.

Kam is with me this evening because she agreed to witness my conversation with a government assessor from the Department of Work and Pensions. Mixed with the sound of our confab an album is playing and the current track is, "Walls Come Tumbling Down!"

My front doorbell then serenades a brief rendition of, "Edelweiss." 'I'll go,' says Kam.

'Thanks.'

Shortly, Mrs Olga Koror comes into view, and Kam says, 'Please, after you.'

'Hello, I'm Alex. Please sit down.'

I point my foot in the direction of an armchair opposite my sofa.

'Yes, please. Thanking you. My name is Olga Koror.'

Immediately, Olga then offers a hand for me to shake. I look directly at her eyes and smile, 'Excuse me, I am not able to lift my arms. I never have and never will. Welcome, and how do you do, too.'

'Would you like a cup of tea or coffee Mrs Koror,' asks Kam.

While sinking onto the armchair, Olga replies.'Tea would be nice thank you. Just one sugar please.'

'Alex?'

'No thanks Kam.'

Olga is looking all around the room. 'You have a nice home, Mr Forrester,' she says.

'Thank you. Please call me Alex.'

'How long have you lived here, Alex?' Olga asks.

'Eight years.'

Olga opens a folder laying across her lap. She smiles and asks, 'I would like to check you received my letter requesting this evenings appointment?'

'Yes I did Olga, thank you.'

'That is good. In my letter, it explained reasons for us to reassess everyone who receives Disability Benefits and for you it is.'

Olga hesitates as she turns over pieces of paper. 'Are. It says for only Disability Living Allowance but both components. Is this still correct Mr Forr..., Alex?' Olga asks.

'Yes,' I reply.

Kam enters the room carrying a tray with two mugs of tea and a small plate with some macaroons on it. Kam places the receptacle on a coffee table, hands Olga her drink and asks, 'Would you like a biscuit Mrs Koror?'

'No thank you,' replies Olga.

Olga takes a sip and puts her drink back on the tray.

'Alex, for clarification why I need to be here, do you have any questions before I start?' Olga asks looking at Kam more than me.

'To be honest, I would like to make a suggestion more than just ask a few questions please?'

'Yes, of course,' replies Olga who then retakes hold of her mug.

'Thank you. How to start?' I ask as I swivel to sit upright facing Olga across the table.

I then continue, 'With two rhetorical questions. Why has the Government also insisted on reassessing those deemed as, "Lifers?" Lifer was the official word printed on documents before this new descriptive use of "Indefinites" came into use. By the way, literally, with a stroke of a Minister's pen! Still, that's democratic consultancy for you!

Why not implement your new classifications without

needing to spend thousands, who knows maybe millions, of what is insensitive and insulting assessments of, to use your words, the "Indefinites," of Britain's society?

I am beyond cynical when I hear anyone, let alone a politician in power, say; it is to ensure efficient use of taxpayers money. Frankly, Olga, if efficiency is the holy grail, so so to speak, how is it every MPs wage is sourced by taxpayers money?

If there weren't pain for some people reassessed, I would laugh at the majority of MPs and to some also spit in their face, at their hypocrisy! At their verbal clap-trap to justify actions that are ultimately designed to give their city of London business friends an even more substantial slice of Britain's GNP pie!

So, Olga, I will sign whatever new forms you have with you to fill in today, while all the boxes are blank! You already have all the information you need to complete this latest assessment. Which, by the way, is yet another form of the same boxes and questions but with, yet another different eligibility criteria!

I pluck a folded piece of paper from my right foot and place it on the table between us and say, 'There is a blank cheque. Who fills the details in or whether anyone does, depends on you and your managers, superiors or whatever other titles he or she may have? I also know from your previous assessments of me, you and or others decide what I'm entitled to or not? I look forward, with interest, receiving your decision in writing accordingly.

Thank you for coming at this time of your working day, and I sincerely wish you a safe journey home. Where do I sign please Olga?'

***

May 17

Sadie and I are hosting a house-warming party at our shared second home. It took nearly three months, but we managed to agree on a change to the name on the deeds to Three Counties

View. I like it so much here I'm tempted to leave my job in Wymondham and live permanently in this beautiful Gloucestershire village.

I'm currently crossing our hallway, and I'm heading to the living room where most of our guests are mingling. I hear a knock on our front door. I stop and spin my rider one hundred and eighty degrees and stretch my leg upwards to push the handle down. I then open the door, 'Hello Clive, it's fantastic to see you! Oh, and of course you too, Helen and Lilly! Come in. How are you all?'

'Not too bad thanks. You?' replies Clive.

'Great thanks.'

'Hi-ya,' says Helen who along with Clive has stepped in leaving a shy teenager still standing in the doorway.

'Come in Lilly. Sadie's daughters will be pleased there is another teenager at the party. How are you doing at college?'

Lilly shyly enters as she says, 'I love it thank you, Mr Forrester.'

'I'm pleased you are enjoying it, Lilly.'

We all then head into the kitchen because Clive has bought the biggest bottle of Vodka I've ever seen. I introduce the newcomers to a mixture of friends, relatives, village neighbours and colleagues.

One of the latter is delighted to see Clive, 'Hello Clive. Great to see you again. What do you want to drink mate? Alex has come up trumps, look.'

Clive's eyes follow the direction of PP's pointed finger, 'He's only got a bloody great barrel of Batemans in the house.'

'Great,' agrees Clive.

Still carrying the vodka, Clive's ushered toward the 'bar' by a very enthusiastic PP, 'Nicola and Harriet are here, and they will be thrilled to meet you! Are you still in the same job? And...'

'What would you like to drink Helen? Lilly?' I ask.

Before either answer, Sadie wraps an arm around my

shoulders, and she says, 'So glad you've both made it. Bet Alex hasn't told you we've combined this house-warming party with also celebrating his birthday. Well, it's actually on Tuesday but I do not think anyone would have made it here on a weekday, do you?'

Helen smiles and replies, 'No, and no you haven't mentioned it have you Alex! Many happy returns for Tuesday. Is it a special big zero then Alex?'

'My thirtieth,' I answer with a wry smile.

'You wish,' says Sadie laughing.

'Sadie's jealous because I can get away with it sounding plausible, can't I sweetheart? Truth is Helen, no it's not a big zero, just another year older that's all.'

Sadie offers Lilly a hand and says, 'Come with me Lilly, and I'll introduce you to my daughters Estelle and Cherisha.'

***

My front wheels are on the front edge of our star-shaped patio which extends quite a distance from our conservatory. I can see Clive standing alone on the bank of the river which flows past our cottage's rear garden. I take a relaxing draw on a cigarette and stub it out into an ashtray resting on a table not far behind me. When I turn back around again, Clive is strolling toward me. As soon as I am within earshot, Clive says, 'This is a wonderful home Alex. They must be paying you too well.'

I chuckle and say, 'As if. No, it's all down to inheritance, and it's still sinking in how fortunate I, we are.'

'I bet there are some wonderful places to go fishing around here. Not that this would excite you. I remember you telling me fishing is not your scene,' says Clive.

'Well, funny you should say that Clive because since you kindly invited me to join you that time, I've considered my reasons for declining. It was prejudice on my part. So, if you are willing, I would like to spend a day fishing with you sometime. Then at least I can form an opinion having experienced it first hand.'

Clive laughs and asks, 'You're winding me up, right?'

I want to stop my smile. My failure to do so does not prevent me trying to sound genuine and convincing, 'No kidding Clive. I really would like too. Feel free to let me know when and where?'

Still looking sceptical Clive says, 'OK. You get bank holidays off too, don't you?'

'Yes, unless there is an exceptional circumstance going down,' I reply.

'It's the spring bank holiday week Monday. Have you got anything planned for that day?' 'Nothing that cannot alter,' I reply straight-faced.

'Alright,' says Clive, 'How about one of my favourite spots which are accessible to you. It's walking distance from a pub. Do you know "The Swan" in Ringland?'

'Yes. Went there to try crocodile. I have a colleague who lives in Ringland as it happens. If you don't mind, I'd like to ask Sally to join us for a pub lunch perhaps? If she's around of course.'

'Yes, fine by me. You OK for getting there,' asks Clive.

'Sure. Probably get a taxi unless Sadie insists I don't need to,' I reply.

I feel a tap on my shoulder. I look behind, and it is Finley who says, 'Found you at last. Oh, hello Mr Verity, didn't see you down there. How are you?'

'Fine thanks,' replies Clive who rightly thinks it is one of the officers he met at his families funeral.

'Was there anything you especially wanted Finley?' I ask.

'Great party Alex. And yes, Kristina wants me to pass on her apologies for not coming. Unfortunately, this weekend clashes with a pre-arranged theatre visit in London. Tickets given with expectation both of us would join Mrs Thorpe and what looks more and more like Kristina's potential step-father. Anyway, I chose here which as you can imagine hasn't scored me any brownie points. But watching Les Miserable isn't my idea of a fun time.'

'Please thank Kristina for her sentiment,' I say as I become aware the music has suddenly stopped.

I look behind again, and Sadie is standing in the conservatory holding an enormous cake. Some guests are lighting up, I later learn, forty-six candles. The music restarts and it is "Happy Birthday" by Stevie Wonder.

Within seconds everyone comes outside and begin dancing, singing and clapping. Sally and Bernice grab a handle each of my manual, belt and side-less rider. Their speed means I'm convinced I'm going to tip off my seat. But somehow, my wildly flailing legs help me remain attached.

They push me into the central area of the star. Sadie is now right in front of me, and I understand her mime telling me, 'Love you, happy birthday and make a wish.'

Sadie then lowers the cake and most cheer as I fail to distinguish all the candles in one breath.

***

May 24

Maxine and Luke arrived at the Waldorf Astoria Hotel in Amsterdam at eight o'clock this morning. They are staying until Thursday when they intend to take a train to Strasbourg. They want to make sure they taste the flavour of both cities before attending the EU summit taking place a week today.

Their, Public gallery, VIP passes for the historic debate and vote are one of three pairs in the first place given by Judge Reginald Chalice-Hermitage QC to the Chief Constable of Norfolk Constabulary. Frank then gave a couple to DC Sally Underwood. Sally was thrilled when chosen, but part of the thrill was going with Sylvia, so she handed them on to Maxine.

Maxine also accepted a favourable redundancy package to leave her job at the County Council and instead enjoys being a volunteer for a charity who support victims' of crime. The horrendous embarrassment Maxine felt when exposed during White's trial, meant she fought for and gained a redundancy package more favourable than is usual protocol. Luke still enjoys his job at the Research Institute in Norwich.

It is now a few minutes before five in the afternoon. Maxine and Luke are in their hotel suite getting ready for their first night out in the wonderful city of Amsterdam.

'Maxine, I cannot find my favourite dress of yours. I've just checked you're suitcase so I know you haven't packed it. Has it been left behind?'

'It's in yours, Hun.'

'OK. Nice one. Thanks.'

Luke fumbles in his suitcase which is laying open on a settee. Beside the case is a paper bag with two cakes Luke bought earlier from the "Mellow Yellow Coffeeshop." He soon finds what he's looking for and positions his hands behind his back, 'Close your eyes please Maxine,' he asks.

Maxine is on a stool in front of a large oval shaped mirror applying make-up. As Luke walks to stand behind Maxine he can see her smile as she picks up her Maybelline pink lipstick. She asks, 'Why Hun?'

'Trust me, please. Go on, close them.'

'OK,' Maxine complies.

Luke stretches an arm around each side of Maxine's head with his fingers holding his surprise. It is slightly away from her face but level with her eyes. 'You can open them now,' says Luke excitedly.

The first thing Maxine sees are neon blue violet painted nails. And now her vision is clearer she reads: The Leidseplein Theatre presents **BOOM CHICAGO** with their **CLIMATE CHANGE COMEDY SHOW** – This show is full of hot-air from environ-mentally retarded comedians. Not your typical eco-warriors, Boom Chicago, are nonetheless worried about the Netherlands, their little Atlantis of the future. Ticket valid for Saturday, May 24, 2008. Doors open at 18.00pm. Show starts at 20.00pm.

'Oh Luke,' shrieks Maxine as she grabs the tickets. 'I've always wanted to go there. Fantastic. Well done and thank you.

Such a lovely surprise.'

Maxine leans her head back in tandem with wriggling her posterior and kicking her legs. And they kiss smacker style. It is a long time since Maxine expressed so much brightness in her face as she says, 'Don't think even in Amsterdam they'll let us in with you only half frocked. So, shall I help you with that dress then?'

'Yes please, though we've even got time to have our cake and eat it too,' Luke whispers into Maxine's right ear.

***

Spring Bank Holiday

In the end, it was more practical I joined him fishing between nine and ten as opposed to six. Clive did though, give me very detailed instructions on where exactly to find him.

The journey to the Swan took twenty minutes in a Green Frog Eco – Friendly taxi. Adjacent to the pub's car park is a patch of grass, and I crossed over this and took a narrow path in a north-easterly direction.

I am now on the last stretch as I cross the River Wensum thanks to a concrete footbridge which replaced a wooden one used by horse-drawn traffic in the 1920's. Clive suddenly comes into view fifty yards or so ahead. 'Morning Clive. It's a great spot,' I say cheerfully.

'Well done for making it. Down to my spot on directions I reckon. No obstacles for the wheelchair either,' Clive replies.

'No, none at all thanks. And, feel quite chuffed I didn't get lost for a change.'

'Seems more appropriate to say good afternoon', jokes Clive before adding, 'Yes, it is wonderful isn't it. Love the peacefulness too.'

'Have you been here since six?' I ask.

'Landlord of the pub is a good friend of mine. Been here since he chucked me out about two this morning,' Clive answers.

'Anything in the cooler box?' I enquire.

'A couple of Barbel, one looks around fifteen pounds,' says Clive casually.

'Impressive,' I reply assuming this is a good catch.

'So, Alex! Is there any way I can assist you to have a go. I've brought my old rod if you want to try.'

I reply, 'Thanks for being thoughtful but the answer is, it's not feasible.'

'OK. Sure. ERM... I've wanted to ask before and now seems a good moment. Can I ask you a personal question please, Alex?'

'You can ask,' I reply matter of factly.

'Was you in an accident? I mean, is that why you use a wheelchair? Hope you are not offended me asking. I'm genuinely interested,' Clive explains.

'I'm not offended. No, was born this way. Meaning, I was born without some of the usual muscles or bones found in limbs. And in my case, some are also missing in my shoulders and hips. It's not degenerative or hereditary. And I've not known how it feels to lose what you probably think I've lost. In this crazy world, the universe even! Shit happens, and life carries on evolving. Right?' I ask.

'Well, yes. I guess so. And it makes some sense when I think of the crap dealt out to my mate Ripper. Do you remember me telling you about him?'

'Yes. I agreed to approach our local MP to try and help. Did Denise get in touch with Ripper do you know? Were things sorted, so Ripper and his family didn't have to move house?'

'Yes to both as I'm pretty sure she did,' replies Clive who then adds, ' The last thing I want to do is sound patronising or embarrass you Alex, but I admire you. You've got real guts.'

'Not a patch on what you and Ripper have. So ditto Clive, ditto,' I reply.

You may be surprised to hear me say despite having been asked suchlike questions Clive has just done countless times in my life, I rarely anticipate their delivery.

At this moment it's sidetracked my intention to tell Clive why I've come fishing with him today. And judging by Clive's next question, it might take a while to get on the required track, 'But surely there are some things you wish you could do. You know, if it hadn't been for nature?'

'That's easy to answer. Yes, a footballer at any level of competitive competition.'

'And that's number one?' asks Clive.

'Not exclusively. But, it is one of the 'some things!' Being able to squeeze a lover's bottom and riding a Harley Davidson at least one hundred miles an hour on a highway in New Jersey are others for example,' I reply.

'Why New Jersey,' Clive asks looking a bit bemused.

'Because Sadie would be my passenger and we're both be listening to...'

'Born to run,' interrupts Clive.

'Yes, the whole album.'

Clive laughs and says, 'I see. Similarly, there must also be things that piss you off?'

'That's also easy to answer. Not being able to swot an irritating fly! Though there is a more serious close second,' I reply.

'What's that then?' Clive asks.

'It's being asked countless times by someone, as their opening shot in a conversation and who at the time of asking is a complete stranger to me, "What's wrong with you then?" Don't know about you but in such situations, I say something suchlike, "Hello" or "Nice to meet you" or "Excuse me" or "My name is Alex, what is yours?"'

'Really!' exclaims Clive before asking, 'What is your answer?'

'Depends on the circumstances, location, context and attitude of impartation. Any...'

'What do you mean?' asks Clive.

'If the delivery is, rude! I have sometimes answered, "Nothing that only needs a good shag to put it right, thanks." When it's sounded clumsy but delivered with genuine curiosity, I say either, "There isn't anything wrong with me, thanks" or "I'm human, just like you"! Of course, as many, probably more, are not rude or clumsy when they ask and in those circumstances, I answer in an open and friendly two-way chat. Like, we are doing now.'

Clive chuckles, and I smile. Clive then asks, 'You're not joking are you?'

'Nope.'

***

Two hours later.

'Time to go and meet Sally. Are you sure you want to stay here Clive,' I ask.

'Yes. Not being rude. I like the break from the outside world. Besides, have lunch in the cooler. Look forward to seeing you both when you return.'

'OK. I'll bring some more beer given the dent we've made in your stock. Anything you want in particular?' I ask.

'Yes, please. I'd like to stick with bottles of Shepherds Neame. Do you like it, Alex?'

'I do. Before I go, Clive, would you please help me get something out of my bag which is hanging on the back of my rider?'

'Sure. What is it you need?'

'In the largest section which is zipped up, please take out a beige coloured ring-binder file.'

'OK.'

Clive retrieves the file and is standing facing me.

'Thought you might be interested to see how the investigation into the murder of Hawker has concluded,' I suggest before adding, 'But, of course, no obligat...'

'No, I mean yes I am. Thanks. A couple of detectives came to check my whereabouts? I think I was the first to be questioned actually.'

'Yes. I know. It's a complete copy so when I return we'll send it up in flames, OK?'

'Right. Yes. Sounds sensible,' says Clive who is opening the file.

'See you in an hour or so. Are you sure you didn't bring those two Barbel in that box, with you?' I tease before heading off.

'Cheeky sod. Enjoy your lunch,' replies Clive as he opens the file.

***

'Watch – ya. Lovely day isn't it,' says Sally while also making me jump a little by tickling the bald patch on the top of my head.

Sally then adds, 'Thought you'd be in the garden having a smoke. Sorry for being late. You been waiting long?' and by now Sally is sitting on the opposite side of a wooden table.

'Hello, Sally. Hello Bernice. You both look well.'

'Hi Alex,' replies Bernice.

'Actually, been here hours. Clive hasn't turned up.'

Sally laughs, 'Oh no. Hold on; you're kidding right?'

'Can you see Clive anywhere?' I ask.

'No, well as it happens, it's me who needs to say sorry to you. We are popping in to see my dad on our way for a fish and chips on Wells beach. So, was only staying for a pint with you guys as it's...'

I laugh. 'No worries Sally, I was kidding. Clive doesn't want to break his chance of catching another fish. Asked me to say hi and said he's happy to have visitors. What do you think?'

'You bugger. Yes, let's say hello to Clive, and we can have a pint before we head off,' replies Sally.

***

'Any more luck then?' I ask Clive.

'Not yet. It was nice to see Sally and Bernice. Are they good mates too then?' asks Clive.

'I honestly don't know Clive. Though close friends. Which is nice as understandably Sally is still feeling raw.'

'Sure, of course,' says Clive.

'Has your lunchtime reading been useful? There's some beer in these carrier bags hanging on my handles. Help yourself.'

Clive reaches the nearest bag without getting off what looks like a stool for a six-year-old. 'Cheers Alex, shall I open one for you too?'

'Yes please.'

Clive then fills both glasses before he answers my question. 'Yes. It's intriguing. Is it really true there are no leads to go on other than establishing the type of gun used by the killer?'

'Yes. Not a sausage,' I state emphatically.

'What do you think? Do the police have any theories?' asks Clive.

'Probably a random act by a vigilante assassin. So, like finding a needle in a haystack given the breadth of public condemnation of Hawker, don't you think?' I reply.

'Well, yes that is the favourite. But why now? My gut instinct is, Hawker knew his killer!'

'Frankly Clive, I don't have concrete answers. In fact the opposite. For example, is it coincidence Hawker is found killed a matter of only two weeks after his mate White is found guilty of murdering Jill? Or, another question I ask is, is this timing significant and relevant to finding out the identity of the killer? Who knows?'

'Least the bastard can't hurt any more children. And who cares about Hawker anyway? It says in the file, even his parents and sister disowned him months ago,' Clive asserts with feeling.

Clive grabs the file and as he stands up says, ' I'd like to send this up in flames now! If that's OK with you, please Alex?'

'Absolutely,' I reply.

***

MAY 31

Maxine and Luke are staying at La Résidence de l'Orangerie hotel while in Strasbourg. It is just four hundred and fifty yards from the European Parliament and Court of Human Rights. Today, the former is hosting an extraordinary EU Summit. At which, a vote on whether Britain should be expelled or not from the Union will take place?!

Within a week of Britain implementing, "The Justice Act 2007" Sweden submitted the resolution for today's discussion. Their resolution demands to expel Britain from the Union. Their reason is a belief Britain's new penal system breaches Human Rights.

There is an uneasy feeling Britain will be left out in the cold. Concerns and less so, support, are voiced by British politicians from all parties, the majority of its Government's cabinet, it's political analysts, it's Establishment Business Tycoons and it's various media conglomerates. I am intrigued as it is perceived, albeit, without a national referendum, a majority of citizens in Britain do not share these sentiments and see leaving the Union would be a good thing!

The tension is palpable for everyone here in the Hemicycle building which is the home for the Parliamentary Assembly of the Council of Europe. Amongst the attendees in a row of seats near to the roof in the public and press gallery are most of those, who've travelled from Norfolk. They are Frank and Violet Toddenham, Maxine and Luke Stewart and then Lady Eva Chalice-Hermitage sitting next to her friend Cynthia. Beside Cynthia are the only two empty seats in the Hemicycle.

Sadie and I are on the ground floor next to an usher. Judge Reginald Chalice-Hermitage QC is standing on the podium and has so far been speaking for half-an-hour.

Even for a person who possesses an ego, self-love and confidence as high as Reginald does, Reginald was genuinely surprised and humbled when the British Prime Minister asked him to be their representative in today's debate. A debate which will conclude with a vote for or against what is an unparalleled and extraordinary resolution set before the Members.

Except for one MEP from Latvia who recently died, every Member is present. The vast Majority seem genuinely attentive to what is the fourth speech to argue for not expelling Britain. Reginald will also be the last because the debate ends by giving the floor to the alleged offender so to speak.

 The choice of Reginald is because he is an admired performer and favourite member on all sides of the House of Lords. And his duties as a respected Judge, who lives in the County with the first-hand experience of the new Penal system, meant the Prime Minister made a calculated judgement. The Prime Minister believes such a representative has the best opportunity to persuade the tsunami tide to recede.

I stop looking at the floor and refocus on listening to Reginald.

'Britain is proud to be a member of this Union. A Union to preserve peace in a previously war-torn continent over not a few hundred years but thousands. We are a Union allied to our dependable friends who are the citizens of the United States of America.

Yes, a superpower country formed by independent states who maintain their allegiance to their Unity, even though some individual States have a judicial system that includes a Death Penalty sentence as an option.

So, I say to everyone and especially those voting today, not just, Why can't we? But we can and must be allowed to do the same! Thank you for your consideration.'

Reginald takes a few backward steps from the Guest podium. Behind him sat at a table the President and his staff lead the applause.

***

Half an hour later

The usher steps beside me again and I correctly see this as a cue. Sure enough, the President is back at his table, but he does not sit down. He picks up a microphone and says in English, 'I first wish to thank everyone for a very respectful debate. And before I read out the result, please remember whatever it is, there will be an opportunity for an appeal to the European Convention on Human Rights. If this happens, their Judges will decide if our resolution should be ratified or not?

The president then begins to open an envelope and from it retrieves its content. He moves it nearer to his face and says, 'The Votes for, is three hundred and seventy-five and the Votes against is also three hundred and seventy-five. And, alas, there is one enforced abstention.'

With the President now shrugging his shoulders he also makes a gesture using both arms which convey, "Help" and is followed by him saying, 'So, no winner.'

A frantic hum is heard swarming around the Hemicycle like Bees do when homing. Some British MEPs sitting in a section of the floor allocated to European Conservatives and Reformists then cheer along with punches into the air.

I think, and it's only my opinion. I'm not claiming I'm right or accept I'm wrong. But yes, I believe the celebrating is because the goal is not just a step nearer but there is now only one more step to take, for a winning score!

***

In one of La Résidence de l'Orangeries two Guests Only Bars is Maxine. All sofa's, armchairs, cubicles, seats and tables are occupied. Maxine is on a two seater sofa and next to her is Reginald. Reginald has just taken an opportunity to leave a table he is sharing with his wife, Cynthia, Frank and Violet.

'I didn't know you were coming too, Maxine. Frank said he passed on tickets to members of his team. What an outcome eh?' asks the Lord.

'DC Sally Underwood kindly gave us her pair of tickets. My Luke is at the bar. What do you think will happen next Reginald?' asks Maxine.

'How long are you staying in Strasbourg?' replies Reginald.

'I'm not interested your Lordship which is not something you've misunderstood; more you still choose to ignore in the hope of another conquer to scribe on your bedpost! But, I am interested in you answering my question please,' Maxine replies.

'Oh well, and as for what happens? I think it's crystal clear Maxine. They did not vote to expel us, so no further action required. Carry on with the usual business I say, or do you think differently?'

Maxine answers, 'I think those determined to expel us will have a re-vote as soon as is permitted after the new Latvian MEP gets elected on the tenth of July. I also imagine Latvia's Government and Business interests will revel in their chance to prosper from an ingenious, albeit accidental, lucky throw of a dice!'

Reginald says, 'You never used to be so cynical Maxine. And such a shame you left the profession. I remember saying to myself on seeing you in action, I might not live to see it but here is a candidate for the first woman to reach the top.'

Maxine is relieved to see Luke returning, and she looks straight into Reginald's eyes as she says, 'To your first assumption I say, Am I? And I am not sad to have left. So, Reginald, my Luke needs his seat back because we just now want to enjoy the rest of our vacation alone but together. I'm sure you understand.'

CHAPTER TWENTY-ONE

June 6, 2008

'Hello,' I say having just answered my office phone by pressing the hands-free button.

'Hi-ya. It's me, Maxine.'

'Hello Me Maxine.'

'Ha Ha. Can you talk Alex?'

'Yes, I was told since I was two.'

'You seem to be in good spirits,' says Maxine with a laugh.

'Did you enjoy Amsterdam and Strasbourg, Maxine?' I ask.

'Great time thanks. What do you think about the vote?'

'Excellent.'

'Why excellent?'

'I like a close finish in a race. Especially one that leaves you with the possibility of enjoying the excitement of a rematch,' I explain.

'I see. Just relieved we weren't expelled,' says Maxine.

'And how is Milena? Is she keeping in touch?' I ask.

'Yes we are and thanks for asking. Milena's doing really well at college and seems to be happy. Miss her like mad, but I admit Alex, Milena even sounds more grown up. It's been a good thing.'

'I'm pleased for all of you Maxine. Nice to hear, it really is!'

'Cheers. And I'm counting down the days to July eleventh.'

'Are you going to Australia to see Milena then,' I ask.

'No, better than that. Milena's coming home for four of the seven-week College summer break.'

'That's fantastic Maxine, no wonder you sound so bright.'

'Can't wait,' says Maxine before then adding, 'There is another reason for calling you Alex. In fact it's more I'm calling for a favour.'

'OK,' I say.

'Is it a convenient time to ask,' asks Maxine.

'Sure. I'm all ears.'

'Good. Do you remember a few weeks ago Sadie joined Jackie and I to see S Club Seven at Blickling Hall?'

'Yes, Sadie said the concert was brilliant.'

'That's true. Well, that evening Jackie mentioned some problems her husband is having. Perhaps Sadie might have spoken about him? His name is Chris Lambert.'

'Oh yes. He's the guy who is suspended from his job as deputy head of care at a residential home for young adults with autism. Do I remember right?'

'Yes. Did Sadie share why Chris got suspended?'

'Yes.'

'Well, I'll be honest Alex, I'm asking because I trust Jackie. Haven't ever met Chris. Jackie truly believes the allegations are false and malicious.'

Maxine stops.

I say, 'I see. How can I help?'

'Promised Jackie, I'm pretty sure you'd at least give Chris a call. Have consent to share his number.'

'I see,' I say again. I then add, 'Sure, what is the number then, please?

'Hold on a sec. Ah, got it. Zero seven five nine three six zero nine two three five.'

'OK. Will call now if that helps?'

'Right. Yes, great! Speak again soon and thanks, Alex.'

'Take care and enjoy Milena being home. Bye.'

I tap the numbers given by Maxine.

'Hello.'

'Hi Chris, my name is Alex. Maxine Stewart asked me to give you a call.'

'OH, hello. Yes, Maxine promised she'd talk with you.'

'Do you know I work for the police, Chris?'

'Yes.'

'How might I be able to help you, Chris?'

'Maxine believes I 'd benefit from talking with you, as someone who knows the processes involved. Just think some advice can help. But understand if you'd rather not?' replies Chris.

'OK. I prefer face to face. I can meet you lunchtime today if that's any good?'

'Why, I mean yes. I appreciate your offer, Mr Forrester. Where is your office?'

'Before deciding where Chris? Can you tell me your full name, date of birth and address please.'

'Sure, Chris Lambert 4th January 1976 and the address is 1 Barclay Lane End Road, Norwich, NR1 0ZZ.'

'Thank you. So, you are a neighbour of the local football team eh! Does this mean you're a big fan?'

'Yes. Hope it doesn't mean this is something that can go against me?'

I laugh, 'No, but the way they play might,' I reply.

'ERM...'

'Do you have any children please Chris?'

'Yes. Ryan who was born on 17th August 1997 and Michelle whose birth date is 4th March 2002.'

'Thank you. I know your wife's name is Jackie, but can I please have her maiden name and if appropriate any other marital names?'

'It's Jacqueline, actually, and I am her only husband, and maiden name was Burlington.'

'Thanks, Chris, very useful. For a meet-up, I'd like to suggest the Canaries pub. I can take an extended lunch break without a guilty conscience today. It's on the corner at the end of the road you live in, isn't it? I've never been in there, but told Delia's food is very good.'

Chris laughs, 'Yes it is. What time?'

'Say around one please?'

'Fine. I'll be standing against my car in the front car park. It's a yellow and green AMG Mercedes,' says Chris helpfully.

I'm unable not to laugh as I reply, 'Wow, you're brave but thanks for that. I will arrive in a Best-way taxi. See you soon.'

'Bye.'

I am relieved on Maxine's behalf that all the checks are negative. So, I press the button again and call to book a taxi. Be good to have a break from a report about the likes of, "The 'Mad' Iceman," I muse.

***

From a taxi, I learn that even the chimney pots on the roof of the Canaries pub are painted yellow and green. I then hear Marcel ask, 'Do you want me to drop off in the pub's car park Alex?'

'Yes please.'

As we enter the car park, I can see Chris attentive with his mobile phone. Marcel chooses a space near to the front door, and we complete the routine of me getting out of the vehicle.

'Cheers Marcel. See you soon,' I say.

'Have you booked a return,' asks Marcel.

'No need thanks, Marcel. Need to pop into County Hall. Can drive my rider from here. Then once the business is over, I will take the scenic route home.'

'Nice one. See you anon.'

'Bye,' I say, and I then turn left to make my way toward Chris Lambert.

'Hello, Mr Forrester?' asks Chris who is also offering a hand and is now I counter feeling a little embarrassed?

'Hello, Chris. I'm Alex Forrester. Pleased to meet you. And please don't worry, you weren't to know. I appreciate and reciprocate the gesture. Shall we go in?' I suggest.

'Yes. I'll buy the drinks. Believe it or not, it's the first time

I've been to this pub without it being a match-day,' replies Chris as he leads the way and kindly holds the doors open until I am inside.

'Nice one. Thanks,' I say.

My first impression of the pub is how dimly lit, dark even; it is inside. The windows are small and the walls and ceiling unsurprisingly are awash with yellow and green.

We reach the Bar, and Chris asks, 'What would you like Alex?'

'Half a bitter shandy, please. Is it OK with you that I find a useful table please, Chris?'

'Right. Yes. Will easily find you.'

'Nice one.'

I soon spot a place where my rider won't block any one's path. I'm browsing the menu when Chris puts our drinks on the table. I say, 'This is some local for a Norwich fan to have eh? It used to be an ambition of mine to buy a home in North London.'

'Are you a Gooner or a Hotspur?'

'The most successful of the two,' I answer.

'Why do you say, used to be?'

'It's now one of the flats built on the sacred turf of Highbury.'

'Are you in favour of the move?'

'Classic clear as mud answer. No, and yes.'

I'm chuckling as Chris asks, 'Why both?'

'No, because a new bigger stadium seems less atmospheric, less intimate. Where the 'Invincibles' became just that! Yes, because the stadium is in the same locality and is still representative of the team. Namely, it has more style than any other in the country.'

Chris smiles and our conversation is interrupted by a waitress dressed smartly in a yellow t-shirt and green skirt. Hello, my name is Chloe, and I'll be looking after you today.

Would you like to order something to eat,' she asks.

It feels like my eyes are deceiving my brain and yet my reply is somehow composed, 'Just a ham and mustard sandwich for me thank you.'

'And you Sir,'

'All day breakfast please.'

'Certainly. I will be back shortly,' says Chloe.

Needing to refocus, I divert my attention to a picture on a wall behind Chris. I ask, 'I recognise Steve Bruce in that big picture behind you. But what was the occasion?'

Chris doesn't need to turn round, and he answers. 'It is a picture I also have displayed at home. It captures a moment every Norwich fan relishes because it is Steve Bruce about to head the winning goal against the scum, I mean Ipswich, in the semi-final of the nineteen eighty-five Milk Cup.'

'Did you win the final?'

'Yes, we beat Sunderland one nil.'

'Did you go to the final?'

'My first away match. My father is a steward, so he was able to get enough tickets for a few of his friends and their kids too. They hired a van for twelve of us. It was a great day. Have you seen Arsenal at Wembley?'

'Yes, three times. Including witnessing Ipswich outplay us in the seventy-eight FA Cup final. So, I understand a little about the pleasure you have in seeing your rivals lose. Though to be fair, Ipswich fully deserved their victory that day.'

Chris does not respond because Chloe is back, 'Here we are, gentleman, one breakfast for you and a ham and mustard sandwich for you Sir.'

'Thank you, Chloe,' I say.

'Yes, likewise,' says Chris.

'If you need anything else don't hesitate to ask,' says Chloe and she leaves again.

'Have you seen England live,' asks Chris.

'Once and to be honest, that was because the opposition was Brazil. You?'

'Yes, many times. I'm an official member of the supporters club. I've seen them play in the last three World Cups.'

'Bet you had a great time. So you saw Brazil beat us in Korea then?'

'Yep. The heat got to us in the second half; otherwise, I'm sure we'd have gone...'

'Oh no, please don't say it. England to beat Brazil pure fantasy in my opinion. But I do understand why you hold the dream. Would be great to be alive when England win it again eh?'

'I shall keep going to every tournament we qualify for to ensure if the fantasy becomes a reality I can say I was there.'

'I admire your optimism,' I say with a wry smile.

'Right, guess I should now concentrate on talking about the situation I still find difficult to believe I'm in. Is that OK with you Alex?'

'Yes, absolutely but before you do I need to explain a couple of things first?'

'Sure, fire away.'

'I want to be open and tell you that since we ended our conversation on the phone, I put your name and every other name you gave me through every computer register used by protection agencies in this country. The good news is the results are negative which ironically means it is more accurate to say they're positive.'

'Glad you did. Have nothing to hide.'

'Sure. Despite this though, it is important from my point of view to share something about the check-lists, risk registers, monitoring forms, call them whatever you like? They are not full-proof. Which means, sometimes too much reliance is placed on such written records. This is because it is a fact that most people on such written records are found out after a history of concealed offending. Please don't be offended by my bluntness.'

'Sure. Get it,' replies Chris.

'Good. Just one last thing before it's over to you Chris. If I ever feel I don't believe you haven't committed an offence, I will tell you so and leave.'

'Understood. It all began when...'

***

Chris left five minutes ago. I'm writing some notes in a text to myself. They're reminders of information shared during our conversation. As I tap, I can see Chloe in the corner of my eye. She is picking up glasses, dishes and debris from tables. I look up, and Chloe says, 'Would you like another drink, Sir?'

'No thank you, Chloe. And please, my name is Alex. Forgive me Chloe, but I can't resist asking you, do you support Norwich? Like wearing yellow and green, even?'

Chloe laughs and then replies, 'Well, funny you should ask that. We live in Suffolk, and my husband supports the enemy. Thus, he's banned from wearing this in my own bloody house. Selfish bugger cuz it means to start every shift I have to allow for extra time to change here. Can't even take it home to wash. Fortunately, the Landlady lets me do it here. He nearly banned me from choosing to accept this job, but we need to pay the bills!'

We both laugh, and I say, 'A Suffolk lass then eh!?'

'Yep, raised in the heart of Constable country I'll have you know.'

'Lovely area. Which part?'

'A small place called Dunwich. Why do you ask?'

'Used to visit Saxmundham quite a bit. Remember to get there we went through Dunwich which is one of a few lovely places along that part of the coast, isn't it! Just wondered if you are a true blue? If you are it amuses me to think Norwich fans mingle in here unaware of the presence of an enemy from within!'

'Fair enough,' replies Chloe with a brief laugh which is

followed by a friendly smile. Albeit, with a hint of scepticism in it' delivery?

'Oh well. Better head off. Break from work has ended. Thanks for a nice lunch Chloe.'

'No problem. Enjoy the rest of your day,' says Chloe cheerfully.

***

Instead of taking the direct route to County Hall, I am approaching an outside table of a café located in an area of Norwich known as "Riverside." My mind is reeling, and I need some thinking time. Talking with Chloe was, 'Well it could have been Maxine, and I wouldn't have noticed,' I verbalise for an umpteenth time since leaving the pub. The more I say them there is a definite decrease in my tone of disbelief.

I force myself to recall a conversation I unwittingly overheard between DI Oaks and Frank Toddenham. Only, this time, I'm telling myself to try and remember the detail too.

Of all places, I was in a toilet cubicle of a large gleaming lavatory. Facilities included a spacious area designed for parents and toddlers and some of the people who use a rider. Amusingly, I think, and ironic, I can shut this cubicle door, but I can't lock it.

The location of this 'For Public Use' lavatory is nearby a reception area of a unit on Breckland Business park. The occasion was a MAPPA annual review of a mother of five children who was on probation following ten years in prison for abusing, in a variety of ways, over fifty known children. The meeting was held two days after our all night E. n. E. M. A. in July last year.

Oaks came in first. The chief constable was close by because immediately after I heard the entrance door open, Oaks said, "All good. No-one in here."

Is the fact Chloe exists is to what they were referring? Should I say or do anything? If so, when? With who? How? But Chloe is evidence Maxine has a twin! How will Maxine react?

And what a shock for Chloe too? They're birth twins. I'm ninety-nine point nine, nine, nine, nine recur... No, certain they are!'

What follows is the rest of what I heard in the toilet.

"Are we still in the clear.'

'Yes, but I could have done without the drama of Monday night at my age. I'm retiring in a couple of years and want my old ticker with me.'

'What was said?'

'That's just it Alan; it wasn't said. No one mentioned anything to give you or I even a sniff of a reason to suspect they might know? Promise!'

'And minutes in order?'

'Yes, come on Alan! Let's get out of here! I'm chairing a review, and you are on sick leave for Christ's sake. You shouldn't be here, and you knew I'd contact you. I did need to sleep you know!'

'Yes, of course. Sorry, it's just..."

As they walked away, both voices faded to leave me hearing silence, very loudly.

***

June 11, 2008

Isaac is parked in a lay-by near the 'Countryside' filling station on the A148. This road meanders across Norfolk between Kings Lynn and Cromer. In the car beside Isaac is his twin displaying a huge grin. 'Hello, Broth. Bet you can't believe I'm here eh! Look, the same birthmark. Great to see you and how are you mate?'

'Don't mate me. You're right mind you, all I've ever thought is, hope you never come back or get caught,' replies Isaac coldly.

'Don't be like that Broth. We're stuck together forever, remember!'

The twins then hug and pat each other on the back.

'It really is good to see you,' repeats Oliver.

'You too, I guess. But I promise you one thing, Ollie. I will never do time again. Get my drift. For no one! Do you hear?'

'Yes, Broth. My name is Robert now. Robert Hardeen.'

'How long you been in Norfolk?' asks Isaac.

'Living with a woman from around here who I met earlier this year in the Gambia. Arrived here in March.'

'Love is it? And by the way, right here, right now, to me, you are Ollie! Someone, the whole world it seems, tells me, "You're that dirty bastards twin brother aren't you?" So Ollie, cut to the chase, why the fuck are you here?'

'My new name was suggested by Harold White. Remember him? Bet you don't know Robert Hardeen was the real name of Houdini? Very funny eh Broth?'

'Why are you back Ollie?'

'To save Harold White from the fate prison has in store for him. Th...'

'You're fucking mad! You have no chance! You're more than likely end up like that Hawker friend of yours, shot dead! You're crackers! Go home wherever that is?'

It was James then, thinks Oliver as he responds with, 'I told you, I owe it to Harold. And after following you undetected for two weeks, I'm very confident I can succeed.'

'Following me?' exclaims Isaac angrily.

'Yes. Well, be fair Broth, I can't exactly knock on your front door and say Hi, can I!'

'Why wait two weeks?'

'I stopped my surveillance over a week ago. I figured, if the pigs are watching you to find me then I would have left a trace for them.'

'What? Jesus Christ Ollie. Isn't getting away with your disgusting tastes enough for you? Why risk capture for an old man fucked up enough to murder his crippled wife?'

'I note one of the blokes you work with also moonlights at...'

'Whoa! That's enough. I'm not getting an innocent man like Dan harmed by you. No way!'

'I won't harm, Dan you say. Just need you to look after him for an hour or two, that's all...'

'I'm off Ollie. Get out.'

Hardeen does. But, twenty minutes later!

***

June 25, 2008

I am in Norwich Crown Court Number One. It is the final day of White's appeal which is being heard by the President of the Queen's Bench Division, a Lord Justice of Appeal and a High Court Judge. A clause in the J Act dictates the venue. It states, "Any appeal has to take place in the same court where the offender was convicted." The said judicial personnel will, if appropriate, also disclose their decision with regard to Clive's application for the death penalty to be administered to White!

A hush suddenly falls as the three-man panel enter. Within a few seconds, the President of the Queen's Bench Division starts today's proceedings by saying, 'Good morning everyone. We have been deliberating since yesterday's proceedings concluded with both sides submitting their arguments. Before I share our judgements, on behalf of each of us, I wish to state our disappointment that Harold White is feeling too unwell to attend today.

Concerning Mr White seeking his conviction for murdering his wife getting quashed, we have unanimously decided to deny him this. Similarly, we deny a request for a retrial. However, we do recognise Mr White has demonstrated he can be honest with his more recent acceptance it is a fact his wife did commit infidelity within their marriage.

Nonetheless, we do all reject the argument put forward by the defence council yesterday! We do not agree there is doubt about the validity of any of the evidence presented in the original trial. A trial which demonstrated Mr White murdered his wife.

Furthermore, while it is possible Maxine Stewart could have stolen a set of Mr White's house keys thirty years ago, it is impossible to believe she murdered Gillian White as suggested by the defence. This is because it does not alter the truth of Maxine Stewart's alibi, supported by documentation from BT, that she was working from home and having a telephone conversation with a colleague during the time the murder took place.

Therefore, this leaves the issue of what is an appropriate sentence? After scrutiny of the criteria within the Justice Act, we find in favour of Clive Verity's request for Mr White to be administered a death penalty. In line with the law, the date will be August 29, 2008, and the place of execution will be Norfolk's Justice Centre at a time be determined by the Governor of the said Centre.

However, we remind this court, should Clive Verity wish to change his mind, he has the right to do so between now and up to five minutes before the actual time Harold White's execution is planned. Thank you.'

***

June 27

I am relieved to the doors are open and then see Chloe at work on entering the Canaries Pub. This said I am anxious and nervous too. I am meeting Maxine for lunch. It was eventually exhausting trying to convince Maxine this pub has such good food and has become a regular haunt for me which she really should experience for herself.

Given the circumstances and facts which are known relating to the separation of these birth twins, I am optimistic Maxine and Chloe will at least believe my intentions are honourable.

I go straight back out and see Maxine turning into the pub car park. With only five cars here Maxine is heading to a free space nearest to me. Now front on, Maxine waves and then steers left. I spin and rush back in toward the bar, 'Hello, Chloe isn't it?' I ask with a friendly smile.

'Yes, I remember you. What can I get you to drink?' replies Chloe.

'Sorry, but could you please help my friend by opening the double front door to this pub?

'Of course, I can,' replies Chloe.

As Chloe stretches, looking out, to unfasten a latch at the top of the door, I see Maxine come into not just my view but that of Chloe too. Maxine stops, quite literally, in her tracks. Chloe lets go of the latch and they are looking at each other and there is not a sound coming from either.

Inevitably I begin to panic that this will be a disaster and I hear Chloe say, 'Jesus Christ, you look like me. Sorry, it's the shock. Here, come in.'

Maxine doesn't move and says, 'Totally understand, you look so much like... ERM, I was adopted as a baby, were you?, ERM, I'm Maxine.'

Maxine then offers a hand to Chloe.

'I was actually, how did you know that? Is this some sick game going on. Annette?

Oscar? Need some backup, please. We've got a nuisance customer,' shouts Chloe.

By now I'm at the other end of the bar hidden by its height.

'There is no need,' Maxine protests, before adding, 'I'm not playing anything. I'm meeting a friend here for lunch. I saw him come in not long before I did. He's easy to recognise as he uses a wheelchair.'

'What's going on Chloe? Are you alright?' asks Oscar.

'No I'm not bloody well al-right Oscar. Look at her, made up to look like me. Says she's come to meet the...'

'Me,' I say,' and add, 'Maxine has come to meet me. Chloe, I am sorry. I thought a natural bump into each other would... Sorry, Maxine.'

Chloe interjects, 'Wait a minute. Are you saying you've set

this up?' Chloe asks pointing to me. She then places her hands on her hips incredulous and says, 'Get out, the both of you. Oscar, tell them they're barred,' demands Chloe.

'Hello Oscar, my name is Maxine. This man,' says Maxine gesturing toward me, 'has invited me to lunch here today. He is like any of us, not perfect. But, I'd trust him with my daughter's life.'

Maxine then looks at Chloe, 'Chloe, as soon as I saw you, I understood why Alex was so adamant we ate here. Chloe, did you know I was coming today?'

'Of course, I didn't,' retorts Chloe.

'Nor did I know about you, Chloe. I used to be a lawyer, and I first met Alex through his job with social services many years ago. Alex knows I was adopted and frankly, I'm certain you won't contradict me when I say Alex has seen you before today, hasn't he Chloe? And, I'm hazarding a guess it was quite recent too, right?'

'Yeah. Once or twice. So?' asks Chloe.

'Did he say anything to you suggesting you just might have a twin sister, Chloe?' asks Maxine.

'No.'

'If Alex had said anything to me or you, he knows I already know I, we, could not have found out anything about one another from formal, well informal channels too as it happens. Believe me, Chloe, I am in shock too but how would you have felt if Alex had just told **me** about his suspicion? And say, I then came here to see you alone. I think Alex was trying to consider us fairly and equally. It is arguably clumsy by Alex, but if we're not twins, then I'll come back and let you and Oscar throw me to the wolves, let alone your car park! Please let the three of us talk together? But first, lets just you and I go somewhere right now and talk. Please?' Maxine asks.

Chloe doesn't answer, and Oscar puts an arm around her shoulder, 'Have to say, Chloe, the similarity is uncanny pet. You can have a cuppa with Maxine out the back in private like. Annette or I can stay with you if that helps you like. Come on, what do you say pet?'

'This is all just so mad. I want you to stay with me, Oscar. And I want to ring my husband before I do anything else,' replies Chloe as she walks quickly out of sight.

CHAPTER TWENTY-TWO

July 18, 2008

It is a beautiful morning. Three Counties View lit by colours of dawn at its peak. The river's surface shimmers a bright mixture of yellow, green, brown, and blue by way of the sunlight bouncing off foliage near to river's edge.

Sadie and I are on annual leave today. In about six hours our first job applicant will arrive for what is their second interview. Last Friday Sadie met each candidate when they came accompanied by their respective pet dog.

Sadie said all of the dogs got on well with Bridie and Polly, but as is usual, she has a favourite. Our advert said we are, "Looking for a full-time Housekeeper who loves dogs. Must live in. The small neighbouring cottage provided rent-free."

Sadie, still dressed in a black signature cotton Sleep-shirt, is carrying a tray. The rays of the sun mean white graphic letters displayed boldly on the front of the shirt is unreadable. I don't need to use my eyes to know it says, "Sadie's Secret" and there is a red heart embroidered in the gap between these two words.

'Gorgeous day isn't it,' says Sadie.'

'Certainly is. You look wonderful too. And, Cream Teas with the best home-made strawberry jam ever, for breakfast. Thanks.'

'Get away with you. Haven't even brushed my hair,' replies Sadie.

'Beauty is in the eye of the beholder! Are you sticking to not giving me any clue which of the applicants owns your favourite dog?'

'It's more they were Bridie and Polly's favourite. And no I'm not. We struck a deal. Today the hard work is yours,' replies Sadie with a devilish smile.

'Be great if our choices tot up to be the same,' I say sincerely.

'Will have to wait and see, won't we sweetheart.'

***

The last candidate closes our front lounge door behind her. I look straight into Sadie's sparkling blue eyes like I've never looked at anyone before. With my heart thundering, I somehow speak, 'I can honestly say I have never been more gobsmacked about anything else, which given what Jill disclosed to me, is quite a statement!'

Sadie is grinning and desperately trying not to laugh. She says, 'I know. I was watching you as soon as Milena walked in.'

'You must have known it was Maxine's Milena from the short-listing you done?'

'Yes, of course. So, the decision is a no-brainer, isn't it! Milena is perfect and needs it too,' suggests Sadie in her friendly self-assured and decisive manner.

'Sadie, I'm not even sure Milena is eighteen yet! And to say it will blur professional boundaries is an understatement of the like. Well, I'm still unsure if everything that's happened so far today is a dream. Or perhaps nightmare is more accurate. It's...'

'Rubbish Alex. You know very well what Maxine and Toby have told us about the change in Milena since she moved to Australia. I...'

'But I can't see Frank giving his blessing. Can you? And it's great the progress Milena's made. But, that's a major concern for me too. Milena will want to enjoy what those in their late teens usually do. Living here will be too boring and isolating surely?' I interrupt.

Sadie leans forward and holds my hand and says, 'Please Alex, hear me out first?'

'OK.'

'The seed came from a chat between Maxine and me at your birthday party. During our conversation, I mentioned our plan to hire a housekeeper. Please understand it is Maxine, Toby, and Milena too, who've poured the water to cause the seed to grow.

Maxine begged me not to say anything in case Milena changes her mind about wanting to return to live permanently in England. I listened to all three and trust me, please, it is because I live with you, why Milena has asked us to help?

Milena told me herself that spending time with her Dad has been brilliant. She also loves the art course and college life. Is happy her mum and dad are friends again but misses her mum and England. Milena wants the Housekeeper job because she can have an opportunity to talk to us, well you. Said you really helped helped her at the funeral when she spoke to you about losing Aunt Valerie.

Milena wants somewhere to live where she can paint. She wants to earn enough money so she can support herself to pay for driving lessons. Wants to earn while studying at Gloucester college. Even mentioned aspirations to go to university.

Yes, I think your right. Frank will take some persuading. Sir Roger has high regard for Maxine and has promised he would be willing to try at least! Believe me, Alex, there is one hundred percent consent and support from both parents. Naturally, Toby is sad, but I think both are putting their child first. Which is good, right!'

Still feeling speechless I say, 'An eighteen-year-old woman on her own in a remote place like this? Sadie, you know what I'm saying.'

'Yes, Alex I do! Look, we've both discussed us leaving our jobs. I accept we were thinking in a year or two. But Alex, I don't mind leaving sooner. You can choose to leave whenever you like. Of course, I would prefer sooner than later.'

'Ditto, though probably next year for me. Nonetheless, you being here surely negates the need for any Housekeeper to look after Bridie and Polly, doesn't it?'

'I know, but we can now do something for someone I know you think has been dealt a few tricky hands during her childhood.'

I shuffle in my seat and lean forward to kiss Sadie gently on her lips and then say, 'You're incredible! Give me a bit of time to digest it all. Must be honest though, this could well be one of those situations where somehow we will move forward agreeing to disagree. So, let's see what happens.'

'Fair enough,' says Sadie who then reaches a hand into a hip pocket of a pretty multi-flowered pattern summer dress. Out of it comes an envelope and she says, 'This came in the post yesterday. I saw it when popping in to get Bridie and Polly before picking you up from work. For what are now obvious reasons, I thought it best to wait till after the interviews.'

'My eyes aren't deceiving me are they Sadie? That is a Californian postmark isn't it?'

'Yes. Exciting eh! So pleased for you, knowing how much she means to you.'

I have tears creeping slowly down, and I say, 'Shit me. It's crazy. This time last year I didn't even know I was a dad! Since we had our impromptu holiday in San Francisco in January, I admit to recently giving up hope the first time together won't be the last too! Shit Sadie, I hope Nicene does want to see her dad again? Wow...'

'She will Alex. I just feel it. Do you want me to open it or put this on the floor?'

CHAPTER TWENTY THREE

July 22, 2008

'Not for me thank you DI..., Alan,' I reply.

'Why are we here?' asks Frank impatiently.

I explain, 'To help two people is the most succinct reply I can give Frank.'

'Help? Who? Why? I assume it's not professional, given we've all been in HQ all day?'

I don't mind admitting my calm exterior and confident delivery is at total odds with, excuse the pun, frankly, shitting myself! I begin, 'On July nineteenth last year I overheard a conversation between you two. Until this very moment, neither of you knew this to be the case. Your conversation took place, not five hundred yards from where we are now sitting. Do either of you wish to acknowledge which conversation I am referring too?'

Alan's facial expression suggests he's cottoned on and Frank replies, 'Conversation? Blimey, we've had hundreds. Alex, what is this all about? My wife is expecting me. We are taking the grandchildren to see "Peter Pan" at the Theatre Royal tonight.'

'Sorry, I didn't know that. Still, it's five-thirty so plenty of time,' I reply noticing Frank made very little eye contact with me while talking.

What have you found out?' asks Alan who sadly does not look a well man since his minor stroke?

'Fair question Alan. And, before giving my answer, I must make it absolutely crystal clear what has led to this meeting happened by accident. I could call on witnesses to this if it became necessary.

So, in answer to your question Alan, what are the right words? On June six this year I met a woman who started her life attached to her identical twin sister. I had lunch in, and trust me on this one, the Canaries Pub on Barclay Lane Road

North. The woman's name is Chloe, and she is employed as a bar-person in the said pub. Has either of you ever been to the pub recently? Well, during the last five years for that matter?' I ask.

Frank stands up to leave I assume. I press to send a text stored in Draft. Frank's expression screams anger, and he says, 'This is ridiculous...'

'Please don't leave Frank...'

I stop because all three of us hear the doors of the Old Fashioned Café open. I don't need to look to see who has walked in. Instead, incredibly, I'm watching Alan turn an even "(A) Whiter Shade of Pale." I also note Frank's jaw has dropped and as he sits back down he says, 'It can't be!'

'You both know Maxine Stewart of course, and so I would also like to introduce you to, Chloe Ryedale.'

'Hello,' says Maxine.

'Hello,' says Chloe.

Alan and Frank look at each other and neither reply. Chloe and Maxine sit next to each other with Maxine beside me. I then open a thin cardboard A4 size folder laying on the table and say, 'Naturally, Chloe and Maxine are more interested than anyone to ask you some questions. Before they do though, we agreed I would convey to you not to be in any doubt about what they already do know!

So, first I will read part of the minutes of the E. n. E. M. A. meeting you chaired last July, Frank. Debbie Eagle, from Children's Services, said, "Valerie and Maxine have separate sets of unrelated birth parents. Challengingly, we have only found out the identity of one of the four. Amongst Norfolk's official medical records and inside its archive files folder we found a scanned copy of a single piece of headed paper dated the sixth of June nineteen seventy-two. All that is written on it is, "TA-Successful caesarean delivery. Too young to raise children. Adoption immediate. GP present. Heritage-NFN. No Further Action Required. ME." On this day all other caesarean sections in Norfolk involved women aged over sixteen. The name of the GP present who signed Maxine's birth certificate is a Logan Baird who was also David and Henrietta Hurst's GP."

I pause to look up before continuing, 'There is not even a sniff of an attempt to advise those at the meeting, that the newborn baby girl, namely Maxine, taken by Logan Baird to the Hurst s' is, as you can see, one of at least two. Maybe more? Who knows?'

Frank leans forward quite menacingly actually, staring right at me, 'Be careful Forrester, you are sailing in, more than close to, the wind with this. I will not be cornered by yo...'

I interrupt, 'With respect Frank, that's just it! This is not about suspicion, recriminations and judgement! It is not about any of us men here! It is about Chloe and Maxine having the right and need, given all the circumstances involved, to have an opportunity to ask questions. Questions to the only people ever identified who can share information which hopefully helps both sisters understand why what happened did happen? I sincerely hope Frank, both of you actually, that I am reassuring you about your initial concerns about motive?

Frank is now sat back with his arms folded over his rotund belly and looks less threatening but is fuming.

Alan says, 'To be honest Frank, it's a relief for me.'

'Your call Alan,' interjects Frank.

Looking at me, Alan offers, 'I will do my best to answer questions. I think it's also fair to mention actions taken by Frank a year ago were to protect me! Frank was not a party to events in nineteen seventy-two.'

'OK. Thank you, both of you. If Chloe and Maxine agree, given Alan's comment Frank, and your engagement this evening, perhaps you would like to leave? I reply.

Frank sits more upright again and glances at his watch and then looks at the twin dressed sisters (I found out later for their first time) and he says, 'I apologise. It must be a tremendous shock to discover what you have. I would like to stay if you don't mind? But need to leave no later than six-thirty.'

Chloe nods agreement, and Maxine says, 'Thank you, Frank. Fine by me too. Thank you also, Alan. Chloe, do you want to begin or...?'

'Thanks, Maxine. Prefer if you do please.'

'What is our mother's name please Alan?'

'Trudy Atwood.'

'Is there any way we can try and find our mother?'

Alan puts his hands together and addressing both sisters asks, 'Shall I tell you what I know first and then answer your questions afterwards?'

'Sure,' and, 'Thank you, Alan, yes please,' reply Chloe and Maxine respectively.

'I do feel I must warn, some of what you are about to listen to may well be hard to hear! Please stop me if it becomes too much to take in all at once. Now that everything is in the open I am fully prepared to meet you both further,' Alan says with sensitivity. He then adds, 'I am not offering my next comment as an absolute justification for my actions. But, please understand the law and culture were very different shy on forty years ago.'

Maxine mimes, 'OK.'

'Trudy was the youngest child of Keith and Iona Atwood. She had seven brothers. The family home was in Great Yarmouth. They moved to Norfolk from Bootle in Merseyside with what was five sons at this time.

Before becoming pregnant when aged fifteen, Trudy was well known to the local authorities and police and had been for at least five years. Trudy had been a frequent runner from residential homes and foster placements. When aged fourteen, Trudy was arrested for the first of many subsequent occasions too, for soliciting in Norwich with two female adult teenage sex workers. Along with these 'friends,' Trudy was addicted to harmful drugs.

The family environment was, to be candid, chaotic and unhealthy on many levels. Keith and Iona and most of their sons had fingers in lots of different pies. Each son, bar one, who was Trudy's twin brother, had or did end up doing time in prison. Their eldest son, Stanley, was sentenced to three years when found guilty of rape against Trudy in nineteen seventy.

As a result of Stanley's conviction, Trudy was in various foster or social services children's homes over the next two years or so. The rest of her family disowned Trudy for what they saw as disloyalty to them and all stated the disclosure to be a lie.'

Chloe holds her sister's hand.

'I seem to recall it was around Easter time in nineteen seventy-two. Forgive me as I cannot be certain about precisely when? Trudy was found to be around six to seven months pregnant. Thus, Trudy was given support in a privately run home called Protectors? And, this support service was jointly funded by the NHS and the Local Authority. Trudy was of slight build and this was the prime factor in the need for a caesarian operation. Sadly, Trudy didn't know who your father is? Not even a right name to try and identify possible cand. Sorry, this is...'

Maxine stretches an arm and gently taps Alan's hand and says, 'Don't worry Alan. Is there more?'

'Thanks, and yes there is. Do you want me to continue?' Alan asks.

Both twins nod yes.

'I was present at the hospital just after both of you were born. The twin birth had been anticipated but the GP Logan Baird was adamant, due to a lastminute hitch is all I was told, that only one of you could be taken to Mr and Mrs Hurst.

I had been summoned to undertake a clandestine journey. I was told by Logan to drive to an address in Suffolk. A nurse from maternity held you in the back of my car Chloe. When we arrived at our destination, we were in Yaxley where I met a man who said his name was John Smith and that he was a GP. It is my understanding, Mr Smith was then personally going to take you Chloe to your new parents. Sorry, I was never told their names or address.'

Chloe and Maxine's eyes are moist.

Alan is glad he's able to say, 'Nearly finished. It is very hard to tell you both that sadly two years after you were born, Trudy died. The cause was, what is genuinely believed to be, an 'accidental' overdose of Heroin. I am so sorry.'

***

Wedding Day

Hazel Billing rings the doorbell of the home belonging to the mother of her very soon to be daughter-in-law.

'Amanda, can you be a darling and see who's at the door, please? I can't leave at such a delicate moment with getting Kristina's hair to look it's best.'

'No problem Mrs Thorpe,' says Amanda cheerfully as she walks with a spring in her step to open the front door.

'Hello Mrs Billing, how are you? Please come in.'

'Thank you, dear. I'm very well, you?'

'I can't complain,' replies Amanda.

'Is that handsome boyfriend of yours here too?' asks Hazel.

'No, he's helping Finley keep calm I hope.'

'Shame, still I'll see him later won't I?'

'I would like to know where he is if you don't Mrs Billing. Feel free to join Rosa and Kristina. They are in Kris's bedroom. Would you like a cup of tea?' asks Amanda.

'If you don't mind dear I'd much prefer a glass of brandy, please Amanda.'

'No problem, anything with it?'

'Some hot milk would be nice please.'

'Certainly, I'll bring it up to you.'

The sound of talking indicates to Hazel which direction to go now she has reached the landing. The bedroom door is open, but Hazel still chooses to knock.

Kristina can see Hazel through the reflection of a mirror

that is the centrepiece of her hand-made solid oak dressing table.

'Hello Hazel and come in. I love your dress,' says Kristina.

'Thank you, dear. Not as pretty as you and the one you're going to wear today. Then, I don't think it's possible that any other woman or dress could be. Finley is a very fortunate man. Hello Rosa, do you agree?' replies Hazel.

'Lovely to see you, Hazel. Yes, I do. I am terribly biased of course,' replies Rosa with a chuckle.

'Stop it. Both of you. You're embarrassing me. Besides, marrying Finley means I am the lucky one!'

Kristina's modesty is genuine, and her smile alters to a laugh on hearing Hazel ask, 'Where is Robert then Rosa?'

'Robert flew to Vietnam two days ago Hazel. He...'

'Good grief Rosa. I am sorry to hear that. Rotten thing to do and his timing isn't exactly clever either. Still...'

Hazel moves her head back in surprise at hearing Rosa laugh.

Rosa then says, 'No, nothing like that Hazel. Robert got a call from Phuc who he's employed to run things in his absence. It is good news, Hazel. There is a buyer for Robert's business. So, needs must. Robert's solicitor thinks taking care of things should mean Robert will be back for good in three weeks, tops. You miss him too don't you Kristina.'

'Yes, mum.'

Kristina then swivels her head to look at Hazel to add, 'Don't worry Hazel. I've done the dutiful grilling daughter bit. No man can get ten out of ten, can they! So, I scored him nine and a half.'

Hazel smiles along with Kristina and says, 'Relieved to hear that dear. All of it!'

'Here you are Hazel,' says Amanda.

'Thank you, dear. Very sweet. May I sit in the chair beside your dresser Kristina?'

'Yes. Of course, you can.'

***

Finley asked Bernice Buck to be his joint best 'man.' Amanda's boyfriend Neil, practically a lifelong best friend, is the other half. All three are in Clip-street Farm which used to be the village of Bale's last functional one. It is now a private residence owned by Mr and Mrs Hipper. Finley is in the house's snooker room enjoying a game in which he's teamed up with his best man against Neil's father, Jacob Hipper.

Neil's mother is showing Bernice, Bale's wood carved village sign depicting the ancient bale oak tree. A tree which once stood with branches over seventy foot high and lived for over five hundred years.

'Impressive isn't it Eliza?' asks Bernice.

'My mother was present at its unveiling ceremony.'

'How wonderful. When did that happen then?' asks Bernice.

'To tell you the truth I never remember without looking at some photographs of mum. Before I was born, so a long time ago,' replies Eliza jovially.

'Real shame Finley's sister can't make today?'

'It is that Bernice. Fortunately, Finley understands the commitment to duty too and is very proud of Lucia. We all are.'

'Sure. With good reason,' Bernice comments supportively.

'Bernice. Have you met Rosa's, ERM, man-friend sounds more appropriate for those of us in our middle years shall we say?' asks Eliza.

Bernice notices Eliza seemed even to frown when asking. 'No I haven't. Why do you ask?'

'Just wondered. No reason as such,' replies Eliza nonchalantly.

'But?' asks Bernice.

'Well, don't get me wrong. I can see the attractions. Robert is his name. Robert has always been pleasant when our paths have crossed. It's just he looks so different to how people usually are round here. It's probably all sounding very silly I know, and then there is, how shall I put it? Yes, in many other ways too, Robert is so different from Rosa's husband. May your soul continue to rest in peace William.'

Bernice hesitates and then says, 'I hope I'm not speaking out of turn. It sounds as if you and the village were fond of William and still are of Mrs Thorpe. Perhaps anyone new coming in would make you feel understandably protective.'

Eliza smiles broadly and says, 'A wise head on young shoulders you have Bernice.'

Eliza then briefly and gently touches Bernice's bare shoulder and adds, 'No wonder Finley has spoken so highly of you. Have you married Bernice?'

'Not yet.'

'Well, whenever you do, he'll be a lucky man, I'm sure,' Eliza says while bending down to remove a sweet wrapper from the base of the village sign.

Bernice, in truth, feels annoyed with herself. But, she chooses not to explain to Eliza, why indeed such a man would be very lucky! Instead, Bernice asks, 'Mrs Thorpe's man-friend will be at the wedding, so I look forward to giving him the once over for you if you like?'

Both laugh and Eliza says, 'Funny you mention him again. What, with Rosa appearing so attached to him, I admit, I was fearful Robert might be chosen to give Kristina away. I felt even more guilty when Kristina and Rosa visited us especially to reassure Jacob that honour remains his. You see Bernice, Jacob and William were best friends from their first school-days.'

'To be honest Eliza. I think hearing about the village gossip will add to my enjoyment at all the celebrations today. Everyone in Bale has been invited haven't they?'

'Yes. We need to get home young lady. The first of all our guests from beyond Bale will soon start arriving. I do hope Jacob and the boys are still wearing clean suits.'

Eliza and Bernice begin to stroll, and Bernice says, 'I think it's great coming to a wedding where everything is happening within the village both the Bride and Groom were born and raised all their lives. And, where their new home is too. Really sweet.'

'It is that Bernice. It really is.'

***

Hawker would have expected the last person to be making himself at home in his secret hideaway is Oliver Stubs. Stubs is now in the most dangerous phase of his plan to free White. No more blending into village life.

The hideaway is, in fact, one of a number of outside brick built dwellings belonging to Bylaugh Hall. Stubs and Hawker found it when both were in their mid-twenties. It was by accident, but at a time they were driving around with an unwilling passenger.

The Hall is very isolated and the estate contains over 19,000 acres of land. The nearest villages are Lyng and Elsing and even further away is the town of Swanton Morley.

Bylaugh Hall was built and privately lived in from around 1851 until the Second World War. During which, the Hall was requisitioned by the RAF as the headquarters of 100 (Bomber Support) Group. By 1950, the house was in disrepair. It was stripped of its lead and interior fittings and has been abandoned ever since. The outbuilding chosen to be their hideout involved Hawker and Stubs assembling a new door with a padlock system.

Inside is spacious and windowless. The bare basics aren't a problem to endure, and some of the boxes are full of things Stubs will enjoy delving into. It is the need to look exactly like his brother and not be Robert Hardeen that is proving to be, **the** test to pass. Stubs is presently preparing to leave the hideout.

To relieve boredom Stubs drives around, in a car bought by William Thorpe, like a tourist is probably the aptest description! He grabs keys off a mattress along with a travellers bag. Amongst other items, this bag contains a complete set of clothes Isaac typically uses when at work. Stubs used to mock Isaac for his skinhead look but thankful for a second time he wears this style.

Today, Stubs has decided to visit Ely and in particular, its striking Cathedral. 'A stay in a nice Cambridge hotel for a few days sounds a pleasant idea,' Stubs tells himself as he locks up the hideaway.

***

Rosa, Hazel, Kristina, Amanda and Helen Thompson are enjoying a brief moment to relax. They are sat in a conservatory. Kristina looks utterly stunning and is much calmer now that Helen has just completed the finishing touches on her wedding dress.

'You are very talented Helen,' says Rosa.

'Yes. Marvellous,' adds Hazel.

'Very clever,' says Amanda.

'Bloody fantastic I think,' says Kristina who then adds, 'Thank you so much, Helen. Everything I ever wanted in a dress for this day!'

'You're welcome Kristina and to all of you, thank you for your kind sentiments,' replies Helen shyly.

Rosa stands up and says, 'Kristina sweetheart, you're father spoke about feeling so sad he wouldn't be giving you away on such a day as this. I know he would have been so proud and happy for you.'

Rosa bends to retrieve her handbag off the middle multicoloured rose patterned cushion laying on a wicker style two seater sofa. On opening the bag, Rosa takes out a small gift-wrapped box. Rosa says, 'Sweetheart, your father asked me to give you this today.'

Kristina accepts the present and says, 'Thanks, mum. What is it?'

'Take a peep and see,' replies Rosa.

Amanda, Hazel and Helen are watching with bright grins

already. Kristina unravels the wrapped paper which reveals a tiny purple coloured trinket box. Kristina opens the box and sees a ring. 'Oh mum, thank you. You've spent loads already on today. You didn't...'

'It is your father's wedding ring, Kristina. He, we want you to keep it and wear it if you wish?'

'Awe, how lovely,' says Hazel.

Rosa and Kristina hug. 'It's a wonderful idea. Thanks, Dad,' says Kristina looking up.

Kristina then wipes a tear away and adds, 'And, thanks, mum. Please mum, you choose which finger?'

Rosa takes hold of the ring and pauses to decide which of the fingers pointing toward her is best. Rosa makes a choice.

'Beautiful mum,' and Kristina kisses Rosa again before adding, 'Truly mum!'

'A toast,' says Rosa who looks for her glass of champagne. Finding it, she holds it up and the four ladies in her company follow suit. 'To your father sweetheart and to my Willie. Forever in our hearts.'

All five glasses clink, and as variable sips are being taken they hear a loud knock on Croft House Farm's front door. 'I'll go,' says Rosa to Amanda.

Jacob Hipper has arrived so he can walk beside Kristina through to the other end of the village. Where upon, Finley and all guests are waiting in an almost full "All Saints Church."

***

Rosa, Hazel and Helen went ahead and are taking their seats in the front row when Kristina and Jacob come into the Chaplain assistant's view, 'Sorry for being a little late Reverend.'

'I do believe it is a bride's privilege,' replies Hilary joyously. She adds, 'We are all ready Kristina. Are you?'

'Absolutely.'

Hilary nods to Father Browning who is waiting in front of

the altar. He, in turn, sends a signal to the organ player. A second later the instantly recognisable melody of "Here Comes The Bride" chimes out gloriously. That is both inside and quite a way out of the church. All in the assemblage that can stand up.

Finley peeps behind him, and his eyes adore Kristina who he hasn't seen for three days. He marvels at the dress which he's observing for the first time. Finley then smiles and mimes, 'You look amazing. I love you.'

Managing to keep hold of a posy of flowers in colours that match the dress, Kristina uses fingers to sign, 'You too.' The bride's smile is also radiating enough energy to put Eco-Warriors out of business.

Arm in arm Jacob and Kristina continue to make slow, relaxed strides up the aisle. The lilac, pink and white dress has an embellishment using hand-sewn flower crystals which induce the hemline to sweep train softly on the floor in front of Amanda. The fabric used for the wedding dress is chiffon, the waistline is natural, the neckline is a sweetheart, and this beautiful handmade dress is both backless and sleeveless.

Kristina arrives to stand beside the groom, and as she and Jacob embrace she whispers, 'Thank you, Jacob. It means a lot to me, both of us.'

'An honour for me to do so,' replies Jacob who then separates from the bride. Before taking his place for the ceremony, Jacob shakes hands with Finley.

The church is now in expectant silence. Only until a moment later when Father Browning says, 'In the name of the father, the son and holy ghost may god be with you, Amen.'

In unison, nearly everyone else repeats, 'Amen.'

'A warm welcome to all of you. Today...'

***

Bernice sits down having just finished the second best 'man' speech. Sally, who is at a table nearest to the head one, notices, for the first time, her friend looking stressed. The freckles on

Bernice's face have imploded into a bright orange-red that matches her hair.

Neil then stands up again, 'Ladies and gentleman, girls and boys. I am thrilled to announce it is time for the partying to start. To mark the official beginning, I now ask the bride and groom to have the floor to themselves and lead a dance to our first song. The song was chosen by both independently from the other. So, with no further delay, I give you Finley and Kristina Billing.'

Immediately there are cheers, whistles, words of encouragement and clapping right around Bale Village Hall. Hand in hand the happy couple make their way to the other side of the head table. They get in a position as if they are contestants about to perform a waltz on, "Strictly Come Dancing."

Neil gives his Dad the nod to press play. Everyone then hears Leona Lewis sing, "What if I told you it was all meant to be."

Bernice leaves her seat and is soon standing in front of Sally. With no words exchanged Sally accepts Bernice's outstretched hand, and they are the second couple to dance. By the time "Moment Like This" reaches the part where the chorus is heard for the second time the floor is covered by guests, including Sadie and I.

I anticipate Sadie will soon place her arms around me, but at present, she's displaying her magical smile while waving the posy Kristina threw behind her back. Sadie's motion is vigorous, and the roses brush my nose yet again, and it probably isn't going to be for a final time.

***

July 29

The neutral ground was agreed by all of us who are congregated at the foyer of The Assembly House in Norwich. Maxine stops talking with the restaurant's receptionist and turns to face us. 'OK guys our room is ready,' says Maxine.'

We all then follow our head waitress and Maxine into the Hobart room. This is one of a few places in this fabulous Georgian building in which you can dine privately. Though, we are not dining as such and instead will choose from the Afternoon Tea menu. It is nearly a year since I last met Milena. The change in her demeanour is evident. She seems more confident and best of all, happier!

'Which chair shall I move Mr Forrester? And, can I sit next to you please Sadie?' asks Milena.

Sadie moves a chair I replace with mine, making it now the one on the right of a row of four. Sadie then says, 'It's OK Milena, you sit on this one, and I'll sit next to you here on the other side.'

'Nice one Sadie,' says Milena who then slides past me to take her seat. She then adds, 'Thank you for coming here today, Mr Forrester.'

'We're both glad to see if we can help you, Milena. Fingers crossed eh.'

Milena chuckles, 'And toes Mr Forrester. I remember you telling me how some words can form a sentence which describes something correctly and incorrectly at the same time.'

I smile before replying, 'Yes. Fair enough. Toes are crossed too.'

I then hear Maxine say to Brooke, our designated waitress, 'Please can you give us five minutes to decide?'

'Certainly madam.' replies Brooke who then leaves the room.

I then look at the person sat directly opposite me and ask, 'Sir Roger, Is Frank still attending this meeting?'

'Yes Alex. Frank's been delayed by a traffic jam on the A11. Another nasty mess on the A47 bypass I'm sad to say. He's just text. He hopes to be here in two minutes.'

'Thanks. What happened?'

'Not sure. Three motorbikes weaving between cars. Five dead at the scene, fourteen others taken to the hospital and some with serious injuries.'

'Awful,' I say.

Frank then walks in, 'So sorry to keep you all waiting.'

I am relieved Frank chooses to sit at the head of the table at the other end.

'Oh, hello Frank,' says Maxine while switching on her ipad which had till now been arrested on the table.

'Good afternoon Maxine,' replies Frank looking the most relaxed I've ever seen him.

'Hello Frank,' says Karen Trinket who is sat opposite Maxine and next to Luke.

'Very nice to see you, Karen. Is all arr. well?'

'Yes, it is Frank. Thank you.'

'Good. Glad to hear that,' Frank replies cheerfully before adding, 'Hello Roger, quite a novelty us being in civvies gear eh?'

Sir Roger is thinking, 'perhaps uniform is a better option for some,' yet he replies, 'It is Guv.'

'Hello Maxine,' is heard by everyone around the table. It is Toby Trunch sat in an armchair at his home in Perth.

'Hi, Toby. Are you well?' asks Maxine.

'Fine thanks. How are you?'

'Hi Dad,' says Milena leaning half of her body on the table with the remainder laying over Sadie and Maxine's laps.

'Hi-ya Princess. You look happy. Have you enrolled at the Arts college?'

'Yes, Dad. Sadie leaves her job at the end of August. Isn't that great Dad?'

'Yes. That's good Milena,' Toby agrees.

'Hey, Milena we need to order before our dis, the meeting starts,' interrupts Maxine sensitively.

'Speak to you soon Dad. See ya.'

'Bye princess.'

'Toby. Everyone can hear you. So, please bear with us while we choose from the menu.'

'No problem Maxine. Carry on.'

Frank says, 'Before we start I also want to reassure everyone here my, our, presence is a voluntary choice to see if we can help Milena?

CHAPTER TWENTY FOUR

August 14, 2008

Shelly Stubs is drunk. 'Why are you back Ollie? And Isaac, why have you let him into our lives again? You can be stupid sometimes!'

Shelly gets off the sofa from between the twins. When she starts crawling more than walking up a staircase, Shelly shouts, 'I don't want him here when I come down in the morning. Do you hear me, Isaac? I want your brother out, never to return! It's the children and us first, or we're finished for good! I mean it. Get him out of here! If you don't, one way or another, I will!'

'Blimey Broth. How do you put up with that?' asks Oliver.

'Shut up Ollie. I want you out too.'

'Begone tomorrow. won't I Broth.'

'Why don't you forget about White. Get away while you can Ollie. Your plan is too risky, crazy in fact!'

'Other than helping me to use Dan, you don't know what my plan is?'

'I know the place is not somewhere you can simply stroll in,' reposts Isaac.

'The least you know the better for both of us,' Oliver states self-assured. He then adds, 'This place I'm leaving your car. You're sure it's discreet enough?'

'Yes.'

'OK. And, I promise I won't hurt Dan.'

'If you do we will have a fight to the death,' and Oliver can see Isaac's eyes are expressing he means it.

***

August 15

An X29 bus turns right onto St Stephens Street in the city of Norwich and the passenger is sitting alone on a sideways seat

313

behind the driver is looking straight ahead. Through the window, this passenger, whose name is Sharon Greengage, recognises it is Isaac Stubs connecting a tow-bar from his recovery truck to a broken down car.

Sharon is a teacher at St. Clotho school and so far today has relished the luxury of a Friday off. Albeit, she reported in sick this morning. Sharon is happy to have visited the city to buy what she needs for tomorrow. She is also enjoying time out without the hassle and expense of driving and parking.

***

The bus is pulling up beside a shelter for the next X29 stop which is the penultimate one for Sharon. Sharon still has a seat to herself, and there is one bag between her feet and two more tucked in tightly under an arm. She notices two men are waiting to get on at Lenwade. The man at the back of the queue is carrying a large holdall across his back and has just left a car in, 'The Bridge Inn,' pub car park.

To assist with depicting the depth of horror Sharon is soon going to feel, I think it's useful first to share what happened on January 21, 2002.

"... and with the last child of her last Art class of the day disappearing out of sight, Miss Sharon Greengage is sitting on her desk. She is close to giggling as she looks around the classroom.

Sharon is happy to see walls sprayed with paint by some children who had no intention of creating a picture. It does not matter to Sharon because the children have expressed themselves.

Sharon then looks at her recently employed classroom assistant. 'I think the children enjoyed their lesson Michelle, do you agree?'

'Yes I do Miss Greengage, and some of the pictures are really good. Especially Jordan's drawing! Have you seen it? I watched him for a minute or two, and I think it shows we might have a little genius in our midst.'

Sharon suddenly feels old. And while listening to Michelle, she also mused, You look as though you should still be at school yourself.

Determined to hide her emotions and not to admit she hasn't seen Jordan's picture, Sharon delivers a careful and untrue reply.

'Oh thank you for reminding me Michelle, yes I did have a quick look. Now – where is it?'

Michelle watches Sharon walk to the back row of desks and sit where Jordan had sat only five minutes earlier. Within two seconds Sharon is statue-like, perched precariously on a small chair.

Michelle is completely unaware the class teacher's frozen in time posture is due to the combination of absolute shock, horror, disgust and the straining of every muscle to prevent herself from being physically sick.

In Jordan's picture is a man, a boy and at each end of a settee is a girl. On the floor is a pair of scissors, a comb, a couple of toy cars and scattered pieces of Lego.

Sharon continues to stare with absolute disdain, and her face reddens to make her two round cheeks the colour of a ripe strawberry. Tears are bubbling, and Sharon wipes the first drops away.

Michelle, shocked to witness Sharon's distress, runs over to put one arm around her. 'What is it Miss Greengage?' asks Michelle gently. She then follows Sharon's stare at the picture and realisation hits home. 'Oh my god,' says Michelle.

Sharon responds by saying, 'I'm afraid our working day is not over yet Michelle.'

Without another word between them, Sharon composes herself. She scrolls up the picture before then walking to her desk and from a cabinet gathers Jordan's file along with rota logs.

With Michelle now beside her they saunter toward the headmaster's office.

The Headmaster Mr Joseph Otter shuffles his eyes between

Sharon and Michelle. 'I Have asked Renee Yeastfield to join us, Sharon. She's on her way. Renee is our DCP, sorry, Designated Child Protection Link Officer, Michelle. Renee will advise us what's best to do next.'

Both women's faces remain blank and do not feel the Head's use of a jolly tone is appropriate. Sharon sighs with relief because of the school secretary, Catalina Rose is now bringing in some tea and coffee. She places the tray on a rectangle table. 'Sugar Miss Greengage?'

'Half a teaspoon please Catalina.'

'Michelle?'

'Nothing for me, thank you. I have my bottled water.'

Renee walks in. 'Tea or coffee Miss Yeastfield?'

'Black Coffee and three sugars please Catalina.'

Catalina duly completes serving and leaves the room.

Joseph hands the scrolled up painting to Renee, and as she unfolds Jordan's drawing, both of her female colleagues place their chins tightly to their chest.

Renee surveys the picture and seemingly, without any emotion. But she quickly understands why Sharon and Michelle are so affected. She too is overwhelmed with anger and disgust.

The uneasy silence is eventually broken by Renee as she turns the picture upside down on the table, 'Sharon, what can you tell me about Jordan please?'

Sharon looks up and is still shaking a little inside. 'Jordan is seven and a half years old Renee. He lives with his mother and step-father whose names are Deborah and Oliver Stubbs. Other children in the household are Jordan's younger full sister Lori and his half-sister, Mina.

Jordan and Lori's father is Damien Wye who Deborah divorced eighteen months ago. Mr Wye is in regular contact with his children. Deborah is perfectly happy for him sometimes to bring Jordan here or collect him from school.'

Sharon pauses and takes a deep breath.

'Damien has a reputation due to a long criminal record for petty offences relating to theft, assault and burglary. Although, I'm sure **petty** is unlikely to be the word his victims' would use. Anyway, Mr Wye's manner and behaviour with the school staff has always been polite, warm and friendly.

Deborah informed us about her marriage to Oliver Stubs fifteen months ago, and since then no member of staff has seen him, let alone talked with him.'

Renee tries to interject, but Sharon raises her hand.

'Please, if I may share a bit more Renee. When comparing Jordan's most recent annual report with his previous one, it is evident from many teachers that Jordan has regressed. For example, comments used include words such as quieter, withdrawn, dreamy, lack of application and uninterested.

Physically, Jordan always presents as smart and clean, although last year's class teacher did say some colleagues also noted Jordan does not seem to have the same healthy appetite as he once had.'

Sharon stops because this time, it's Michelle wiping away tears. 'Would you like to go home Michelle?' asks Sharon.

'Thank you, Sharon, but no. I'll be OK.'

'Is there anything else I can help with Renee?' asks Sharon.

Renee is thinking, 'I need to speak with Debbie about this one.' She then says, 'Just a few more questions please Sharon. Has any member of staff had any conversation with Deborah Stubs about Jordan's apparent regression? Has she ever shared observing the changes we at the school have seen, at home? If so, has she expressed any concern at all? Oh, and what is Deborah's maiden name please?'

'Simpson, and no to the other three. I've checked the files, and there is not anything to indicate Deborah has.'

'OK, thank you again,' says Renee at the same time she's thinking, it's entirely possible that a conversation has occurred. But unintentionally or otherwise someone omitted to record it on Jordan's file.

Renee then says, 'Joseph, I am going back to my office, and

I will discuss our concerns with Debbie Eagle, who is the manager of the Children's Services Access Team.'

Joseph is in too deep a shock to realise his behaviour of denial. Couple this with his sense of fairness to explore the content of Jordan's picture, being just that; a snapshot of family life, he meekly asks, 'Do you agree before involving Children's Services it would be prudent of us to consider other possibilities for why Jordan created his painting?'

None of the three women answers until Renee states her view with assurance and conviction. 'No Joseph. This matter must be reported to the appropriate agencies now! Jordan's picture strongly suggests children are likely to have suffered or are suffering significant harm. Oh, and remember Joseph, our employer is Norfolk County Council's Children's Services.'

Renee is now standing and has already tucked the scrolled again picture under her right arm. She then picks up the files Sharon brought from the classroom. Joseph offers no repost. 'I will keep you informed Joseph. Goodbye Sharon and Michelle. Thank you for your prompt action. There is no need to delay going home any further.'

'OK. As long as your sure,' replies Sharon.'

'Yes, of course, it is. And yes, well done both of you,' Joseph agrees.

Renee is already walking back to her office. She is doing so with a heavy heart, and her current analysis only further increments its weight. From my experience, a disclosure of the type Jordan has made usually means the chances of a successful prosecution will be dependent on the witness statement and cross-examination of a child. In this case a seven-year-old frightened and unhappy boy. The only way Jordan and possibly his two sisters can avoid the trauma and stress of such a process is if Stubs confesses. And the chances of the likes of Stubs spilling their beans is nearly below zero percent.

Renee's reluctant predictions proved to be reasonably accurate. Following a strategy meeting between the police and Children's Services, Jordan and his two siblings, as well as his mother and father, were interviewed. The parent's respective reaction could not be more different. Damien promised the police, "I'll kill the fucker!"

While Deborah told them, 'I refuse to believe Ollie would do such a thing.'

Oliver Stubs denied all allegations. He was bailed to reside in a safe house until it turned out, as you know, he faced trial. The safe house was quite away from his home because the threat to his life from Damien was taken seriously by the police.

Jordan's interview with child protection officers resulted in a witness statement. Couple this with a medical report following a consultant's examination of all three siblings, meant, the Crown Prosecution Service boosted the investigative team's morale. They agreed Oliver Stubs must defend his actions in a court of law. So, he was charged with committing five category B crimes relating to "Gross abuse and assault." The only additional words the Custody Sergeant, who issued the official charges document, had the stomach to record when completing it was, "against a minor or minors."

Sharon moves the bag between her feet to behind her legs because the first man getting on is using a walking stick. Sharon then sits upright again. Her light-headedness and nausea are instant because she knows she is staring at Oliver Stubs.

Stubs is looking straight ahead paying for his ticket. Thoughts are exploding in Sharon's mind; It has to be you. I'd recognise those eyes anywhere. Besides, I saw Isaac only half an hour or so ago.

Sharon is very hot and bothered and is having flashbacks to moments she and Stubs had eye contact during his trial. Realising her eyes are on Norfolk Constabulary's most wanted man she dips her head, scratches her nose and nearly falls off the seat when Stubs puts his bag in the luggage space before sitting right next to her.

Sharon shuffles to her right although there is no contact between them. Thank heavens my stop is next. What if he gets off too? But why would he? There's nothing in Bawdeswell. Get a grip girl. More important, surely the police don't know he's roaming the streets free! They soon will, Sharon decides.

***

'How long has your wife been waiting in Guist post office then, Isaac?' asks Dan Jurtten as he drives past the sign for Bawdeswell village.

'Shelly phoned about one-thirty. I was picking up that car on St Stephens. When I returned to our depot, I checked to see if the bus had got going again? Shelly said the bus is knackered. And, the driver told them the next bus on the timetable isn't running. So, they'll have to wait for the one that leaves Fakenham at two thirty-five. Told Shelly we might as well rescue her. Not all bad though. Shelly is making the most of lots of tea and cakes from the post office café courtesy of First Travel. So, least she isn't waiting in the rain.'

'That's something,' agrees Dan who then adds, 'Should be there for three.'

Isaac receives a text. 'He's gone. Thank god!'

'Told u he wud. Dan and I r on a call out in Fakenham. Will b home la8. Will eat out + Dan will go stra8 2 wk from the depot. C u soon. X' replies Isaac.

CHAPTER TWENTY FIVE

Dan pulls up outside Guist post office. Won't be long mate,' says Isaac who then rushes into the café. Dan changes the radio station to Talk-Sport. He sits up again and sees what he thinks is Isaac returning on his own.

Stubs points to the back door and so Dan, believing Shelly will be sitting in the front, unlocks both rear doors. Stubs is soon sat behind Dan having placed his unfastened holdall across the back seat beside him.

Dan looks in his mirror and Stubs says, 'Shelly on her way.'

'Powdering her nose I expect. What with all that free tea,' says Dan chuckling.

With a knife, Stubs pushes the sharpest point in between Dan's shoulder blades. At the same time Stubs demands, 'Do as I say and neither you or your wife will get hurt. Are you getting me, Dan?'

'Fuck me. You must be Ollie. Shit a brick. I don't want to...'

Dan feels the knife press a little harder as he hears, 'Do you understand Dan?'

As Dan replies, 'Yes,' Isaac gets back into the front seat. He then says, 'Sorry mate. Just do what the dick head says, and we'll both be safely home in a few hours. Trust me, Dan. Everything will be alright.'

'Don't push it Broth,' warns Stubs.

'He's got someone else with Connie. How the fuck can I not worry? Tell me, Isaac?' says Dan bravely.

Isaac looks at his brother, 'No he hasn't Dan. Have you Ollie!'

'No. 'But I know where you live.'

'Thank...'

Dan stops because he is relieved he no longer feels the knife as Stubs says, 'Go back to the Bridge Inn car park. Now!'

***

Sharon hasn't done anything since being home, other than initiating a frustrating conversation with the police. Eventually, to be informed, ten minutes ago, that DC Sally Underwood and a colleague are on their way to speak with her further.

It is now five past three.

***

Bernice arrives at the home of Isaac and his family and rings their doorbell. From the shrieks of children playing she is pleased her journey won't be fruitless.

Shelly shouts, 'Quieten down you two,' and opens the door. Bernice raises her ID badge and says, 'Hello Mrs Stubs. My name is DC Bernice Buck. I need to speak to Isaac, please. Is he in?'

'What do you need to talk about?' replies Shelly coldly.

'Is Isaac in Shelly?'

'No he ain't as a matter of fact. You're welcome to check if you like,' replies Shelly who now has her children leaning against a leg on each side of her. 'Who is it, mummy?' asks Devona.

'The lady is a police officer petal. Now then, both of you go and watch the telly while mummy talks to the lady.'

Both children comply, and Shelly asks, 'Well, are you going to look around?'

'Where might I find Isaac please Shelly?'

Shelly replies, 'At work I suppose. He sent a text about half an hour ago as it happens. Said he might be home late. A car broke down in, Fakenham I think is what he said. What's going on? What's he supposed to have done?'

Bernice gets her mobile from a trouser pocket. 'What is his number please Shelly?'

'Tell me what it's about, and I'll consider your request?'

'We have reason to believe Isaac's twin brother has been seen in Norfolk today. Are you aware if Isaac knows this? Has Oliver been to your house recently at all?'

'Are you crazy? Ollie in my house. We may not be perfect, but neither of us would let that disgusting human being anywhere near our kids. Whose seen him? I predict they're mistaken. He'd be mad to come anywhere near the White Cliffs of Dover, let alone here at The Lodge Breck in bloody Drayton. I'd swear on my children's lives; Ollie hasn't had any contact with Isaac since that low life talked my stupid husband to do porridge for him. But, only Isaac can answer your questions.'

'OK. Thank you, Shelly. So Isaac's number please?' asks Bernice a little impatiently.

'I'll go and fetch my phone. Pity it's still raining,' says Shelly who then politely shuts the door in the face of the DC.

Bernice looks in all directions. Surely there is a good chance of at least one of these neighbours noticing a second Stubs about, she considers.

The door flashes open. 'There you go,' says Shelly handing Bernice a torn piece of notepad paper.

'Thank you, Shelly.'

Shelly watches Bernice make a call. Both remain silent and hear the call go straight to voice-mail. 'Switched off,' says Bernice inconsequentially. She then adds, 'Does Isaac have a work number, Shelly?'

'Only the depots,' replies Shelley who then looks at her watch. 'It's three-thirty. Sorry, I can't help. Can I get on with cooking the children their tea now please officer?'

'Just a final question Shelly. What clothes does Isaac wear for work? And, if different, what was he wearing when he left for work today?'

'That's two, and a please would be polite. Isaac leaves before any of us are up, so I don't have a bloody clue what he put on this morning. Their uniform is blue with the Eastern Garage logo splashed all over their back. Is that it now officer?'

'Yes. I know the garage. Thank you, Shelly. As soon as Isaac contacts you or comes home, please let him know we need to speak with him. Here's my card.'

Shelly snatches it and says, 'Will do.'

'Oh Shelly, if I don't hear from Isaac in the next few hours, I will be coming back.'

'Do what you like,' suggests Shelly who then slams the door shut.

***

Finley brings in a cup of tea for Sharon, and Sally too. 'Thank you,' they say in unison.

Sally then asks, 'Miss Greengage, how...'

'Please, I prefer you use Sharon.'

'Sure. Sharon, how can you be so certain it wasn't Isaac you saw get on the bus?'

'Well, like I've already explained, I...'

Sally's phone starts ringing. 'Sorry Sharon, I need to take this call.'

'Of course.'

'Hello, Bernice. I see. Right. Interesting. Yes. OK. Good. We'll be going to the Fakenham Station from here. Suggest you go there straight away too. Yes in Bawdewell. Great. Thanks, Bernice. See you soon, bye.'

***

Police officers at Fakenham station are buzzing with activity. Two of the three Sergeants are patrolling their area in a car looking for an Eastern Garage recovery truck. Similarly, on foot is a Constable and three Police Community Support Officers. Plus, a member of their Safer Neighbourhood Team agreed to try and comfort Sharon Greengage who is still very frightened and shocked.

Inside the station, Sergeant Liam Brady is revelling in hosting the presence of Sally and her two colleagues. 'Do any of you guys want a coffee,' asks Liam.

'Not for me thanks,' replies Sally.

Bernice's phone begins blasting out, "Crazy For You." She answers, 'Hello. Oh, hello Isaac.'

The room falls silent.

'Where are you? I see. No. Will be with you in twenty minutes, half an hour at the latest. No. Thank you.'

Bernice ends the call and says, 'Isaac is home, Sally.'

Sally glances at a clock on the wall. It's ten past four. She then looks at the sergeant, 'Liam, call all searching off, please. Ask every available officer you have to return here. I believe Miss Greengage has seen Oliver today and with the owner of Eastern Garage informing Bernice, as far as he knows, there was no pick up in Fakenham today, I think Isaac knows his brother is around and probably has just returned from being with him. But of course, I cannot be sure.

So, the priority is to quiz Isaac before opening our search again. Depending on what Isaac says, we may need to broaden our strategy by calling in other sources of personnel at our disposal.

I can't stress enough sergeant, the need for no publicity whatsoever! Until at least after I've seen Isaac. When I then will report to Sir Roger during which, no doubt, there will be a review of my decision.

Our suspect is very clever. He's better at escaping than Houdini. Of course, Isaac may well have alerted Oliver we are onto him. But, while there is a chance we may be a step ahead of Oliver Stubs, no publicity is my call. And, you can quote me as saying I accept the responsibility for it as mine alone. OK sergeant?'

'Yes Guv,' replies Liam doing his best to dampen his excitement.

'Bernice, please arrange for trailing of Isaac's mobile and landline numbers. Then, follow Finley and me to Isaac's house. Oh yes, Liam, can you please ask the head of CID in Sheringham to ring me asap. Here's my card. Let's go, Finley.'

***

Dan and his wife, Connie, are with Stubs in his hideout. Connie is rattling more than shaking. She is blindfolded and wearing a green uniform worn when working in a residential nursing home.

With force, Stubs makes Connie get off a mattress and onto her feet. His grip is firm enough to hurt. Connie attempts to defy him by struggling to sit back down.

'It's going to be alright love,' says Dan.

As Stubs shouts with menace, 'Do as I ask and no harm will come to either of you,' he is also literally shaking Connie.

'Oh Dan, stop him,' Connie pleads.

Dan's handcuffed to a disused tap on a wall. He is trying to break free such is the extent of his helplessness. He cries out hysterically, 'For Christ sake man, Connie is with a child. You hurt Connie or the baby I will rather die than do what you're asking of me.'

Stubs lets go of Connie and looking at Dan retorts, 'What?'

Still shouting Dan replies, 'Yes. Our first. We'd given up hope, and now after twenty years, it's happened. So, please don't be rough with Connie. I really will do what you want if it means no harm coming to them. Get me, Oliver?'

Stubs stare at Connie is piercing, and he says, 'Right. Are you ready now?'

'Do as he says Connie. Better we cooperate the quicker this will be all over. Trust me, love. You are his security. You know I will do anything to keep you unhurt. I will die to save you from the same fate. Without me Connie, he's got no plan. His way will mean we both keep our lives. Trust me, Connie.'

Connie complies and is desperately trying not to cry.

As Stubs then suddenly leaves the hideout, with the door open Dan peeps out and thinks he can see the high-level Braithwaite water tank.

'What is he doing Dan?' whispers Connie.'

'Not sure Con but we're be going to the JC soon. Just keep

calm Connie, and everything will be fine.'

White re-enters and smiles at Dan before saying, 'Yes, you're right, we are ready to go.'

***

'I can't work out why the pigs think Ollie is back?' asks Isaac once again and in truth, rhetorically.

'It's bloody obvious, and I told you. Someone's spotted him, and told the police,' answers Shelly scornfully.

'I know that Shelly. But why not assume it was me?'

'Have you let Ollie know?' asks Shelly.

'No point. His phone will be off.'

'Why did he come back? And don't bullshit me, Isaac!' insists Shelly.

The doorbell rings.

'Please go and let them in Shell and leave the talking to me,' Isaac sort of asks.

Shelly does so, 'Hello officers, come in. Isaac is in the living room. First on the right.'

'Thank you Mrs Stubs,' says Sally as she steps in with Finley close behind her. Sally then adds, 'My colleague who visited you earlier Mrs Stubs should be arriving here soon.'

'I'm going to bath the twins,' Shelly informs Sally before rushing upstairs.

Sally and Finley join Isaac.

'What's this crap about someone's supposed to have seen Ollie?' asks Isaac brusquely.

'I'm DC Sally Underwood, and this is my colleague DC Billing. May we sit down please Isaac?'

Isaac points to a smaller sofa and says, 'Well?'

'What time did you get home this evening, please Isaac?' asks Finley.

'What's it to anyone what time I got home. A free country

isn't it!'

'Please answer the question, Isaac,' requests Sally.

'Between three and four, the usual time for a Friday. Why?' asks Isaac.

'Shelly told my colleague you'd contacted home to say you might be late due to a pick up in

Fakenham. Where exactly had this vehicle broken down?' asks Finley.

'At the time of calling Shelly the details had just come through. Soon after it turns out to be

Frettenham, not Fakenham officer.'

'Frettenham you say?'

'Yes, that's right officer,' confirms Isaac.

'What time did...'

Bernice rings the doorbell, and Isaac says, 'Excuse me, officers.'

On re-entering the room Isaac tells Bernice, 'You can use a dining chair if you want.'

'Hello Bernice,' says Sally before asking, 'Can you please confirm if Frettenham was one of

the calls out locations for Eastern Garage today?' she then asks.

Bernice replies, 'Give me a moment, and I'll check my notebook. Ah. Here we are. Yes, last one of the day Sally. The job given to a Patrick Vieira is what I think I've written. Does this help?'

'Thank you, Bernice,' replies Sally.

Finley then says, 'Mr Stubs, this afternoon we received a report of a sighting of your twin brother Oliver. We...'

'That's ridiculous,' Isaac exclaims laughing and interrupting Finley.

'We are taking this information seriously Mr Stubs. I agree it is a surprise, but it's not necessarily fanciful or impossible. As you know Mr Stubs, for the past six years Oliver could be anywhere?' suggests Finley.

'Yes. Give you that officer,' says Isaac still laughing. 'So, where and by whom has Ollie been spotted then,' he asks mocking.

'Can I look at your mobile phone please Isaac, ' asks Bernice.

Isaac looks at Sally. 'I don't think you have a proper reason for making me heed that request! Do you, DC Underwood? I'm helping you with your enquiries. Right?'

'Yes. Which means I can seek such authorisation very quickly if I have a proper reason to believe you're not helping,' replies Sally.

'Fine. Here it is,' says Isaac as he leans forward to place his mobile on the dark blue carpet.

After what seems an age, Sally nods. Bernice scoops up the phone and then begins a search.

'You asked a reasonable question, Isaac. The person who contacted us recognised Oliver for two reasons. The second is because some thirty to forty minutes before our witness saw, at the Lenwade bus stop, Oliver get on the twelve fifty-five pm going to Fakenham, she saw you. You were seen standing near an Eastern Garage recovery truck on St. Stephens Street in the city. You left to attend the scene of that call out around twelve-thirty pm today, didn't you Isaac?'

Isaac is rolling a cigarette. 'Yes,' he says nonchalantly. Isaac then licks the Rizzla paper before asking, 'What's the first?'

'Our source had met both of you during Oliver's trial six years ago. By a difference in your eyes is the explanation,' replies Sally honestly.

'Yet, you cannot be sure Oliver was seen, can you?' counters Isaac.

'As certain as you are uncertain I'd suggest Isaac,' replies Sally.

Isaac lights his smoke. Sits back and places his right foot on his left knee. He then inhales and slowly releases the smoke out of his nostrils. 'So, is there anything else I can help with DC Underwood?' he asks.

Bernice hands Isaac his phone while looking at Sally and says, 'Nothing obvious amiss Guv.'

'Have you been in the company of or had contact with Oliver today, Isaac? And, for that matter any time since you helped him escape from the trial?' Sally asks.

'None,' answers Isaac at no one. He then eyes BB and says, 'You have beautiful hair, Bernice.'

'DC Buck to you Mr Stubs. What you think of my hair is an irrelevance to why we are here and even more so, to me!'

***

17.17pm.

'Hello. Is that a DC Buck? Good. Anton Hershel, owner of Eastern Garage. Well, you asking about a non-existent job in Fakenham has been niggling at me detective. I usually stay behind for a while after the workers' end their shift. Today though, my eldest son is performing at Cambridge University for the first time. Sure. I'm pretty certain Isaac left in Dan's car. We shut at two on a Friday. Dan doesn't live in Fakenham, but you take the same roads out of the city to get to his home.

The bus you mentioned would have taken a route including Drayton too. Dan and Isaac are mates DC Buck. I know they meet socially, including with their respective wives. Mainly at each other's homes is how I understand their friendships. I was hoping you'd think that. But, I also know Dan has a second job on weekends. Dan is a sound bloke, and I want to be clear about that DC Buck.

Dan's second job is a prison warder at that new prison, or Justice place, whatever it's called. I know.

Sure. No problem, glad to help. Yes, of course. Bye.'

'Sally, I think we need to turn round and revisit Isaac,' Bernice advises.

On hearing the update, Sally not only agrees with BB, she decides to arrest Isaac and bring him in for questioning.

CHAPTER TWENTY-SIX

The Justice Centre, where Harold White is waiting to die, is a contemporary new build. It's located near a border which divides Norfolk and Suffolk on land which was a caravan leisure park in a small village called Ditchingham.

Dan is a matter of five minutes away from beginning a most extraordinary shift. He looks in his windscreen mirror for an umpteenth time at Connie handcuffed in the car behind. Connie soon twists her head to keep looking at Dan as Stubs takes an exit off a roundabout onto Ditchingham Dam Lane. Dan is taking his usual exit onto the A143.

Dan is glad it's stopped raining and is comforted a tiny bit by a burst of dusk sunshine twinkling on the river which almost forms a moat around the JC. Dan then turns right off a large roundabout and then in a matter of seconds takes another right. Directly ahead is a literal first barrier to negotiate. Dan pulls up with his window down and ID already in hand.

'Hello, Dan. You had a good week?' asks the security guard.

'Not too bad, thanks, Ralf. You?'

'Next three weeks will be better. Off to Florida with the wife and kids,' replies Ralf.'

'Sounds great.'

Ralf then gets out of his station Hub and completes a thorough search inside and out of Dan's car. Dan takes this opportunity to have a cigarette and asks, 'Do you want one Ralf?

'Just put one out thanks. Blimey, Dan. Some draw you're giving that fag. Are you OK?'

'Yes, with Connie pregnant, I'm rightly banned from smoking in our house,' replies Dan with a forced a grin.

'I know what you mean mate. I'm gearing myself up for when I'm sure Tiara will soon insist, I do the same. There you go. All spick and span,' replies Ralf.

Dan gets back in his car and says, 'See you later Ralf.'

Dan waits for the barrier to lift and drives through toward a large car park. He follows the sign for spaces used for D Wing staff only. Like for most shifts, there is only one other car in this front left-hand area of the park.

Dan picks up his lunch and newspaper from under his seat and heads into work. Dan veers left onto a footpath which has a row of Silver Birch trees on both sides. D wing is physically separate from the rest of the building and hidden from view too. D Wing is a lot smaller than A, B, C, E, F and G. White is the only occupier of a cell in D at present. He's in number Eight.

Dan places his badge in front of a red smarty styled buzzer, and the beep sound signals the main entrance door is open. Dan walks to an alcove where there is a lift and presses a button for Floor One.

On stepping out, he heads to the staff kitchen. He leaves his paper on a table and food in a fridge. Dan is surprised a bit as the Warder about to end a shift says, 'Hi Dan. Was going to get us a brew and a biscuit to enjoy while completing our busy handover,' says Isabel Chimer, chuckling.

'Hi-ya Is. Was beginning to wonder if you'd left. How are you? No drink for me thanks. I'll make you one though. You put your feet up in the office. Bet you could do with resting after such a busy shift eh,' replies Dan.

'To be honest Dan. I need to dash off if that's OK with you?'

'Sure, Is. No problem. Go on. Get yourself home.'

'Cheers mate. See you tomorrow. Bye.'

Dan makes his way to the Warder office. From a locked drawer, he takes the key to a cabinet where there is what are known as Visitor suites. Each suite is an all in one outfit used by D Wing's prisoners when they need to attend the Visitor's Centre.

Dan removes a suite from a box labelled, Length 1.8M + Waist 0.8M to 1.0M. He then places the box on his desk before then unlocking a safe. From which, Dan removes a card key that opens all cell doors in D Wing. Still in the forefront of Dan's mind, as he walks to cell number eight is Connie's, frightened face.

Dan doesn't knock before swiping the key like that when paying for goods using a credit or debit card. White is laying on his side and twists his neck to look at Dan, 'What the hell is going on? he asks.

'Do you know what Mr White, I really don't believe you know, do you?'

'Know what turnkey?' asks White impatiently.

'You need to put this on please Mr White,' says Dan and he leaves the suite close to White's feet, which are, bar underwear, naked like the rest of him.

'Not till I know what for?' replies White snappily.

'I hope you believe me when I explain it is because my wife will die if I don't get you into an ambulance drove, as I understand it, by a friend you haven't seen for a while. His name is Oliver Stubs.'

'Oh piss off turnkey! Is that the best you can come up with to get a kick at my expense,' counters White.

'Am I laughing or smirking. Connie's life is at stake. Get dressed now, please!'

Dan begins to unravel the suit and says, 'I'll be back in five minutes.'

White watches Dan exit the cell leaving the door completely open. White stares at the doorway convinced Dan would soon pop is head into view laughing at him.

Dan sits at his desk and calls Ralf. 'Hello Ralf, Dan here. No! Major emergency. Heart attack of a prisoner. Yes, tell me about it. Anyway, a local community first...ERM, yes, that's right, a CFR is already on his way. He's employed by the East of England Ambulance Service as a Paramedic so is using that vehicle. That's great Ralf. Already alerted the prison doctor. Oh yes, nearly forgot Ralf. The name of the CFR on duty is Ray Kennedy. He said he'd not long arrived home as he's just got back from picking up his wife from the nursing home she works in. So, she's with him too. Better go, our doc should be here any second. Thanks. Bye.'

Dan fumbles hurriedly for his Blackberry phone and texts Connie, 'Tell him now. Stay brave.

Lv.u X' He then looks up and is glad to see White standing dressed in the doorway of the office.

Stubs says, 'We're on,' and turns Connie's phone off before dropping it in her lap. Connie is worried about the baby, Dan, herself and yet at this precise moment, she is revolted by having to help this dreadful man.

Connie forces herself to refocus as Stubs says, 'You will soon be rid of me, and I didn't know you are pregnant.'

'You'd have still used us if you did,' Connie reposts more cuttingly than a knife through butter.

Ignoring Connie, Stubs continues to speed along Broad Street until at a roundabout he slows to drive straight across it. From here it is a matter of seconds when Stubs and Connie witness the barrier going up with Ralf enthusiastically waving them through. Stubs is quick to see Dan standing where the birch tree footpath merges with the tarmac of the car park.

Before Stubs comes to a halt, Dan runs back inside D Wing and says, 'Right Harold get ready to lay on a stretcher.'

'I'm not going anywhere turnkey,' says White who then immediately sees Stubs and his nurse running with a stretcher toward them. Dan reopens the doors.

'It really is you,' says White with a facial expression akin to seeing a ghost!

'Sure is Harold. Come on, get on here for Christ sake man! We need to leave now!'

Dan helps Connie hold her end and a very bewildered and confused White gets under some blankets to lay in heart attack victim mode.

Stubs is soon walking backwards until he then manages to keep hold of the stretcher while climbing into the ambulance. Dan and Connie let go of their end as soon as the descent of

White begins.

Dan grabs Connie's left hand and shouts, 'Come on we've done enough. Run.'

Stubs is still disentangling himself.

'Keep running Connie,' says Dan who lets go of her hand and stops to face Stubs. He then adds, 'Go on, get the fuck out while you still can. CCTV cameras everywhere. Go on, don't think shooting me will help you?'

Stubs stare is toxic. Yet, realising his options, he turns and races into the ambulance. And, in more ways than one literally flashes away. Which means, at 18.12pm precisely as they hurtle through the still open barrier, White becomes the first prisoner to escape from the new much supported and yet also much maligned, Justice Centre!

***

Dan places two cups of tea on his office desk, 'All hell is about to erupt so make the most of this time Con. I'm so relieved we're all alive.'

Connie says, 'But you were stupidly bloody brave to confront the evil psycho. Hope his capture results in the police having to kill him!'

'What the hells going on Dan?' Shouts John, tonight's head warder. John then points while he also asks, 'Who is she?' And is White seriously ill? Why didn't you escort him to the hospital? We...'

Dan stands up, 'I saved Connie and our baby's life sir. She, as you put it, is my wife! That's the most important thing that's happened, sir! So, with respect sir, please sit down,, and I'll tell you the rest. But, before I do I strongly advise you let me report an escape of a prisoner to the police,

Sir. So that every penal organisation that needs to be informed can start hunting that Stubs bastard and our escaped prisoner down, Sir!'

***

19.02pm

The chief constable and Sir Roger Bright have returned to HQ. They are in Frank's office with Sally,

Finley and Bernice. Dan and Connie are in a Suffolk police car taking them to Wymondham and at the beginning of this journey, Dan used his mobile to engage in a lengthy discussion with Sir Roger.

Connie has been seen by a Doctor at the JC and advised all is well.

Isaac is in a custody cell already interviewed by Sally and Finley. Isaac told the police everything he could. Which doesn't include the precise location of the hideout?

All ports and airports in the country have been alerted to intercept anyone who fits the two men's descriptions. All the same, all in Frank's office agree with him. A more local departure has probably been chosen to flee the country.

Presently, Frank is talking. 'Right, Isaac has suggested he met his brother for the first time in six years not far away from Bale. Therefore, I'm more than interested in what Finley has shared about the stranger who became the new kid in town, as it were. If you haven't already done so Finley, explain to your wife and mother-in-law about the potential danger he casts. Ask, well tell them please, to get here as a matter of urgency. And please stress the chief constable personally requests to speak with them.

'Yes Guv, straight away sir?' asks Finley.

'Yes.'

Finley leaves the room.

'Bernice, use the wonders of the web, please. To search and identify possibilities for the hideout in the vicinity of the Braithwaite water tank. We will then discuss merits or otherwise of any findings.'

'Yes, sir.'

Bernice leaves the room.

'Sally, once Finley has spoken with his family and we decide which of Bernice's findings we target, I want all three of you to go there right away. I know Dan Jurtten has informed us he's not seen Stubs with a gun but he has reported Stubs threatening with use of a weapon. Namely, a large knife. Therefore, I have decided to put two ARV units on standby as a precautionary back up to an operation, I want you to lead DC Underwood.

I note Sally; you are one of our reserves should we require cover or additions to AVR operations. Sir Roger has also informed me you graduated with the third highest marks-person score in the history of any such equipped police squad ever formed in this country. Telling me, you are what is known in the trade as, "A Crack Shot."

But, I want both men, three if you include Robert Hardeen, captured alive! If we can, I'd much prefer to apprehend them without a shooting match show being put on. Instead, arrested with no spill of blood by unarmed capable detectives. Of course, this is my call, and I am sincere when I say you are absolutely at liberty to refuse such an operation? As are DC Buck and Billing. Please, Sally, I value your thoughts,' asks Frank.

***

'Go on your own Ollie. I am grateful for your gesture. I truly am. I will be a hindrance and without me, I know your stay free. To be honest, Ollie, since you got away, this country has become, in the main, intolerable of the likes of us. You really shouldn't have risked coming back.

Sorry, Ollie.'

Stubs switches on a battery operated shaving razor, 'Head back Harold. Any advice you give me is rarely wrong Harold and the one I've used above all others is to remember the plan with the highest risk is most likely to succeed!'

White cannot respond and is glad for the hair on his face to disappear. Ollie is careful, attentive and thorough in completing the shave. He then blows bits of hair off the blade and asks,

'Did you kill the girl too, Harold?'

'Yes. But, I didn't kill Gillian.'

'Why?'

'She was never going to stay shush.'

'Right. Just a shirt and jacket and we're ready to hit the bright lights of Amsterdam! Harold, do you remember that week, James and we had there? For James and I, it was our first adventure abroad. The...'

'Ollie, I'm not going with you. You can throw me in your car, and I can't stop you. But Ollie, the only pleasure I have left is knowing the pigs haven't found you. Go now, without me.

And, no drippy goodbyes Ollie. For Christ sake man, don't make me beg, fuck off out of here!'

'I can't leave you here,' reasons Ollie.

'You should heed another piece of advise I told you more than once.'

'What's that?' asks Ollie.

'Sometimes the police get a break. Believe me; Dan would never have confronted when he did, if he couldn't have achieved the best of both worlds.'

'What do you mean Harold?'

'You bought him and his wife here first, you said.'

'Yes. What of it?'

'He knew you couldn't and wouldn't shoot either of them at that moment, especially from his point of view, his wife? And, I'd stake my life on him knowing something to pinpoint here. Which means he made time not in your original plan to inform the police of everything he knows sooner rather than later! They'll be here, I feel it. Tonight wouldn't surprise me. Let them find me, please Ollie. "When a good plan doesn't go to plan, face the problem by tweaking it so it can still, succeed." Remember it now?' asks White.

'Yes. But...'

'Either you leave me or shoot me?' interrupts White angrily.

Stubs clasps fingers around his chin.

'OK.'

Ollie then gathers what he needs before walking out briskly, slamming the door behind him.

With the door still shuddering, White starts to cry. And soon he hears Ollie drive away.

***

Sally, Finley and Bernice are standing close to the Braithwaite water tank. The sun is beginning to set. Sally speaks, 'Doesn't need much detecting which outbuilding is the den of inequity, does it?!

Neither colleague respond. Instead, both watch Sally make a call, 'Hello Guv. OK, Guv.

Hello Sir. Yes, we've found the hideout Sir. No vehicle present Sir. Yes, only one building has a door wide open Sir. We are two hundred yards or so from the target Sir. Permission to go inside, please Sir. No Sir, looking around I'll be surprised if we find either Sir. No Sir, no need to change their location. Yes Sir, thank you. Hello, again Guv. Yes Guv, we feel safe. Thank you Guv. Bye.'

'To cover all eventualities, we need our car to be out of sight. Finley, please drive it behind the building with a corrugated roof on the far right,' asks Sally.

'Sure.'

'Hold on Finley. Then, walk the quickest route to meet up with Bernice and me so we can all make our way to look ate our target. Come on Bernice.'

'Will do,' says Finley.

***

Fifteen minutes ago Stubs took the exit off the Norwich road

A140 roundabout that returns you onto the Ipswich Road. As he did so, Stubs increased speed and said out loud, 'Should still make the ferry.' He then thought I couldn't leave you to the pigs, Harold. Shit, why didn't I just pick you up in the first place?

***

Sally stops and waves for Finley to hurry over. Do you see any breathing,' Bernice asks.

'Not sure. We'll watch while Finley catches up,' suggests Sally.

Harold has already spotted them and is just resigned to the inevitable. She's bloody good is that sidekick, he muses.

Finley arrives and joins his colleagues watching White in the hideout. 'Let's go,' says Sally.

At quite a pace the three detectives head forward and when they cross over the doorway in a line White says, 'What took you so long Sidekick? You've missed your prime catch too.'

'Do you know where Oliver Stubs is Mr White,' asks Finley.

'Who?' replies White who then chortles and sits upon the mattress.

'Cut the crap please, Mr White. No prize for guessing where you are...'

Sally suddenly stops because all four hear the sound of a car getting nearer with every second. 'Maybe not eh detective,' says White.

Sally grabs White by his left arm. 'Finley, help me move White out of sight,' she orders.

Once White is off the mattress, Bernice drags it next to a side wall. White is then bunged onto it and Sally kneels behind him. She then holds one hand around his neck and the other over his mouth. White tries to resist and grunt, but all he can do is smell the sweat on Sally's hands.

'Both of you against the wall each side of the door. Bernice, you take the side behind the door.'

Within seconds they are in their places. The vehicle come to a halt. Ollie rushes out and shouts, 'It's only me Harold. I just couldn't leave you...'

With Stubs literally in the doorway, Finley rugby tackles him around the waist. Not to the ground though. From the other side, Bernice attempts an arm-lock, but Stubs is too strong. With her left hand, Bernice grabs Stubs collar and with her right his belt at the front.

Finley has slid to the floor and is trying to topple Stubs over by taking a foot from under with his hands. But, failing to do so, Finley lets go and tries to scramble up a leg instead. Not high enough soon enough though to prevent Stubs reaching into a thigh pocket to bring out a gun. Stubs fires instantly, and while the trigger was pulled, momentum of Finley and Bernice's respective struggles now cause Stubs to lose grip on the gun which flies away from the melee.

'Oh no,' cries Sally.

Sally feels a hand belonging to White swipe her ankles as she scrambles in an attempt to win the race for the gun. Fortunately the trip sprawls her to fall toward the bouncing gun which is careering over the concrete floor. It comes to a halt after crashing against a wall under a tap and Sally wins the race to retrieve it.

Awash with fear spreading inside her like a catastrophic waterfall crashing into the sea from a breakage in a glacier, Sally swiftly struggles to her feet. The gun is secure in her hands and repeatedly she switches pinpointing it between both men and shouts, 'Stay exactly where you are.'

Two AVR vehicles are speeding along Bylaugh Hall's extensive driveway. Ollie ignores Sally and advances toward her. Sally fires, aiming at a calf. Stubs howls and crumbles to the floor and White retreats heading for the mattress. Sally moves near to the feet of Stubs and as she stabs with force her right shoe heel against where the bullet imploded, she shrieks, 'You fucking bastard.'

CHAPTER TWENTY SEVEN

I am unaware of events unfolding at Bylaugh Hall because I took a train to join Sadie at Three Counties View two days ago. Sadie drove here with our dogs last Sunday having left her job a week ago today. Although Sadie's official leaving date is the last day of August, she had annual leave days and TOIL owed so bringing her departure forward.

Around 5 pm today, Sadie, Estelle, Cherisha, Maxine and Milena left Three Counties View to visit Birmingham. Their first destination is the Hippodrome theatre to see Mary Poppins.

They are staying overnight in a Premier Inn Family Room, so they can hit the malls and lanes nice and early in the morning to do some extensive fun shopping. The priority is to fill Milena's new wardrobe, apparently.

I have just come back from a five-hour walk for Polly and Bridie which included a lengthy refuel pit stop at our local pub, "The Saracens Head Inn." I am hungry and cruise into the kitchen. I press play on a CD player wondering which album Sadie has left in it. I then shuffle along to heat up a dinner prepared earlier by Maxine and Milena. As I press my nose on buttons embedded within a microwave oven, I can't help note the time is 22:24. I also hear "Mothers Pride" being sung by

George Michael.

Four minutes later I dine alone at the kitchen table, but I have a pair of eyes looking up each side of me. Bridie is also dribbling bucket loads. They watch my every move with anticipation and expectation even, that a bit might just 'accidentally' fall there way.

I then hear the doorbell and think I imagine I did. I swallow a mouthful before dropping a piece of chicken to each of my friends. I hear the bell again and this time I make a move to seewho on earth is at our door at this time? At least I don't have to hear that song now playing. Will I ever not think of you whenever I hear it, I ponder as I leave the kitchen. The song is called "Waiting For That Day."

Unusual for me, I am approaching my destination with my rider and myself both facing forwards. I look at the half glazed door for a clue to the identity of my totally unexpected visitor. I immediately stop. My heart appears to miss a beat. I'm on fire more than hot under my collar.

'Surely not,' I say trying to convince myself I must be mistaken. Trouble is, I'd recognise the person on the other side of the door amongst a crowd of trillions.

I open the door. 'Hi-ya,' says Angie, 'Bet you weren't expecting to see me. Given the amount of effort I've made to track you down, not to mention the length of time I've waited around these parts this evening, I'm hoping for at least an invite in. Could murder a cup of coffee.'

'Jesus Christ Angie, it is you,' is all I can say.

'Sure is,' she says smiling.

'Yes. Sorry, of course, you can. Come in.'

My brain is saying, You look fantastic as always, but as I back up to open the door fully I say, 'You look well. For a second time Angie you have truly taken my breath away. Where the heck have you come from? How long have you been waiting?'

'I'll make us a cuppa first, shall I?' replies Angie.

Angie then bends and kisses me briefly with her scintillating eyes wide open. She then says, 'Hello, gorgeous. It's so brilliant to see you again. It's been such a long time.'

Not sure if I'm going to laugh, or cry even, I reply with a light heartiness I hope will quell both, 'Oh, I don't know. Fifteen years is only a drop in the ocean of time I guess. How are you?'

I lead us into the kitchen, and our entry prompts Polly to greet a new friend. Bridie is standing over my dinner plate which I didn't even hear nudged onto the floor, wondrously unbroken. There is a pool of gravy on the plate, and Bridie is licking her lips while shuffling her look from me to the food unsure now whether to continue. 'Go on,' I say, and Bridie never needs a second invitation for such a treat.

Angie is fussing Polly and says, 'Hello. Aren't you lovely? What is her name, Alex?'

'Polly,' I reply.

Noticing the love Polly is getting, prompts Bridie to nuzzle against Polly to vie for attention from Angie too. Angie duly obliges.

'And this is Bridie,' I say stroking Bridie briefly at the same time.

I then pick up one of my zip sticks and switch on the kettle.

'How long have you lived here,' asks Angie who, unseen by me, sits on the kitchen table.

I spin round, and bare thighs are closed and right in my level of vision. Angie lowers a shoulder to allow her Balenciaga Classic Town handbag to rest beside the hem of her short Valentino striped broderie anglaise skirt. I look up and reply, 'Not long, less than a year. Well, it's a second home. It...'

Whoa, get you. Mr two homes eh' interrupts Angie who then adds, 'Good on you I say. It's a beautiful home. Even nicer than the time I last came here. Though an hour or so ago when there was no reply I confess to taking a peep around the outside this time. It's lovely too isn't it?'

In an instant, it's not so much a penny dropped because it feels more like a ton of them landing on my head. I reply, 'Yes. I'd honestly forgotten. We called in to visit Aunt Rochelle on our whistle-stop tour around the Cotswold during that otherwise unforgettable long weekend.'

I am convinced I look as embarrassed as I feel.

'Yes. We did,' replies Angie with a wry smile. She then says, 'And don't worry, the second half of your recollection more than makes up for not remembering the first.'

'Aunt Rochelle kindly left this little bit of heaven to me in her will. I still live and work in Norfolk. Come here as often as I can.'

Angie looks at a photograph on an Oakland dresser with a

wine rack and asks, 'You can?

Who is the lucky woman?'

'Sadie is her name. Pretty sure the kettle has boiled.'

'And where is Sadie?' asks Angie as she leaps off the table before brushing my face with two fingers on her way pass me to attend to the kettle. Angie then half twists her body until she has one leg crossing behind the other. She's holding the kettle and uses her other hand to gently places some of her Gothic black wavy shoulder length hair behind an ear.

With a smile bright enough to light·up the universe Angie's eyes, I admit, are capturing me again like no others I've seen. She then says, 'Would love to share a bottle of vodka and some tomato juice with you again. What do you think? And, I'm still waiting to hear where Sadie is?'

'Well, not sure...'

'You don't know, really?' asks Angie devilishly.

'Staying in Birmingham over the weekend with her daughters and friends. Shopping bonanza!'

'I see. Where is the vodka kept then Alex?'

'Amongst the bottles in the wine rack. There is a carton of the juice in a cupboard above your head. I'll get the glasses,' I reply.

'No need. Tell me where they are. Then you can remind me how to find you in the room with that magnificent fireplace. Assuming you haven't changed it.'

'No, it's too good to alter. Glasses are on the bottom right shelf of the dresser. You go left out the kitchen and then take the first door on your right. See you in a minute.'

I exit the kitchen after turning the CD player off, relieved strangely. Knock me down with a feather doesn't even come close. To distract myself I switch on the TV which is already tuned into Radio 4 extra.

I listen to a comedy called "Old Dog and Partridge" until Angie brings in our night cap.

'I used a tray next to the kettle. Trust this is OK. Love this straw with a chick on it,' Angie says.

'No probs. Thanks for the drink. Had the straw for years. Bought four of them in a gift shop called Woodlander in Ashby de-la-Zouch.'

'Ashby de-la-Zouch! Really?'

'Yes. Honest,' I reply.

'The place where we met. Cute. And, do you remember originally my last placement was planned to be in Coventry?'

'Yes, I was going to joke, you had a lucky escape. But maybe neither of us did eh?'

Angie steps out of a pair of scrolls which are decorated with pink leather straps and a white pink spotted butterfly bow on each buckle. She sits facing me with one foot tucked underneath the thigh of her opposite leg. Angie then says, 'Thank you for making my whole degree worthwhile.'

'Don't be daft. I wasn't your placement practise teacher. That pleasure was Jenny Houseman's wasn't it?'

'Yes. Are you still doing social work?' Angie asks.

'No. 'ERM, Angie, while it is truly wonderful to see you again. Albeit, a touch surreal to be talking to you, now, on this sofa! I would like to understand why, and how you found me please?'

'Which one would you like first?'

Angie leans to my right, and puts her glass on a nearby coffee table. And, as she sits upright again, she bends both her arms. Angie then, in wave fashion with one hand after the other, asks, 'The how or the why Alex?'

I'm grinning and thinking, 'It's a shame but I'm going to move my gently squashed toes from under your thigh Angie.' Instead, I dangle my foot over the front edge of the sofa and reply, 'Why please?'

'I want to know for sure whether I can unmake or not, my worse mistake? That's the truth in quite a big nutshell, I acknowledge.'

'Mistake?' I ask not wanting to make the mistake of

assuming.

Angie retrieves her glass and takes a good sip. She then swaps her glass for mine and lifts it near enough for me to syphon a large gulp. Angie then shuffles closer, and taking hold of my hand says, 'I was wrong. I think I knew this minutes after my friend met me at Christchurch airport.'

'What were you wrong about Angie?'

'I did enjoy travelling and can't regret seeing so much. It's just, it was then I first accepted to myself that I was in love with you. It was too late because, well you know why I.'

I lift my left leg until my toes reach Angie's face, and I carefully brush the hair off her cheek.

I say, 'Because you wanted to see the world and probably thought you'd discover it had something more, maybe even better, to offer.'

Angie holds my foot and helps direct it, so my big toe wipes away a tear or two. I say, 'We both understood it was one hundred percent impractical for me to have done, that particular type of journey with you. It's great to hear you enjoyed it. How long did your journey take in the end?'

'Five years. After...'

'Five! That sounds amazing! Do you have a favourite Country?'

'Yes. ERM, Two. Cambodia and Canada. Especially Vancouver!'

'How long did you stay in Cambodia?'

'A year.'

'You did like it. And Canada?'

'Six months. Vancouver was the last stop as it turned out. Three months into our stay there, Maia chose a cruise liner trip to take her home. I was chewing over whether to settle in Canada or not? But, Mum became seriously ill, so I came home. Mum needed a triple heart-bypass, and glad to say she and Dad are still going strong.'

'That's good to hear. Do they still live in Upton upon

Severn, is the right name isn't it?' I ask with a chuckle.

'Yes,' replies Angie before replenishing our glasses. She then fumbles in her bag and exclaims, 'Got it!'

'What?' I ask quietly as I watch Angie clench both hands into a fist.

Angie replies, 'Which hand?'

'What is it?'

'That's not answering my question. Go on, which one Alex?'

I reply, 'Your right hand.'

Angie opens the said hand to reveal a miniature red tin with an intricate décor depicting life and culture somewhere in Asia by the looks of it. As Angie opens the tin she says, 'Just what you asked for. A sample of the purest sand in the world gathered by my own hands in Whitehaven on Whitsunday Island.'

'Oh Angie, how brilliant is that,' I say, and I lean forward so we can share a thank you kiss. It will be the crème of my collection,' I add.

'It's more than nice to finally be able to give it to you. Sorry, it took, so long.'

'It is what it is. Talking of which, I'm intrigued to know, how did you find me, Angie?'

Angie puts the tin on the coffee table, and answers, 'Eight years ago, aged thirty-two, I finally moved out of Mum and Dad's lovely house, and into my first and only permanent home. I live down the road in Ross-on-Wye. I...'

'No way!'

'Yep. I have two dogs too. They were with me when I tried earlier, but after going home and deciding to give it another go, I left them at home. You won't be surprised to hear I also have three rabbits, five cats, eight chickens, three goats and a tortoise I named Forrester.'

We both laugh. You know, the kind you find difficult to stop and which water your eyes.

Somehow, amongst my spattering, I say, 'You cheeky

bugger,' which makes us laugh even more.

After gasping for breath, Angie asks, 'I need to clean my face. Where is the bathroom, please, Alex?'

'The nearest is off the kitchen and you get to it via the utility room.'

'Oh, I think I saw the door. There's a large map on it isn't there?'

'Yes, that's right.'

Angie takes hold of her handbag, and as she leaves the room it's evident the vodka has gone to her head a bit. I take a chance I've got at least five minutes. So, I go outside for a smoke.

I am back on the sofa just as I hear a cupboard shutting. When Angie walks into the lounge I can see she's brought in another carton of tomato juice. She says, 'Just in case. No, you don't,' and Angie swivels my legs off the floor and onto, this time, her lap. She then asks, 'Where were we?'

'Ross-on-Wye Zoo wasn't it?'

'Haha,' replies Angie who then adds, 'Right. Yes. It was early July this year I saw you at a distance walking Polly and Bridie in Lady Park Wood. I had not long left the park, and was in my car with Mum and Dad. We had not long finished a nice walk in the same park with Zig and Zag, and I genuinely...'

'Sorry to interrupt. Pity you didn't take Forrester with you too as they'd have been time for both of us to spot each other eh!'

Angie chuckles and says, 'Don't start me off; I don't think there is much paper left in that toilet now.'

'You're not banned from the others,' I advice with a grin that feels as wide as a Cheshire cat.

'May I continue?' Asks Angie mimicking a teacher's disapproval of a naughty child.

'Yes Miss. You may!'

'I was genuinely shocked seeing you and even tried to convince myself it was probably someone who looked like you.

Say nothing. I work part-time in a job share post for Life-ways as a hands-on manager of their outreach services. My base is their community resource centre in Stroud.

I also work part-time as a trainee vet which includes one day a week for studies. This means every Friday I attend the Abbeydale Vetlnk Veterinary Training Centre. At six this evening I left the centre, and saw the three of you from my car while heading home via the A40. You were on a path near the Wyastone Business park. I tried to find you, and to cut a long story shorter, drove pass the Saracens Head Inn.

I saw you smoking at a table in the pub's garden around eight. The garden was chocker, so I chickened out at this moment. But, remembering this house, I came back to see if, what was a pure hunch, is right? As you've heard, I tried earlier and it was around nine. All very innocent for such a complex explanation eh!'

We both laugh. 'Yes, I agree. Thanks for explaining though.'

'So, what do you do work wise now, Alex?'

'I think you are going to be surprised, so hold on tight.'

Angie parts my legs, and sits between them with her bottom on her ankles. She then grips each of my knees tight and says excitedly, 'OK, I'm ready!'

'The police as...'

'Never,' gasps Angie, and instinctively, I presume, it is Angie's surprise which causes both of her hands to grip both of my knees even harder.

'Careful babe. Oh sorry, I...'

'No need, honestly,' says Angie who then claps, raises her bottom and jiggles her hips before adding, 'Yes! You're the only person to ever call me babe. Yes!'

Truth is, it was not intended but with Angie it's always been natural, and feels right.

Angie then says, 'Well, you couldn't and wouldn't have been a plod. And, I'm still wondering if you're winding me up? So, are you involved with something related to well-being services for front-line staff.'*

'Nope. I am front-line. Do you want another guess?'

'Yes. Let's think.'

As Angie's brain ticks our eyes are locked together, and I can see myself in hers. She then says, 'Oh no, surely not! You aren't Norfolk's "Cracker" are you? I remember you were a big fan of that series.'

I laugh and then say, 'I'm no Cracker, but well done. Yes, I'm a Forensic profiler and also do SIA duties for Norfolk's MASH unit. Really interesting to hear about your intention to change profession too. You'll be in heaven with looking after so many animals eh! Good luck with the studying. How long till you qualify?'

'If I qualify? Two more years and done three so far. What are SIA duties?'

'If felt appropriate or requested offer advice for colleagues who interview suspects. By the way, I promise to be a customer and recommend you to others.'

'Thanks for the faith you have in me. And, well done you too. Must be bloody interesting, to say the least. Definitely a great reason for a celebratory drink.'

Angie refills both glasses and we, through Angie, duly click and she says, 'To new beginnings.'

I accept another invitation to sip through my chick again. After which, I watch Angie place my glass back on the table, and then retrieve a postcard out of her bag. I recognise it. The card is the first gift I ever gave Angie other than my self.

'Do you remember this, Alex?'

Angie holds it in her hands like when a shopkeeper sometimes does to check a bank note is not fraudulent. I hear Angie ask, 'Please read it out loud one more time, for me. Pretty please?'

'Hey Angie, this is a bit unfair,' I protest politely while also knowing Angie won't give up.

'For me, us Alex. Please?'

I equally know it is inevitable I will concede. So, I read:

"Hello from sunny Ashby-de-la-Zouch.

Trust you are revelling in being on yet another student holiday."

Below is my favourite "Meaning of life" definition. This is how I felt a nanosecond after we met and do feel every moment I am with you. I have never said this to anyone else and my heart tells me I never will.

Life is not measured by the number of breaths we take, but by the moments that take our breath away.

Missing you. See you soon. Me."

While reading I even heard Berlin singing their song used by the makers of the film "Top-gun."

'I'm not sure what to say. Other than I haven't, and tonight proves it is not inconsistent.

Nonetheless, I do feel...'

'I was first though Alex,' interrupts Angie.

'And the only one to give me my breath back.'

Angie bends forward putting her arms right around my waist. Her face burrows and nestles into my chest. I hear faint crying, and Angie says, 'I truly love you, Alex. So, I'm sorry too.'

In a whisper, I say, 'I believe you, Angie,' and I kiss her forehead. I then add, 'I can't lie. I've never stopped being in love with you. Just had to bury it, and still will after tonight. Did you get, are you married? Have any children Angie?'

Silence, other than talk from the radio for what I think is at least half a minute. Then Angie answers, 'No to both.'

More silence, though not as long this time. 'Have you kept what I gave you when we did our own little episode of "Swap Shop?" Angie asks.

'Yes, of course,' I reply still whispering. 'And, you?'

'Yes. You said earlier I still take your breath away, and you need to know I still want you to "Show Me, Heaven," replies Angie.

I say, 'I assume you found my note in the sleeve of the three track CD I made, and dropped into your handbag during that awful moment we pretended we'd see each other in a few months?'

'Yes. I cry every time I hear any of those songs,' replies Angie.

We remain still. Except for Angie is using fingers under my shirt and inside my trousers to caress the lowly area of my spine. She then asks, 'And, your tattoo is still here? Where I still wear the other half too!'

As I wrap my legs around Angie's waist and hug gently though tight, I ask, 'Two zero on you and zero two on me, equals?'

'Us,' replies Angie.

I think I also hear in Angie's tone of voice, a diminutive note of acceptance she may not succeed, as she says, 'I haven't given up yet, you know.'

***

16 August 2008. 05.14 Am.

Angie went upstairs over an hour or so ago. She is in one of our spare bedrooms. With Sadie away it was always the case I wouldn't undress for bed tonight. If I had I wouldn't then be able to get dressed in the morning, so depriving Bridie and Polly of a walk before the shoppers return. At what I'm confident will be a time much later in this day.

I would have slept dressed, but with tonight's events still feeling a bit surreal, I know I won't sleep. Instead, I've had two coffees and three cigarettes on the patio outside the room I am now in. I call it the small room, although Sadie's use of Study is far more accurate.

When I came back inside a few minutes ago, I spotted a red light flashing on the landline, alerting me to a message on our answering machine. Having just this second put the computer on with an intention to complete the eighteenth chapter of this story, I grab my zip stick and press the play button.

'You have four messages. First message.

Hello Dad, it's me, Nicene. Sorry for not ringing sooner. It was great to get your letter, thank you so much. We do have Skype Dad. My number is eight three one seven six three seven zero six three. Just want to say I am so glad we're now in touch Dad. And yes, I'd love to visit you. I'm thinking when I'm next on vacation perhaps? Be great to give us a chance to know each other better. I'd come tomorrow if I could! Only joking. Mum is well and returns her best wishes to you. Shame to have missed you. Wanted to tell you I've been asked to take a trial with the San Francisco Nighthawks next week. Beats college studies any day.

I'm not sure how much you know about soccer over here Dad, but the Hawks are a Women's premier league team. I'm so excited and know it's a privilege to get this opportunity. Fingers crossed. Would love to see your team one day. Such a cool name is Arsenal Gunners. Are they one of the top teams in England? Really am sorry you guys are out, will try again soon. Take care Dad.

Bye for now.

Message saved.

Second message.

Hi, expect you're out with Bridie and Polly. All is well here. We're just leaving to walk to the theatre. Take care, love you all. Bye.

Message deleted.

Third message.

Hello Mr Forrester, ERM... Alex. It's Chloe. Maxine said you wouldn't mind me calling you at home. I know I thanked you at the time. It's just, well I, well my whole family want me to invite you and Sadie to have dinner with us, please? We want to show our appreciation for not only reuniting Maxine and I but for the children now knowing their Aunt, uncle and cousin.

My husband is very keen to thank you too. I know you are a busy person, so I'll be delighted if you can return my call, please. Hopefully, arrange a date etc. Our number is O one nine eight six one two three four five six. Maxine, Luke and Milena are also coming. Look forward to seeing you both. Bye.

Message saved.

Fourth message.

Hello, Roger here. Message for Alexander Forrester. Sorry to ring so late. Not expecting you to return my call until the morning, so it can wait. But, please call then at the earliest convenience Forrester. My work mobile is always on. It is important Alex. Bye, speak tomorrow.

Message deleted.'

Deciding to have another smoke, I rest my stick on the keyboard and hear a toilet from upstairs flush. I reverse to look up the staircase, and wait. With my left foot about to push me across my study toward the patio, I see Bridie trotting down the stairs. Closely followed by Angie in silhouette.

Bridie soon says hello by licking my hand and then turns to go upstairs again and passes Angie. I presume, to return to the luxury of being allowed to sleep on a bed.

Seconds later, Angie reaches the bottom of the stairs, and I can now see she is dressed in underwear. I look at her face, and say, 'Oh Angie, now this is very unfair,' at the same time I'm thinking, 'You're determined not to lay down easily, aren't you!'

Angie doesn't say anything. She straddles me and then, taking hold of my face, passionately kisses me. The landline then starts to ring. Instinctively my mouth opens slightly to say something suchlike, 'Need to get that.'

Instead, my lips are pierced by a fervent tongue. I close my eyes which means my defence is being breached. Then, with an eruption of volcanic proportions everything that is Angie breaks through unhindered, so bringing to life what, till this moment had laid dormant deep inside me for far too long.

The exploration going on is soon mutual. The sparks caused by our frenzied frictions, create lava, so to speak, to spiral out even hotter! This ambrosial mixture cascades and swirls within me, sending shivers down my spine. With this freedom, my heart is dissipating fast, a suppressed yearn.

Only for a short while though. I slowly and gently retreat my face from Angie's. 'Am so sorry, but had a message from work earlier. Think it...'

'The person you have called is unavailable. Please leave a message after the tone.

Hi-ya, we have just left the hotel to come home. After the show, we heard the awful news on telly about what's happened in Norfolk. None of us can sleep nor fancy going shopping in the morning now. I expect you've seen it too. It makes me feel sick to even wonder which officer has been killed? Isn't Oliver Stubs that SPO who has been on the run for years? Bastard! Oh yes, I haven't got my keys. So, please wait till we're back before taking the dogs for their walk. Though given I'm talking into a machine, will probably be back in time to wake you up. Love you. Bye, see you soon. About an hour to an hour and a half at most I reckon.'

I delete Sadie's message and say say, 'Sorry Angie, be...'

Angie interrupts, 'Sure. Yes, of course. Do you know the officer that's been killed, Alex?'

'I fear the answer will be yes. I need to call Sir Roger.'

I am already tapping the number and Angie kisses my cheek, reassuringly I think, and says, 'Will get dressed. May I have a cuppa before I leave? We have time, don't we? Would you like one, Alex?'

'Coffee, please. Will join you in the kitchen after...'

'Hello, Detective Chief Inspector Roger Bright speaking.'

'Hello Guv, Alex here.'

'Ah, Forrester. Good. I'm sure you've heard...'

I interrupt Sir Roger, 'Guv. I've literally only just heard about Stubs arrest. Is it true an officer has been killed by him too?'

'Good god Forrester, you mean...'

'Who has been killed Guv?'

'DC Billing I'm afraid. His wife is inconsolable and...'

'Shit, how awful.'

Conscious I keep interrupting, I listen to Sir Roger outline the trail of events that led to Finley being killed!

EPILOGUE

My Diary entry – August 28, 2008

I am inside Norfolk's newly built Justice Centre. One of quite a few now scattered onto the British landscape. I'm in D Wing's Family visitor's suite to be precise. It is 11.30 pm, and to write this entry, I have just stopped what is thus far a pleasurable read of a story called "The Question?" by Jane Asher.

Frank and Sir Roger agreed to nominate three members of MASH willing to undertake the duty of witnessing, at first hand, a state death sentence. The prime purpose is for laypersons to evidence the process is completed as required under the law. Kindred to important principles inherent in Jury duty I reckon! Any adult person can apply or be nominated for consideration to go on a rota for the witness panel, but no-one can be forced to sit on it.

A few minutes under two hours ago, I left the office and company of the night Warder on duty in D Wing tonight. His name is Dan Jurtten. My honest motivation to introduce myself with a knock on his door, so to speak, was to offer my heartfelt empathy for what he and his wife went through because of Oliver Stubs. We had a good chat, and I like Dan. I was fascinated by what Dan shared verbally, and what he showed me about Harold White's behaviour in his cell.

When Dan put the Warder's Headset on my head, he then said he needed to answer a call of nature. I heard White talking and to be honest, I simply couldn't resist! Next, is our conversation!

"… and, I can still ensure you pay with your life!'

'Hello, why do you think it is, Maxine, is what you said isn't...?' I ask using a British dialect different to my own.'

White interjects with, 'I knew I'd be chosen to provide some entertainment tonight! So, turnkey, fuck off and leave me alone!'

'I'm not a turnkey. I'm moonlighting, just for tonight!

Like all prisoners in D Wing, White was naked except for

underwear. At this juncture, White unravelled to sit upright against a wall. No doubt he could feel the permanent warmth radiating from large padded tiles of which, all cell wall and floors in D wing are built. Then, with a sudden rush of fear mixed with my nervousness, I asked myself, 'Has my voice been recognised?'

It was difficult to gauge an answer from an infra-red vision. Yet, relief flooded through me as I heard, 'So, who are you?'

I chuckled softly, and then said, 'That's just it! You don't know who I am! Or, more importantly, what I know! Goodnight, sleep tight!"

When I returned to my room, I switched on my ipod and chose a music play-list I'd especially created (For this tale in truth). I press shuffle before activating the last song on the list. Immediately, the irenic haunting sound of the instrumental introduction began. I listened intently, and knew twenty-four seconds later I would also hear the magical voice of Heather Small singing her brilliant composition, "Proud."

***

My Diary Entry
August 29, 2008

Today began with Dan Jurtten knocking my door to make sure I didn't oversleep. After a brief chat Dan left, and I had an hour to kill before attending a gathering of today's Witness Panel. Therefore, I watched an open university programme about the amazing Waorani tribe who live in Ecuador.

When Sir Roger first heard my name had been pulled out of the hat, so to speak, he immediately visited me in my office. Sir Roger offered to apply on my behalf for an exemption. On the grounds, it would be an unacceptably emotional challenge given the nature of all the police's involvement with White and his accomplices.

I genuinely thanked Sir Roger for his considerate thought, and politely declined his offer. However, Sir Roger was pleased and determined to fulfil his agreement with my request to be given clearance, on practical grounds, to stay within the JC from yesterday evening.

In fact, Sir Roger seemed almost joyous when he confirmed I had permission to use a family suite within the D Wing building. A suite offered to loved ones for up to forty-eight hours before the prisoner's sentence is due to be completed.

I reported to the receptionist in A Wing at three minutes to five. From here I was escorted to a room which had a sign on its door which reads, "Witness Observation Point" with underneath, "Strictly staff entrance only."

On entering, I quickly noted I was the eighth witness to take my position. The latter being one of two unoccupied desks which had a computer screen standing on it. Before I settled at desk number two, I caught glimpses of live pictures streamed from cell number one.

At 5.10 am the sound of a buzzer meant the event of today was ten minutes from happening. I watched White's cell door open, and a man of Christian cloth entered with a Warder each side of him. I could not hear the conversation White had with the chaplain, but I can tell you it lasted one minute and fifty-two seconds. Then, the chaplain nodded to one of the Warder's who then, in turn, opened the cell door, so that four more people could enter. Two of them carried a bed similar in design to a stretcher. They placed it in the centre of the cell and it was evident White was ordered to lay on it.

White refused and I could see he was shaking, but it is difficult to try and hide your fear and dignity at the best of times, so, as you can probably appreciate it is impossible when you have been stripped naked. Two warders then held an arm each, and put White on his back. Then, two of their colleagues strapped White in, pinning him down against his will. One of the Warders then left the cell, and with him when he returned were two medical Doctors and Clive Verity.

With my eyes almost popping out, I realised sound is now permitted. What follows is what we all heard.

"Mr White, as is Mr Verity's right under the law, he has

asked to talk with you. To decide whether or not to change his mind about you receiving a state death?' said the prison chaplain.

'Hello Eddie,' said Clive as he knelt beside the stretcher.

White looked terrified but locked his eyes on Clive's stare.

Clive then said, 'According to the police, you and Tristan are responsible for murdering our Jo. Is this true? If it is, then I will stop this attribute of your sentence happening. However, if it is, I need more than a simple yes. I also need, to be as sure as is it is possible to be, something which substantiates your answer, either way! The police, nor anyone else for that matter, know how Jo vanished at the fête? So, White! Are the police right?'

'I'd preferably die now. Better than to exist in this place,' replied White.

Clive stood up, and said to the chaplain, 'Call it off, please. My final decision.'

White said, 'Wait, if I tell you the truth will you let me die now?

'Yes,' replied Clive. (But this proves to be a lie).

White then said, 'Yes, I killed your girl but it was James and Reginald who kidnapped her from the fête.'

'Who is this Reginald?' Clive calmly asked White.

'Ollie knows him too! He's a Lord and Judge and lives in Heydon."

Acknowledgements

I would like thank Michael Terence Publishing for their support, assistance and encouragement to achieve publication of my novel, *Does Anyone Care?*

In no particular order, I thank the following for their constructive feedback and patience when providing a sounding board for discussion about my creation of this story.

My Aunt Sheila

Sharon Bunce

Chris Bunce

Chris Rose

Anne Ellen

Tim Ellen

Gemma Moss

Beverley Rowe

Nick Tingle

Robert White

Carly Giglio

Louise Shrimpton

Andy Bridges

Steven Trinkwon

Steven Trinkwon was born on the Isle of Sheppey, England in 1962. When aged 3 months he was taken to Chailey Heritage Craft School in Sussex. This was a Local Health Authority run residential environment. He left, aged 16 years and accepted a place at a residential college in Coventry.

Steven studied at Lanchester Polytechnic and immediately after graduating in 1989 began a 25-year professional career. Some of his posts meant working in partnership with law enforcement officers involved with adults and children in need of protection. Or, they were a victim of a crime which often required interceding with those who perpetrated against them.

Steven lives in Norwich and uses experiences in his life and his profession to produce an extraordinary and thought provoking Crime Fiction story called *Does Anyone Care?*

A story set primarily in Norfolk and which will challenge you not to at least ask, "What would I have done?"

Available worldwide from

Amazon

————————

www.mtp.agency

www.facebook.com/mtp.agency

@mtp_agency

28672141R00218

Printed in Great Britain
by Amazon